Holly Wainwright is a writer, editor and podcaster who lives on the south coast of New South Wales with her partner and their young family. She's an Executive Editor at women's media company Mamamia. *He Would Never* is her fifth novel.

Also by Holly Wainwright

The Mummy Bloggers
How to Be Perfect
I Give My Marriage A Year
The Couple Upstairs

HE WOULD WOULD NEVER

Holly Wainwright

Pan Macmillan Australia

Pan Macmillan acknowledges the Traditional Custodians of country throughout Australia and their connections to lands, waters and communities. We pay our respect to Elders past and present and extend that respect to all Aboriginal and Torres Strait Islander peoples today. We honour more than sixty thousand years of storytelling, art and culture.

This is a work of fiction. Characters, institutions and organisations mentioned in this novel are either the product of the author's imagination or, if real, used fictitiously without any intent to describe actual conduct.

First published 2025 in Macmillan by Pan Macmillan Australia Pty Ltd
1 Market Street, Sydney, New South Wales, Australia, 2000

Copyright © Holly Wainwright 2025

The moral right of the author to be identified as the author of this work has been asserted.

All rights reserved. No part of this book may be reproduced or transmitted by any person or entity (including Google, Amazon or similar organisations), in any form or by any means, electronic or mechanical, including photocopying, recording, scanning or by any information storage and retrieval system, without prior permission in writing from the publisher.

 A catalogue record for this book is available from the National Library of Australia

Typeset in 12/16.5 Adobe Garamond Pro by Midland Typesetters, Australia
Printed by IVE

Map on page vii created by Christa Moffitt, Christabella Designs

The author and the publisher have made every effort to contact copyright holders for material used in this book. Any person or organisation that may have been overlooked should contact the publisher.

*For my own camping mothers' group.
Mel, Becky, Sam, Sarah, Ciara.
And Leanne, who saved my sanity many times
but draws the line at tents.*

Character List

Site Four
Ginger and Aiden
James, Abigail and Maya

Site Five
Juno and Emily
Bob

Site Six
Dani and Craig
Lyra and Brigitte

Site Seven
Liss and Lachy
Tia, Grace and Ollie

Site Eight
Sadie
Trick and Lucky

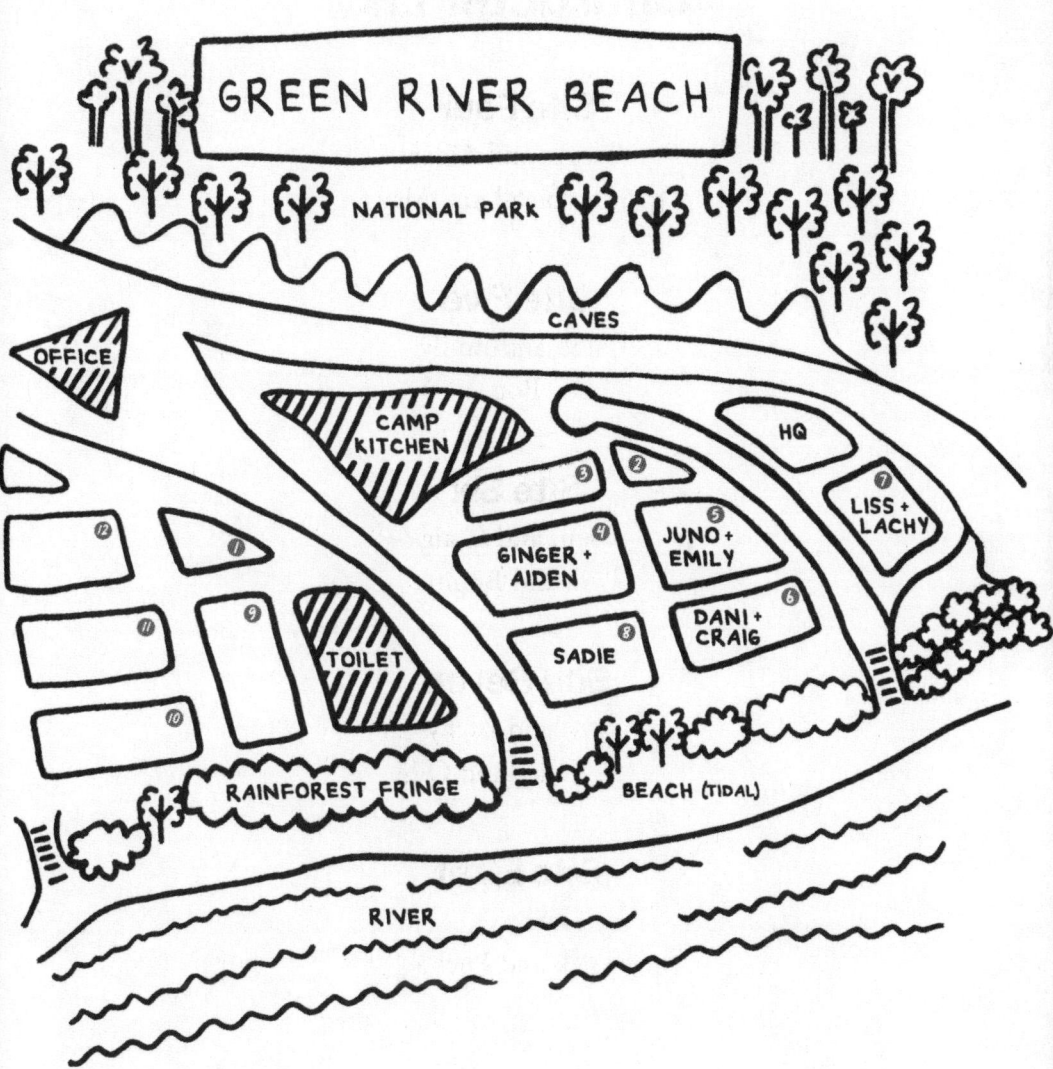

Prologue

Sunday night, 11.55 pm

Green River Beach

This would be a fitting place for Lachy Short to die.

On the edge of a splendid beach he hated with a passion.

If you believed in the afterlife, which Liss definitely did, or ghosts, which Dani most definitely did not, then Lachlan Short's troubled soul would be bound to walk this stretch of river for eternity, bitching about the absence of decent surf or a proper coffee, and picking tiny shards of crushed lilac river shells out of the soles of his calloused feet.

Some would think it was entirely appropriate for him to end his days in the place that most made him doubt his marriage, his masculinity, his very life choices: a campground.

A hell for a man who liked the finer things. Beds that weren't in close proximity to the ground. Food that couldn't be cooked on a one-ring stove or in the coals of a ban-defying fire. Drinks not served with ice scooped from a sandy esky by a sunscreen-smeared hand. No, if Lachy Short was to be doomed to camp for eternity, he would find a way back to the light.

Because, actually, he wasn't dead yet.

He was lying on the rainforest floor, somewhere between consciousness and unconsciousness, somewhere between the campground and the sand. And someone would find him soon, surely. Liss, or Dani, or Aiden, or Tia. They must all be frantic, beside themselves.

This strip of wilderness wasn't wide, but it was dense and tricky, as all the Green River Camp regulars knew. At night, you could step away to pee between trees and a thick, dark-green curtain would close in, leaving you banging into branches and tripping over roots, embarrassed at your rising panic.

The forest vibrated with a low thrum of life. Always hungry, inching forward, manoeuvring to reclaim its stolen space. Marching insects and scuttling rodents. Advancing spiders and snakes and slugs and snails. Nibbling, sucking, sliming, gnawing. The strangler vines always reaching. They'd have a thick, nobbled tendril around Lachy's ankle by morning.

It was strange that no-one was calling his name.

He was still breathing, but not so you'd notice. Shallow, now.

His loud Hawaiian-print shirt might just save him from this terrible misunderstanding. Its hibiscus-bright yellow and pink was still faintly glowing even as the campground's lanterns and fairy lights flicked off for the night, stealing the last glimmers of light.

The shirt had been ironic. Which was now, of course, extremely ironic.

At the beach, only a few steps away, the river was rising. Lapping closer to the tree line with every sweep in, every pull out. The crabs' sandball-scrawled masterpieces were being washed away, the fish heading in from deeper water to swirl around the anchors of the dormant boats.

Try to breathe with the waves. It won't be long. Can't be long.

A crunch, finally, of footfall. Getting closer. No talking. No chatter, no urgency.

HE WOULD NEVER

A phone light, held low, sweeping left to right, right to left, below the eye line of campers on the other side of the tree curtain. Invisible to anyone hurrying to the toilet block in their pyjamas and thongs.

Who was coming? His wife? His children? They'd been on the makeshift dancefloor with him, only hours before, bumping, jumping, shrugging to the beat pounding through the trees, out to the sandy flats of the beach and tipping into the river.

The girls had jiggled through clouds of embarrassment, eyes averted, aware of the phones pointed their way by cooler kids. But his daughters would still dance with him, if he asked. They weren't too old for that.

Nor was Lyra Martin. That little idiot. It was because of her, surely, that Lachy was lying in the roots of this giant fig on the forest floor and not sinking into the double-flocked inflatable mattress inside his giant tent, beer-snoring into Liss's tolerant ear.

Lyra could have said something. Changed all of this.

The crunching. Closer. Stopping.

'Lachy. There you are.'

Someone was bending to him.

Feet in thongs by his flickering eyes. Toenails pink and shimmery in the phone's blond light.

'Thank God. We wondered how far you'd got.'

A voice as familiar as his own.

'Such a terrible mess.'

Yes, this would be a fitting place for Lachy Short to die. If you didn't like him. If you didn't trust him. If you thought he'd spent a life tainting beautiful things with his touch. If you thought he'd taken something from you, knocked you off course, tormented a person you loved. If you believed the lies spread about him tonight, last night, all weekend.

'Do you need help?'

Such a question, to a body in the woods. Asked in such a sweet tone.

There could be no answer from swollen, numb lips.

So yes, there might be people who wished to damn Lachy to eternal rest below this fig, but they would be wrong. That wasn't who he was. Not what he deserved. And there were people here, people only steps away from this mossy, ferny dump who knew that. Knew that he loved his wife. Loved his children. Knew that every decision he made was in the service of protecting them. Even the wrong ones.

Hot breath mingling with the hot breeze. So close it would ruffle the hair above his ringing ear.

'Good night, Lachy.'

The crunching. Retreating, this time.

An impossible act from a person so beloved.

A roar was building inside him. A rush of furious indignation at having been so misunderstood. A heart-fluttering terror at the idea his children might grow up thinking he was someone he was not.

All of it charging at him now. The ritual of the camping trip. A friendship grown too close. A teenage girl too sure of herself. A marriage almost done. A secret unwrapped and scattered around the campsite like bait.

And now, the worst of it. Humiliation. Betrayal. Abandonment.

Liss. Dani.

Lachy Short would never stand for this.

If only he could stand.

Part One

1

Friday, 1 pm

Green River Campground

Liss

Liss pulled up her underpants and kicked a little dirt over the steaming spot between the roots of the great old fig.

'Hello to you, too,' she said to the tree, letting her skirt fall to her bare feet.

She performed this same, small ritual every time she arrived at Green River Beach. Stepping away from the campsite's yawning car boots and scrubby tent squares and onto the forest floor in just a few steps. She'd been doing exactly that, in this exact spot, since she was six years old; so long that she liked to imagine she was a little bit the fig and it was a little bit her.

She drew breath and looked up into the canopy, the vine-draped palms, the reaching branches of the gums, the drooping blousy blossoms, and she exhaled. *Happy place.* It was a cliché, an Instagram meme, but it was also accurate. Liss felt happier in this place than any other, and she had never wanted to share her first look at Green River with anyone else.

'Liss!'

Soon enough, Lachy's voice, through the trees. He'd be asking her where the tent pegs were, or telling her that the kids needed drinks, or calling for help finding the mallet.

'Hold on!'

She pushed through the vines, instinctively stomping out a warning to snakes, reaching the edge of the green-brown fringe and stepping over the old kayak her kids kept stashed in the tree line, out onto the golden brown of the beach. The tide was out, pulling the water far from her.

Liss pushed her hair back from her sticky face. Despite the proximity of the campsite, there wasn't a single person on the beach. Tourists didn't like the mudflats of low tide. There were just the two old fishing tinnies, upturned at the far end of the cove as they always were, two pelicans turning their weighty heads towards her from the stumps of the rotten pier, as they always did, and the exposed pegs of the moorings of the one lifeboat, anchored way out beyond the tideline, waiting for an emergency, as it always was.

She shoved her toes into the mud and looked out to the other side of the river's bank, where a few homes, accessible only by boat, studded the far river line. No McMansions yet.

'Liss!'

The campsite wasn't far enough away. Which was the point, really. Where else could you pitch your tents on the fringe of a rainforest and step straight onto beach, into water? Here.

Lachy, apparently, needed her back at Site Seven. By now he would have unlatched the roof racks, the rolled-up bags of tents, the folded chairs, the air mattresses, the stretcher beds. Everything she'd remembered to pack.

Liss took another deep breath, before throwing her head back and letting out a little whistle. *Hello, beach. Hello, river. Hello, hello, hello.*

HE WOULD NEVER

'You always disappear,' Lachy was saying as she walked back along the sandy path to the Land Rover, back to the pile of jobs. 'Just as the work starts.'

Liss smiled. It wasn't even remotely true. The work of constructing the long weekend's temporary tent town would be going on for hours yet.

'Oh well, I'm back now,' she said lightly, surveying everything she'd carefully stacked and packed into the car boot now tossed all over the sandy ground. 'Get Tia to help you with the tent. I'll sort the furnishings.'

'Furnishings,' Lachy snorted. 'Like it's the beach house.'

'You'll survive, babe, you always do.'

'And as if Tia's helping. As if any of them are. They've already gone . . .' He gestured, with a clenched fist, towards the beach, the forest.

This mood was typical of the arrival day of camp weekend. What was being asked of Lachy was an hour or two of physical labour. Lifting things, staking things, pulling ropes and fixing pegs. Invariably it would be too hot, or too cold, or wet, or windy.

And when it was done, he and the other men of the group would put down their mallets, pick up their beers and leave the next three days in the hands of the women.

'I'll go and find the kids,' Liss said to him, out loud. But in her head she was already talking to Dani.

Poor Lachy, having to do some actual work for a change.

But Dani wasn't here, yet. And anyway, she'd heard it all before.

Liss walked away, following the shouts of children. They were running the campsite's looping central track, naming familiar things.

'The swing!' Still there. Hung from the biggest fig on the forest's edge by Juno, four years ago.

'The wasps' nest!' A dimpled, deflated waxy balloon, still clinging to the weatherboard edge of the toilet block, where last summer it had caused a speedy evacuation.

'The den!' A hollowed-out cave on the far side of the campsite, on the edge of the national park, where rocky outcrops formed a barrier between the campers and the wilderness. Giant toothy crags, pocked with caves and squeezy passageways into the wilds on the other side.

Little Liss had pushed herself through one of those scrubby gaps alone only once, scratching her knees and puncturing her hands as she scrabbled, determined to ace a game of hide-and-seek. But when she'd found herself on the other side, and with the cousin she'd been chasing nowhere to be seen, it only took a few steps on spiky ground to realise she was too small to be alone there, dwarfed by trees, spooked by rattling scrub in the shadow of those rocks.

Her mother had found her; of course she had. It must have only been a few long minutes really, before she appeared, also dirt-streaked and sprinkled with bush, wide-eyed but laughing. 'I thought I'd lost you, little one.' She'd smiled, and taken Liss's hand to lead her back to the campground via a less treacherous route. 'Your cousin's hiding near the kitchen, you know we don't come this side of the rocks.'

Liss's children had the same rules – *don't play in the national park.* But the rocky barrier itself was full of welcoming shelters, which, Liss's mother had explained to her that day, would once have been kitchens and bedrooms and living rooms for the people who had always lived here, for millennia.

Now the caves were the territory of holidaying city kids, with candle stubs, joint butts and mouldering cushions jammed into the smoke-blackened ledges. It was a rite of passage for camp kids to build their dens here, and to venture beyond them, into the woods. Liss eventually had, and now her children ignored the rules, too.

Liss followed the trail of voices to a sighting of her three children, about to head off into the trees to where, doubtless, more secrets were stashed.

'Tia!' Liss called out. 'Don't go too far, the others will be here soon!'

Her eldest, comfortable here in a way she wasn't always, threw her a withering look. 'They know where to find us,' Tia said, and disappeared into the green murk, her little brother and sister at her heels.

Liss kept on walking, following the loop of the campground's path, counting sites, taking stock. It was what she always did, after her tree-wee.

Everyone lucky enough to have the rights to sites at Green River was deeply invested in nothing ever changing. They arrived each year praying that the rented sites hadn't been halved to squeeze more dollars from twice as many visitors. They'd welcomed hot showers in the bathroom block but were quietly pleased that news of the update hadn't made it to the park's neglected website. They'd rejoiced when powered sites were introduced, but signed petitions to keep caravans out, swearing that the winding road down the peninsula was way too narrow. They professed to want to protect this pocket of wild beauty but were entirely opposed to it becoming a part of the national park.

If you had the connections or the dumb luck to have bought one of the twenty sites at Green River Campground back when you could, you held on to them tightly. And Liss had her father to thank for that. One thing on a very short list of things he'd Done Right was to secure the right to these camping sites for his family, all summer long.

Now Liss felt a swelling pride in sharing it with her closest friends, if only for these few days every year. As she padded out the boundaries of her special place, she fizzed with the excitement of seeing them all again. Of *hosting* them all again.

Five families whose bond had been forged in the white-hot fire of early parenthood. The first of those babies were teens now. Some of the men had come and gone, but the gathering of these women, in this place, year after year, was Liss's own achievement. *Welcome, family*, she wanted to say to them, *let's bunker down and nurture each other.*

She could hear Dani's cynical snort from here.

Sadie? Dani would say. *Who wants to nurture Sadie?*

Liss did. Even Sadie. Despite everything.

She passed the office where Ron and Shell had been doling out strict rules and cold ice for decades, fiercely guarding both the campsite entrance and the peace.

'I hope that mob of kids isn't getting to troublemaking age,' Shell had said when they'd arrived, leaning on the counter, one eye on the horseracing on her tiny portable TV, the kind you never saw anymore.

Liss had agreed, since it had been the subject of much group-chat angst this past week. Was it the year the kids were going to sneak out of their tents to pash each other on the beach at midnight? Raid the parental eskies for booze?

'They start off so adorable,' Shell had said, handing over the new code to the boom gate and the toilet block, but not the wi-fi, since there wasn't any. 'Doing doughnuts on their pink tricycles. And a few years later you've got a gang of rampaging yobbos.'

'Hope we've got another couple of years yet,' Liss had answered with a bright smile. 'It's the dads you've got to worry about.'

'Always.'

It was Shell and Ron's vigilance that stopped the whole camp being swallowed by nature. The tentacles of the rainforest would have snaked through the place years ago if it weren't for Ron's constant chopping and Shell's whirring cleaning buggy, with its buckets of bleach for scrubbing back the mould and lichen from the toilet block. If it weren't for the rat traps circling the camp kitchen and the mesh wrapped around the trees that edged the tent sites. Ron and Shell kept this wild place tame enough for city types to come here and play at being wild.

Liss padded on, past the camp kitchen with its tree-trunk foundations and its heavy wooden doors. She could see a woman in there, boiling noodles on the hotplate while her two small children sat staring at iPads. It could have been her, just a few years before.

There were ghosts of old versions of herself everywhere at Green River. Little Liss, being chased by her laughing mother. Teenage Liss, motherless, smoking spliffs in the trees with her cousins. Newlywed Liss, desperate for Lachy to love this place as she did, fucking him at sunset in the rockpool tucked away around the headland. It hadn't worked, she knew; he resented every trip here just a little more than the last. New mum Liss, trying to get babies to sleep in carry-cots under mosquito nets, willing herself to stay awake long enough to see the stars. And then, for years, it seemed, the version of herself that looped this path at a trot, chasing children on trikes and bikes and scooters, willing them not to fall, not to stray into the bush with its spiky, bitey dangers.

Now, maybe, this version of Liss could exhale, just a bit.

Although, *Lachy*.

She was almost back at Site Seven, Liss's lucky number and the best spot on the campground. There was no argument about which family would get Seven every year. Liss had fought off her brothers for her familial right to this place on this particular weekend and so it was only fair that she and Lachy would settle in prime position, and the others accept the spots nearby.

Seven was closest to the beach, furthest from the ammonia smells of the bathroom block, and next to the boardwalk that took you through the forest to the sand. It was also the biggest, and opposite a communal site where – with a silent understanding from Ron and Shell, whose adherence to rules softened just a little for VIPs – they could set up a communal HQ, the beating heart of the camp.

The men would pull on ropes to hoist a tarpaulin roof and lay long plastic sheets on the ground for a sweepable floor, held down at the edges by eskies and barbecues. The women would unfold a long trestle table, where meals would be served and drinks would chill in buckets and always, always on the first and last nights, speakers would pump out music that, from the hallowed position of HQ, wouldn't bother the handful of other families who'd made it to Green River. Instead the beat would roll out over the mudflats, a pulse of nightlife in the wilderness. Dancing barefoot under swinging lanterns was the opening and closing tradition of every summer long weekend.

'You're back.' Lachy was huffing as Liss arrived at Site Seven. 'Thank fuck, can you hold this?'

Liss tucked her long skirt into her knickers and squatted again, to hold the pole her husband needed steadying.

'Where are the kids? Where are the others?' He was hoisting the flysheet over the big old canvas tent Liss insisted they bring, year in, year out. So much more soulful than those modern lightweight numbers, although harder for Lachy to erect.

'They'll be here,' she said. 'They're just giving us our moment.'

'I see you've slipped into Zen mama mode,' Lachy muttered, but he was smiling as he reached and pulled. 'I could do with someone a bit less Zen, though, to help out.'

Liss smiled off into the forest. *Breathe.*

HE WOULD NEVER

There was the scrape of tyres and the shadow of a car pulling up at exactly the right moment. 'Liss!'

Lyra Martin catapulted herself from the door of an enormous shiny red Jeep.

Liss dropped the tent pole to the sound of a soft swear from Lachy and fell backwards as Lyra's arms and legs wrapped around her torso, hard. It was the same greeting, this high-speed koala-attack, that Lyra had given her since birth, always reaching, always enveloping, always burrowing in.

'Hello, darling,' she said into Lyra's hair. 'So good to see you.'

'Lyra, you nutter.'

That cool voice definitely belonged to Brigitte, Lyra's little sister, who would never consider wrestling an adult to the ground in enthusiasm.

Liss laughed, spiky bindis at her back, the joy of her god-daughter's love squeezing the breath out of her. Perhaps Lyra hadn't yet got the memo that the only acceptable teen disposition was permanent irritation, as if you were perpetually interrupted doing something of far greater importance by someone inexcusably stupid.

'Lyra, leave Liss alone. She's pretending to help her husband get the tent up.'

And there was Dani. The only person Liss was happier to see.

Lyra rolled off, unfolding her long, gangly limbs, tossing back her thick black hair, beaming the smile that seemed to stretch from one ear to the other as if her head were about to hinge open.

Liss had read enough columns and listened to enough podcasts to know to never comment on the appearance of a young girl, but she couldn't deprogram the part of herself that appreciated Lyra's beauty.

'If this was the eighties,' she'd whispered to Dani last year, 'your girl would be jailbait in a French film.'

'Don't say jailbait,' Dani had said. 'We definitely don't say jailbait.'

Now Liss took Dani's hand to pull herself up off the grass and hugged her tight.

'Dan, we made it!'

'Another year, who would have thought,' Dani said into Liss's armpit. 'Put me down, darling.'

'I'm just so fucking happy to see you.'

'And I'm happy to see you, Craig.' Lachy was talking to the man standing behind Dani, bouncing a little on his toes.

It was Craig's second year there, and Liss could sense how eager Dani's boyfriend was to show that he knew the ropes, that he was itching to start unfolding poles and hammering pegs.

'I bet, mate.' Craig had also got the memo that the outnumbered men must appear put-upon.

'Nice car,' Liss whispered to Dani, arm around her shoulders.

Dani shrugged. 'It's his. There's a bit of me that thinks he bought it for this trip.'

'To impress who?'

Dani nodded at Lachy, who was walking over to the huge Jeep, whistling behind his teeth, errant tent pole in hand.

'Nice wheels, Craig. New?'

Lyra Martin made a finger-down-throat gesture.

'Where's Tia?'

'You girls are going nowhere until you've set up your tent,' Dani said, and Liss felt a twinge of guilt at the thought of her kids off roaming, helping no-one but themselves. As usual.

'We have a lot to talk about, friend.'

'But first, tents.'

'Thank God for the cavalry,' Lachy was saying, his interest in the car exhausted. 'Lyra, say hello!'

HE WOULD NEVER

Lyra danced over to Lachy – she'd never been a girl to walk when she could dance, or run when she could skip – and gave him a brief hug, only shoulders touching.

Liss moved to give Craig a polite kiss on the cheek and he said, 'I thought we might set up on Site Five this year,' gesturing at the bigger spot, a little further from Liss and Lachy.

Liss felt a twitch of discomfort and looked at Dani. 'You're on Site Six, Craig,' she said. 'Dani's always been there, it's right across from us, and we've always –'

'I just found it a bit cramped last year, wondered if we might spread out a bit.'

Lachy walked back to the tent poles, head down, staying out of it.

'Well, I don't think . . .' Liss reached around for a reason to say *no, we won't be changing sites*, but she couldn't quite find one that didn't sound petulant. 'I don't think it works. Everyone's assigned their sites already.'

Craig was opening his mouth to say something when Dani touched his forearm, ever so lightly. 'It's okay, Craig, we'll be fine on Six.'

Liss knew Craig saw himself as a straight shooter. The kind of person who asks for what he wants and doesn't apologise for it.

But he was also the kind of person who could read status. Hierarchies.

'Okay. Fine,' Craig said, his shoulders ever so slightly lower as he turned back towards the red car. 'Let's get this show on the road.'

It was Dani's turn to catch Liss's eye. 'Countdown 'til sundowners,' she said as she went to join him. 'And all the catching up in the world.'

Lyra was obediently hauling down the sleeping bags from the roof racks. 'Are we ready for disco night?' She shook her hips as she threw a bundle of fleecy blankets to her sister. 'Bridgey, are you ready to party?'

The two Martin girls dashed off to Site Six as Craig climbed into the Jeep and it roared into life to move just a few metres along the track.

As she watched the car pull into its spot, it occurred to Liss that Dani hadn't said hello to Lachy. That her best friend and her husband hadn't acknowledged each other, hadn't exchanged their usual bear hug, hadn't thrown a sarcastic dig in the other's direction.

'Hey, Liss?' Dani called, loudly, from across the path.

'What, darling?'

'Have you already pissed on your tree?'

And Liss felt a wave of intense love for her smart, tough friend as she raised two middle fingers in her direction, and the Martin girls fell about laughing.

2

Friday, 2 pm

Green River Campground

Dani

'It's bullshit.' Craig kicked at the gumnuts that scattered Site Six with the tip of his boat shoe. 'I'll wake up with one of these up my arse.'

'I've seen that mattress you bought,' Dani said, unfurling the first of the tents from its sausage-skin bag. 'You won't feel a thing, Princess.'

She watched Craig pull his frown into a straight-line smile with considerable effort. His ego was dented by Liss's refusal to upgrade their site, but his status as a visitor in Dani's inner sanctum made sulking a precarious choice.

'It's not like these people are actual campers,' he huffed.

'Craig, please.'

'Don't they own a beach house up the road? They're just play-acting.'

'Craig. Shut up.' Dani bumped him with the tent. 'If you're the real camper, help me with this.'

Case against Craig: Sulker.

Dani was collecting tokens of evidence that her relationship was doomed. She wasn't sure why yet, except that, after two years of dating – an impossibly youthful word for what they'd been doing but really the only applicable one – she could no longer ignore the twinges nudging her towards an escape hatch.

Case against Craig: He was late picking her up in that ridiculous new car.

The giant red truck had rounded the corner when she and the girls had been standing outside her apartment block for more than ten minutes, Dani's irritation growing with every second.

'Surprise!' he'd called, double-parking and lowering the window with a barely audible *zip*.

'I thought he drove a Tesla,' Lyra muttered to her mum.

'He does. But clearly not camping.'

Lyra had hesitated as Brigitte clambered up to the back door with a squeal. Dani could see her elder daughter's excitement at the prospect of riding in this huge, shiny spaceship rubbing against the required disapproval at such a gas-guzzling, performative monstrosity. 'It's a bit . . . much,' she said finally, grabbing her holdall.

Dani had wanted to drive them to Green River in the Rav, like she always did. There were few things she hated more than turning over her schedule to other people's patchy punctuality. But Craig had begged for a change of plan. Now she knew why.

'You're late.'

'But worth it, right? Picked her up last night.'

'Her?'

'Of course. Such a beauty.'

Case against Craig: Ugh.

He'd climbed down from the driver's side, oblivious to the cars banking up behind, honking and attempting to pull around him on

Dani's narrow street. He'd pressed a button on a little black box in his hand and the ute tray began to slide open.

'Ventilated retractable cover. We could sleep in here, if it came to it.'

'It won't.' Dani could hear the snark in her voice. She didn't like it. She couldn't help it.

'One year there was a storm and we all ran away,' Brigitte called from the back seat where she was stroking the leather, pulling at handles, counting the drinks holders, breathing in the new-car smell.

'Drove away,' Dani corrected. 'At speed.'

'And another year it rained so hard we all slept in the camp kitchen.'

Craig visibly shuddered as he tossed the chairs into the tray, weight-curling arms on display in his tight, white polo shirt. 'If that happens this weekend, we're finding a hotel.'

'Good luck.' Dani laughed. 'There's nothing available on the peninsula on a long weekend.'

'It's who you know,' he said. 'Like everything. We won't be sleeping in a mouse-house on my watch. Say the word and we're in a suite at The Arcadian. So, are we ready?'

Dani wanted Lyra to go and check that she'd locked the door for the third time but, looking at the car queue, she swallowed the urge to ask her.

There were three security screens between their flat and the street anyway. Gleaming and modern and a realistic distance from the beach, Dani had put a deposit on her piece of this building before the slab was even poured. A safe, clean, purpose-built home devoid of history was precisely what she wanted, and exactly what she'd finally moved into, a year ago. 'We're ready.' She'd pulled herself up into the passenger seat and Lyra whispered to her again.

'Mum! Has Craig always been so rich?'

'Don't be crass,' she said, but Craig had heard and was smiling.

'Did you really buy this car to go camping?' Brigitte asked as he strapped himself in, and Dani did the same, her feet dangling like a child's, nowhere close to touching the floor.

'I've been looking for an excuse.'

'Did you sell the Tesla?' asked Lyra, eyes wide.

'No, I just extended the garage,' he said, with a wink.

Did the wink mean that was a joke? Dani had felt Lyra's confusion from the back seat. She knew, of course, he wasn't joking. Craig's dream of a three-car garage twenty minutes away in North Bondi was coming true, one neighbourly objection at a time.

Case against Craig: Too materialistic. Bad example to the kids. She caught herself. Good example to the kids. Self-made. Independent. Works hard.

Not that he spent much time around Lyra and Bridge, even after two years. Their strict twice-weekly date schedule meant Dani rarely stayed over at his house and if he was at hers, she brought him back late and hurried him out early. It irritated Craig, actually. She knew he'd like them to progress to a more blended-family model. But Dani also knew that was because he'd like the convenience of folding his own son, Anders, into the mix, and she wasn't that stupid. Dani wasn't looking to mother anyone new.

Now they were here: him feeling personally affronted by gumnuts and an inferior tent site; her trying to stop herself from kicking at that escape hatch.

She looked around. Where was Lyra? She'd just been here, unfolding poles with Brigitte.

'Bridge, go find your sister, she'll be looking for Tia.' Those girls were like magnets. 'I asked her not to go anywhere until the tents were up.'

HE WOULD NEVER

Brigitte flitted away as Dani and Craig started building the skeleton of their home for the next three nights. Working quickly, efficiently, while flies dive-bombed their sweat-studded foreheads.

Dani stepped back, wiped her hands on her shorts and was looking around for the flysheet when Craig suddenly came close, cupped her chin and lifted her face to look into his.

'Baby,' he said.

Dani blinked. Did Craig usually call her baby?

'It's good to see you. Good to be part of this.'

She nodded, his finger moving up and down with her head.

'I want you to know,' Craig's voice was deep and round, one of the things about him that Dani found both seductive and irritating, 'there are no other people on the planet who could make me go camping.'

He dipped his head and kissed her mouth.

'Yes,' she said, pulling away from his lips, his hand. *Not now*, she hoped her movements said. *Not here. Calm down, buddy.* 'But I didn't make you.'

'Make me *want* to go camping, I mean,' Craig course-corrected and pushed on. 'Just to be around all of you; to be part of something important.'

Case against Craig: All of this.

'But I was thinking,' he continued, 'maybe we can start making our own traditions and rituals. You know, just for us, and the kids.'

'Oh.' Dani was deciding what to say when Lyra – God bless her – came bouncing back to camp, Brigitte behind her. Beyond them, down the path, Dani could make out Tia with Liss's two younger kids, pushing and shoving each other. 'Of course, I – Lyra! You're back. You and Bridge need to put your tent up this year. It's time you two started helping more.'

Craig dropped his hand and turned back to their flysheet. 'Lyra,' he said, trying on an authoritative tone. 'Help me get this over the frame and I'll help you girls with yours.'

'Did I interrupt a romantic moment?' Lyra's voice was tilting, mocking.

'Hardly. Can you do what Craig's asking, please?'

Lyra looked back to where Tia Short had stopped on the path. She was jiggling, reminding Dani for the umpteenth time that inside this young woman's body was an impatient, unsure child.

'It'll take two minutes.'

'I have to do what *he* says?' Lyra whispered.

'Just get the tent up, Ly.' Dani sighed. 'Don't make it about that.'

Her daughter slunk over to the far side of the tent frame and picked up the corner of a plastic sheet. 'Where does this go, boss?' she asked, pointedly, and Dani felt a jolt at the attitude in her voice. That was new. Wasn't it?

Craig hoisted the sheet over the top of the frame then returned to picking at his favourite scab.

'It just always surprises me, you know, that you're a camping family.'

'We're not.' Dani started unpacking the box of plastic plates and cups and torches, laying them out on the Formica card table. 'This is it. One weekend a year and then all this goes back into storage.'

'But, you know, Liss and Lachy – those old-money people are not usually campground types.'

Dani sighed. 'Liss is not a flashy person. And it's not any old campground, is it?'

'If I'm sleeping in something that's not an actual bed and shitting next to a stranger, it's a campground.' Craig snorted. 'It just feels a bit fake. Why camp when you don't have to?'

HE WOULD NEVER

'It's not all about Liss and Lachy. When we first started coming, as the mothers' group, it was democratic. We all come from different backgrounds, different budgets, different situations. Camping is manageable for everyone, rather than renting a holiday house, or –'

'But they *have* a holiday house not far away.'

'It's not big enough for everyone.'

'And the whole mothers' group thing,' said Craig, banging in his final peg. 'I get that at the beginning, but the kids are all so big now, there's no real need to stay friends with people who aren't on your –'

'Social level?' Lyra called as she walked over from her side of the tent. Such a smart-arse. Dani threw her a smile.

'Wavelength.'

Case against Craig: He was a snob.

'Liss is family to me. This weekend is important to her. We've been through a lot, and the girls and I have got good at pretending we're campers, haven't we?'

'It's my favourite holiday of the whole year,' Brigitte confirmed from her and Lyra's decidedly wonky tent.

'Because we get to do whatever we like,' Lyra added.

'You do not.' Dani grabbed Lyra's hand as she passed and looked her straight in the eye. 'The mums will be deciding the rules later. How far you can go, when you all have to be back to camp. Bedtime.'

'We're not babies.' Lyra pulled her hand away.

'Only the mums make those rules, do they?' Craig asked.

Dani ignored him. 'Lyra, I love you, but being fourteen is not the same as being an adult. There will still be rules.'

'Can I go now?'

'No. Your sister needs help.' A wave of exhaustion hit Dani at the prospect of three days of boundary-setting and rule-enforcing with a group of teenagers all straining at their leashes of various lengths. It would be easier to let them *Lord of the Flies* it.

'Fine.' Lyra went to Brigitte and the piles of tent.

She was a good girl, Lyra. Dani had never caught her lying, found a vape in her pocket or cider on her breath. She didn't have the school on the phone, or a lunking boyfriend hogging their lounge. Lyra played soccer and netball and swam. She got solid Bs. When her friends came around they said please and thank you for the snacks and drinks foraged from the fridge. Lyra was where she said she would be when Dani checked the family app, and she called her father as promised. When Dani worked late, Lyra came home and fed Brigitte. She smiled and giggled politely when her grandma critiqued her clothes. She followed the house phone rules – the bane of every teen parent's existence – plugging in overnight in the living room and doing her homework before scrolling TikTok, most days.

Dani had no choice but to set things up like that. There was no time for an unruly teen; she was a single parent with a big job. She had chosen a school – Catholic, girls-only – that would reinforce the boundaries she could not always police. Dani knew that schoolfriends' parents might whisper about whether hers was a house they'd want their girls at – that one with the working mum and the overseas dad – so she counter-programmed with a tight ship.

But every year this camping weekend was both a release and a threat. Some of the parents were happy to let the guide ropes slacken. They opted to take their eyes off the kids, to shrug off teenage 'experimentation'. They trusted that everything would be fine. But Dani couldn't. When the kids were little, she was constantly vigilant. 'Where's Bridge?' she'd repeat any time her younger daughter wandered out of view. Now it wasn't the forest or the unknown campers that worried her, it was the other children. Who knew if they were as good as Lyra? As boundaried and responsible? Who knew if they were already necking (was necking still a thing?), smoking, wagging?

'Show's on the road,' Craig exclaimed, gesturing to the tent. 'We might be on the crappiest site, but our home is our castle and the castle is up.'

'Sadie's on the crappiest site,' Dani said, without thinking, taking her eyes from her daughters to Craig. 'It looks good.'

'I live to serve.'

Case against Craig: He spoke in clichés. In public, at least. When they were alone he was capable of honesty, originality, even vulnerability. But Public Craig was programmed to communicate like a marketing campaign. And she was about to spend a very public weekend with a very public Craig.

Now the tents were up it was time for the beds and the sleeping bags and the blankets, all tightly packed away in those plastic sacks she'd sucked all the air out of with the Dyson.

Craig would find something more physical to do, she knew, over at HQ with Lachy. She looked across and saw Lachy was leaning against the Land Rover while Liss rummaged in the open boot. He was on his phone. *Typical*, she thought, looking up from her own armfuls of fluffy covers to see that Craig was doing the same.

'Hey,' she said. 'Don't set a bad example.' She nodded towards the girls.

Craig pocketed his phone and came over to kiss her forehead and take a blanket from her. 'Of course. Although I know you – you'll be checking your work messages as soon as you've got two hands back.'

She would.

'Only when the girls aren't looking.'

Craig's eyes were back on Site Seven and Lachy. 'That guy is not about life's humble pleasures any more than I am.'

'For God's sake.' Dani sighed, ducking through the tent door, a spike of intense irritation pushing into her chest. 'I thought we were done with that. If you hated it last year, if you don't want to sleep in a tent, if you think Lachy and Liss are pretentious – Just. Go. Home.'

'Whoa!' Craig followed her into the strange pale blue light of the tent. 'I'm just talking, babe.'

'Mum!' Lyra's voice, from the other side of the canvas. *Shit.* Kids who'd spent their formative years in the eye of a disintegrating marriage were sensitive to raised voices and emotional temperatures. She'd seen Lyra run from a loudly exclaimed curse.

'All good, Lyra.' Dani turned to glare at Craig and mouthed a quick shush.

He shrugged. 'I'll go inflate the mattresses, the new car's got a plug-in for –'

'Thanks.' She turned her back on him before he could finish.

She was being a bitch. Sometimes the magic of Green River worked on her the way it worked on Liss, unravelling her tightly wound anxieties, smoothing her frown lines, lowering her shoulders. But at other times the disruption from routine and the forced extraversion made her tighter, harder, spikier. She knew to choose the former today. But the latter was pricking at her temples.

Her phone, shoved in the back pocket of her navy shorts, buzzed.

Just as Craig had predicted, work.

He reappeared in the tent's doorframe as she dumped the blankets and reached for her phone.

'I want you to know that I promise to embrace the hard ground and have a good time,' he was saying. 'Couldn't be happier to be here. As if I'm going to miss what your mad mate Sadie is going to do this year. She's really something.'

'Yes,' Dani said, absently, waking her phone screen. 'Let's hope this year she's not something to worry about.'

Craig smiled, pulled his head back out of the tent and returned to mattress inflation.

HE WOULD NEVER

I need to talk to you. Urgent.

It took a minute for Dani to realise that the message was from Lachy.

Jesus. She shoved her phone back in her pocket, pictured her friend's husband over the path, leaning on the car, poking at his screen. Not again.

3

2010

Randwick Community Centre, Sydney

Liss

Strip lighting and padded walls and the faint smell of bleach covering a pungent hint of infant shit.

Liss was discovering that parenthood forced you back into public spaces in a way you'd avoided since school.

She'd had the obstetrician with the most letters after their name and a waiting room complete with Italian *Vogue* and kombucha on tap. She'd had the birth suite with the fairy lights and piped-in rainforest sounds to drown out the screams, but it now seemed inevitable that at some point she was always going to find herself here, in a room decorated with laminated orders not to smoke around babies and that feeding them anything other than breastmilk was murder. And she was perched on the slightly sticky Formica chair that formed part of a sharing circle in which at least half the women looked like they hadn't brushed their hair since their placentas plopped out.

She was questioning her decision to come here as she looked down at baby Tia, who was swaddled in a geometrically patterned knitted wrap that had been ethically sourced from a female-centred co-op in Central America. Liss's sister-in-law had bought it for her, possibly to compensate for the complete lack of support she'd shown during pregnancy and birth because, you know, she was dealing with her own stuff and she was sort of at capacity and surely Liss didn't want to be crowded, etc.

Liss saw that Tia had a strange blooming rash peeking out from under the collar of her 100 per cent cotton limited-edition Bonds onesie and her mind filled with one clear thought, *I have no idea what I'm doing. Here or anywhere else. Clearly my baby is allergic to me.*

And then she was saying that thought, out loud. 'I think my baby is allergic to me,' and all the heads in the circle, the blow-dries and the birds' nests, turned towards her.

'When my husband holds her, she goes to sleep,' Liss kept talking. 'But when I'm home with her she never sleeps, and most of the babies I know like to be held but she's more likely to be quiet when I put her down than when I cuddle her, and when I hold her, she snuffles and coughs and cries and kicks her legs and now she's got a rash that I think only comes when she touches my skin . . .'

The facilitator of this session was a woman called Anne. It was printed on her name badge in full-caps Comic Sans. **ANNE**, *Early Childhood Centre Community Lead*. Anne had a cheery pink clipboard, and Liss knew that her own name was on it, along with baby Tia's, and that likely what was being written next to it right now was the word *anxious*.

Liss also knew, in what was left of her right mind, that this woman saw a new group of mothers every six weeks: the latest batch of women in the postcode who'd given birth. They sat, they talked, they shared. Then they graduated and were quickly replaced by the next wave. It was clear that Anne had seen everything, was unimpressed by histrionics and could pick a troublemaker a mile away.

Liss suspected she was the troublemaker, because it didn't feel like the things she was worrying about were the things the other women were worrying about, not by the way they were responding to her babbling, with raised eyebrows and tongue-clicks and head-tilts and little sighs of shock. Anne, though, merely looked irritated.

'Your baby is not allergic to you,' she said. 'You're tired.'

Well, that's obvious, thought Liss. *I haven't slept much at all in the past four weeks. Or the three months before that, because everything about pregnancy gave me reasons to stay awake. The constant need to pee, the constant need to worry, the constant need to tell Lachy every thought that was plaguing me.*

'You never used to be such a worrier,' Lachy had said to her somewhere around month seven, when he'd come home from tennis to find her crying on the lounge, her well-meaning baby book open at the 'When to Panic' chapter. 'Try to go with the flow.'

Well no, she hadn't been such a worrier before. Because before, she wasn't growing a human inside her. And before, she hadn't been aware of just how much could go wrong. She hadn't considered how high the fuck-up factor was for pregnancy until she was in it and suddenly, all around her, there were seemingly casual references to miscarriage and stillbirth and birth defects. And bleeding and pre-eclampsia and perineal laceration. And she'd been so bloody focused on getting past all those terrifying ideas that she hadn't allowed herself to think past the pregnancy, to the bit where she would have a human to take care of and keep alive, and it had actually never occurred to her that being a mum wouldn't be the easy part.

'I thought I'd know how to do it,' Liss said to the circle of strangers. 'Everyone said my mother was a natural. I thought this would be the easy bit. And Tia's so perfect and she looks so pretty and my house is full of perfect little tiny things and I've got the right pram, you know, the Wasp, with the wheels that rotate in every direction and the cover that clips on but has just the right amount of ventilation . . .' She could see she was losing some of the women now, their eyes sliding down to the floor, their attention pulled away to their giant nappy bags. 'And I've got that Danish cot with the rounded edges and that red wooden highchair from Sweden. But Tia doesn't seem to need a highchair or a cot. And that seamless flat bear with the wipeable weave? No? Anyway, I thought I'd got it all right. She just doesn't seem to like me very much.'

On cue, Tia shouted and then let out a loud, wet fart. A couple of the women giggled. Most did not. Tears blurred Liss's eyes.

Anne just looked down at her clipboard, then looked up and across the circle.

'Does anyone have any questions about the six-week check-up?'

Liss's face burned. Why had she said all that? What exactly had she said? Did she sound absolutely crazy? The rash on Tia's neck seemed to be reaching a finger-width higher every time Liss looked at her.

'I don't think that can be true,' a voice said, from somewhere on the other side of the circle of chairs. Liss was blinking hard and she'd stopped looking at the women's faces because their expressions were making her stomach flutter.

'Pardon?' asked Anne.

'I don't think your baby could dislike you,' this woman said, and when Liss looked up and focused on her face, it belonged to a small, slight woman with tired eyes that mirrored her own, but with enough mascara to signal that she'd tried hard today. 'Because that's not how babies think. You're just . . . her home.'

'Yes,' another voice said, this one clipped, sharp. 'She doesn't know you're even separate from her yet. She thinks you're all one and the same thing. So, really, if she doesn't like you it probably just means –'

'She's having a bad day,' said another voice. There were a few of them. A chorus, who'd stepped in to fill Anne's awkward silence.

'And I think we've all had a lot of those lately, right?' A nervous giggle rippled through the circle; heads nodded. 'Maybe you're having one today. I had a shocker yesterday but today I seemed to be able to put my shoes on the right feet.'

'Anne?' the second woman's voice called out. 'Doesn't that sound right?'

'Sadie,' Anne said, in the tone of a sigh. 'Where's your baby?'

Liss looked at the woman who'd offered up her inability to get her shoes on the right feet. Oh. She was the only woman in the room who didn't have a tightly wrapped bundle in her arms, or one eye on a pram parked, as per instructions, around the edges of the room.

'I left him at home with Charlie.'

'This is a mothers' and babies' group, Sadie,' Anne said, with a heavy dose of resignation in her voice. 'I've told you that before. You were only allowed to re-enrol on the condition that, this time, you brought the baby with you.'

'It doesn't work for his sleep schedule,' the woman said. She looked up, making eye contact with Liss. 'I'm a Routine Mum.'

A little gasp from the crowd. In the eastern suburbs of Sydney in 2010, Routine Mums were as frowned upon as formula feeding and crack cocaine.

Anne lowered her tasteful white bob to the clipboard and ran a pen through something on it. 'Sadie, please leave.'

A ripple of discomfort looped the room. Silent babies were bounced, heads went down, nappy bags were re-rummaged.

Through her own strange haze, Liss tried to understand what was happening. Could you throw someone out of a mother and baby group? It seemed heavy-handed. It also seemed like the most exciting thing that had happened outside her own head for months. Someone crazier than her, out in the wild. Liss felt a fast flush of energy.

HE WOULD NEVER

'Do you even *have* a baby?' one of the other women asked, her voice spiky with indignation, too loud for the small, silent room.

'This is a bit much.' It was the voice of the first woman who'd spoken to Liss, the one who had told her she was Tia's home. It might be the nicest thing anyone had ever said to her. 'Maybe Sadie – it's Sadie, right? – just needed a break. Don't we advocate for that?'

Advocate? Liss couldn't quite place the woman's accent. It was Australian, but there was an edge to her vowels that sounded a little transatlantic.

Anne ignored this comment. 'Sadie. You're welcome to come back next week. *If* you bring baby.'

This was the excitement of being in the real world, Liss thought. You never knew who you might rub up against when you couldn't curate the crowd.

She harnessed the nerve to look around the circle. Fourteen women, all trying to unpick the shock of a sudden, awesome responsibility.

'I just have a question about sleep,' called out a new voice. 'Because I don't care if this woman has a baby or a puppy in the Moses basket by her bed. I bet I'm not the only one here who wants to know when my baby is going to start to sleep, like, for more than thirty minutes?'

A validating murmur of confirmation from the crowd. Liss was surprised. She was confused about a lot of things, but she had never expected her baby to sleep. If a fourteen-year-old wrote a list of things they knew about babies, wouldn't that be at the top?

Anne shook her head. 'You women always want to know that. For now, your babies need feeding every three hours, twenty-four seven. None of those books you're reading are going to change that fact. If a full night's sleep was high on your priority list, you shouldn't have had a baby.'

There was a collective gasp under the strip lighting.

'What?' It was the woman who had told her she was Tia's home. Liss focused on her. Small, dark, beautiful. The bundle in her arms was neatly burritoed in a tasteful navy-blue waffle-woven wrap, a dummy (a dummy!) dangled from a clear-manicured finger. A clean white sneaker tapped up and down on the faux-wooden floorboards. '*You women?* Are you even allowed to talk to vulnerable new mothers like that?'

'Vulnerable?' Comic Sans Anne's voice had raised an octave and had a tremor in it that wasn't there before.

Oh, Liss thought. *We are not the only ones having a bad day.*

'*You women* are not *vulnerable*. You are entitled princesses. I sit here, week after week, listening to you being eternally surprised that babies don't run on a schedule convenient for your other priorities. Guess what? Your priorities have changed, and right now, they're shitting in your laps.'

And into the shocked silence of the circle, Anne tossed her name badge onto the floor, carefully rested her clipboard on her blue chair and walked, only a little unsteadily, to the door.

There was a moment of stunned silence before Sadie, the woman without a baby, said, 'Best. Mothers' group. Ever,' and the women erupted.

Liss stared after Anne's back. 'But she was meant to help me,' she said.

Sadie stood and picked up her tiny handbag, the only one in the room that wouldn't fit a cat. 'This has really been fun. And you,' she pointed at Liss, 'you need to see a mental health professional. And that's not an insult. It's chemical, what you're feeling, and there's nothing these bitches can say that's going to help you. There's nothing wrong with you some meds won't fix.'

No-one – bar Sadie, who was striding towards the door, swinging her bag – could decide what to do.

Thirteen babies were stirring, cries floating up to the greying ceiling panels and dusty air-conditioning vents.

Liss felt Tia flinch in her arms. This had not been what she was expecting.

'Come with me.' It was the little woman, the first one who'd spoken up after Liss's messy rant. 'Coffee. Anne's not coming back. I'm Dani.'

She would always struggle to explain why, but when her eyes met Dani's, Liss felt something like calm settle across her shoulders, her chest. Breathing seemed easier.

Liss looked down at Tia, so tiny in her tasteful blanket. The rash looked like it might be fading.

'Yes,' she said. 'I'd love a coffee.'

4

Friday, 3 pm

Green River Campground

Sadie

Site Eight was closest to the toilet block and on a hot afternoon – and in January, there was no other kind of afternoon – if the wind was blowing in from the south, it was possible you'd wake from a post-lunch nap with a nose full of ammonia and piss.

Sadie was unpacking on Eight now, wondering at her son's ability to make himself almost immediately invisible, cursing at the bindis already stuck in her knees and feeling certain that her progress was being closely observed.

Twenty minutes before, she'd been parked at the side of the one dusty road into Green River, two wheels in the grassy ditch. The car was crammed to the roof racks with sleeping bags and clothes hastily stuffed into any available space. Her head on the steering wheel, she was breathing in the triangular way her therapist had taught her. Three in. Hold for three. Three out . . .

'Mum.' It was Trick. 'We're right here. It's a bit late for a freak-out.'

Shush. Three in . . .

'Never too late,' said Lucky. 'This is Mum we're talking about.'

It sounded to Sadie like Lucky was using her father's voice.

'It's okay, kids,' she said, staring at her bare knees through the gap in the steering wheel, noticing lines that weren't there before. 'I've got this.'

'Looks like it.'

'Just centring myself.'

The afternoon was still heavy-hot, and the insects were beginning to whirr. The entrance to the campground – with its single rusty boom and its vine-wreathed wooden arch – was right there, if she lifted her head.

'Come on, Mum.' Trick's voice softened. 'It's fine. Let's go.'

One more breath, and Sadie pulled up and out of her ditch and bumped down to the gates, feeling the kids rise up a little in their seats, heads swivelling, looking for their friends. Sadie, meanwhile, kept her eyes down, in no hurry to see any of hers.

The old lady who ran the office was still there. Sadie tried not to look up as she walked in to check her name off the handwritten list, nodding as she was lectured about the sanctity of the code to the toilet block.

'I know you,' the woman said, handing her the familiar piece of paper, the one with the map and the code and the warnings. *No noise after 10 pm. Take out what you bring in.*

Sadie shuddered. But as well as equipping her with breathing lessons, her therapist also liked to tell her that people aren't thinking about you anywhere near as much as you think they are. This woman saw hundreds of people coming through here each season, so it was unlikely that the expression Sadie didn't want to look up into really was one of disgust.

'Yes,' she said, lifting her head to look into the woman's cloudy eyes. 'I come every year, with the Shorts.'

'Welcome back,' the woman said, her voice sour and flat. 'Be good.'

She was looking out through the glass door to the car as she said it, so it was perfectly possible she was addressing the kids through the Kia's open windows. But it didn't feel like that to Sadie.

'Oh, I will!' she said brightly, tapping the counter with a little punctuation that was firmer than she'd meant, setting the leaflets for river boat tours and national park walking trails shuddering.

And then there it was, Site Seven, and Liss Short waving wildly from outside her tent, a huge smile painted on her naked face.

One more deep breath, and Sadie threw the car door open.

'Liss! You bitch, can't believe you've managed to get me back here again, after all the bad juju we've dumped on this place,' she'd yelled, hugging Liss and waving at Dani, who raised a hand but didn't move from where she was unfurling sleeping mats on Site Six.

'It's so good to see you too, Sadie,' Liss had said into Sadie's neck, the teeth of her smile hitting skin.

And there was Lachy Short. At the open boot of the black Land Rover. The way he moved, as he unfurled himself and turned her way, was unchanged. The way he smiled that half-smile. The way he looked at her, which was the same way he looked at everything, like he owned it.

'Lachy.' Sadie had nodded in his direction.

'Always a pleasure, Sadie,' Lachy had responded, with an infuriating little bow. 'Can I get you a drink?'

His words hit Sadie like a piece of wet paper shot from a biro tube in class. She flinched, inhaled, and turned to survey her site. 'My place hasn't had an upgrade, I see.'

'I thought you liked . . .' Liss's forehead creased in worry.

'We go through this every year, Liss. It's not that I *like* being near the toilets, it's just, since I've been coming on my own . . .'

'So the whole time then,' Lachy said.

'Fake news, Lachy. Remember Jacob? Remember Lewis?'

'Do I?'

'Shut *up*, Lachy,' Liss snapped. 'You know you do.'

'Anyway, since I've been coming alone I feel more comfortable with the shortest distance to walk in the night . . .'

'It's not like the rest of us are walking to the toilet block in twos, Sades.'

'Lachy, again, shut up.' Liss, Sadie knew, was perfectly content for her to be willing to take the worst site. Someone had to, after all.

'Just taking the piss,' Lachy said. 'Sadie can handle it, she's a grown-up.'

Sadie shrugged, her stomach fizzing, her throat dry. 'Missed your chivalry, Lachlan Short.'

'Ignore him,' Liss said, in the way you might about an outsized puppy knocking things over with its wagging tail. 'I'll send him over to help with your tent in a minute, we're nearly done.'

'Please don't,' Sadie had said. 'I'm a *grown-up*.'

Now here she was, trying to work out which side of the tent had the door in it, billowing bright polyester everywhere.

'Trick!' Sadie called again, in the direction of the trees. No answer. The reunited teens and tweens had fused into a single organism as soon as they were together, and slid off somewhere, doing who knew what.

'Can I hoist your fly for you, madam?'

It wasn't Lachy who walked onto Sadie's site, although there were plenty of similarities. The same confident lope, the same patronising smirk. The same well-pressed khaki shorts and polo shirt embossed with the little horseman waving his stick about.

Sadie looked up from the polyester puzzle. 'You're Dani's boyfriend.'

'Craig. We met last year.' He looked a little disappointed, like he was not a man used to being forgotten.

Sadie hadn't forgotten.

'I'm trying to block out last year,' she said, looking at the mountain of puffy yellow material at her feet rippling in the slightly stinky afternoon wind.

'Oh no, it was fun,' he said, and there was a smile around the edge of his mouth that made the back of Sadie's neck go cold. These fucking men.

'Let me help you.' He bent down, picked up the edge of the tent and began to walk backwards in neat, fast steps to pull it out square.

'I don't need your help. My son is –'

'Off being a teenager with the other teenagers. He hasn't realised you're a person yet.' Craig pushed the first metal corner peg firmly into the ground and moved on to the next.

'Oh, he knows I'm a person,' Sadie said, mimicking his movements. 'No getting around that, unfortunately.'

She caught Craig's quick glance up at her, his head going straight back to the tent. 'The door's here,' he said, lifting a flap.

They moved quickly now, Sadie remembering that it always took two people to put a family tent up, and just how bullshit unfair that was.

'How long have you and Dani been together now?'

'Almost two years.'

'I'm amazed she brought you.'

'That feels like an insult.'

'I'm also amazed that you wanted to come back.' Sadie clipped her side of the tent to her new pole and, together, they hoisted the roof of the tent. 'This is a pretty tight crew. And Dani's . . . tough.'

'I like what Dani likes. And she loves you people, so, you know, she's not so tough.'

Sure, Sadie thought. *That sounds convincing.*

Dani, she knew, was tough like granite.

The tent was up, now there were only pegs waiting to be knocked into the hard ground. Craig looked around, dusting his hands on his shorts. 'Got a hammer?'

'No. For fuck's sake.' Sadie looked over to where Lachy was fiddling with the barbecue, with Liss up a ladder draping her signature solar fairy lights over everything in sight. 'Can you go and ask that idiot for one?'

'You two haven't made peace?'

Sadie didn't remember much about Craig, but she did know better than to trust him with any kind of intel. He was, after all, an outsider.

'No idea what you're talking about, we just give each other shit. We've all known each other a long time.'

'Oh, sure.' Honestly, the smirk on the man. He was as convinced by that as she'd been by his 'I like what Dani likes'.

'I'll go,' she said, and walked away towards Site Seven.

There wasn't a child to be seen, but Sadie took a moment to stop, face the trees and, just as her therapist had urged her, check in on her breath. It was still there. The sun was beginning to track back down towards the tree line but the air was soupy warm. The kids would be flinging mud at each other by the river, or rediscovering old hidey-holes in the forest.

Dani was bustling between the two tents on her site with armfuls of doonas and pillows pulled from the tightly packed bags in the back of that ridiculous red truck. Sadie called out to her and Dani looked up, offered a quick smile and nod, and went straight back to her blankets.

Right.

By the time she reached Site Seven, there was no longer any sign of Lachy. Liss, her floaty skirt tucked up in her pants, her strong, dimply thighs on full display, looked down from her ladder.

'Craig's helping you?'

'I don't like him.' Sadie sank down to her haunches. 'Got a hammer?'

'Lachy's got it. Not sure where he's gone. You okay?'

'I'm just recalibrating.'

'It's going to be difficult for you, this weekend, isn't it?' Liss climbed down, leaving a long line of lights in the shapes of giant chilli peppers to swing free.

Sadie reached a hand up to Liss, who pulled her to standing. 'I just need everyone to let me be a different person.'

'We will,' Liss said, squeezing Sadie's hand.

'They won't.' Sadie nodded over to her site, where she could now see Lachy. He and Craig were pulling her guy ropes out tight and banging them down with the missing hammer and what looked like excessive force.

'They'll move on.'

'It's funny,' Sadie looked right into Liss's face, 'you have the most reason to be mad with me, but you're the only one who isn't.'

Sadie had thought about not coming this year. She'd thought about it a lot. If friends were, as Instagram quotes insisted, for a reason, a season or a lifetime, how did you know if and when your season was over?

'No moral high ground here,' said Liss. 'Anyway, we go way back.'

'We really do.' Sadie squeezed Liss's hand again, then shook her head quickly, as if to dislodge a thought. 'That guy, though.' She nodded over towards Craig.

'Give him a break,' said Liss, even though Sadie was sure her feelings were identical. 'He's with Dani. And the person who's going to suffer the most that he's here isn't you, or her. But –'

'Aiden,' they said in unison. And it was as if the word magically conjured the car that came bumping up the track towards them. It was the same station wagon that Aiden and Ginger had arrived in every single year, covered in what looked like the same dust and dirt.

Sadie watched as Dani threw the pillows she was carrying through the flap of the tent and came trotting over, beaming and clapping. Clearly, this was a friendship whose season was still in full bloom.

The rear door of the station wagon shuddered open with what looked like pressure from a foot belonging to a gangly teenage boy.

'My God, James, you've grown a foot!' Dani went in for a hug, but her head only hit his chest now, and he stood so still and frozen she could have been embracing one of the palms that lined the beach.

Two more overgrown children followed, their faces set in the expression of a child who's been told to be polite with these overly familiar adults. *We think we know them*, Sadie thought, *but we have no idea.*

And then the front passenger door opened, and it was Ginger, in denim overalls, a baseball cap and bare feet, and a smile that split her wide, freckled face. She had a bottle of champagne in her hand and she lifted it triumphantly towards the women.

'Supplies!'

The kids all cringed. 'Where is everyone?' asked Abigail, peak twelve in her tracksuit, hood up, hands in pockets. Just like Lucky.

Liss was hugging Ginger to within an inch of her life as Dani continued to cluck over the children. 'Out there somewhere,' Sadie told Abigail, 'far from us.'

James and Abigail began to move off, staring down at their phones as if they were homing beacons that would guide them to the location of their old friends. Which, in fact, they were. Maya, the littlest and not yet of digital age, followed at a skip.

'Make good choices!' Ginger called after their backs.

Aiden climbed out of the driver's side, crumpled in an old band T-shirt and oversized denim shorts. His hair stuck up in different directions, his rough chin speckled now with tiny grains of grey.

'*That* was a drive.'

'You are such legends,' Liss was saying. 'I know it's a big ask for you to leave the farm.'

'It's not a farm,' snorted Sadie. 'He's a teacher and she's a nurse.'

'They grow everything!' said Dani. 'It's like paradise out there.'

'You visited?' Sadie didn't know that. 'Who else went?'

Liss said nothing and Ginger busied herself with the car door. Aiden walked around and pulled Sadie, who was half a head taller, with a stronger grip, into a hug. 'It's paradise with an endless to-do list and too many mice. You're welcome any time, Sades.'

'Okay.'

'Are we popping this, or what?' Ginger asked, waving the bottle. 'You know I'm better at setting up camp with a bit of a buzz on.'

Sadie looked at her feet, knowing Liss was looking at her rather than rushing to pull out the plastic champagne flutes that were always the first thing unpacked.

'Maybe let's wait until the sun's over the yardarm.'

'Oh, it's definitely over,' said Ginger. 'I've been up since five. My body clock thinks it's midnight.'

Sadie knew that if she lifted her gaze from the ground, Liss would be nodding at her, perhaps even mouthing something to the others. Dani, she knew, would be rolling her eyes. Here was the midlife fuck-up, spoiling everything for everyone.

'Oh, don't mind me,' Sadie said. 'I've still got to sort the tent out and I've brought some of my pretend beers.'

She watched Ginger and Aiden's faces click into recognition, as if they were remembering something they'd been told, maybe around a farmhouse kitchen table that Sadie hadn't been invited to.

'We can wait!' Ginger dropped her hand with the champagne bottle down by her side, and a little behind her, as if she was rethinking its existence. 'Probably getting a bit old for tipsy tent-building anyway.'

Sadie could have sworn she heard Dani tut, ever so quietly, before Liss jumped in. 'Well, it's disco night, so there's plenty of time for bubbles and fake beer once we're all settled in and Juno gets here.'

They all paused, looking up the path, as if Liss's magic would work again to produce their friend from thin air, but Juno's family wagon didn't appear.

Sadie nodded over to where Lachy and Craig seemed to be wrestling over inflating one of the kids' blow-up beds on her site. 'Better get back to it before the alpha men explode in a testosterone mushroom cloud.'

'Nice to have some husbands for hire, though, hey,' Ginger said. 'All care, no responsibility.'

'Not a husband,' Dani interjected very quickly.

Aiden, Sadie noticed, was not rushing over to join the men, who raised their heads and hands in recognition before turning back to her flaccid mattresses. Instead he was stretching, rolling his neck and looking around. 'I'm going to go and say hello to the beach before we start work.'

'Check if the kids are down there,' Liss said.

'And if they're entirely covered in mud,' Dani added.

Sadie knew Trick wouldn't be covered in mud. She knew he would be slightly apart from the others; there but not there. She knew he'd be quietly stewing on what these next few days would be like. What *she* would be like.

A familiar sensation burned the back of Sadie's throat, made her tongue tingle.

'Okay,' she said, slapping her denim shorts. 'Call off your husbands, friends, I'm going to go ruin my manicure finishing off the site.'

'They can help,' Liss insisted, as Ginger and Dani, arms around each other's waists, headed off towards Site Four, the wide, open spot in between Sadie and the camp kitchen, a convenient space that wasn't in the line of the poo-breeze. 'It's the least he can do,' she added, quietly, as Aiden wandered off towards the beach path, leaving the dusty station wagon still packed, doors flung open in the middle of the track.

'Thank you, Liss.' Sadie ran her hands through her hair, fishing around for a smile to offer her friend. 'I'm so happy to be here, I am, but the less I have to do with your husband this weekend, the better.'

5

2010

Bean There, Done That Cafe, Randwick, Sydney

Dani

Almost as soon as they walked out of the early childhood centre, Dani was regretting rescuing Liss.

This woman was so fragile and strange. And her thoughts in the very weird mothers' group that day seemed to have been flitting around the room before settling, in fear, on her baby.

Dani had clocked the other women's faces tweak with disapproval when this bronze-blonde in loose linen and the kind of leather sandals you couldn't buy in Kmart had been listing all the things she'd bought to fix motherhood. She'd seen the eye rolls.

But she'd offered a lifeline. And once you did that, you couldn't reel it back in. At least, not straight away.

She'd steered Liss to the only cafe nearby she knew, and only because she'd been in this shopping centre the week before, groggily pushing Lyra around with a dazed Seb by her side. She'd pointed at the sign and said, 'If the name's that terrible, imagine how shit the coffee is.'

The coffee at Bean There Done That was, indeed, terrible: watery and toothless. But there were wide communal tables, some room for parked strollers and sugar.

Liss had paused outside the door when she'd realised that she'd have to lift her baby out of the pram to go into the cafe. 'She doesn't like me holding her,' she'd said, and Dani marvelled, again, at a person who would say something so honest to someone they hardly knew.

'Of course she does,' said Dani. 'You just need to be confident.'

It was a trick, of course. Dani had no more maternal nous than Liss. Baby Lyra was an exhausting mystery; a puzzling little creature Dani immediately couldn't live without.

She smiled encouragingly at Liss, nodded down to the pram and, soon enough, Liss bent and scooped little Tia up, her muslin wrap trailing like a bridal train as they walked to a table.

They'd only been there a moment, and Dani was working out what to say next to this scattered person with the whimpering bundle, when an enthusiastic holler of recognition signalled the arrival of the woman without a baby.

'Sadie,' she said, standing right next to their table, a manicured hand on her chest. 'I won't shake hands, I can see you've got yours full.'

For Dani, Sadie's voice was half a decibel too loud, her gaze too direct. Chaotic energy buzzed around her like a swarm of bees.

Behind her were two more women vaguely familiar from the session. The one with the American accent. And the one who looked so tired her eyes were retreating back inside her head. One was holding a baby with the most impressive head of vertical black hair, while the other's was barely visible inside one of those complex linen wrap-around sling things that made Dani anxious.

'Juno and Ginger,' Sadie said, gesturing to the women in turn. 'I rescued them.'

'That sounds like an ice-skating duo,' said Liss.

Dani was starting to think that it wasn't honesty fuelling Liss but rather that she was so tired that whatever words came into her head were falling straight out of her mouth.

'Ha!' Sadie said loudly, rather than actually laughing. 'Can we join you? Form our own group? A rebel alliance?'

Dani shrugged. This was not what she'd imagined when she had confidently told Seb this morning that she was 'going to make a friend today'.

But Liss was nodding, and Sadie, in what seemed like slow motion, was leaning down and cooing in Tia's crumply little face. 'You're not a naughty baby, are you? You're just a tired little poppet, aren't you?'

'Aren't we all?' The American woman, Juno, was sitting down next to Liss, opposite Dani. She held her baby, the one with all the hair, outwards, and he was awake, eyes open, staring at them.

'This is Bob,' said Juno, and Dani considered the confidence it took to give your child such a very ordinary name.

'And this is James,' said the other woman, Ginger, nodding towards the squishy linen lump on her chest.

'Well, this is Lyra, I'm Dani, and this is . . .'

'Liss. And Tia.'

Sadie was taking Tia from Liss as she spoke, deftly tightening the wrap around her, firmly patting away at the baby's bottom and bouncing on her toes at the head of the table.

'And where is your baby, Sadie?' Dani asked, because someone had to.

'He's at home, with his dad.'

A couple of impressed murmurs.

'Why?' Dani asked. Everything about Sadie pricked at the worries that had been hard to shake lately.

Sadie just kept on bouncing Tia, who had stopped her squeaky, halting cries and looked like she might be about to sleep. 'Because he's his dad.'

'But why today, with mothers' group and everything?'

'It's mothers' group,' Sadie said, still a touch too loud, with emphasis on the *mothers*. 'Not baby group. I wanted to make friends.'

Dani wondered if Liss was beginning to get nervous about the woman holding her baby. Was she about to run from the cafe with Tia under an arm? Maybe Liss was secretly hoping she would.

Sadie looked around at the women's confused faces.

'We're separated. He comes over in the mornings for a couple of hours, I let him be with the baby. Here.' She nodded at Liss. 'She needs feeding.'

'How could you be separated . . . already?' Liss said, with a hand up her shirt, presumably rummaging around for a bra fastener.

A young woman in a tight cut-off T-shirt arrived to take their orders. 'Coffees?'

'I couldn't remember my baby's name this morning,' Ginger half-whispered, 'never mind what coffee I drink these days.'

'You drink a latte,' said Sadie, loudly, as she bent down to manhandle Liss's exposed breast. 'Big Special K mouth, little one,' she instructed Tia. 'Lattes all round, please!'

'Um, no.' Dani couldn't remember the last time she was so irritated by a person, and she'd been living in New York City until four months ago, so that was saying something. 'I'll have a decaf long black, please.'

'And I'll have soy,' Liss said, over Sadie's bent head. 'I think my milk is irritating Tia.'

'Only at mothers' group, or possibly a strip club, would I have seen your nipple before I knew your last name.' Sadie laughed, straightening up. 'There you go. Better.'

The waitress looked around. 'Long black, lattes, soy,' she said. 'Anything else?'

Three women said 'banana bread' at once. Dani wasn't one of them.

'So what happened? With your baby's dad?' asked Ginger when the young woman had left.

'I deserved better,' Sadie said. And no more.

Dani looked at Lyra and tried to imagine summoning the will to make another major life decision.

'Yeah,' she said, finally. 'I get that.'

Dani didn't tell them that she was reckoning with the fallout of a seismic life choice herself, only that she and her husband had just moved back from years overseas. She didn't tell them how hard it was for her European husband to adjust to this new reality in her home city, how she could feel his resentment hardening against her like firming cement. She didn't tell them about how the family she'd moved back to be close to had actually turned out to be the last people she wanted to be around. That she desperately missed work, where she'd felt competent and in control. But that also, she couldn't imagine leaving the house every day now, without her baby, to go to an office. She didn't tell them that she was sometimes so lonely it was hard to breathe.

Liss told them she lived in Bronte. She had been on a hiatus from work when she got pregnant. She just needed to understand what was happening; why this was so much harder than she'd imagined. When she knew that, she said, left breast exposed to the entire cafe, she'd be so happy. She just knew it. She was made for this, she was certain.

Juno said she and her partner, Emily, had discussed who would carry their baby and she had volunteered because she wanted a holiday. Everyone at the table choked on their coffees. Now,

Juno said, she realised just how badly that plan had backfired. 'Emily,' she said, with just the right amount of drama, 'is an evil genius.'

And Ginger was a nurse who lived in an apartment block just a few doors down from the shopping centre. She didn't offer much more information, every word sapping energy she didn't have. But there was a husband, Aiden. A teacher. Back at work.

At least today's outing had armed Dani with an actual conversation she could have with Seb that night. Something beyond the poo diaries and feeding updates that met him when he walked in the door from the job he clearly thought was beneath him in this city he disdained.

'Promise me you'll speak to someone,' Sadie said firmly to Liss, outside the cafe as they were saying goodbye, as if it was definitely Liss who needed help, and not she, the woman who was on her second round of baby-less mothers' group meetings.

'I'm fine,' Liss said, but her voice was too light, too thin, as if it might splinter.

'Of course you're not fine,' Sadie declared, full volume, pulling Liss into an awkward, cross-pram hug. 'None of us is fine.'

And then she walked off, swinging her tiny bag, heading home to – who knew? An imaginary baby? A custody handover?

'See you next week!' she called over her shoulder.

Dani and Liss had found themselves in the quiet of the underground car park.

'Well,' said Dani, 'it's been good to meet you, Liss.' The urge to get away from her, from all the women, with their unpredictable chaos that mirrored her own, was palpable now.

She heard Liss take a deep breath, saw her hands white on the handle of the pram.

'I came to this group,' she said, 'because I can't tell anyone who knows me that I've lost my mind.'

Dani looked at the fragile, odd woman, who was trying so hard not to cry. 'Why are you telling me?'

'Because you have no idea who I really am,' said Liss. 'And so you can't be disappointed in me.'

Dani knew that her urge to run away might not, actually, be the right one. 'That's true. You're the last person I'm going to be disappointed in. Listen, why don't you let me come over tomorrow and we'll organise to get you some help. No-one needs to know.' Dani sensed, without knowing why, that she should add this next bit. 'Not even your husband. If you don't want him to.'

When Liss looked up again, shaking her head, tears were running fast down her face. 'He thinks I'm happy. Who wouldn't be happy,' she gulped, 'with a baby?'

Dani took one hand off Lyra's pram and put it over Liss's. It was stuffy and murky in the car park. 'I think we've just answered that question upstairs.'

Liss smiled. 'That was one of the more batshit mornings of my life.'

Dani pulled her BlackBerry out of her nappy bag. This woman, whose red-raw nipple had been on full display in a crowded cafe, who'd told a room of women what brand her highchair was, who had let a complete stranger cuddle and comfort her baby, who couldn't get through a sentence without crying – this woman was about to become the friend she'd made today.

'Let me get your number,' Dani said. 'I'm coming to your house tomorrow.'

'My house,' Liss was breathing more slowly now, calming her tears, 'shocks people.'

'Then it will make me feel better about mine,' said Dani, and she held Tia's pram handle while Liss tapped her number into her phone.

'Maybe,' the strange woman said. 'What about next week?'

'You mean, Sadie's renegade group?'

'Yes.'
'Do they make you feel better?'
'Yes.'
'Then we'll do that, too.'
And as Dani headed back to her car, Lyra just beginning to cry for her next feed, right on cue, she felt something she hadn't felt for a while: useful.

6

Friday, 4 pm

Green River Campground

Liss

The flame trees had left puddles of blood-red bellflowers all around the entrance to the beach path.

The women, barefoot and giggling, picked their way through, kicking up splashes of colour.

Juno and Emily had arrived, their new electric SUV gliding to a stop at Site Five like a spaceship landing in a swamp. Now it was time for the first female tradition of the weekend – a swim before the chopping and grilling of dinner began.

Liss knew that their appearance on the beach would send the sand-splattered child-pack running back to the tents where they would nag the men for the sugary drinks they would certainly get.

'Yoo-hoo!' she called to the gang of bodies already in bikinis and boardies at the far side of the sand. 'Yoo-hoo! Want to swim with your mothers?'

'Child repellent.' Emily laughed as the children turned their heads towards them and then scattered, some waving, some heads-down darting, into the fringing tree line.

'Thank God.' Ginger sighed. 'Now I can swim without all the commentary.'

'Commentary?'

'Why are you wearing that, Mum? Put it away, Mum. Is that how you swim, Mum? You look silly, Mum.' Ginger's voice was high-pitched, whiny. 'Who knew we'd given birth to our monstrous inner critics.'

'Speak for yourself,' Sadie said. 'My children worship me like a goddess.'

'Yes, I've noticed.' Dani, earning a swift look.

The women dropped their towels and sarongs where the sand was still dry and turned to the water. The tide was washing back in, the river sandy golden-brown-green as it lapped the shore.

Liss pulled off her shirt, dropping it in a sandy heap. 'Let's go!'

For Liss the weekend truly began when the river closed over her head. When she shut her eyes under the water, rolled and stretched out on her back, floating under the dipping sun. Her skin tingled now, knowing that feeling was coming.

She had been wearing her swimmers – a 1970s one-piece printed with a toucan she'd found in a long-forgotten box of her mother's things – all day in anticipation of this moment. She imagined that the shiny, thinning fabric held tiny molecule remnants of swims her mum had taken, maybe here, at the river campground. Liss could clearly remember those early summers; she could paint a vivid picture of her mother, in a toucan swimming costume, tossing a toddler version of herself up in the air from the water, just as she had with Tia, with Gracie and Ollie, revelling in the freedom and safety of the river beach. No breakers. No surfboards. No blow-ins.

Lachy called it her campsite uniform, the floaty vintage she always wore for this trip. He didn't know, or maybe care to remember, that these were her mother's literal clothes. That in the place she felt closest to her mum, she held her next to her skin.

HE WOULD NEVER

Liss ran into the river now, gasping as the cool water hit her calves, her thighs. She knew that Sadie and Ginger would be right at her heels, flinging themselves forward into the rippling tide. She knew that Dani, Emily and Juno would stay standing and swaying at the river's edge, avoiding getting their hair wet, avoiding the palaver of drying off, avoiding the salty, brackish tang that would stay in your mouth after a river swim, a sensation Liss loved.

Liss shot back up through the water, sending rainbow droplets through the air. 'Heaven!'

'As long as the jelly blubbers don't get you,' said Dani, who was, as always, up to her thighs but looking around anxiously for a tentacle.

'They don't hurt you, Dan, you know that.'

'I don't care, they're a disgusting feature of this beautiful place.'

'So Australian, that there would be something gross and dangerous,' Juno agreed, 'even here.'

Emily snorted. 'No stingers in the land of the free, darling?'

Liss noted the tone. Some of these women – like Dani – she saw as often as she could, for as many coffees and walks and dinners as it was possible to cram into boringly busy adult lives. Some, like Ginger, she saw rarely. Distance and difference intervened.

So now was the time to read the faces, gestures and comments of her friends.

Dani was as tightly put together as ever, in her tasteful French navy bikini with its white edge, the only mark of age a few extra stripes at the loosening skin on her shoulders and at her thighs, her slicked-back dark hair entirely free of silver or frizz. But Liss knew Dani well enough to see signs of turbulence. Nibbled skin at her fingernails. An indirect gaze. Right now, as the water tried to pull her deeper, Dani was turning away from it, glancing back towards where the children had disappeared into the forest, unable to keep herself here, with her friends.

Sadie was tall and strong and fragile and weak all at once. She was gliding freestyle through the water in her high-cut, bright-lime one-piece. Liss knew she would stop only after making sure everyone had seen her stroke – calmly confident and capable. The stroke of a woman who wanted you to know she was no longer falling apart.

Ginger was porpoising in her faded black knickers and bra. She thought swimsuits were for posers and would rather skinny-dip, as she declared every year, and at some point certainly would. Ginger was unbothered by the stares that would come her way from any of the other campers. Especially any who might notice that one side of her lacy black bra was yawning empty, a space where a traitorous cancer had been, two summers before. Now she burst out of the water tossing back her tangled hair. Liss worked hard at appearing easy-going, a dose of Bohemia in a manicured, middle-class world, but Ginger was the real thing.

Juno was holding Emily's hand and wobbling on the muddy riverbed. She wore a wide black bikini and sensible waterproof sandals. Emily – slight and angular in a crocheted one-piece that looked as old as Liss's, as pale as Juno was dark, as hard as Juno was soft – didn't seem as indulgent as usual with her wife. Juno was hooting, loudly, about what she might step on, how the water was colder than last year, about bull sharks, which no-one had ever seen in these slightly murky waters. And Emily was looking down at her free hand trailing in the water, sending up little arcs of diamond drops. Absent.

'What do we want from this weekend, friends?' Liss called out, treading water just beyond where her feet could touch the bottom. 'We should ask the river for it.'

Dani squinted at her with a familiar, affectionate frown, hand above her eyes. 'Again, Liss?'

'It's called a tradition for a reason.'

'Okay, okay.' Dani shook her head, closed her eyes for a moment, let her breath go. 'Cliché, but I want peace. Even the school holidays have been too damn fast this year. I want three days of nowhere to be and nothing to do.'

'You do not.' Liss laughed. 'You hate nothing to do.'

'Well, luckily we're camping, so there's always something to fucking do.' That was Juno, still unsteady at thigh-height. She was every inch a city person and Liss loved that she still came every year despite it. Bob, she was sure, had a lot to do with that. 'I'd like,' Juno sighed, and held up Emily's hand towards the sun, 'some quality time with my elusive wife.'

'And some good content, no doubt,' said Emily, still looking at the water. Juno, who'd been a book publicist when she'd had Bob but had since passed through careers in PR, talent management and massage therapy, was now busy 'building a brand'. She'd become 'big on lesbian TikTok', she'd told Liss.

'Aren't you a bit old for that?' Liss had asked, thinking of her daughters glued to their glowing screens, to the incessant whiny repeat of catchy music hooks, shouty comedy lines and tearjerking stories about dogs. Juno had laughed. 'You have no idea,' she'd said. Liss still hadn't seen any of Juno's 'content', but Dani told her there was money being made. That new car, for starters.

Now Juno was shaking Emily's hand in hers. 'Of course there'll be a little content,' Juno said. 'Camping's too good not to post. But look at me now, honey, I left my phone in the car.'

'Congrats.'

'Emily?' Liss pushed, smiling.

'I'm with Dani,' Emily said. 'I wish for a year here where things don't get messy.'

'Ouch.' Her wife pulled at her hand.

'She means me,' yelled Sadie, from her floating spot. 'But it's okay, Em, I've cleaned up my act. Going to be boring this year.'

'I didn't mean you,' Emily said, gently. 'And you could never be boring.'

'She means me,' Juno called to Sadie.

'And what about you, Sadie?' Liss asked.

'I want to stay away from the men,' yelled Sadie. 'They're pigs.'

Ginger laughed. Dani and Liss did not.

'They ruin everything,' Sadie continued. 'I've sworn off the lot of them.'

'Welcome,' said Emily, smiling.

'Well, I want to have fun,' said Ginger. 'No animals, no chauffeuring the kids, no patients. And, sorry, but I *will* be drinking.'

'Thank God,' said Juno.

Liss looked around at her women, beaming now at the comfortable back and forth. It was going to be okay. They were always okay.

'I want to be with you all,' she said. 'And, of course, our beautiful kids.'

Dani laughed. 'How many of them are there again?'

'Eleven.' A man's voice.

Lachy was standing at the water's edge, one hand in the pocket of his khaki shorts, the other holding a glistening beer bottle. Something Italian.

'Where did you come from?'

'Came to check up on you.'

'No need, darling, we'll be back soon.' Liss waved her hand, raised her eyebrows.

'Those eleven kids are hungry,' he said. 'They're asking where the food is.'

'I'm sure you men are capable of figuring out some snacks.'

HE WOULD NEVER

'Yeah, we're decompressing here, Lachy,' Juno called to him. 'You're not helping.'

'Okay. Okay.' Lachy looked at an imaginary watch on his bare wrist. 'It's five o'clock.'

Liss saw how Dani kept her back to Lachy. How Sadie ducked back under the water and swam several determined strokes further out.

'We don't need a timekeeper, darling,' she tried again, keeping her voice bright. 'We'll start sorting out dinner soon.'

'I meant it's shark o'clock.' Lachy's voice was full of suppressed laughter, as if he were talking to a group of naughty children. 'Don't want you to come back in pieces.'

Liss's irritation hardened into flat-out annoyance. 'We're fine, you don't need to keep an eye on us.' But she knew he would.

'He's got a point,' said Juno. 'Dusk, and all that.'

'It's not dusk. And there aren't any sharks.' Ginger kicked up her legs in exactly the kind of splashy, rhythmic display that would attract them if there were. 'Lachy's just trying to scare us. As usual.'

Lachy raised his beer and turned to walk back to the red-stained beach path. 'We'll put some snacks out and turn the barbecues on,' he shouted. 'We just want our women to come back alive, you hear?'

'Our women,' spat Sadie, shooting a mouthful of river water towards the shore. Still, she started her strong stroke back towards the sand, and the others all began to leave the water too, murmuring now about what they'd brought for dinner, and whose salad they might use today and whose cheese they might save for tomorrow.

Lachy had broken the spell.

7

2010

Bronte, Sydney

Liss

'It's like falling in love,' Liss had told Lachy as he was trying to break into her breastfeeding bra. 'Dani gets me.'

'I get you,' he'd said, burrowing into her aching, oozing cleavage.

'Babe, no. Not the boobs, not now.'

He didn't get her at all. Not lately.

It had been one month since the mothers' group revolution and everything had changed.

With a combination of Dani's hustle and Liss's own spending power, she was on the books of an expensive therapist.

Tia's feeding had settled into a more predictable rhythm.

And she had people to talk to.

'You're having sex?' Dani had gasped, when Liss told her about Lachy's pawing. 'Already?'

'I don't remember a lot of advice my mother gave me,' Liss had said, rubbing Tia's head as she fed. 'But she told me to always be in the mood to fuck your husband.'

HE WOULD NEVER

'No offence to your dead mother, but that's the worst advice I've ever heard.'

Baby Tia let out a surprised squawk as Liss's boob shook with the unfamiliar feeling of spontaneous laughter.

'My mother had a lot of shit advice. Wonderful mum, terrible taste in men.'

Dani was in Liss's too-big, sunny kitchen, sitting at the thick wooden island bench on a squishy leather high stool, balancing Lyra on her knee and unenthusiastically picking at the bland bran muffins she'd brought along.

Liss didn't usually invite people to her house. But this last month Dani had been in and out regularly, with muffins, lattes and well-timed welfare checks.

The house could be intimidating. Six bedrooms. Sandstone. Set in gardens behind Bronte Beach. You could see and hear the ocean from the deck's swimming pool. Liss knew there were so few old houses this size left in Sydney's eastern suburbs that living in one marked you as Other. Which was why, she also knew, fancy old money hangs around with fancy old money.

When Dani had pulled up the first time, and lifted Lyra out of the car in her little capsule, Liss had stood at the gate to her driveway, watching Dani take it all in.

Dani had turned and looked directly at Liss, who was wearing an oversized, stained lacy Victorian nightgown and battered sheepskin slippers. Liss knew she hadn't brushed her hair yet, and couldn't remember whether she had brushed her teeth.

Dani smiled with half her mouth, a kind smirk. 'So, you're rich. Doesn't seem to be doing you many favours.'

Then she'd seemed to examine Liss more closely. 'You know, you could have opened your fancy electric gate, and not walked out here looking like that. Your poor neighbours.'

'Like what?' Liss had asked, and Dani laughed.

Dani was not intimidated or awed by the house. Just confused.

'Why haven't you just got a night nurse, and some sleep?' Dani asked a little while later in the kitchen.

Liss was padding about in her slippers, trying to make tea. 'We hired one when I first brought Tia home.' She turned on the tap, turned it off, shook the kettle, and turned the tap on and off again. 'I was too embarrassed for her to see what a disaster of a mother I was.'

Dani had stepped in, taken the kettle, filled it, switched it on.

Four weeks later, kettles were less of a challenge and Dani was stuck on Liss's dead mum's sex advice.

'My mum can't even say the word fuck. And Seb isn't even a little bit interested in having sex with me until this,' Dani gestured broadly to her body, 'pulls itself together.'

'Everything looks pretty together to me.'

'He's worried about . . .' Dani's hand travelled lower.

'Your vagina? Well, he might be waiting a while for that to pull itself together. Tell him not to be so fussy.'

The immediate intimacy Liss felt with Dani and – to a lesser degree – the other members of the renegade mothers' group was remarkable. She was trying to remember any other time in her life when she'd felt so comfortable with strangers so quickly.

University? Certainly that had been Liss's first attempt to shake off the social circle she'd been allotted and rewrite her assigned script. All her clever friends went off to do law at ANU and medicine at Melbourne Uni while she opted for a degree in Fine Arts at UNSW, a school her father and grandfather considered beneath her (they meant beneath them). It provided Liss with an escape and she'd made fast friends in clouds of pot smoke in the share houses of Sydney's inner west. But all those people had fallen away in the years since, the years she'd spent slowly heading back to where she'd started.

Her travelling friends? After uni, Liss had delayed the inevitable by embracing the cliché of a couple of years overseas. Getting as far away from her father as possible was the driving force. Of course, he kept turning up wherever she was. Liss was sunbathing, topless and high, on a beach in Skiathos and he'd stepped off a ferry with his oldest friend's ex-wife. Liss was pulling pints at a pub in Chelsea and he'd walked in with her middle brother for a summer afternoon Pimms.

'Come home, darling,' he would say. 'A beautiful life is waiting for you.' So she went to India, where she knew he wouldn't follow.

But the friends she'd made in those years? The boyfriends and the girlfriends and the drinking partners and the ravers? Facebook, now, mostly. And all of their lives looked like hers these days, which meant she couldn't talk to them, not really, about what a shock all this was.

These mothers' group women didn't know her. They expected nothing of her. And they didn't know Lachy.

Four weeks of fast, firm friendship, of multiple daily texts and endless cups of tea, yet Dani hadn't met Lachy and Liss hadn't met Seb.

They were existing in a women's world.

When she'd pushed Lachy away from her last night, Liss knew he'd be trying another angle within the hour. He loved her. Adored her. Always, always wanted to fuck her.

It's not that he was aggressive about it, it's just he was always so dejected if it didn't happen. Such a moper. And Liss didn't like to see him sad. Since the day she met him, his smile was her motivation. It wasn't always easy to get, because he was hard on himself, driven, disciplined, and that came with its pressures and stresses. So a moment of joy, of unselfconscious release, was rare. And for Lachy, like lots of men, Liss imagined, that moment came in bed.

Before she could introduce Lachy to Dani she would need to explain him a bit. He could be the kind of man you could take the wrong way. And although she'd only known Dani for a month there were two things Liss knew about her. She did not like dickheads. And Liss wanted her approval.

She had heard about Dani's husband, Seb. He was French. He and Dani had met in New York. Dani said that he was pretty much the opposite of any man she'd imagined herself being with – impulsive and creative and spontaneous, whereas she had never met a spreadsheet she didn't want to optimise. Dani handled things, quickly and capably. Liss got the feeling that their relationship was complicated, trying to settle into Sydney and parenthood at the same time. But Dani was not an oversharer. Liss absolutely was.

'Before you meet Lachy,' she started.

'I'm meeting Lachy?'

'Of course you are, we're friends now. And I'll be meeting Seb. And we'll all go away together one day for one of those couple weekends new friends like to do to see if they're compatible.'

'We will?'

'It's inevitable, Dani, don't fight it. Anyway. Before you meet him, I need to prepare you.'

Dani was making faces at beautiful little Lyra, who was having her 'stimulation' half hour, or whatever the latest stop on Dani's increasingly complicated schedule was. 'Does he have a thumb for a nose?'

'That's a strange place to go to.'

'Something *my* mother would say. Go on.'

'He can be a lot.'

'How?'

'He's handsome,' Liss started.

Dani laughed. 'Come on, I can handle handsome. Do you think I'm going to try to hit on him? I promise, I do not have the energy or the will for that.'

'And he's confident. He talks a lot at first . . .'

'I feel like you're speaking in code.'

'I just want you to know that if he comes off like a bit of a prick, he's not. He would never do anything to hurt anyone.'

Dani held Lyra up to her face and kissed her nose. 'This is beginning to sound scary. Is he scary?'

'No!'

'Anyway, I don't have to meet him. We can stay in our bubble.'

'I don't want to,' Liss said. 'I told you, I'm in love.'

Dani smiled in a way that made Liss feel warm. 'You know how you said Lachy's a lot? You're quite the generous serving yourself.'

'You saved me.'

'I did not.'

'And so whether you like it or not, we're bonded now.'

Dani was clearly not comfortable with all this naked emotion because she stood up and jiggled the baby, changed tack. 'Tell me how you and Lachy met. I like those stories.'

Liss lay Tia on the kitchen island – the one Lachy wanted to get redone in Italian marble – and windmilled her little legs as she told Dani the story of how she'd only just returned from a few years travelling overseas when she was summoned to her eldest brother's birthday party.

It was the kind of party her sister-in-law insisted on calling a barbecue. Her brother's harbourside new-build was full of caterers, and waiters bringing around mouthfuls of things on Chinese soup spoons, and a man in a bow tie mixing cocktails in the corner. Not a barbecue, in Liss's opinion.

'Piper loves money.'

Dani raised her eyebrows. 'Doesn't everyone?'

'I don't,' Liss said, and caught Dani swallowing a splutter.

'You're thinking it must be easy to pretend you don't care about money when you've got it, but it's more complicated than that.

There are rich people who love money, who dedicate their life to keeping it close and getting more of it, and making sure everyone knows they have plenty of it.'

'Your father?'

Liss nodded. 'And there are almost-rich people who are always chasing an invisible number, some mythical amount that will make them safe. Like Lachy. His family was . . . he's driven by wanting to be a different kind of rich. I know that was part of his attraction to me.'

'Brutal.'

'No.' Liss scooped Tia towards her and began unfixing her bra. 'It's just true.'

Dani still looked amused. 'Well, I'm not rich, but I'm chasing that invisible number, too.'

'Most people are.'

'And you?'

'I don't care about it at all.'

Tia feeding was the most satisfying feeling Liss had ever experienced. Now that it was working, it was better than any drug. Maybe it was acting as a truth serum, because she could see that the longer she talked about this, the more irritated Dani looked. And she didn't want to irritate Dani.

'Come on. All this? The view, the house, the right pram? You'd give it all up?'

Liss decided she'd gone far enough. 'I don't care about money, but that doesn't mean I don't appreciate what it's done for me. Or that I am an idiot.'

Dani laughed. 'So, Lachy? And the fancy barbecue?'

Piper's party had been fairy lights in trees and a string quartet playing Metallica. Liss's overwhelming memory of walking into that evening was of feeling displaced. After the time she'd spent travelling in India, everything back home seemed wasteful, frivolous, gross.

HE WOULD NEVER

Her dad, her brother, Piper and the ugly new house, all of it repulsed her. She didn't fit here. She didn't fit in stinking, throbbing, exhilarating India either. There she'd felt slight, faded, sketched, like an impression of a person rather than the full, bold-colour version. Thing was, she felt like that here, too.

She was by the cocktail cart, avoiding her father. She was about to take the first glug of her third lychee martini when a man stepped up to her.

'Who are you hiding from?'

Liss knew she didn't look like the other girls at the party that night. She was wearing a long, loose dress from a market in Goa, the colour of overripe peaches. Leather sandals wound around her big toe and snaked up her ankle. She was slight from the inevitable Indian flu and her hair was untrimmed and frizzy. The other women, in their little cocktail dresses and tasteful diamond-stud earrings, blended in. Liss stuck out. Was that why Lachy had noticed her?

He must have realised that she was only there out of obligation.

'I'm hiding from my dad,' she'd said, with a freeing lurch of honesty.

The man was kind of beautiful. Tall and wide-shouldered with a direct gaze. But she had seen enough, in the few years she'd been out in the world, of handsome men who knew their power.

'Would you like me to tell your father to fuck off?'

'I wouldn't. He's paying for the drinks.'

Was that the moment? Maybe. But what Liss could still conjure, as she sat at her kitchen island, was how she'd felt when he leaned in towards her, his mouth so close to her ear his lips brushed her hair as he said, 'I'll still do it. Is it him?' He turned his head, pointed. His hands, she noticed, were big and wide, but clean and soft.

Liss's father wasn't hard to pick from the crowd. Everything about him said 'holding court'. This wasn't technically his party, or his house, but his entire demeanour said that none of this would be happening without him. The way he threw his head back and laughed one notch louder than anyone else. The way he put a hand out, casually dangling an emptying glass, knowing that it would be plucked away and swapped for a frothy replacement within seconds. Even in his mid-sixties, Michael Gresky had a glow about him.

'Yes,' Liss said, her lychee martini stopped at her lips, her eyes now looking up at this man. 'That's him.'

Lachy turned abruptly and walked away. Down the three stone steps to the pool deck, along the edge of the glowing turquoise oval lit from below. Right up to where Liss's father was talking to three of Piper's most attractive friends, all women less than half his age.

Liss watched Lachy stop, wait for the couple of seconds it took for her father to register his arrival. This tall man smiled a glorious smile and then leaned to her father's ear and spoke. Liss actually gasped as she watched her father's face change. His expression shifting from polite curiosity to disbelief to anger. His lips moved, most likely in exclamation, but the younger man was already on his way back to Liss. Her father's eyes settled on his back. And then moved to Liss.

The stranger was smiling, walking ever so slightly faster than he had on his way there.

When he reached her, Liss knew, she was going to put her sickly drink down, and he was going to grab her arm, careful but firm, and she was going to be swept along with him.

'We'd better go,' he said, still smiling. 'I just told your dad to fuck off, as discussed.'

'As discussed!' Liss allowed herself to be steered towards the house, towards the front entrance and the leafy, ink-dark street, almost giggling with fizzy excitement as she pictured the look on her father's face.

HE WOULD NEVER

They stopped on the street. It was late summer, the insects were a cheering chorus, the air was sweet and warm.

'I'm Lachlan,' he said. 'Lachy.'

'I'm Liss,' she said. 'Alyssia.'

'What do you want to do now?' Lachy asked. This big man, in a suit. She had never before gone anywhere with a man in a suit. She could feel the last traces of India, of the version of herself caught in the threads of this peachy market dress, floating off and up into the evening like fireflies.

'I'd like to go for a walk,' she said, 'by the water.'

The harbour beside them lapped at still, quiet beaches that ran along the front gardens of huge homes, lit up like shopping malls against the navy sky.

The big man surprised her by putting out one of his hefty paws, as if to shake on it. 'Can I hold your hand?'

'It's cheesy, but I knew my next adventure was him,' Liss told Dani, raising Tia to her shoulder and patting her tiny back.

'No shit,' said Dani, her finger hooked in Lyra's mouth, her body rocking back and forward. 'That's a great story.' She bent to strap Lyra into the capsule. 'Okay, I'll meet the guy. Who wouldn't?'

8

Friday, 7 pm

Green River Campground

Dani

Juno was filming Ginger making margaritas.

'Shake it, sister,' she was saying, as Ginger duck-faced for the phone, her hair damp and frizzy around her face, dark patches on her denim overalls where her river-wet undies were soaking through.

'No kids had better turn up on these TikToks,' Dani said as she passed, carrying a tray of sausages in the direction of the barbecue.

'Calm down, Grandma.' Ironic, considering Juno was a few years older than the rest of them.

'I mean it. Seb would kill me.'

A tut from Juno. 'As *if* Seb's on social.'

'You never know.' Dani kept moving, calling over her shoulder. 'We're all trying to stay relevant, lady. Anyway, hard rule: none of the kids on your channels.'

'Channels? You're so cute.'

First night dinner was barbecue. The roles had been so well-honed over the years that Dani could tell you exactly what everyone would bring. By unspoken courtesy of Liss and Lachy, rib-eye for all. Everyone else offered a plate of polite gesture – supermarket burgers from Sadie, something tofu from Ginger. Dani brought lean chicken skewers. And between them there were enough plain beef sausages to feed the children three times over.

The trestle table was scattered with colourful plastic bowls of gluten-free chips and optimistic carrot sticks. Foil lids were waiting to be peeled back from shallow tubs of hummus, and Sadie and Liss were talking intently as they cut and buttered a bag of bread rolls. Kids ate first, and kids ate sausage sandwiches.

But where were the kids? Dani wasn't sure she'd seen them since the beach. She had washed off the river in the shower and changed into her evening camp uniform of long linen everything to fend off insects. She would love to be spraying the girls with something repellent right now.

'You seen Lyra?' She was handing the sausages to three men who, blissfully unaware of their predictability, were standing around the barbecue with bottles in their hands, waiting for the only catering request that would come their way all weekend – *Grill this, please*.

'Can't keep track of your kids, Dani?' Lachy Short made pointed eye contact before turning back to the gas.

'You know where your kids are, do you?' Dani asked, knowing she shouldn't rise to Lachy's bait but still feeling a hot flush of guilt in her chest.

'Of course not. That's the whole point of camping these days, isn't it?'

Aiden's eyes locked onto Dani's. *Help*. He had clearly already run out of conversation topics with the camp's other males.

'Go and get a margarita, Aiden,' Dani said. 'I'm giving you permission to enter the estrogen zone.'

'What about me?' Craig put his arm around Dani's waist and pulled her in, nuzzled her ear. 'Do I have permission to enter?'

Dani felt a wave of something like panic. Repulsion.

Watching Lachy watching Craig behave like this was worse than Craig behaving like this.

'Whoa, you two.' Lachy's voice was sly, his eyes narrowed. 'The fire hasn't gone out yet, then.'

Dani shook Craig off. 'Give me a break. I'm going to find the kids. Don't burn those.' She nodded at the sausages and stepped out onto the track. She felt Liss's head lift and turn as she walked away.

Case against Craig: She was still with him. Her crime, of course. But it was a mistake to bring him here again.

Craig was the result of a loose port connection. Her firm had been presenting to his, and she was the lead on the marketing plan she hoped would tip the bid for collaboration their way. Dani's presentation had been flickering on the giant screen in one of those wireless, open-plan offices that compete with each other for kitchen views and foosball tables. Dani hated off-site presentations. So many things were out of your control.

If a client walked into her space on the marketing floor of her fund, she knew that the boardroom would be ready for anything. Water would be the perfect temperature in the smudge-free glass jug in the centre of the table. She knew that the breakfast muffins had to be small enough to be eaten in one bite, but also that no-one would touch them because having your mouth full in a multimillion-dollar meeting wasn't *it*, as Lyra would say. She knew that her assistant had already asked the guests' assistants for their coffee orders, and hot cups of barista-made would be waiting.

And she knew that the fucking laptop adaptor would fit the fucking black box in the centre of the boardroom table.

HE WOULD NEVER

'Let me help you,' Craig had said, leaning over from the other side of the table, after a flustered young marketing assistant from his firm had dashed off for IT help.

'It usually just connects through Bluetooth.' Dani was irritated by finding herself in the exact kind of damsel-in-distress situation she worked hard to avoid. 'I'm sure I can get it.'

But she noticed Craig's hands, and then saw how his forearms filled the expensive grey flannel of his suit. This was not the sort of thing she usually noticed. *For God's sake*, she thought as she took in his predictably strong shoulders, his close-cropped hair, his kind eyes. *Get it together.*

She hadn't dated since Seb. She hadn't joined any of the apps that Sadie constantly sent her. A little while ago, Liss had brought her a super expensive vibrator with a crystal handle as a joke, and Dani was almost offended. It felt like judgement. 'Do you think I need this?' she'd asked.

'Well, babe,' Liss had answered lightly, clearly trying to decide how honest to be. 'Yes.'

Even after fourteen years of Liss's lightly thoughtless honesty, sometimes it still knocked Dani.

Of course Craig had solved the black box problem. It was his boardroom table, after all. His shitty technology, she'd fumed, quietly, when he'd said, 'There you go, no need to stress,' and her deck had sprung onto the screen in full colour.

And so. Maybe still rocked by the crystal vibrator, Dani had let Craig pursue her. It was old-fashioned. Flowers. Text messages with photos of his face, not his penis. Sadie told her this was highly unusual, and scrolled through her own phone, showing Dani dick after dick. 'This is how it is now,' her single girlfriends would say, with a sort of amused resignation. Craig must have clocked early that wasn't going to be Dani's thing.

And he'd had to be patient, because she had the girls and an ex-husband who was out of the country more than he was in it. She was rarely alone and rarely available. Generally, she loved that she wasn't juggling a complicated custody schedule and missing the smell of her girls' hair on a Sunday morning. But after she finally agreed to a coffee and a walk with Craig around Centennial Park, she found herself thinking, for the first time, that the odd free night would be okay.

As it turned out, the time limitations were a feature, not a flaw. She found him physically attractive but mentally exhausting. When Seb was finally in town and the girls were having a night with him at a hotel in the city, Craig planned a dinner. He'd booked them a private room. A tasting menu. A bottle of something vintage she knew she wouldn't drink.

When he started to look disappointed that she wasn't more impressed, Dani had decided to be honest.

'This is very generous but I have to get up early. Could we just go to your place?'

Always his place. Always her timetable. Dani had no idea if he was seeing other women during this time, and she didn't care, as long as there was nothing awkward, no mess involved. They had sex when they could, they ran together two mornings a week, they were occasionally each other's date to a Thing.

Liss didn't even meet him for the first year. 'Please bring the boyfriend,' she'd say, at the mention of drinks, a birthday, a picnic.

'Not a boyfriend,' Dani would say. 'Sex friend.' Not words she would say to anyone but Liss, and only if neither the children nor Lachy were in earshot. Bridge and Lyra had only learned of Craig's existence weeks before last year's camping trip. Another stupid mistake. They had not been impressed.

Now Dani was walking away from camp, around the kitchen, following the path towards the forest edge.

'Lyra! Bridge!'

Dani did not love this side of the Green River campground. Especially at dusk.

These were the trees that you drove through when you left the triple-lane highway heading north from Sydney. As you took the turn-off and the road narrowed and twisted and just kept on going, it felt like you were abandoning order to head into something wild. These endless trees and rocks and mossy caves were the world between the calm expanse of the river and the rushing, tarmacked motorway with its headlights, Maccas stops and Wrong Way Go Back signs. The bush yawned away on all sides, vast, dense, ancient. Travelling through the trees in an air-conditioned car made Dani feel a little uneasy, never mind heading off into them on foot.

'Lyra! Bridge!'

How could eleven children have disappeared?

Dani took a deep breath, heavy with drifting barbecue smoke and the evening sweetness of all this lush green sighing out the heat. She skirted the edge of the rocks, checking the caves.

'Kids!'

They were probably at camp by now. She would likely hear them if she headed back. Dani turned, and as she did, she sensed a slight movement in the trees between the rocks. She felt it before she saw it, as if someone's eyes were on her. 'Kids!' she called again and took a few steps towards the boundary.

It was getting to the time of day when it's still light, but the brightness is being turned down every second. When it feels urgent, suddenly, to get everything and everyone you need together before darkness comes. It was the part of camping that freaked Dani out every time. They could hang all the lanterns they wanted, drape all the fairy lights – but they would only ever form a puddle of light, and everything beyond it would be blackness until the sun came up.

Dani swiped on her phone torch and ran it, twice, over the trees. 'Lyra!'

She shivered and started walking back to camp. The feeling that someone was watching her walk away was just her anxiety spiking. She was annoyed about Craig. Irritated that they hadn't given the kids a curfew. She was being silly.

Craig and Lachy were still standing over the sausages. Craig looked up and smiled as she passed.

'The kids were here, right?' she said, loudly, to everyone. Ginger and Aiden were drinking their margaritas and watching Juno film a slice of lime sprinkled with salt on a pleasing wooden board. Liss was tossing a salad at the table. Sadie and Emily were puzzling over a phone and a portable speaker in the shape of a poo.

Liss looked up. 'I haven't seen them since we went swimming, but Lachy said they were here. Lachy?'

'They were here,' he said, breaking from his bro-talk. 'They all got drinks and chip packets and headed off again. They'll be back.'

'Well, it's shower time,' said Dani, feeling her foot tap. 'Dinner and disco time. We need them back.'

'You need to stop helicoptering,' said Sadie, looking up from the poo. 'They're not babies anymore.'

'They're not all teenagers. Gracie's only seven. Bridge is only nine.' *And I don't take parenting advice from you*, she added silently.

'But the big kids are fourteen.' Liss was using her peace-keeping voice. 'They'll be fine. And they'll smell the sausages soon and find their way back.'

'Who cares if they've had a shower?' Ginger licked the salt from the edge of her plastic wineglass and Juno turned to film her. 'Dancing makes you sweaty again.'

HE WOULD NEVER

'I care.' Dani knew her voice had changed, that she sounded panicked. 'We don't just get to give up on being parents because they're old enough to walk and talk and not go with strangers.'

Lachy held up a sausage on an oversized fork. 'I thought that's exactly what it meant. These are ready, by the way.'

Craig was beside her now and took her hand. 'I'll come with you, Dan,' he said. 'We'll find them. It's okay.'

Dani saw Sadie's eyes flick left and right and lower her chin. Was she smothering a giggle? *Don't*, she thought. *Don't.*

She shook off Craig's hand, walked over to Liss who took her hands out of the rocket and parmesan and wiped them on the towel still wrapped around her waist from her swim. 'It's okay, Dan. When we get the kids back, we'll draw some rules up about where they can and can't go and when they have to come back. Check-in points, like when they were younger.'

Liss got it. She always did.

'Come on,' said Craig, 'let's walk. We'll stumble over them.'

Juno held her phone up and spoke into its screen, 'Different parenting styles can lead to tension on a group holiday.'

'Stop it,' Emily called. 'Not cool.'

'Let's call it the Karen clash.' Juno laughed before she lowered the phone.

Dani tried to look amused.

Just beyond the tarpaulin roof of HQ and its circle of foldable camp chairs, the cicadas started to sing.

'Golden hour,' said Craig. 'Let's do a loop, find the girls. I'll pour you a drink.'

Liss was looking up at Dani, nodding approvingly. Lachy had loaded up all the sausages on a foil tray. Emily must have finally got the poo speaker to work because some angry rap song suddenly blasted through the quiet. 'Sorry, Bob's choice!' she yelled, flicking it off.

Craig was holding Dani's hand again, pushing a faux champagne flute into the other. 'Let's go.'

In the darkening gold gloom, they headed to the beach path and out onto the sand. Craig chattered away as he kept his hand closed on hers, telling her how Lachy had tried to tell him the car was a bad investment, and how clearly it was only jealousy talking. Telling her how nice it was to have a conversation with someone like Aiden, because in 'real life' he never met 'ordinary people'.

'He's refreshing, you know. He's not trying to fuck with you, he's just talking.'

Dani scanned the beach. No kids. Her stomach knots tightened.

'Baby,' Craig said, squeezing her hand. 'None of the others seem too worried about the kids. Maybe don't stress it. They're probably all just messing about.'

'It's not that.'

'Then . . .'

'Do you ever feel extra pressure.' Dani pulled her hand away and shaded her eyes from the sinking sun. 'Because it's just you? Like, if something happened to Anders on your watch, that it would be extra terrible because Gen would blame you?'

Gen, Craig's ex-wife, barely let Anders out of her sight, but Dani had a hunch Craig had probably never thought about this, whereas in Dani's mind, a pursed-lipped, disapproving Seb followed her parenting choices around like a ghost.

As expected, Craig sounded confused. 'She would believe I was doing my best, just like I believe she's doing her best, right now, wherever the fuck they are, probably at Mountain Man's chalet in the woods, dodging bushfires. Not my concern. Do you really worry about what Seb thinks of your . . . what? *Parenting*?' He said the word like it was made up.

Dani sighed. 'They're not here. Let's go back.'

'Dani, look.'

'I'm looking.'

'No, really look.'

Craig wanted her eyes on the horizon, where the sun was about to fall behind the endless forest on the other side of the river, and the skyline was lighting up purply pink and bluey red. She could see its beauty, but she couldn't feel it, not right now.

'You have to relax,' he said, clearly a touch irritated at her distraction from his romantic moment. 'The kids will be fine. Seb's not here. But you're tense, and you're snapping at people. Lachy, which, obviously, I can't blame you for, the guy's a joke, but also Sadie, and she's just trying to get back in everyone's good books after last year.'

Dani looked at Craig, the outsider. 'Bullshit. You don't need to worry about Sadie. That woman will survive the apocalypse.'

'That's what I mean. Harsh.'

'Oh, come on, Craig. You've got this wrong. Worry more about Liss, who was too soft not to invite her back after last year. Anyway,' Dani started walking up the beach, towards the other entrance, 'I'm not worrying about any of them right now. I just want my daughters where I can see them.'

She was moving fast but he was following, she could feel him, hear his sandals slapping softly on the wet sand.

'Go back,' she said. 'All afternoon I've been feeling like someone's watching me. You're making it true.'

'You've been feeling what?' He caught up in a few long strides.

'Like someone's watching. It's probably the kids.'

'So, that would mean there's nothing to worry about.'

'But it's still not okay.'

'No.' Dani could feel Craig reaching around for something to say as they walked, quicker than a couple taking a romantic sunset stroll, towards the southern beach entry.

'Lachy's so protective of you and the girls, you know,' he said finally, in lockstep with her on the soggy sand. 'He talks about you like you're family but I can't say I've ever heard you say anything particularly nice about him.'

'He's my best friend's husband. What's there to say? You don't choose those.'

'You choose to be here every year with him. I've got mates whose wives I've never even met.'

That unsettled feeling wasn't fading. Dani realised the plastic Prosecco flute was still in her hand, and took a big swig. 'We've all been through a lot together.'

'So you keep saying.'

They'd reached the other end of the beach and the other path back into the campground. Dani looked into the archway of trees bending over it, and the gathering gloom.

'Let's go back to the caves, see if they're there,' she said. 'And please God, stop talking about Lachy Short.'

9

2011

Centennial Park, Sydney

Liss

On the morning of the babies' first birthday party, stirred up by nostalgia and awe at how one thing led to another, Liss thought about how the decision to irritate your father by leaving a party with a confident man could lead you to packing sugar-free muffins and watermelon hunks into Tupperware containers to share with a group of people you hadn't even known a year ago.

'I didn't really tell your father to get fucked,' Lachy had said all those years ago, not long after they'd left the party. They had been lying on the sand in their underwear, the harbour licking at the shoreline, the lights of the surrounding mansions streaking the black water with yellow ribbons. They were wet, lightly panting.

'I didn't think so,' Liss had said, rolling over to look at him.

She could tell he'd been nervous when she'd suggested a night swim, pulled off her dress and run into the water. She imagined he'd been thinking about the opening scene of *Jaws* as he hopped around the sand on one foot, trying to pull off his trousers as she stroked away.

Liss had called to him, as he stayed kick-kicking in the shallows, and she was out, beyond the boats bobbing in the front garden of their owners – the world's most beautiful harbour. Liss liked it where the water was black and cool. Before her babies she was reckless like that, believing that if something came for her when she was doing what she loved, so be it. Her mother had passed down her impeccable freestyle stroke to Liss as if it were a family heirloom. Hours in their pool, up and down, up and down. 'We're water people,' she'd said. 'You don't want to be a splash-about, Alyssia.'

But he hadn't swum out to her, even though she could sense he wanted to. He'd stayed where his toes grazed the seaweedy floor and called for her to come back to him. A splash-about, then. She'd powered back into the shallows, laughing as she kissed him with a mouth full of salt.

'So what *did* you say to Dad?' she asked, rolling towards him, eyes narrowed, her body half-caked in crushed shells.

'I told him I was going to marry his fucking beautiful daughter,' Lachy said.

Liss had laughed. And kissed him again.

Bedraggled, crusty and dizzy with almost-sex, they'd carried their shoes back towards the glass box he rented in the city, blackening their soles on the quietly steaming streets.

Her peach dress had clung to her shoulders under her damp hair. She shivered as a breeze whipped along the pavement, cold at the dawn's sharp edge. His suit jacket hung on his arm and for a moment she was sure he would drape it around her shoulders. But he didn't.

'So,' she asked. 'Who are you?'

He knew her brother from school, he said. Tom was a year ahead, but they'd played rugby together.

HE WOULD NEVER

'I didn't really belong there,' he told her. 'Not like your brothers.' He had neither the stellar grades nor a long history of old boys to ease his passage.

'Tom's a good guy. And meeting people like your family is why my mother wanted me and my brother at that school. It was my duty to make friends with him, and his friends. Still is.'

Liss had tried to remember his name coming out of the mouths of her brothers. Tried to remember his face from the blur of boys at formals and parties and presentations. She couldn't. Not that she'd ever paid much attention.

'School was a long time ago,' she said.

He stopped outside a smoked glass door in an old sandstone wall. 'Sometimes it feels like we're all still there.'

'It doesn't have to be like that. You can opt out.'

Liss hadn't understood the hard edge to Lachy's laugh at the time. 'You can?'

He swiped a card and ushered her through the door into his building. Behind the historic facade was a gleaming modernist block overlooking The Rocks, four rooms with glass walls. Everything sharp and shiny. Everything immaculate.

'Do you really live here?' She trailed her finger along the gleaming stainless steel kitchen bench. 'Like, sleep here, eat here?'

'Yes.' He'd stood in the middle of that kitchen, his white shirt damp and unbuttoned, his shoes in his hand. He looked like an action figure, placed on a set. He looked proud and embarrassed at the same time. It made her want to kiss him again.

'Can I have a shower? I'm freezing.'

The light-headedness of lychee martinis and no sleep was settling on her and she needed to cleanse.

He showed her the bathroom – more sharp lines, more dark gleam – with the confidence of a man who knew it would be spotless.

He'd opened three invisible cupboards along the corridor until he found towels – deep, soft, dove grey – then turned on the water for her, and left.

What she remembered most about that morning was that when she'd come out of that bathroom, freshened and wrapped in a cloud of towels, Lachy had been asleep. Completely naked, curled onto his side on the inevitably black sheets – his mouth open, his damp hair stuck to his forehead, his breath raspy as it escaped his slightly too-full lips. He looked so vulnerable, like she could have slipped a knife into his belly.

She dropped the towels right there on the floor and curled up behind him, her body following his, one arm along his back, the other around his waist. And she fell asleep, too.

Now here they were, Liss introducing Lachy to the women who'd got her through this first year of Tia, of parenthood, of her new reality, her next life.

'Be nice,' she hissed to him as Juno raised her hand to wave them in.

'I *am* nice,' he replied, and Liss laughed.

'You can be a bit intimidating,' she said, knowing he liked to hear it.

Aiden. Jacob. Sebastian. The men's names were thrown at Lachy in a flurry of pointing and grinning and hand-shaking. Liss knew he would be pleased that none of them were taller than him. She knew he would definitely comment, later, on Seb's open-toed sandals. She knew he would, at some point today, ruffle Aiden's sandy-blond, floppy hair.

Jacob was new. He was Sadie's boyfriend, quiet, confident and some kind of 'tech' guy. Lachy had asked Liss, on the way to the park, if Jacob was rich. 'It's so crass to ask that,' she'd told him, and he'd looked puzzled.

HE WOULD NEVER

'It's just a fact,' he said. 'Like whether he has brown hair.'

'It *isn't*.'

'It's 2011. Everyone's selling their shiny little tech start-ups for silly money and coming to us about it. I just need to know if he's that guy.'

'You don't need to know that. It shouldn't matter.' But she knew it did. Of course it did.

Liss had hugged all the women, and they'd settled in a loose protective circle around the one-year-olds, watching them stagger and bounce and plop down on their bottoms, exclaiming all the time how quickly time had flown.

Six years ago she'd woken to Lachy kissing the back of her neck, her hair twisted in his fist. What she could remember so clearly, watching him now nod and attempt small talk with these new, unfamiliar men, was that she'd involuntarily gasped a porno kind of gasp as he'd pushed his fingers inside her and then they were lost. There are a few fucks you would always remember, and this was theirs.

It changed everything, as sex sometimes can.

'My apartment,' he'd said, later that day, 'is completely wrong, now I've seen you in it.'

And she'd replayed the image of the action figure in the kitchen. A boy playing house. *See me here, pulling off my tie and lying on my leather couch before my multi-storey entertainment system. See me shaving with my edgy cut-throat razor in one of the bathroom's fifteen mirrors. See the maid moving around these rooms when I'm gone, restocking towels, wiping down the surfaces smeared with the traces of sticky white substances from the countless nights I came home, not alone, from the bar with the boys I have to beat at work every day. See me winning. See me, on my black sheets, in my bed, with* this *woman,* that *woman.*

Liss laughed. 'It's wrong because *I'm* in it?'

'You don't fit here. And so neither do I.'

Within a month Lachy had been trying on a new set. Renting a floor in an elegant art deco block at North Bondi. Learning to ocean swim. His sheets were warm white. His benchtops were marble. He was calling Liss every day, telling her he was tired of 'all that', which she took to mean not the fishbowl home in the skyline, but what came with it. A certain crowd. The constant need to prove yourself. It was time, he said.

'To one year of fatherhood,' he was saying now to the birthday party group, raising his Italian beer. 'We all survived.'

Sadie's tech guy looked away. 'Sorry, mate,' Lachy said, 'do you have kids of your own?'

'The world doesn't need any more babies.' Jacob clearly did not do small talk.

'The future of mankind doesn't depend on it?' Lachy asked.

Jacob shook his head but didn't respond. Dani's Sebastian, in his almost comically French accent, did. 'Funny none of us think we're the problem,' he said, 'when we're buying the little hats and changing the nappies and planning our legacies.'

'Change a lot of nappies, do you?' Lachy asked. He was play-acting Alpha Idiot again.

'My fair share.'

'I bet you do.'

Liss forced herself to stop listening and focus on Tia, who was sitting between her legs, playing with the unlit Number One candles they were about to push into the tops of the healthy muffins. As the fathers stood a few lengths away, talking, the children's chubby hands were reaching for everything, always, and the mothers were in constant motion, pushing them away, offering distractions, moving things out of reach.

She looked around the circle. There was bubbly wine that definitely wasn't champagne and there were cupcakes that allegedly had

HE WOULD NEVER

no sugar in them and there were little Vegemite sandwiches in the shape of stars. How had they all come to know what one-year-olds would want to eat and what wouldn't kill them? The Liss who had walked out of her brother's party that night with Lachy could barely turn on the water in an unfamiliar shower. The Liss who'd walked into that childhood centre with her baby and a panic attack could hardly leave the house. And now here she was, puncturing a grape with her teeth and ripping it in half before she gave it to Tia.

She'd evolved. All these women had been forced to become new, slightly altered versions of themselves. Looking at the men, Liss felt a passing pang of pity. Look at them, still grunting at each other.

'Come over,' she called to Lachy. 'It's time for cake.'

He looked relieved, and so did the other men, to be offered a reprieve from trying to connect. He crouched beside her, resting on his heels. 'You know, babe,' he said, as quietly as he could manage, 'we have enough friends.'

'These are Tia's friends,' she hissed back, gesturing at the kids rolling about on the grass.

'One-year-olds don't have friends.'

'You'd be surprised. Tia loves Lyra but always pushes James in the face.' She kept smiling.

'James is probably a prick.'

'He's *one*.'

'We're born that way.'

Liss had to swallow a laugh. Dani was bending over to light the muffin candles, shielding the flame from the breeze. Sadie started up the birthday singing and, right on cue, all the children started to wail. Tia threw herself onto Liss with force, her chubby little arms whacking her brow as they looped around her neck.

'Toddlers love a party, am I right?' Lachy was just loud enough for Liss to hear under her singing.

No-one was singing louder than Jacob, who was standing next to Sadie with his arm around her waist as Trick, the little boy they'd all once doubted even existed, kicked him repeatedly in the shin, often falling over in the process.

'I have something to tell you,' Liss said to Lachy, as the singing and the crying subsided, and the children's mouths filled with sugarless cake and strawberries.

'That I'm handsome, and charming, and when you look around at these other guys, you're so glad you chose me?'

'You're in a good mood, considering you didn't want to come.'

'I can handle a few new people, Liss.'

'I keep thinking about when we met. Ever since I told Dani the story.'

Liss saw Lachy glance up at Dani. She was holding Lyra as Sebastian fed her little pieces of strawberry. Lyra was squishing the juicy red mess in her little fists, and Dani was twisting, giggling, to try to avoid her baby rubbing them all down her neat navy sundress with its halter-neck. She looked happy, Liss thought. *Good.*

'You tell Dani everything?' Lachy asked, his eyebrows raised.

Yes. 'Not everything. No-one's interested in the dirty bits.'

'I am, tell me those again.' Lachy was smiling.

'I have something else to tell you.'

Juno and Emily were dancing with Bob. Ginger was badgering Sadie and Jacob for details of where they'd met as Aiden loaded James into his stroller, all fistfuls of cake and watermelon.

Incredible. How one thing led to another. And another. She leaned in close to Lachy's ear and whispered, 'I'm pregnant,' a giggle barely contained in her voice.

He pulled back, eyes comically wide. 'You're pregnant?'

'Shush.' She pushed his shoulder with a flat hand, a tight little smile.

HE WOULD NEVER

But it was too late. Lachy, who had never been able to resist an audience, whooped. 'Everyone!'

'No.' But Liss was too giddy to rein her husband in.

Heads turned, shushes were whispered, toddlers were jiggled. Liss buried her face in her hands, then pulled Tia closer to her, stroking her hair. Tummy full of happy bubbles.

'Liss's pregnant!' Lachy yelled.

Dani's eyes were wide as Lyra splatted a red hand on the pristine blue linen. 'What?'

There were whoops of delight or disbelief.

'But, Liss! We were meant to do that together!' Dani was half-joking, half not.

Seb's head snapped towards his wife. 'You were?'

'You're going to be a big sister, Tia,' Liss told her bewildered daughter, whose face crumpled.

Lachy leaned past his daughter to kiss Liss on the lips, then jumped to his feet and raised his bottle.

'I guess that means we won!' he yelled. 'First to number two!'

10

Friday, 7 pm

Green River Campground

Lyra

The mushroom looked like the tree's tiny, exquisite ear. Its flutes of spongey white pleats were so close to the end of Trick's nose Lyra thought he was going to snort it.

'It's not that kind of mushroom.' She nudged him with her bare foot, rolling him slightly from where he was lying on the brown leaf carpet of the forest beyond the caves.

'You don't snort magic mushrooms.'

'How would you know?'

'I know.' Tia twitched between Lyra's knees. She was sitting on the leaves too, slapping ants from her thighs as Lyra plaited her long hair into tight braids. It was satisfying, this pulling and twisting.

'As if you do.'

Trick stretched out on his back, right there in the muck and moss, and flicked the mushroom into an arc that landed in the leafy mess. 'Whatever.'

HE WOULD NEVER

As the light slowly leached from the forest, it felt like the trees above them were trying to close in above their heads. When Lyra and Tia were little, they were afraid of this space just beyond the rocks and caves, the place where the parents told them not to go but knew they would. The two of them would hold hands as Lyra trailed the boys along the path. It had felt so distant from the camp, with the chattering grown-ups and the plastic chairs and the gas barbecues. As the years passed, they would get bolder and dare each other to go further as if they were brave explorers.

Now, she knew they were actually only ever steps from civilisation. That her mum had been a ball-toss away when they'd all just heard her calling for them through the trees. That the kids needed to hiss and whisper and tread ever so softly, if they didn't want to be discovered. She and Tia didn't need to hold hands to step into the woods anymore.

This year something had shifted in the kids' group. She looked at Trick looking at her. The purpose of the hide-out would morph again.

'Nearly finished.' Lyra fixed a thin rubber band around the last of Tia's yellow plaits and rubbed her friend's shoulders. 'Done.'

Tia shook her hair to feel the braids fall about her. 'Want me to do you now?'

'No thanks.' Lyra watched Tia's smile falter just a little bit. 'I mean, not now.'

'It's great for swimming,' Tia said, quietly.

'I don't think Lyra wants your Bali braids,' Trick told her from the floor.

It had only been a couple of hours but the group had cleaved into its inevitable cliques, and it looked like this year strange, awkward Trick had decided to be one of the girls.

Lyra looked over to where James and Bob were sitting on a rotting log, hunched over a phone in a cloud of vape mist.

'Why don't you go see what they're doing?'

'I know what they're doing,' he said, in that voice that was three notches deeper than last year. 'Looking at porn.'

Tia squealed. 'They are not.'

On the other side of the clearing the littlest girls, Gracie, Maya and Brigitte were building fairy houses and bee palaces from twigs and fallen orange leaves while Ollie tried to whack them down with sticks just as quickly. And the older girls, Lucky and Abigail, appeared to be teaching each other a TikTok dance, all jutting elbows and booty shaking, which Lyra recognised as so last year.

'Bless your innocent soul.' Trick rolled onto his side, leaves sticking to his black hoodie, tiny bits of grass in his hair. 'What do you think fourteen-year-old boys are interested in?'

'You're a fourteen-year-old boy.' Tia hooked a finger in his direction. 'And you're here with us.'

'Yes, but I am more than my hormones.'

Trick was stranger than usual, Lyra thought. James and Bob and Trick were the exact same age as Lyra and Tia, but last year they'd still felt like little boys, wrestling each other in the mud, throwing crabs into the girls' hair and peeing into the river off the rockpool edge. This year they were bigger and broader but also quieter, more self-conscious. Only Trick had really spoken, so far, and everything he said seemed deliberately cryptic.

The first day was always clunky. Lyra imagined the others felt like she did – fizzy with the excitement of seeing each other and for the freedom that came with distracted parents and safety in numbers. But also unsure. Most of the kids were strangers for the rest of the year. And everything was changing so fast.

'Boys are so gross,' Tia exclaimed, again, and Lyra wanted her to stop with the performative disgust. It could be useful to have a boy around. There weren't any at her school, and there weren't any in her house. Her friends' older brothers were, apparently, always in their dark bedrooms, watching writhing bodies. It came over them suddenly, her friends said. Like a fever.

And there was Ollie, Tia's brother, who she saw at Aunt Liss's house. But he was eleven and didn't count.

'Do you know any girls, Trick?' She poked him with her toe. She quite liked doing that.

Trick had grown about a foot since last year, and his curly hair was as dark as his mum's was blonde. *Quirky*, Lyra's mum had always called him. 'And I say that with love,' she would add, as if someone other than Lyra were listening.

'Of course he knows girls,' said Tia, standing up, arranging her braids and brushing off her denim shorts. 'Bay High is co-ed.'

'I know girls,' he said.

'Do you have . . . a girlfriend?' Lyra knew her voice sounded teasing. She didn't mean it to but she didn't know how to ask a question like that without making it sound ridiculous. Tia was looking at her strangely now.

'Why do you want to know?' Trick looked right at her. It was the most observed by him she'd ever felt.

'It's time to go.' Tia was obviously uncomfortable with this conversation. She looked over at the young kids. 'Come on! The parents will be mad.'

Groans. Sighs.

'Aren't you hungry?' Tia pushed. 'I can smell sausages.'

Lyra felt her skin getting prickly under Trick's weird stare. 'You're chaotic,' she said to him, getting up to follow Tia. But it wasn't true. He was more still than anyone she'd met.

'Do you see your dad?' Trick asked, causing Lyra to stop where she was.

'Yes, when he's here. You?'

'Yeah.'

'Is he alright?' Lyra knew a few things about Trick's dad from a decade of listening in to her mother's conversations. The vibe she'd generally got was pity. Was that because he had to put up with Aunt Sadie, or because there was something wrong with him? She couldn't remember. Had she ever actually met him? Probably at a birthday party when she was little. She had a vague feeling that he was tall. Otherwise, he was a blank.

'He's alright.' Trick shrugged. 'He has a baby.'

'Oh.' *That must be weird*, Lyra thought, but didn't say. 'Let's go.'

'Yeah.' Trick began to peel himself off the forest floor, bringing half of it with him. 'Your mum will be freaking.'

Lyra thought of how they'd all watched her mum peering into the trees near the caves, looking worried, confused, trying to make out their shapes in the tangle of bush she wouldn't step into. All the kids looking back, suppressing giggles, shushing the little ones. She felt a stab of guilt but also irritation. The other mothers weren't stressed about the kids doing their own thing. They weren't babies anymore. Mum needed to let them live. 'She'll be fine.'

Lyra walked over to Tia, who was pushing the littler ones towards the path. 'You coming?' she called to Bob and James, through the mist that smelled like sickly strawberry and sour chemicals. 'Or are you too cool? Too stoned?'

'Fuck you, Lyra,' said Bob, but he was smiling a slightly dazed, goofy grin at her. Unlike Trick, they were dressed in the board shorts and T-shirt uniforms of teenage boys she saw around the eastern suburbs, even though James lived in some weird country place and she'd almost expected him to turn up with a mullet and one of those waxy-brim hats.

HE WOULD NEVER

'Fuck yourself, Bob. Your mums are going to kill you if they catch you with that thing.' She nodded at the oversized silver vape canister. 'Let's go.'

'He shouldn't talk to you like that,' Tia whispered to her as they began to follow the little kids through the trees towards the campsite. 'He shouldn't talk to girls like that at all.'

'You can tell him that if you want to,' Lyra said, knowing that Tia wouldn't say boo to anyone. It was funny, because Auntie Liss was like the queen of everything. And Uncle Lachy was, well, Lachy was Uncle Lachy. But since they were little, Tia wouldn't do anything until Lyra had done it first. Climbing up the slide instead of sliding down. Jumping from the edge of the rockpool. Stealing 'adult' chocolate from the fridge. Rolling up the waistband of her skirt to go to Westfield.

'I think Bob's turning into a bit of a dick,' Tia whispered, knowing the boys were too far back to hear.

'You're right.' It was Trick, right behind them.

'Why aren't you back there with the vape crew?' Lyra asked, irritated and a little bit pleased that he was still tailing them. 'Asthmatic?'

'Lyra!' Tia elbowed her. 'He is!'

'He's not,' said Trick. 'Grew out of it.'

Lyra looked at Tia, mouthing, *Yeah right*.

'What about you?' Trick went on. 'Asthmatic?'

'Gave up,' Lyra said, not looking back, and getting another sharp elbow from Tia.

'You did *not*.'

Lyra shrugged, and then giggled. It really did feel different this year.

'How would you know, Tia?' Trick asked, his voice laced with a mocking he must have heard in movies. 'You don't go to her school. Lyra Martin has a whole life without you in it.'

Lyra did turn around then. 'Don't be a dick, Trick.'

'Dick trick!' called James, sending Bob into hysterics, and Lyra instantly regretted handing them that.

Tia was quiet now. Lyra could tell, by the set of her mouth and the tread of her foot, that she was upset. She had always been possessive of Lyra. She didn't like stories about a world that didn't involve her, or them as friends, or their parents and their shared history. It made Lyra feel both safe and stifled, to have her oldest friend love her so much.

'These boys feel a bit like strangers now, don't they,' Lyra said to Tia, softly.

'We're only a year older,' Tia replied, eyes still on the path. 'Things were already different last year.'

It was true. That was the year that the mums had suddenly been very quick to throw the girls towels as soon as they climbed out of the rockpool. The year that they'd been told to stay out of each other's tents, that co-ed sleepovers were no longer appropriate. It was the year that the boys, who had always wrestled Tia and Lyra to the ground in mud fights and jumped on their backs to dunk them in the river, had suddenly stood back. The year that they'd gone from being 'the big kids' to 'the big girls' and 'the big boys'.

'Yeah, but now they feel a bit like the enemy.'

'Sometimes I wish we were still little,' Tia said.

They were at the edge of the campground now. The smell of meat grilling and citronella burning rose into the dusk. Lyra watched Brigitte and the smaller kids charge down the path towards the twinkling fairy lights and faint bass pounding of HQ.

'Ah,' called Trick, catching up. 'Disco night. When all the adults get smashed and call it family fun.'

'Speak for yourself,' Lyra said, and Trick flinched at the words. 'I'm sorry,' she said quickly. 'I didn't mean . . .'

'It's okay.' But it wasn't, Lyra knew, from the way the confident tone had left Trick's voice, and his eyes had gone to the ground. She was sure that her words had taken him to the beach, last year. The full moon night. And no-one, especially Trick, wanted to think about that.

'I've heard your mum's doing well this year,' Tia said, her voice high and bright.

'Yeah. Well.' Trick's voice was deep, tired. He sounded old. Thirty.

The three of them were walking in a line now, Trick's hands deep in his pockets. The other boys had stopped near the toilet block, still huddled over a phone, vapes now stashed out of potential adult view.

'No thanks to your dad, Tia,' Trick said, not looking up.

Lyra's stomach lurched and just as she was certain Tia might burst into tears, her mother's voice rang out from over their shoulders.

'Lyra! I've been looking everywhere for you. Where's Bridge? Where are all the little ones? Where have you been?'

Lyra grabbed Tia's hand and they turned towards Dani's voice. Trick kept on walking.

Dani and stupid Craig had plastic wineglasses in their hands. Her mum was all showered and Lyra knew that if they hugged she would smell like her favourite shampoo, her musky body wash and minty toothpaste. Her mum was always clean, tidy, put together. It made Lyra feel safe, and grubby.

'We were at the beach,' she said, taking hold of Tia's hand and swinging it, like they were little girls, hoping to deflect from Tia's face, which she was certain was still stricken.

'You were not. We were just there.'

'You must have just missed us. We went to the toilet block.'

'Lyra, come on.' Dani's forehead crinkled. 'We couldn't have missed you, we were –'

'Don't overthink it, Mum,' Lyra said, smiling what she hoped was her most winning smile. 'We're all fine.'

'Don't overthink it?' Craig's eyebrows were up, his tone joking. 'Hear that, Dani?'

Shut up, Craig. Lyra waited to see if her mum was going to let it go. The chances felt fifty–fifty.

The way her mother's eyes narrowed and the edge of her mouth twitched made Lyra's stomach clench. She didn't want to be responsible for that look. It was worry. And this was meant to be a time when her mum didn't have to worry. A time she got to be normal, like her friends. She and Bridge had heard it enough. *Can't I just relax for a few minutes without you girls giving me a heart attack?*

'I've been braiding Tia's hair.' Lyra pushed Tia ahead of her, as evidence.

Her mum's face relaxed. Anything Lyra used to do a year ago, three years ago, made her mum happy. Anything new made her worry.

Craig's big man hand looked even bigger resting on her mum's little shoulder. It was a mystery why her mum kept Craig around, with those big hands, and that fake voice.

'Let's get back to the party, shall we, ladies?' he said now, his arm tightening around her mum's shoulder.

'Are you okay, Tia?'

Dammit, her mum didn't miss a thing.

'I'm fine,' Tia managed. 'Just hungry.'

'Your dad's been cooking sausages. They'll be cold.'

'We don't care,' Lyra chirruped. 'We love cold sausages.'

Suspicion returned to Dani's face and Lyra could have kicked herself. Time for the big guns.

'Come on, Mum, let's go and dance.'

She stepped up, gently pushed Craig's hand off her mother's shoulder and wrapped her in a hug, knowing it would make her melt. It was weird being as tall as the person who'd always been able to cover you with cuddles. It felt, sometimes, like someone who had always protected you was shrinking, and you were left exposed.

'You can do better than this,' her mum said into Lyra's hair. 'But let's go find Bridge.'

Craig's arms were left swinging, with no hands to hold and no shoulders to rest on. He took a sip from his plastic cup and followed a few steps behind them, as Tia and Lyra and her mum walked arm in arm. He was the tail, not the head. Always would be.

'Is my mum worried?' Tia asked.

'No, your mum's much better adjusted than me.'

Music started pumping towards them as the solar lanterns flicked on. Something old, something techno. Something that would have all the adults' hands in the air in about two minutes flat.

'Disco!' one of the kids called towards them and Lyra could see, in the flicker of the fairy lights, Sadie with her hand on Trick's shoulder, talking into his ear. She could see Aunt Liss, spinning one of the little girls around what passed for a dancefloor. And she saw Lachy Short standing near the barbecue, tall and upright, cheersing their arrival with the beer in his hand.

Lyra felt herself tense, and she could have sworn that her mum and Tia did exactly the same thing.

11

2012

Thai Time, Randwick, Sydney

Liss

Ginger's mum was a rodeo rider.

Juno was born June in bland suburbia but craved more drama.

Dani's family never forgave her for marrying a Frenchman in New York City.

And Sadie's mother poisoned her father.

These were the stories Liss didn't know about her new friends until they were spread across the table at an average Thai restaurant, next to green chicken curry, jasmine rice in a tarnished silver dish and a plate of slowly congealing satay sticks.

Liss had arrived at the high-street restaurant with a classy bottle of pink wine in hand that she had no intention of drinking. She was pregnant again.

This wasn't the baby she had so confidently announced at the first birthday party. That unknowable little person didn't stay.

It had all seemed too easy at the time, but photos of that day in Centennial Park were hard to look at, knowing what came next. Two more weeks, then the blood. Then the tears. Then the emptiness.

Now here she was again at that precarious early stage, carrying herself carefully in fear of scaring off whatever was quietly unfurling inside her.

Babies were everywhere. Ginger was heavily pregnant. Sadie, for God's sake, was having Jacob's baby, much to his confusion. Liss's sister-in-law Piper was having her third, which just seemed greedy. Lachy was impatient, both with her sadness and at her inability to make another baby happen. He'd spent a day stroking her hair after the last little-big loss, before asking her when they could try again.

Dani met Liss outside the restaurant in her work clothes – a silk shirt and tailored pants, the kind of things no sane person would wear around a two-year-old. She looked at the bottle in her friend's hand and pulled her into a hug.

'This one's the one,' she said. 'If my grandmother was here, she'd say she could sense it.'

'Like a disturbance in the force?'

'You're getting your folklores muddled.'

'Sorry. We had no culture on the North Shore.' Liss squeezed Dani's hand. It was a wet night and the cars swooshed loudly as they passed, casting orange and red light on the slick black road. There were tiny dark spots of rain on Dani's green silk shirt.

'How's Seb?'

Dani shook her head. 'I haven't been home,' she said. 'I assume he's fine.'

That wasn't what Liss was asking and they both knew it. But this was not the time.

Inside, Sadie and Juno had already decided on what everyone would eat. Sadie's well-established baby belly was draped in some sort of silky gold dress that only someone who didn't get out much would wear to a Tuesday night dinner. She was declaring her baby 'baked enough' to be pouring a glass of Juno's sauvignon blanc for herself.

Ginger arrived just after Dani and Liss squeezed into their seats, the curve of Ginger's own almost-baked baby in a floaty cheesecloth number Liss had seen on sale in Tree of Life when she'd been pushing Tia through Bondi Junction the other week.

Just like Liss, and unlike the others, Ginger hadn't been working since James was born. But unlike Liss, it was making her poor. The word was that Ginger and Aiden were talking about moving out of the eastern suburbs, and Liss wasn't surprised. They were pretending, really, that a teacher and a nurse could live here. It was just doable for two people without children on an ordinary double income. Impossible for two people who urgently needed another bedroom, especially when one of them was about to be busy with the unpaid work of breastfeeding.

Still, you're so lucky, Liss thought, looking at Ginger's ringed eyes and wide smile. *You and Sadie sitting there stroking the babies that are reassuringly rolling around inside you. You have problems I don't have, but you have that.* Conscious that this thought was troubled in about five different ways, Liss gulped her fizzy water and smiled around the table.

Moneybags and spring rolls were delivered – Liss knew better than to resist the fixed-price banquet with this group of friends – and Juno made an announcement. 'So my father died on Thursday,' she said, dipping crispy pastry into neon-pink sweet chilli sauce. 'And I'm not flying home for the funeral.'

Liss swallowed, blinked. 'I didn't know you had a father,' she said, and immediately internally shushed herself as Dani shot her a raised eyebrow.

'We all have fathers,' Juno said, still chewing.

'I don't,' said Sadie.

'Me neither,' said Ginger.

'You do all *have* fathers,' Juno pushed on. 'Dead or alive, they exist.'

'Does Bob have a father?' Sadie asked, sipping on her controversial wine.

'Fuck off, Sadie.' But Juno was smiling.

'I'm so sorry,' Dani said, reaching over the spring rolls to put her hand on Juno's hand.

'Ah.' For a moment Juno looked wild. 'It's okay. He was an asshole.'

'What level of arsehole are we talking?' asked Ginger.

'Regulation-issue asshole. All-American man. Outdoorsy. Intolerant. Dull, really. My sister is telling me not going back is borderline abusive to my mom but, you know, I don't think she liked him much, either.'

'Your mum?'

'Yeah, I think she'll be okay. Emily and I were planning on taking Bob next winter, when we're a bit straighter with the cash and,' Juno was looking down and turning a spring roll around in her fingers, 'I think Mom might need us more then, when all the pies have stopped turning up.'

'It's hard, being far,' Dani said.

Juno shook her head slightly, blew out through her mouth. 'We don't talk about our families. Like, our original families. I think it's time for the stories about all the dead dads.'

'And dead mums?' Liss, already sitting in her anxious envy over her friends' well-established bumps, couldn't help herself. She realised that for all they did know about each other, through those midnight messages and hormonal tears and terrifying, up-ending, giddy early baby days, their own back stories were not much discussed.

Juno, of course, began.

The wild north-west coast of the States. Everything grand-scale and rain-washed, apart from her suburban three-bed on a symmetrical new development in the shadow of mountains. Her dad didn't talk much, other than to complain about being in a house full of women. Her mother was in real estate, practical, driven, tidy. Juno was different from both of them. Dreamy. Creative. Growing up, she wanted to be a writer. She got into college in LA, stayed, changed her name – 'I was just plain June but I wanted to be more interesting' – got a job as a publisher's assistant and met an Australian screenwriter called Agnetha – yes, like ABBA – who was so bewitching Juno followed her all the way to Sydney, where she got a job with a literary agent and where Agnetha broke her heart by starting to sleep with men, 'awful ones, too'. The split was long, drawn out, messy, and Juno decided to go home. The night before her flight, she was tempted out to a bar in Erskineville and she met Emily. Beautiful, solid Emily. 'I fell fast, I always do. But this time it stuck.' She didn't get on the plane.

Liss wasn't expecting much from Ginger's story, if she was honest. Ginger had always been a side character in Liss's mothers' group world. At first, just quiet and very, very tired. Liss had never found herself wondering about Ginger's life, the way she had about Sadie's. Ginger, she suspected, was dull.

Liss was wrong.

Ginger was originally from the country. Not the kind of country with green rolling hills and a quaint bakery serving artisan bread, but the kind of country where 'town' was an hour away and 'school' was a shortwave radio.

Her mother had been a rodeo rider in the 1980s. This information caused the whole table to pause, mid satay stick, for exclamation. Ginger's mum had learned from her own dad, who died of a broken neck in exactly the manner you'd expect. Ginger's parents trained horses to do tricks and travelled the dusty, boozy show route with the babies under their arms. Ginger was named with the circuit in mind, and could stand up on the back of a galloping pony by the time she was nine.

'Stop it.' Liss was open-mouthed. She considered the pony her father had bought her after her mother's death. Anatole had lived in stables at Centennial Park and been taken out for a trot once a day. 'That's wild.'

'It was wild.' Ginger nodded, rubbing her bump. 'And then it got sad.'

Her mother fell from a horse when she was teaching a teenage boy how to perform a trick called a spritz stand. Google it, Ginger said, it's hard. She broke her back.

It was, Ginger went on in the quiet but authoritative voice that Liss had finally begun to hear, the defining moment of her childhood. Her mother, needing full-time care and not getting it, drank. Her father, who'd always been a selfish prick, left. Ginger and her brother tried to keep things going in their little home in the middle of nowhere until a grandmother took them to live with her in the nearest actual town.

Her mother never really recovered. Her father never came back, and the moment Ginger turned sixteen she left that town, with its smell of woodsmoke and stale beer set deep in her skin. A teacher had insisted this wild little girl was smart, so she got a job in a racecourse stables, took herself to TAFE, became a nurse and, as soon as she started getting paid an actual wage, never looked at a horse again.

'Horses hate us,' she said, plucking up a fishcake with her fork.

Liss thought about Anatole, whose mane she loved to brush and whose neck she loved to nuzzle. She had always fed her pony sugar cubes. And then one day, Anatole nipped her. It was best not to mention it.

The table erupted in questions and Liss considered Ginger with a new wonder. An entirely self-created, capable creature, formed under extreme pressure. Where were the hints of this person? In the few words first spoken? In that purposeful, slightly heavy-footed walk? In the way her hair could look a bit like an unkempt shrub?

'It's your turn, Liss,' insisted Juno as the mains rolled out.

Liss felt a deep burn of discomfort.

'No rodeo riders here,' she almost giggled, mortified at herself as she heard it bubble from her mouth. 'Boring Sydney story.'

'Not boring,' Dani said. 'Go on.'

Liss pushed some plain rice around on her plate and drew some broad strokes.

North Shore. Money on both sides but more from her mother, who came to Sydney from London, where she'd met Liss's father at a 1970s arty party. That's what she called it, when she'd tell Liss the story of meeting this confident Australian, a dealer not a painter, but a man moving through a world she'd wanted to join, with her own tiny little paintings that brought her joy. Liss's mother was from properly posh people, with generations of owning things: mills, land, people. But she was wild, and loved the idea of an adventure on the other side of the world.

They set up home in Liss's father's grand house and, as Liss told it at Thai Time, the next chapters unfolded quickly – two baby boys and her, then the illness, the death, her teenage rebellions under the eyes of new stepmothers. Liss pushing away expectations of an art history degree and a gallery job that was really just a husband waiting room and leaving to travel. She came back, met Lachy, moved east . . . The rest, they knew. Please pass the satay.

But her friends had questions they had been waiting to ask.

'Did you ever have a job?'

'I did teacher training.' Liss felt a little embarrassed to admit the number of times she'd started things and abandoned them, including her teaching career, which had lasted a week's placement in a school too many suburbs away.

'Did you marry Lachy for the money?'

'Quite the opposite.'

'He married you for your money?'

Dani shifted in her seat. 'Pass the sweet chilli please, Sadie.'

'Not exactly. But my mother left me some.'

'How much is some?'

'Sadie!'

'Enough to not have to have a job, if I didn't want one.' A ripple of wonder around the table, as if that were as unusual as being able to stand on the back of a galloping horse. Perhaps it was.

The truth was that Liss's mother, at the point when she was sick enough to know it mattered, but not too sick to make her wishes plain, had explicitly stated in tight legal language that she wanted the lion's share of her own inheritance to go to her daughter. In less legal language, she'd told a confused young Liss that she didn't want her Alyssia to ever have to rely on a man for money. It was a strange, barbed blessing. An assumption, perhaps, that the boys could make their own way but her girl could not.

Still, Liss had come to understand that her mother had meant it as a shield. And she'd known that the men in her family would be much too proud to ever challenge it. And so it was.

'But how much?'

'Enough.' Dani pushed a plate of pad thai towards Sadie. 'Have some noodles.'

'I've never had a rich friend before.' Ginger laughed. 'You have to excuse us.'

Liss's face tingled with pink. She couldn't lift her eyes off the table. *This was why*, she knew Lachy would say, *you should have gone private.*

Dani started to talk, Liss was almost certain, to save her from having to say any more.

Dani told the table about her outer suburbs upbringing, of the pressure of being the eldest daughter. How hard she tried at everything – school, chores, sport – and how it somehow made her more disappointing to her parents than her sisters who didn't even bother. How she struggled to feel like she belonged in this close but critical family. So much so that when she left uni and got into the graduate program at a bank in the city, she chose the one with the option to send her overseas. She thought her parents would be proud. They weren't. Why was she always running away from them? For eight whole years she lived on the other side of the world in New York City. She loved it, she hated it; it was a challenge and a stress and it was complete freedom. Dani came home with a French husband and a baby in her belly, and her parents were still barely speaking to her about it.

'But isn't that what they wanted for you?' Juno was confused.

'I did it wrong,' Dani said. 'Seb was a stranger to them and they were furious at me for getting married in New York. They still are. Although Lyra's hard to resist.' She smiled, sipped. 'That's me.'

Liss watched all heads turn to Sadie. Alongside the smell of lemongrass and coconut milk, anticipation was hanging over the table. They all wanted to hear the story of the woman who went to mothers' group without a child, who decided to dump her partner while she was pregnant, who draped her baby bump in gold lamé as she sipped sav blanc.

'My story's so boring,' she said, drawing a heart in spilled water on the table with a pink-tipped finger.

HE WOULD NEVER

'I bet it is not,' said Juno, leaning in.

Sadie grew up just a couple of suburbs south, she said. Her father was a local politician. Dani, clearly more across news than Liss was, nodded at the mention of his name.

Sadie's dad was a pillar of the community with something on every night – a shop opening, local businesses awards, a fundraiser. As Sadie spoke, Liss saw another layer of recognition crossing Dani's face. Oh.

'Yes, that's him,' Sadie said, noticing Dani's expression.

Sadie's mother was at home. A 1950s housewife in 1980s Sydney suburbia. It was all mornings by the pool, home-made pies and lipstick on at 5 pm. She accompanied her husband to most things, children allowing, in a rotation of beautiful dresses. Many of Sadie's early memories were of lying on her mother's bed, watching her get overdressed. She'd come home in a fug of perfume and gin and kiss Sadie and her little brother before they went to sleep. Sadie would usually wake to hear her father coming in much, much later, and her mother offering him some saved dinner, or a hot cocoa, because she knew it would help him sleep.

Her mum seemed to make so much effort for her father, little Sadie thought it was like she lived only for him. Which was why, when it became clear that the upstanding local MP's evenings away from home involved too much alcohol and several affairs with several other women in his district, Sadie's mum did something extreme.

'She made him a pie,' Dani said. 'I remember the story.'

On that particular night, Sadie and her brother were sent to a neighbour, highly unusual but quite the adventure. She remembered that her little overnight bag was shaped like a woolly lamb, and you unzipped its fluffy stomach to reveal your pyjamas and toothbrush. And while they were a few doors down, being indulged with after-dinner TV and extra ice cream for dessert, Sadie's mum made a very special meal for her husband.

One that would see her in court, charged with baking a pie that contained poisonous mushrooms. One that would see her charged with attempted murder.

Liss was sure her mouth was hanging open. 'Your mother killed your father?'

'Not quite,' said Sadie. 'He wouldn't die. But he went to hospital and never really came out, and she went to jail and then got sick so also never really came out, and that was the end of our childhood.'

Ginger was the one who put a hand over Sadie's, next to the banana leaf piled high with jasmine rice.

'Anyway.' Sadie drained her glass and smiled. 'I don't suffer fools. And I don't trust easily and,' she looked around the table with a playful glare, 'you don't want to cross me.' She laughed, but it was high-pitched, hollow.

'What happened to you and your brother?' Dani asked.

'We went into foster care for a while,' said Sadie. 'Until my mum's sister came back from overseas and decided to take us in. I have to tell you, I was the best-behaved teenager on the planet. I knew what the women in that family did to you if you betrayed them.' Again, a laugh. 'So we spent the last few years out at Richmond.'

'And the by-election called because your dad was incapacitated won the next prime minister his seat,' said Dani. 'So, you know, your mum changed history.'

'Yeah, and died of breast cancer.' Sadie filled her glass again. 'Karma, I guess.'

'What happened to your dad?'

'This life story has gone on for too long,' Sadie declared. 'Why's there no egg fried rice at this place?'

It's Thai, Liss couldn't help but correct, in her head. *Not Chinese.*

HE WOULD NEVER

Nobody knew what to say for a moment. They just looked at their food and then at the rain through the huge, rattling window. It was coming down harder now, in that determined way Sydney rain has of getting it over with.

Dani squeezed Liss's hand under the table.

'Is it nice to be the boring one for once?' she whispered, with a grin.

Liss returned the squeeze. These women, walking around with all their big and small stories, with a mess of reasons for wanting to build a family beyond their own.

She sipped her water and took a mouthful of rice and felt a twinge she chose to ignore. Because what else could you do?

When Liss got home that night she found a splash of scarlet blood in her underwear. She put a pad in her pants, swallowed two Nurofen and went to her daughter's bed, climbing in and curling into a comma around Tia's tiny back. She felt the soft soles of her daughter's feet pressed against her thighs and breathed in her soapy smell. She lay there all night, in and out of something close to sleep, feeling the possibility of a new life slipping away, and conjuring women who could stand tall on the backs of horses and bake poisonous pies.

12

Friday, 9 pm

Green River Campground

Sadie

The twinkling lights blurred the edges of Sadie's vision. She was sunk low in her oversized camping chair, cradling a zero beer, open jar of supermarket salsa balanced on her knee, just a few steps from the makeshift dancefloor where there were drinks in every hand. Children under feet. The little ones were chasing each other around the legs of the swaying adults. The big kids were divided – some indulging their parents with a sideways shuffle dance, eye-rolling all the while, others hanging back on the edges, cradling their glowing phones, tapping, filming, scrolling.

Sadie was watching Trick watching Lyra Martin and Tia Short. He was slouched, in the way he was always slouched, against the now-cold barbecue, the angle of his body and the direction of his head suggesting that he would rather be anywhere else. But Sadie could see that his eyes were focused on Lyra. That they moved when she moved, as she and Tia shrugged their shoulders ever so slightly to humour their cajoling parents.

HE WOULD NEVER

This was new.

Juno was in the camp chair beside her, phone up, filming. But it was difficult to talk above pumping bass and the screaming insects.

'Look at those great big babies!' Juno yelled, nodding over at the big kids. 'They're too cool for all this now.'

Sadie had always loved the opening night disco, a tradition since the kids were tiny, that very first weekend. Back then the children had lived for it, pulled on tutus and painted their faces in glitter to twirl around the dancefloor holding hands, and she'd joined them to spin and jump and lift them high in the air. There was always a little boy, usually Bob, who would dance unselfconsciously in a way that would make all the adults laugh. Thrusting hips, shaking little bottoms. Sadie had always been the one with her hands in the air like she just didn't care.

Most of the older kids had grown much too cool for disco night. Certainly her Trick was. There had been an in-between time, when the whole crew would studiously prepare a routine they'd learned in dance class or been served in their algorithms and knew off by heart. But now the hard-earth dancefloor was mostly the adults' domain, a place to embarrass their children, possibly joined by Ginger's little Maya, and Liss's Gracie.

Under Trick's eye, Lyra and Tia were half-in, half-out, standing on the edge of the circle, swaying lightly, shoulder to shoulder, skin touching, mouthing words to the songs they'd doubtless heard their mothers play a thousand times.

Juno was up and dancing now, phone in the air, spinning around, drink held high. Sadie sank back into her camp chair and closed her eyes.

This was so hard without a drink. Her zero beer tasted like sour water, and time was crawling by at an unbearable plod. When was an acceptable time to go to bed? And could a sober person really pretend that a foam mat was a bed?

Sunset without a glass of something fizzy was just about manageable. Steak and salad without red wine was a challenge. A multi-generational dance party with a flat pretend beer in hand was almost certainly impossible.

'Hey.'

Sadie opened her eyes. It was Lachy Short. He was bent over at the waist so that his face was near hers. 'Don't fall asleep on us,' he said, close enough that his voice was just under the music.

'Not sleeping. Relaxing.'

'You should have a drink.' He dangled his beer between his thumb and his middle finger, swinging it back and forth in front of her eyes. 'Loosen up a bit.'

Lachy's face was slightly sweaty, the fine lines around his eyes gritty with campsite dust. His eyes were open wide, daring her. 'Go on.'

'I don't do that anymore.'

'Boring.' He straightened up, looked around at the group. 'You used to be the most fun.'

'Fuck off, Lachy.'

'Rude,' he said loudly, then he sank into the empty chair beside her. 'Don't you think it's a bit late to pretend you're the Virgin Mary?'

If she closed her eyes again now, Sadie knew, what she would see was a vision of herself pushed up against this man. Her hands on his chest. Her fingers fumbling at the zip of his pants, her face in his. She would feel his hands on her shoulders, hear his voice, 'No, Sadie,' loud enough for others to hear. 'Stop, Sadie.'

But she wouldn't close her eyes. She would maintain eye contact with the prick. 'I'm not pretending anything, Lachy. Please leave me alone.'

HE WOULD NEVER

'I wonder why you came this year.' He leaned sideways, towards her.

Across the dancefloor, Sadie saw Liss's head turning. She would be over here in a moment, no question.

'Liss asked me to.' Sadie felt exhausted. Heavy. 'And you could be kinder.'

Lachy let out a little laugh. 'What did I do?'

'Hi.' It was Liss. 'You two okay?'

'We're fine, babe. Just offering Sadie a drink.'

'Sadie doesn't need a drink, Lachy, you know that.' Liss lowered the glass in her hand. But like Dani, Liss was that infuriating kind of drinker who could have one, have two, and slow to a stop. Never a wowser, but never a mess. It was a balance that had never been available to Sadie.

'Who said anything about an alcoholic drink?' Lachy asked, putting an arm around Liss and squeezing her shoulder. 'I could fetch the lady a Coke. Or a tea.'

'Oh, shut up.' Liss kicked his foot with hers. 'You're not fetching any *ladies* anything. Go and dance with your daughters.'

Lachy shrugged and nodded at Sadie. 'Enjoy,' he said and danced away.

'You okay?' Liss took the chair. She was breathing fast from her turn on the dancefloor, her bare feet still tapping.

'I wonder how many times you're going to ask me that this weekend.'

'Sorry.' Liss smiled. 'I'll get over it.'

Sadie remembered these words from the final morning, last year. When she'd come to find Liss in the chaos of packing up, her head a heavy mess of ache and regret, her mouth dry, her arms still a little bit tender to touch.

'Don't worry,' Liss had said, even then, in the weak early light, surrounded by deconstructed tents. 'I'll get over it.' And then a sliver of steel. A hand on an arm. 'You need to look after yourself better. We could help with that.'

Liss was still smiling now, looking out, nodding to the music. Her lips moved lightly to the words. She raised her plastic flute for a sip of cold wine. It looked delicious.

'It would have been easier if I hadn't come, wouldn't it?' Sadie asked.

Liss swallowed. 'Easier for who?'

'Everyone. You. Lachy. Dani, who's trying very hard to pretend she can tolerate me.'

Liss tilted her head as if she was considering this, toe still tapping. She was still looking straight ahead. 'Would it have been easier for you if you didn't come?'

It took Sadie a second to understand the question. 'Yes.'

The song changed. Lyra and Tia gave out a little shriek as some banging bass filled the space and they bunny-hopped into the circle, as if they were still those little girls in tutus and glitter, only now they looked like women. Or they looked how women are told they should look: slight, lineless, happy.

'Imagine if you hadn't,' said Liss, watching the girls. 'Imagine if you were at home, doing your yoga, Trick and Lucky wondering why they were excluded. Would that be better?'

Sadie looked at Liss, trying to read her tone. It had a harder edge than she was used to.

'No,' she said, finally. 'I guess not.'

Liss took another sip of her drink and pushed herself up from the chair. 'We do hard things for our children, don't we?' She shimmied away, towards Dani, who she pulled out of the circle.

Sadie's eyes started to swim. She took a swig of the awful water-beer and swallowed hard. *Breathe. Three in. Three hold. Three out. Come on, get it together.* Her heart felt like flapping wings.

HE WOULD NEVER

All she could see now, as she looked around the camp, were glasses and glasses, some still half-full of yellow or purple wine. Open brown and gold bottles. Cans discarded, half-drunk.

Nope. Nope. Nope. Don't think about that.

The scratching thump of 'Single Ladies' started and Juno, Emily and Ginger started pumping their arms in unison.

'Come on!' Juno yelled towards her. 'Sadie, come dance!'

But she couldn't. She just wanted to be gone. To be lying on her mattress next to her daughter, willing this first damn night to be over.

She scanned for Lucky and Trick. He was still over near the barbecue, pretending to look at his phone but actually transfixed by Lyra Martin, who was turning her hand this way and that in time to the music.

Where was Lucky? It would be a novelty to be one of the parents ushering kids to bed and reminding them to wear thongs to the toilet block when they brushed their teeth, rather than the parent who was the last one on the dancefloor, the one falling through the tent flaps long after the kids had taken themselves off to their inflatable beds.

'Single Ladies' morphed into 'Crazy in Love'.

The bass was almost as loud as the cicadas, the sound of bare feet slapping the plastic-covered floor as dancers bounce-bounced up and down. The smell of beer and popcorn and stale, sunscreen-spiked sweat. The men were dancing. Lachy and Aiden and even Craig, shuffling from foot to foot, behind the women.

'Mum! Come!' Lucky's voice. Sadie raised her eyes across the dancefloor to where her daughter was whirling her arms and shaking her hips, alongside Juno, who was filming Emily. 'Come!'

Yes. Dancing with her daughter was exactly what she should be doing. Making fucking memories. *Come on, Sadie*, she told herself. *Get up there, show that man he hasn't completely shamed you to the sidelines.*

She bent to put down her drink, move the salsa and chips from her knee. She straightened up, stood, and then she saw them.

It was impossible to tell, honestly, if his bare right hand was touching her bare right thigh.

If that thumb pressed into her waist was circling, ever so slightly, up and down, round and round. Marking her with a fingerprint. It was difficult to see if he really did have his other hand on her waist, stroking the skin of her exposed midriff with his thumb. Or if he was dancing too close, his front pushed into her back, their hips moving together to a beat that throbbed from the tents through the muddy dusk into the thick rainforest and out across the flats of the beach, tipping out into the river.

Did he really bend down in the glow of flickering fairy lights strung between trees, scoop the hair back from her neck and whisper? Words from his thick, stubble-edged lips trickling into her ear with its neat line of tiny, shimmering hoops?

The music was even louder than the cicadas now. Somehow the noise made it harder to see clearly.

The push, the noise, the movement, the whole scene was a glitching blur.

But Sadie was certain of what she was looking at.

And what she was looking at was Lachlan Short with his clumsy big-man paws all over little Lyra Martin.

That was what she was seeing. Surely.

It was a beat, a split second, before Lachy pushed himself back from her, arms in the air, gave out a whoop and turned to grind behind Aiden, thumping his fist in the air.

Sadie wasn't sure she was moving her own legs as she started to push towards Lyra, who was still jiggling, pulling faces now into Tia Short's phone. Sadie shoved past the dancers, stepping over the smaller kids.

'Lyra!' she shouted over the pounding, feeling like she was calling out through water, in one of those dreams where you're screaming hoarse but no-one can hear you. 'Get away from him.'

Inexplicably, the girl was laughing now, tongue out to the camera, waggling her head. She turned to Sadie. 'What?'

'Turn it off!' Sadie yelled in the direction of the music.

Where were Dani and Liss? Nowhere.

It was unusual for those two women not to be in the middle of this, refilling the drinks, gathering up drooping children. Liss was usually in a constant motion of clearing and hosting.

On the far side of the dancefloor, Lachy and Aiden, Emily and Craig were all still dancing, shouting in each other's ears, swigging from cans.

'What?' Lyra was asking her again. Did she look afraid, or annoyed?

'It's okay, Lyra, darling. You're okay.'

The noise in Sadie's head was louder and louder. The cicadas, the bass, the shouting. The adults beginning to look at her with confusion, their faces blurred. Some of the kids had their phones raised, neon rectangles pointing towards her.

'Mum!' It was Lucky, whose arms had stopped whirring, looking at her in horror. 'You're being weird.'

'Sadie!' It was Juno.

Sadie was pointing at Lachy, her arm straight out, her finger shaking a little. She hadn't realised her arm was doing that. 'Stop!'

Lachy had his hands up, in the way you might if someone was pointing a gun, rather than a finger, at you. He was twisting a little this way and that, smirking. 'What did I do?'

'Are you okay?' Sadie asked Lyra, grabbing the girl by the shoulders. Lyra shook her off, stepped away to Tia, who looked terrified.

Someone, finally, stopped the music. And at that moment, when the relentless beat fell silent, Dani and Liss stepped into the circle.

Dani had a laugh just fading from her face, and was holding a bunch of ice creams by the corners of their slippery wrappers. Liss was holding a tray of ruby-red watermelon, sliced in rounded quarters, laid out in a pattern of overlapping petals. Or tongues.

'What?'

'He –' Sadie was still pointing at Lachy. 'He was . . .'

'He was what?' Liss's eyes were flicking from Sadie to her husband.

'I was nothing.'

Her finger swung to Lyra. 'He was groping her.'

The words sounded inadequate. He was a predator. A monster. He was what poisoned this group and this place. He was what made her stomach tilt and her mouth fill with sour saliva when she thought of Green River.

And yet, all heads turned to Sadie.

'What?' Dani's eyes fell on Lyra.

Lyra Martin was shaking her head. Lachy Short was actually laughing.

The teens' phones turned, too. One of them, she knew at some level, was Trick's, his face obscured by the black mirror he turned on his mother.

'I saw it,' she said. 'I know I saw it.'

Why was Dani so calm? Walking to the table with the quietly sweating ice creams. Why was Liss not tearing at her husband's infuriating smirking face, but instead holding up the tray of watermelon and saying, 'There's so much here.'

'Are you mad?' Sadie was properly shouting now. 'Are you all actually mad?'

Dani walked over to Lyra, held her by the shoulders and looked in her eyes.

Sadie could see Liss's knuckles were whitening as she said, 'You need to be quiet, Sadie. I've always defended you, but this is too much.'

HE WOULD NEVER

Sadie took a choking breath. 'Don't you want to know who he is?'

Liss actually laughed before she turned away to the table. 'I know who he is.'

'Come on, Sadie.' It was Lachy. 'Calm down. I know you have a problem with me, but come on. I would never do that.'

It was the firm, seductive voice he'd been using his entire life to get away with things. 'I would never.'

Sadie felt like the ground was unsteady under her feet. None of this was making sense. 'Trick, put the phone down,' she said. 'We're going.' She turned to the other adults. 'Are you all crazy? Are we just ignoring this? Really?'

But the others, even Juno, began to turn away, to gather their open-mouthed children, to mutter about teeth and pyjamas and bedtime.

Dani had already led Lyra away, with Brigitte dancing along behind. Ginger let out a long, low whistle. 'Way to ruin a party,' she said before putting out her arms for Maya to fold into. Aiden just looked confused.

Trick had disappeared. Lucky had run off to the bathroom, probably wishing herself invisible. Liss and Lachy had gone to sit by the trestle table, almost regal in their authority, hands clasped in laps, heads together.

The darkness around the camp felt like it was pushing towards them. Sadie stumbled a little as she bent to pick up her bag. She needed to get away from them.

She passed Dani's tent and heard the low murmur of mother and daughter. There were some kids up ahead near the bathroom, giggling. Juno's unmistakable voice telling Emily, 'Who could be sure of why Sadie sees the things she sees, or says the things she says, these days?'

Fuck. Why did the shame that should belong to that man always stick to her?

Site Eight was silent. You didn't need to put your head inside the tent to know it was empty. The door hung flapping open, a sign that one of her children had been here, and was angry or embarrassed enough to disobey the only camping rule they usually adhered to: *Zip up the damn tent.*

Lucky, she knew, would be at the toilet block, talking fast to pretend what just happened hadn't happened. Trick would be God knew where, alone or with the other teenagers. She wasn't sure which would be worse for him.

'Shit,' she said out loud, dropping her bag through the tent door and straightening to put her hands through her hair, rubbing at her head as if the thoughts and pictures could be massaged out with just the right amount of force.

She didn't have a torch, and her phone was somewhere deep in her bag. Now the lanterns of the surrounding sites were flicking off, Sadie was almost in darkness, and felt a wave of intense exhaustion. Would she just wait here for the kids to come back? What if they didn't?

There was a crack and a snap and some rustling fronds in the palms across the path. Sadie's head spun towards the sound.

Craig stepped into the momentary glow of the toilet block's flickering fluoro. He just stood there. So she could see him. So he could see her. His face was blank, unreadable.

Then he turned and walked towards where Dani and Lyra and Brigitte were clucking around their tent, feathering their camp beds for the night.

And somewhere over on Site Seven, she heard Lachy Short laughing.

Part Two

Part Two

13

Saturday, 7 am

Green River Campground

Liss

Liss woke up irritated.

She'd spent much of the night staring at her husband's sleeping face, so close she could wake him with a puff of breath, his outline illuminated by the full moon's long reach.

She knew him so well she could end his sentences, predict every food order and read his mood by his footfall on the driveway. But he could still surprise her. And not always in a good way. This was not how she had wanted this weekend to start.

Saturday was usually a swimming day. A paddling day. A day for watching kids at the rockpool or attempting to lie on the beach and read. A day for walks with your old friends, ones where you might share particularly meaningful secrets or stories you'd been saving for a day like this one.

Now it was going to be a crisis management day. A day of tension and tears, of whispered conversations and apologies, speculation and overflowing emotions.

Lachy slept on. As a woman who struggled with sleep, Liss had spent years lying next to this man, tracking the ripples of his eyelids, wondering how he slept so easily, what went on in his dreams. What things did Lachy not do in life that needed playing out in his subconscious?

And then she'd stopped wondering, because if she was honest, her husband's internal life interested her less, and she became more focused on how she and the kids could dodge whatever mess Lachy's lived-out dreams might make.

He opened his eyes. 'Hey, you. Okay?'

The kids were just a few metres away, in the tent's other 'room'. Soon they would be awake, stirred by the building heat, asking for the phones and iPads and consoles that staved off the confronting nightmare of having to think or dream.

'Not really. Couldn't turn my brain off.'

Lachy closed his eyes again, sighed a heavy sigh. 'Sadie is mad. The end. Brain off.'

Liss sighed. 'I wish –'

'Do you think she's gone yet?'

'I was thinking.' Liss reached out her hand and pushed a lick of damp hair back from Lachy's forehead. 'I don't want her to leave.'

Lachy opened his eyes. 'The woman who wants people to think I'm a paedophile? You want that one to stay?'

'We've never lost anyone before.' Liss knew she sounded petulant. 'And, you know, we've come close.'

'Liss.' The kids hadn't moved yet. He slipped his arms around her waist under the big heavy eiderdown they'd brought out here, rolled tightly and tied with ancient fraying rope, for years. 'You have to accept that things change. Last year was enough, wasn't it? We didn't lose her then, but it's time now.'

HE WOULD NEVER

'But what if she just made a mistake? Thought she saw something she didn't see? A trick of the light, or whatever.'

'Whatever?'

'Does it have to be such a big deal?'

'Being accused of groping a teenager? A little girl I've known her entire life? I'd say yes.'

Liss knew it too. There were all kind of allegations you could throw around and come back from, but not that one. Not in any normal circumstance. But given this was Sadie they were talking about, and Lachy, and Lyra, was this what could be called normal circumstance? She wrestled with how to put this to him.

'I don't think that's what she did.'

'Liss, it's literally what she did.' He rolled over onto his back, his body tensing with frustration, his voice getting louder. 'I can't stand for that. Nor should you.'

Liss could hear – or perhaps sense – Tia stirring on the other side of the tent. She propped herself on her elbow to peer over in the weak early light. Tia was lying on her fold-out bed, eyes wide open, staring at the tent ceiling, just as Liss had done.

'Hi, darling,' she called out, her voice, she hoped, light, bright. Tia looked like she winced at the sound of it, and quickly rolled over to face the other way.

'Hi, Mum,' she finally said quietly. She was as long as Liss now, and looked faintly ridiculous in the stretcher cot she'd been sleeping in for a decade. A young woman's body in a little child's bed.

'You okay?' She sounded like Lachy.

No response.

'You have to back me on this, Liss,' Lachy said, not looking towards his daughter. 'We can't stand for it.'

He could be very convincing, even now. It hadn't taken Liss long to realise, back when Lachy Short was wooing her like his life depended on it, that there had been nothing accidental about their meeting that night.

It took only a few weeks for some obvious pieces to fall into place. His commitment to morphing into someone she would find tolerable and exciting. Her brother's throwaway comment that Lachy Short never accepted an invitation unless there was a party bag in it for him. Details of her family and her life slipping out of Lachy's mouth. The Bondi love nest. The speed of it all.

Liss had spent years avoiding dating the kind of boys who went to school with her brothers. They held no appeal or mystery for her, with their bottomless confidence. There were no surprises. They would live in one of a handful of familiar suburbs. Holiday at Positano and Aspen and Hyams. Spend a few summers spinning around identical dancefloors at each other's weddings, then it would be school fees and sailing and tennis and golf for eternity. This was not what Liss had in mind. And if she had been raised for that life, her mother's death had knocked her firmly off course.

On that day, as her father's cool hands held her shoulders firmly in place, she had stood by her mother's bed, staring at the tufts of fluff on the thick beige carpet under her feet and said what her father told her to say. *Goodbye.* It seemed ridiculous to be saying that to her mum, who was already not there, just a tiny thing lying in the vast bed, eyes flickering under her translucent lids, her skin thin and taut across collarbones and wrists, her fingers trembling.

Liss's mother had wanted to die at home. Eleven-year-old Liss wished her mother didn't want that. She wished her mum had left their house the woman she remembered from before, not this ghostly version of herself. Liss had tiptoed past the door to that room for weeks, trying to dodge the nurses and aunties and her father, who might intercept her and make her go inside. Her brothers, she noted, were gone. Sent somewhere else with balls to kick and throw. They, apparently, were not required to play along with this macabre charade.

Liss knew her mother wasn't in that room. And she also knew that any plans you made for your life were entirely redundant. After that day, Liss had abandoned how things were supposed to go.

It was the very same day she'd started bleeding into her underwear. In one day you could lose your mother and start your period and there would be no-one to talk to about either of those things. This was definitely not how things were supposed to go.

So, no, she wasn't into her brother's suitable friends.

But what had surprised her within weeks of being in Lachy's bed, and he hers, was that, actually, Lachy wasn't suitable at all.

Her father thought he was an imposter. A wolf in the old school tie. It wasn't money that was the issue, but pedigree. Lachy's dad had made his money starting a betting shop franchise in the suburbs. His family were interlopers, with their fortune made from poor men's misery, Liss's dad said. There were no stellar qualifications, no soaring talents. Lachy Short, to Michael Gresky, was cocky. Brash. Unworthy. A symbol of what was wrong with Sydney these days.

The other surprise was that Lachy was far from boring. Their chemistry was intoxicating, and so was his willingness to break rules. He took her to places she hadn't been, literally, sexually. And he treated her with the exact combination of adoration and disdain that she'd been looking for but had always found in the wrong quantities.

They were obsessed with each other from the beginning. So the proposal wasn't such a surprise, when it came, six months after the night he whispered in her father's ear.

The ring was. It was her mother's – a beautiful, delicate cluster of diamonds daisy-set in a yellow-gold band. If Liss had guessed what ring Lachy Short would choose for his bride, she would have imagined platinum, because silver was in fashion, but silver was cheap. And she would have imagined a rock that could be seen across a busy room. An announcement that you had made it, like that awful apartment he lived in when they met. Her mother's ring was subtle and sentimental. Liss had cried.

But it wasn't her mother's ring. Lachy let her think it was for one whole night. And then the next morning, when they were lying in bed at the Shangri-La, a whole wall of window bouncing the morning sun from the harbour view to the stones Liss was holding up to twinkle in the light, he told her.

He had asked her father for the ring at the same time he asked him for permission to propose – a full-circle moment from the night of Tom's party, half a year on. And Michael Gresky had said absolutely not. Even though Liss was his only daughter. Even though it was clear she was wild about this man. Even though this union would see her settling down close to home, which is what her father had always claimed was his heart's desire.

'Did he think it was too soon?' she asked Lachy.

'No, he said he wouldn't give that ring to me under any circumstances. Ever.'

'And so this . . .'

'Is an exact copy.' Lachy's voice was different. Lower, flatter. 'I know a guy who knows a guy. Specialises in duping antiques. Sourced the gold and stones from the same era. Amazing how old things cost more than new things, isn't it?'

'But you said . . .' Liss thought back to the moment she opened the box, at the table at the sky-high restaurant last night, dizzy from two glasses of champagne. She had known, the moment they arrived at the hotel, what script Lachy was following, with the private table, the flowers. And she had decided to go with it. She was certain that when she opened the box she'd gasped, because her mother's ring was such a surprise.

HE WOULD NEVER

'I didn't say it,' Lachy said, taking hold of her hand and looking at his creation. 'You said it, and I didn't correct you, because I didn't want to upset you about your dad being an arsehole. It could wait.' He kissed her hand, let it drop.

'You know that's a strange choice, right?' she'd said. 'To remake my dead mother's ring?'

When he rolled on his side to look at her, he was smiling. 'I wanted you to think about her when you look at it,' he said. 'You deserve that.'

It was a lovely thing to say. She had told him, of course, about the space her mother had left that she could never fill. About how Liss wished she felt her mum with her, like other people said they did but she didn't.

'And every time you see your father,' he went on. 'I want him to see that ring and know what a complete cock he is for underestimating me.' He kissed her. 'And you.'

It was a bit embarrassing now, as a supposedly grown-up mother of a daughter, to admit how incredibly sexy Liss had found Lachy's twisted little stunt.

You get me, she'd thought, then, as they rolled around in the blistering light pouring through the penthouse suite window. But the slight from her father had left a mark. Lachy had got up not long after, and as if a switch was flicked, had looked around the room and declared the hotel overpriced and tacky. That the meal from last night had maybe made him ill. That he really couldn't afford to take the day off, like he thought, because his new boss was an insecure phoney who would try to badmouth him if he wasn't there.

And everything beautiful and special was swept away, leaving Liss feeling uncomfortably hot in the fishbowl room, lying on a wet patch and looking at her deep-fake ring while Lachy ranted and swore about the size and number and thread count of the towels in the bathroom.

And so it was with him. The sun was shining its brightest beam right at him or the world was pissing in his pocket.

Us against the world was one of his favourite scripts, and today, he had decided that Sadie was the enemy who must be eliminated. Did she have to go along with it?

Easier for you. It was a cruel thing to say to Sadie last night, and she knew it. But Liss was irritated by her friend's self-pity. Sadie used to be fearless. A remarkable survivor of a traumatic story. From the very first day, babyless at mothers' group, Sadie was refreshingly other. But the last few years, she'd brought mess to almost every interaction. And Liss's tolerance for mess had shrunk.

She whispered to Lachy, hoping Tia was falling back to sleep. 'Why would Sadie make that up though?'

'You know why.'

'Because of last year?'

'She's obsessed, Liss. You know it.'

'Mum.' It was Tia. She hadn't fallen back to sleep. 'Can I get up?'

It was cute that she was still asking that. There was a rule between Liss and her friends that no child was out of the tent before 7.30 am. Otherwise all the kids would be up, shouting and running and calling for breakfast, and before you knew it, the mothers would all have to be up, too, breaking up fights, picking up plastic bowls, closing cereal boxes and putting the lids back on orange juice bottles. And Liss craved the novelty of a slow morning.

'Can't you wait a bit?' Liss asked, realising in that moment that Tia didn't have her phone in her hand. Weird.

'I just want to go and see if Lyra's okay.'

'Why wouldn't Lyra be okay?' Lachy's voice was too quick, its edge too harsh.

Tia twisted at her long braids and made eye contact with Liss. 'Can I, Mum? We'll just go down to the beach.'

'I said, why wouldn't Lyra be okay, Tia?' Lachy's voice inched up a decibel.

'Just . . .' Tia, Liss could see, was trying to reach around for words that wouldn't make things worse. 'All that fuss with Sadie.'

She'd said the right thing. Liss felt Lachy relax a little beside her. But Ollie and Gracie were moving now, woken by his sharp words.

'Lyra will be fine,' Lachy said. 'She's not a drama queen.'

'Go, darling.' Liss nodded towards her daughter, who didn't say anything else. She just folded her long body up out of her bed and grabbed her wash bag and a sweatshirt, and slipped out of the tent, head lowered.

'Us too!' Ollie cried. 'We want to get up too.'

'Your Switch is in the tent pocket by your bed,' said Liss, simultaneously throwing her phone towards Gracie. 'Half an hour.'

'Lachy. Conference.' She signalled to him to meet her under the quilt. It was one of their small rituals, to pull the covers over their heads and meet in the musky darkness. Once, it was to kiss. Now, it was to whisper.

Liss's eyes adjusted to the gloom, her husband's face inches from hers. He was still so handsome. She saw the way women looked at him. So many of the men in their world had hit forty and sagged and gone bald and faded. Lachy's ego wouldn't survive that. Being attractive, being wanted, was a big chunk of his sense of self.

What did he see, she wondered, when he looked at her under here? Unlike Sadie, unlike Dani, unlike almost all the women at Ollie's school gate, Liss wasn't fighting the ageing process with needles, fillers and threads. Lachy would be seeing the lines around her eyes, a little stripe of silver at her roots, a softness under her chin that had never been there before. Unlike Lachy, physical beauty wasn't a currency she was invested in holding on to. It had never brought her much peace, and she was comfortable with how she was changing.

Lachy could take it or leave it. She knew, as he put both hands on her bottom and pulled her close to him, that he would still take it.

'Lachy.' She shook his hands away. 'What were you doing that set Sadie off?'

'Dancing.' The faint sound of Ollie's Nintendo was audible in their parent cave, and yet, he kissed her neck.

'With Lyra?'

'With everyone. It's disco night. The girls joined in. You know how rare that is these days.'

'I do.'

'We were dancing. It was fun. Until Sadie started screaming.'

'Was Lyra uncomfortable?'

'With what?'

Liss took a deep breath. 'With you?'

'Liss, for fuck's sake.' He took his hands back to his side of the bed. 'Lyra Martin knows me as well as she knows that French fuck of a father of hers. Better, probably.'

'That's not what I'm asking.'

It was getting uncomfortably hot in their blanket cave, but his eyes, now, were unblinking. 'What are you asking me, Liss?'

'I'm asking you if anything happened last night which would explain Sadie's reaction.' Liss swallowed.

He put a finger on her lips. 'Liss. I am not interested in teenage girls, I am not a criminal. I did not touch Lyra Martin. I would never do that.'

Liss exhaled. He kissed her.

'You know who I am,' he said. 'You're the only one who does, really.'

I know, thought Liss. *I know.*

'But it's us,' he said next. 'And you can't let Sadie demonise me like this. I know you don't want to lose a member of your precious gang but if there's a toxic element you've got to cut it out. And that one is determined to fuck me, one way or another.'

'Please don't talk about Sadie as if she's a thing.'

'Liss, you're too forgiving. Have you forgotten last year?'

Liss pushed the covers back, exposing them both to the sunlight shining through the canvas, and took in a big gasp of stale tent air. It was always unbearable to be inside the tents once the sun got to a certain height in the sky.

'What about Dani?' she asked. 'She's the most protective mother I know. Right now, she could be calling the police, or packing up, or plotting to kill you.' Liss was only half-joking.

The kids' heads turned from their screens towards their parents.

Lachy laughed, just like he'd laughed last night when a tipsy Liss had first asked him if Sadie had a reason to hate him so much.

'You don't need to worry about Dani,' he said. 'She's family.'

Bless you, Liss thought. *You have no idea at all.*

14

2013

Bronte, Sydney

Dani

'Lachy thinks I cursed it.'

'The baby?' Dani was dangling her legs in Liss's pool on an oppressively hot Saturday afternoon, as Tia and Lyra splashed in the shallow water in their rings and wings and float vests.

'Every month, when I get my period.' Liss was sitting next to her. 'He says I cursed it by being so sad after Tia was born, that my body's fighting feeling that again. He says he's joking.' Liss pulled her knees up to her chest. 'He's not joking.'

'That seems uncharacteristically superstitious of him.' Dani was talking to her but both their eyes were fixed on the three-year-olds.

'He says he googled it, and that it's not uncommon for a woman who had postnatal depression to suffer a sort of wilful miscarriage.'

'Lachy should leave the magical thinking to the experts.' Dani reached down and spun Lyra like a top, sending up a shower of shrieking giggles. 'You have plenty of time.'

'Is that what you and Seb are telling each other?'

HE WOULD NEVER

'I have no idea what to say to him most days.' Dani brushed drops of water from her thighs. 'Since the New York thing, we barely speak.'

It was true. Seb had two suitcases open on their bedroom floor, the same metallic wheelies he'd brought here a little over three years ago, following his pregnant wife home. Dani watched what was going into them. Neatly folded sweaters he barely wore here. Books he hadn't got around to reading in their real, busy life. A picture of Lyra in a frame Dani had bought him to hold the first ultrasound of their little girl, back when she was just an idea.

She stepped around the open cases, and counted down the days.

'I keep imagining he'll change his mind about the job,' she said. 'He says if I was pregnant, he wouldn't go.'

'That seems cruel.'

Dani shrugged. 'I think he's just unhappy.'

Lachy and Seb would soon be back from a mandated mission to source lunch and more pool toys. Dani could not imagine what they were talking about in the front seats of Lachy's BMW.

She knew that Seb found Lachy brash and thoughtless. She was certain Lachy thought Seb was pretentious and strange. What common ground they had was populated by their wives and their daughters, and Dani couldn't really picture either of them engaging in small talk.

Dani's work and the growing girls had changed the rhythm of her time with Liss, but they had held on tight to their friendship. Liss picked Lyra up from preschool two afternoons a week and brought her back to Bronte. Dani arrived to collect her around six in a frazzled haze, and there would be a cup of tea or a glass of wine – depending on the scale of the frazzle – while the girls ate Liss's home-cooked dinner. Often, Dani would stay for bathtime, and strap a sweet-smelling, damp-haired, pyjama-clad Lyra into the car to take home to Seb.

Weekends always involved a park outing, or a group date at some horrendous indoor play place or, sometimes, a gathering at Liss's. Always Liss's, since she had all of the space and Dani and Seb had graduated from the tiny Randwick flat to a slightly less tiny Randwick townhouse.

There was a part of Dani that envied Liss – sometimes, when she was in an interminable project meeting after a night of scarce sleep, she imagined her friend drifting around this beautiful home, creating thoughtful snacks and craft projects for Tia and her other little friends whose mummies didn't work. Sometimes, when she was feeling the pressure of earning the bigger salary, when she was stuck dealing with Seb's dissatisfaction and resentment, she envied Liss's apparently simpler life. But only for a moment. She knew too much to be completely seduced by the fantasy.

Dani knew Liss thought Seb hadn't tried hard enough to find his dream job here in Sydney before giving up and taking on a contract back in New York. She was probably right.

And Dani knew Liss thought that Dani was trying hard to get pregnant to keep him here. She was wrong about that.

'I think he's pretending to be really torn about going,' she said. 'I think his baby fever is a bit of a front.'

Tia was turning in circles in the pool, giggling as she kicked up splashes of silvery drops. Lyra was swishing her hands back and forth, back and forth, watching the wash.

'Do you think they're off talking about our menstrual cycles?' Liss asked. 'Swapping tips about conception sex?'

'Seb would rather die.'

There was a crunch and a clang and the men appeared at the garden's side gate, brandishing fluoro pool noodles and two big oil-speckled brown bags.

'We return, family,' Lachy called. 'With sustenance and inflatables.'

'We got a roast chicken, salad and bread.' Seb raised a bag.

'A roast *chook*,' corrected Lachy. 'And chips. And garlic sauce.'

'Chipppppies!' yelled Tia from the pool, splashing wildly.

'Absolutely not,' replied Liss, shaking her head at Lachy.

Lachy shrugged, poked out his tongue, put the bag of food on the glass-topped outdoor dining table and lobbed the pool noodles over the fence into the water.

'The daddies are coming in, kids,' he yelled, and Dani watched Seb wince. 'It's about to get fun!'

'I didn't bring swimming shorts,' Seb said, his eyes finding hers.

'Well, that was dumb on a day like today.' Lachy mimed horror at the little girls in the pool, who were watching the dads with interest.

'Don't worry about it, you can borrow some of mine,' Lachy looked over at Seb, 'if they fit your skinny arse.' Lachy was already wearing board shorts that looked nothing like board shorts, and was peeling off his weekend polo shirt.

Dani knew Seb would not wear another man's swimmers. She held his gaze, the one that was begging her to find an excuse for him to not have to wear Lachy Short's shorts or swim in his pool. And she said, 'That would be lovely, Lachy, thank you. I'm sure they'll fit just fine.'

They may have met in the city that spawned a hundred romantic comedies, but Dani thought her and Seb's meet-cute lacked something. Particularly after she'd heard Liss and Lachy's.

She had been in New York for a year and was absolutely not dating. The Dani who'd aimed for the New York office of the megabank she'd worked for since graduation was all business. She thought that her sacrifice and work ethic were her most original and defining characteristics. She was wrong.

She'd hit the target, scored the move to New York City, a place that had always represented success, ambition and the perfect amount of distance from where she didn't want to be – in Concord, living with her parents, grandfather, sister and all their judgements. But everyone else at the bank in New York was just like her. Driven, hard-working, and waving around their own MBAs.

'Why are you here tonight?' the Frenchman at the bar had asked her.

That night Dani had drunk two glasses of wine. Uncharacteristic. She was at the bar because the new marketing boss wanted to shout the team a round of expensive top-shelf drinks, a visible, if token, reward for something-something that the hungry team had won or nailed or aced. Dani didn't remember the details, but she remembered the pride, and the uncomfortably urgent need she had for the boss to know it was her hard work, her project leadership, her MBA, dammit, that had yielded the win. She didn't need his free drinks, she needed him to remember her name.

But the CMO didn't show. Instead, his assistant had turned up at 7 pm with his credit card in her faux Prada clutch and told them all he'd said to drink up.

Dani would have left right then if it wasn't for the latest key tenet she was trying to work on in her self-optimisation program: to be more likeable. Popular co-workers got more opportunities. And popular people didn't shy away from drinking with their colleagues, even if she knew everyone was doing the same mental calculation of the most lucrative path the evening might take from here.

So she didn't usually drink, and she didn't usually talk to men in bars. That was not what the New York chapter of her life was going to be about. It was about promotion and progress in the most competitive arena. And then getting sent to London, or Singapore, where the really big guns were, and then one day back to Australia, where she would buy a great big house about five suburbs away from Concord, to the east, near the ocean.

HE WOULD NEVER

Dani was pretty certain she was thinking about that plan when the Frenchman had approached.

'The person you are waiting for, he didn't come?'

'My boss, no.'

'What were you hoping for, when you came here tonight?'

It was such a ridiculous question for a Wednesday night, Dani decided to leave.

Her small room in her small, clean apartment in Soho was fine for studying, working, sleeping. Her room-mate Nan would probably be home, and there would be mint tea, and frozen yoghurt, and a warm radiator, and *The Simple Life* on their Tivo. All those things were more appealing than this man with the accent trying to pick her up. Dani was not one for being picked up.

Nan, of course, could never understand why. 'You're thousands of miles from your Catholic parents. You'll be thirty any minute. If this isn't the time to sleep around, I don't know when is.'

But Dani knew. Never. And anyway, there were still three years to thirty.

'Don't leave,' the Frenchman had said. 'Really, it's extremely cold out there.' His accent was almost comically seductive, his language oddly formal.

'That's not a reason to stay. In fact, it will be colder the longer I stay here.'

'Okay, then, don't go because it's boring to leave.'

Dani didn't understand men like this. Why did they try so hard? What made him think that, even if Dani decided yes, he was coming back to Soho with her, that any imagined sex would be *fun*? She would be much too nervous and self-conscious to writhe and moan like she was doing inside his head.

'I have no problem being boring,' Dani told the Frenchman.

He had shrugged, turned back to the bar and raised his hand, like people in American bars did in American movies.

Dani slid off her stool and looked around for her ridiculously large coat.

'Got to go, early spin tomorrow,' she'd called in the general direction of her remaining colleagues, gathered around a small table, heads together.

Only one of them turned their head and raised a hand. 'See you, Daniella.'

There was something about the dismissive wave that hit Dani hard. In a flash she saw the sterile walls of her apartment, no pictures hanging, no comforting clutter. Once she walked out of this bar, wrapped in a padded bubble of a coat, and started towards the subway – one tiny person in a city of millions – she realised that if she disappeared into the thin, cold air of this night, all the people who would care were thirty-six hours away.

I am alone, she thought. *I wanted to be, and now I am.*

Dani turned back and saw the Frenchman smiling at her, raising his glass. He wasn't bad looking, and his eyes were kind. His suit wasn't sharp and shiny, like the sharky men who cruised the corridors of her bank, but loose and linen, like it wasn't five below outside. And his shoes were actually ankle boots, with a thick tread. He looked like a safe harbour.

She walked back up to the bar, feeling that at least one of her colleagues at the little round table was watching her.

'If I give you my number, will you call me?' she'd asked him, standing a few footsteps away, leaning at the waist to push the words over the music and into his ear.

'Of course,' he said, too fast. He was surprised, and it was charming.

'But will you?' she asked. 'Or will you just say you will?'

HE WOULD NEVER

'I will call you,' he said. 'If you tell me your name.'

'Even though I'm boring?'

'I doubt that you are actually boring.' He put down his drink and held out his hand. 'I'm Sebastian,' he said. 'Seb, in America.'

Dani shook his hand and then turned hers over, an outstretched palm. 'Give me your phone.'

She took his grey Nokia and tapped in her name and number and she added the name of the bar to the 'business' note, to help him remember who Dani was. 'I'm going now,' she said, pulling her coat around her. 'Don't be boring.'

Seb nodded, and turned back to the bar in a way that made her nervous. As she walked out into the cold and the washed-out black of a city that was never truly dark, she felt faintly nauseous. She'd done something she didn't ever do in a bid to muffle a truth that, until tonight, she hadn't even allowed to be voiced. This was why, she understood, there was the rush and push to swap numbers, to bump bodies together, to have someone call you. To have somewhere to go on Saturday afternoon, other than back to the gym. Why had she thought she was immune to that?

Six years later, beside the infinity pool carved into Liss's sandstone deck, everything twinkled and Seb excused himself. Dani watched him walk towards the open double doors into the kitchen.

'There'll be some boardies in the laundry, to the left,' Lachy yelled after him. Then he looked over at Dani, a smug grin forming. Liss punched him in the arm as she got up to get a towel for the girls. 'You're an idiot.'

They all knew Seb wasn't going to get the shorts.

If their first meeting was tainted for Dani by the sharp realisation of her own desperation, the few months that followed it had been genuinely happy. Whatever instinct had turned her around at the door of that bar had been solid. Their date turned into a romance, which was something, Nan had always assured her, that never happened in New York City.

It had knocked her completely off balance, the way she had allowed herself to fall into Seb. He thought she was likeable. In fact, he thought she was wonderful, and told her, all the time. It brought her a freedom she'd never associated with love, and she'd dived into it. Now she had two things in her life: work and Seb. It wasn't in her five-year plan, but the thrill of being loved had wrapped itself around Dani in an unexpected way.

None of her family flew out to New York for their wedding a year later. It was an act of protest, Dani knew, a physical marker of their strong disapproval. 'You should be getting married here at home,' was the only thing her mother had said, 'so all your people can be there.' Those words conjured a picture in Dani's head, a blurry line of aunties and uncles and cousins from a mash-up of identical eighteenths and twenty-firsts and christenings and engagement parties, weddings and Easters and Christmases. So many backyards with long trestle tables and so many air-conditioned function rooms with grey-speckled ceiling tiles at clubs within a five-kilometre radius of her parents' home. She'd feel their eyes on her, what she chose to wear, who she'd chosen to stand next to.

'This is where we live, Mum, it's our home. We'd love to show it to you.'

Her mother never mentioned it again. When Dani offered to pay for tickets for her parents and Bianca, her mother had just clucked her tongue and changed the subject.

On the wedding day Dani found herself dizzy with relief, knowing the exact set of her mother's mouth at the sight of the calf-length lace dress she'd chosen, at the flower tucked behind her ear. At her bare ankles and flat shoes. It was at City Hall, like in the movies, and then dinner at a restaurant. A wedding was a good idea for visa

HE WOULD NEVER

purposes, because Sebastian's mother was from Louisiana, and his accent was hiding the fact that he was an American citizen. And it was a good idea for love purposes, because she had never felt so wanted. The way Seb looked at her made her feel like she'd done something right. He liked that she was energetic and organised and ambitious. He liked that she was always thinking of what was next. He liked that she took care of him but didn't need him. He liked that she tried so hard, at everything. He didn't cluck his tongue and tell her to slow down, calm down, or climb down from that ladder.

Dani Grasso became Dani Martin at the same moment she broke away from the ranks of the marketing team to become an analyst. It was a good year.

'I'd better go talk to him,' Dani said back at the pool to Liss. She gestured to Lyra and Tia, still bobbing about in the water, urging Lachy to jump in. 'Can you watch Lyra?' The food was still sitting in the bags on the table. 'I'll get some plates. Be right back.'

She'd walked into Liss's beautiful kitchen and out into the hallway. The front door was open. Surely Seb hadn't just left? No. He was sitting on the front step of the ironwork veranda. She could tell, from the way his shoulders sat up near the place where a dark curl kissed his ear, that he was angry.

'Seb,' she said, and watched the shoulders twitch. 'It's just Lachy. It's just swimmers. Seriously.'

'He says you and Liss have an agreement.' He still didn't turn around. Dani glanced back down the hallway then went to sit beside him.

'What?'

'That you want to get pregnant at the same time, together, that she's waiting for you to be ready.'

She leaned forward to look into his face. 'You mean Lachy said that Liss isn't really trying to have a baby?'

He nodded. Dani's first reaction was to laugh. The idea that her friend Liss, who wanted nothing more than another baby, might make some childish pact like that was unthinkable. Did Lachy not know his own wife?

'That's ridiculous. Liss has been in tears every day for a year about this.'

'And you?' As he turned she saw, as she had for months now, that the face that had always been so open to her was closed, tight, hard. Other. 'Are you in tears about it too?' Clearly, Seb did know his own wife.

'Seb.' She reached around for words that weren't a lie but weren't quite true. 'You're leaving. In three days.'

'Not for ever.' It was his turn to reach. 'And you wanted me to go.'

'Only because you're so fucking unhappy,' she said. 'It's just not the time to . . .' She pictured Lachy spinning a giggling Lyra around in the pool. 'Grow our unhappy family.'

'You are punishing me,' he said. He had said it before. 'You have a plan, and I am not going along with all that you want.' He gestured around, as if what she wanted was to be sitting in Liss's front garden, staring at a manicured hedge the height of a truck, stomach lurching, eyes stinging. 'You are punishing me.'

'I don't know what you want me to do,' she said, rubbing her forehead.

It wasn't really true. She knew what he wanted. He wanted Sydney to be a place they visited, not the place they lived. He wanted her to have another baby. He wanted her to see his sadness and fix it. He wanted her to put her needs aside for his.

His misery was infectious, his dissatisfaction tangible, and Dani felt drained every time she walked into the house she'd finally convinced him they deserved to rent.

HE WOULD NEVER

The problem was, out in the world, she felt like she was in exactly the right place. At work she was finally being offered the projects she'd watched previously pass her by. She could taste the life she'd dreamt of when she'd finished studying. The problem was, by marrying Seb and having a child, she'd complicated her permission to have it. Because it was her dream, and not his. And couples, apparently, are meant to have shared dreams.

So, after years of doing work he didn't like for people he didn't respect, when Seb had been offered a contract back in New York, it was true she'd urged him to take it. And then he'd asked her to come too.

'You'll walk back into the Manhattan office,' he'd said. 'And I'll be earning good money again, and we'll be . . .'

Who we were, she knew he wanted to say. But it wasn't true.

'I don't understand why you won't just try it. We can come back.'

When they met she'd told him she wanted to work all over the world. They'd dreamed of a future where they weren't tied to one place, one home, one job. Then she'd changed the script when she had decided she wanted to have her baby in Australia. And then stay.

She was bad at explaining why it was impossible for her to uproot herself again, to walk away from the life she'd created here. She knew that if they were in New York and he was back working in his dream job, she would be the one trying to find the good babysitter, the good preschool, to hustle Lyra's way into kindergarten and elementary, to try to get them into a good building. She knew what it would take to build Lyra a life there that offered anything like their life here.

They'd been arguing about it for Lyra's entire life. And then they'd stopped arguing. And he'd started speaking to Lyra only in French.

It was an idea she'd always loved, but now it felt like their home was divided into two clear camps, and one of them was talking about the other behind their back.

Seb stood up. 'I'm going home.'

'But Lyra's in the pool. She's having a ball.'

'Just bring her home when you're ready. I'll finish packing.'

'It's not true,' Dani called, as he walked to the gate. 'About Liss and me and babies. That's just Lachy fishing.'

'He knows more about you than I do, it seems.' Seb shrugged, then kept walking.

Dani kept watching long after he'd gone.

Fuck.

When she walked back out to the pool deck, no plates in her hands, she stepped right into the end of a conversation between Liss and Lachy.

'How can you be too French to want to swim with your kids on a hot afternoon?' Lachy was saying.

'He's not –'

'He's a miserable bastard, Liss, you know it. And if you can't be happy here,' he tipped backwards, floating in the bright ice-blue for a moment, arms outstretched, 'then fuck off back to France.'

'New York,' said Dani. 'He's fucking off back to New York.'

Lachy straightened up in the pool but then shrugged. 'You know it's for the best.'

'She does?' Liss was looking at her, eyebrows raised.

It was true that Lachy understood some parts of Dani's life better than Seb. Her sisterhood with Liss. Her career drive. It had only been a matter of time, she knew, before their paths had crossed at work.

They had first run into each other at a farewell dinner for an old partner who was leaving Dani's bank. Dani was nervous to be invited, sensing it was a sign of progression but unsure how to act at this level. Of course it turned out that old Frank Altmann had been a mentor to Lachy early in his career, and Lachy had taken her under his wing at that party, introducing her to other useful old bastards as 'the woman my wife loves more than me'.

He'd been kinder than she'd expected him to be. More generous. Since then, she had asked his advice once or twice on breaking into some inner sanctum, or for an introduction to someone she had no business calling. And Lachy had flattered her for it. 'You surprise me,' he'd said, at the end of that first-night dinner. 'You get it.'

'She's too smart for him,' Lachy said now, giving the girls another twirl. 'Let the man go and ruin his life.'

'We are not breaking up,' Dani said, a little too loudly, because Lyra, who was surely still too small to make sense of those words, spun around in the water and stared up at her mother.

Liss stood, grabbed Dani's hand and the food bags and headed for the house. 'Get the girls dried off,' she called to Lachy over her shoulder. 'We'll sort lunch.'

In the sun-dappled kitchen, at the giant, newly marble bench, Liss opened cupboards and drawers as Dani stood, feeling dazed, sort of loose-limbed and useless. It felt unbelievable that all these feelings she had, these resentments, and this stubbornness whose source she couldn't locate, might have led her to the edge of an actual marriage collapse, not just a professional break.

Liss was looking at her, she could see, as she moved around the kitchen, pulling out hefty plates for the kids and linen napkins for the grown-ups.

'The chips will be cold,' Dani said, dumbly.

'Good.' Liss opened one of the greasy brown bags and plucked out the fries. 'We'll chuck them.'

Dani watched her friend pull open her kitchen bin and drop them in, considering what most of the people she knew would think about throwing away perfectly good hot chips.

'Where did Seb go?' Liss's eyes were on her again.

'He's gone.'
'Why?'

Dani shook herself a little, looked up, tried a smile. 'He's just so grumpy, I want Lyra to have a lovely afternoon. I want us to have a lovely afternoon, he's just . . .'

'Was it Lachy?'

Dani looked out through the doors to where Lachy was lifting Lyra out of the pool.

'He says Lachy told him we have a pact about not getting pregnant.'

'What?'

'Weird thing to say, right?'

'It's crazy.' Liss also looked at her husband talking to the girls as he handed them towels and made a show of drying himself off. She looked hurt. 'Sometimes I have no idea why he says the things he says. He knows what I'm going through.'

'I think Lachy thinks it's fun.' Dani moved to the island, to the food bags, and started unpacking the remaining food. 'To fuck with people a bit.'

If this was a shocking thing to say about her friend's husband, Liss didn't show it. 'I'm sorry, Dani. I'm sure that didn't help.'

Dani lifted out the plastic carton of thick, white garlic sauce that only Lachy would eat. 'The thing is, Liss, for me, it's true. I'm not trying to get pregnant. I'm still on the pill.'

'You're still on the pill. But . . .' Liss was looking at her in exactly the way Dani expected. A way she never wanted her friend to look at her. 'What are you talking about, we . . .'

'I couldn't tell you, not after everything.' Why was she telling Liss this now? She didn't need to know.

'But, Dani, you've been . . .' Dani could see Liss was mentally trawling through their interactions for blatant lies. Every month, for months and months, Liss had shared disappointment and shame at her body not doing what she thought it was here for. Dani had made all the right noises, but she hadn't outright lied, had she?

'He's right, I'm not upset that I'm not pregnant. Because I don't think Seb and I should be having another baby right now.' Dani put the cartons on the counter and stepped to Liss. 'But I really, really want you to have your baby, my friend. I promise I'm not pretending about that.'

'You lied to me?' Liss looked outside again. 'Does Lachy *know* that?'

Dani shook her head. 'Of course not. He's just fishing.'

'Did you tell Seb?'

'Nope. He thinks we've been trying.'

The two women stood there for a moment as shade began to touch the edges of the room, and the girls' voices cooed and laughed at Lachy in the garden.

'I promise to tell you the truth, Liss, you really are my lifesaver here.'

'And I thought you were mine.' Liss's hands were shaking as she folded them over her stomach.

'I am. I promise you. Every single thing I said to you about what you've been going through, I meant.'

There was a moment before Liss dropped her hands and picked up the plates. 'Well, okay,' she said.

Dani accepted her friend's signal that this part of the conversation was over. She ripped the foil-lined bag of chicken and lifted the dripping bird onto one of Liss's tasteful platters.

'I think he's going to leave me for good,' she said as she licked her fingers. 'So, maybe I should stop taking the pill.'

Liss picked up the plate with her free hand and turned to walk out to the garden and her troublemaking husband and those beautiful little girls.

'Don't you fucking dare,' she said.

15

Saturday, 10 am

Green River Campground

Dani

Craig was winning friends one at a time with his tiny portable espresso machine. He'd already turned out a near-perfect macchiato for Juno, who'd enthusiastically filmed the process, and Ginger, who was dancing away from HQ with a wiggle in her hips, coffee held aloft. 'Nailed, it, Craig. You can come back.'

Craig was beaming, as if winning the approval of this group of women was his life goal. 'Maybe this will score us a better site next year,' he whispered as he handed Dani her plastic mug of superior blend and their hands touched on the handle.

The coffee would not dissolve the tension in Dani's stomach as she scoured the site for Lyra. Tia Short had put her head through the tent flap this morning and spirited her daughter away before Dani could restart the grilling from last night.

'Nothing,' was the only word she could get out of her daughter when she asked Lyra what happened at the disco while she and Liss were off collecting ice creams from the camp kitchen's stuttering freezer.

'Nothing,' was what Lyra insisted when Dani asked her what she wanted her to say to Sadie.

And 'nothing' was what Lyra answered when Dani, at her most direct, asked what Lachy Short did to her on that dancefloor.

She'd tried to sleep on all these nothings, as Lyra and Brigitte fiddled around getting ready for bed as if it were any other evening. Craig had wisely disappeared for a while and, when he returned, she asked him to sleep in the kids' tent, so she could bring her girls onto the big inflatable mattress with her. Dani had kept her daughters where she could see them, and listened to Craig's gentle snores through the canvas.

'We'll be back together tonight, right?' Craig said, watching her sipping her coffee.

'Were you at the same party I was at last night?' she asked him, her voice sharper than she'd planned. 'I have other things to worry about.'

'It was a lot of nothing.' Craig put his hand back over hers on the coffee cup. 'I'm no big fan of Lachy Short, but it's not a secret that Sadie is crazy. And sometimes, Dan, people bump into each other on a dancefloor.'

He went back to fiddling with his coffee pump. Dani watched his hands while she considered his words. 'Maybe.'

Lachy and Liss, and Sadie herself, were nowhere to be seen, so far. But Trick had been hovering around the smaller kids monstering the bacon and egg rolls, his face unreadable.

'How's your mum?' Dani asked, in as neutral a voice as she could manage. The boy shrugged and pushed a piece of bacon into his mouth.

She tried a different question. 'Have you seen –'

'Beach,' he replied quickly, nodding to the path, mouth still full, his urgency to get away from her clear. 'The girls are at the beach.'

They were. The tide was on its way in, and Lyra and Tia were sitting where the wet mud turned to dry sand, heads together. At first

Dani thought they were talking, staring out at the pelicans perched on the old pier stumps. But as she approached, and Lyra's face turned towards her, she realised they were looking at their phones.

Once the sight of Dani would trigger her daughter's automatic smile. That beloved little face splitting into a grin when Dani appeared to collect her, or arrived home from work, or was spotted in an assembly crowd or at the sidelines of soccer. Now, that face she knew better than her own was finding it hard to hide the inevitable mother–daughter shift brewing between them. Sometimes there was relief, sometimes irritation, occasionally disgust. *It's Mum*, her daughter's face said, *how do I get her to move along?*

'Hi, darling.'

Tia Short's face also turned Dani's way, attempting an old-style smile. 'Hi, Dani.' She looked raw around the eyes, like she hadn't slept. Her face was slightly puffy and pale, dappled with the headless pimples of hormonal youth. Tia looked like she'd been another mother up worrying all night.

'What are you doing?'

'Nothing.' Lyra lifted her phone hand a little. 'Data's terrible.'

'View's good though, right?' Dani nodded out to the pelicans and the girls' eyes went back to their impotent phones at this most predictable of comments.

Dani sat down anyway, making sure that the bum of her denim shorts would be on the dry sand, and her feet not too far into the mud. She cradled her coffee and took a breath. 'Girls, I just have to ask –'

'Mum!' Lyra glared at her. Her daughter nodded at Tia, whose eyes stayed down. 'Can we drop it?'

'Lyra, I'm your mother. It's my job to keep you safe.' It was her most well-worn of teenage parenting lines; still, it was the right one for now. 'And before we all get on with this weekend, I just have to ask you again –'

HE WOULD NEVER

'Again,' muttered Lyra.

'Yes, again. And while Tia is here, too.'

Tia, she could see, was scrunching her bare feet into the mud, like she was tensing her whole body, in her fluffy pyjama bottoms and strappy little vest, almost exactly the same thing that Lyra was wearing.

'I have to ask – no, I have to say – that if anything happens, anywhere, with any of the boys, or any of the . . .'

Tia Short's eyes were squeezed shut now, and Dani wasn't sure what word was coming next. 'Anyone, whatever age,' she went on. 'If anything happens that makes you uncomfortable, or crosses a line . . .'

Why was this so hard, this kind of conversation with teens? Dani wasn't a prude. Dani was straightforward. Dani could have conversations with high-status, wealthy men that they did not want to have. But talking to teenage girls, even when one of them was your own, was terrifying. It was as if they were surrounded by a force field. She blundered on, 'You can speak up. You can tell me. You can tell another adult you trust. You know that, right?'

The girls said nothing. Tia opened her eyes and Dani could see they were glassy.

'You have to tell me.'

'Are you finished?' Lyra asked, finally.

Dani felt a surge of fury at the cheek of her oldest daughter. At the idea of what her mother would have done – or her father, more likely – if she'd used that tone of voice when she was a teenager, growing up in a three-generation house. 'Lyra,' she started, in a voice that both her daughters knew was one step away from all-out yelling. 'You want to watch yourself with that voice. I am trying to be reasonable here. I am trying . . .' her voice was disappointingly shaky now, 'to protect you.'

'From who?' asked Tia, looking up.

'It's a good question.' Liss. She'd appeared, presumably from the south path, a cup of Craig's coffee in hand. Her face echoed her daughter's. Pale, sleepless, but with a hint of a smile around her mouth. 'Can I join?'

'Of course.' Dani patted the sand next to her but Liss lowered herself on the other side, next to Tia, and put her hand on her daughter's shoulder. 'You okay, girls?'

The horror of a dual mother–daughter chat flashed across both the teenagers' faces at the same time. If the circumstances had been slightly different, Dani would have laughed. She and Liss would have laughed. They didn't, though.

'Mum, we don't need another lecture,' Tia said. 'Everything's fine. It's just . . . Dad, you know.'

'No lectures here. Sounded to me like Dani was about to lose her absolute shit.' Liss sipped her coffee, winced a little. 'So you've definitely had the whole "it's our job to keep you safe" chat?'

Dani leaned forward and looked at Liss, widening her eyes in a 'what the fuck?' face. 'Thanks, friend.'

The girls' energy had shifted. They were twitching in their desperation to get up and leave their mothers, this beach, this conversation – the planet, perhaps. 'Mum, everything's fine. Can we go?' Lyra's voice was no longer full of attitude but cajoling, like a little girl.

Tia stood up, a little patch of damp sand on the bum of her pyjamas. 'Dad is so embarrassing,' she said to Liss. 'Can you just tell him not to dance anymore?' An innocent request with a tortured tone.

'Yes, Tia, I can.'

The teenagers started down the beach back towards the path. Two almost-women, only their bare feet and doughnut-printed fluffy pants giving them away.

HE WOULD NEVER

'Get some breakfast into you!' Dani called after them. 'Ginger's made bacon and eggs.'

'Gross,' she heard Lyra mutter, before they were out of earshot, walking in step.

Dani and Liss sat for a moment, watching the river lapping up to them. Dani finished her coffee, pushed the base of the mug into the soft sand and tipped her head back, sighing.

'Jesus Christ.'

'So, who *are* we protecting them from?' Liss asked, eyes still out to the water.

'Everyone.' Dani sighed. 'Absolutely everyone.'

'What did she say happened?'

'Nothing. Nothing is the word of the moment.'

Liss, hands wrapped around her mug, looked like she was choosing her next words cautiously, which was uncharacteristic. Usually words between them were a constant streaming exchange. They had a shorthand, they had in-jokes, they had no filter. Only when it came to Lachy could things get spiky, careful.

'So.' Liss had chosen. 'You think Sadie?'

'Do you?'

'Well, I don't think anything else, Dan. Lachy's a lot of complicated things, as you know, but Lyra? Come on.'

It was what Dani believed, too. Or, at least, it's what she wanted to believe. Believe her daughter, believe her friend. But there was a little block to it in the shape of the growing distance between herself and Lyra. It was inconvenient, but it felt wrong. She shuffled a little closer to Liss in the sand, dropping her voice.

'How do you know what's normal teenage behaviour and when to worry?' she said. 'That's what's keeping me up at nights now. How would I know if something bad had happened to her? Would she tell me? I don't know if that's something I can count on anymore. She used to tell me everything, but now . . .'

'That's not what this is.' Liss pulled her toes out of the way of the advancing river and turned to look at Dani. 'And, Dan, you'd know. You're so close to your girls. You'd know.'

Dani wasn't sure if this was true, looking down the beach at her daughter's retreating back. She and Tia were turning to walk up the path, they were talking to each other now, phones down by their sides. Dani was jealous. To be on the end of a free-flowing conversation with Lyra. To know what was being shared between them, their private worlds and thoughts. Would she really know? Would her daughter look different to her the day after she lost her virginity, say, or the day after something world-shifting had happened? Like . . . a trusted older man groping her? Would it leave a mark that a mother could read?

'Yeah,' was all she said as the girls disappeared up the path. 'So, Sadie?'

'I don't know if she thought she saw something, or if she made it up entirely because . . .'

'Of last year,' Dani finished the sentence. 'If that's true, Liss. If she invented the whole thing, you have to do something.'

'That's what Lachy says.'

'Of course it is.' It didn't quite feel right, even in all its obvious likelihood. Sadie carrying shame, projecting it around.

'Okay, well, I'll talk to her about it.' Liss placed her hands on her thighs in a decisive, 'here goes' gesture. 'It'll be okay. Lyra wants this over. Lachy wants it over. I want our weekend back.'

Dani nodded. It was tempting to just move past this, to erase the first-night disco from the story of the weekend. But there was one more idea she needed to try on first.

'Do you think it's possible that Lachy just didn't realise it was Lyra he was dancing with?'

HE WOULD NEVER

Liss looked at Dani for a long moment. 'Well, he knew it wasn't me, so . . . what are you saying?'

'Nothing.'

'You think he thought it was . . . you?' Liss asked, looking closely at Dani, a smile forming.

'That's not what I meant.' But maybe it was, a little bit. 'Sometimes people bump into each other on a dancefloor, as Craig says. That's all.'

'I think it's Sadie seeing things,' said Liss, calmly. 'Let's stick to that.'

'Yeah.'

The river surged and both women jumped up, their feet in the water, the coffee cups knocked to their sides. They laughed and fished the mugs out as the water retreated.

'Let's go,' Liss said. 'I think I've got some instant coffee somewhere that's better than this.'

Dani laughed, picturing Craig's earnest face pumping away at his espresso machine, easing into the idea that they were pushing this chapter out with the tide. 'Jesus, let's hope so.'

16

2014

Facebook Messenger Chat

LISS: I have an idea.

SADIE: So do I. Let's all go out Friday and get drunk.

LISS: Impractical for Dani and me.

SADIE: Pregnant women are boring.

DANI: Hey. You weren't so boring, if I remember rightly.

SADIE: I was not following doctor's orders.

JUNO: You've never followed orders in your life.

LISS: Focus, please.

DANI: Go on.

LISS: I think we should go camping.

SADIE: Fuck no.

DANI: Fuck no.

JUNO: Absolutely not.

LISS: I bet Ginger would like it.

DANI: She's not here to save you. Moving day.

JUNO: Leaving us for country life. That bitch.

LISS: Hear me out. My family has a place.

SADIE: Does it have a roof and walls and a swimming pool?

LISS: Ha. NO. It's a campsite.

DANI: Your family owns a campsite??? Is there anything they don't own?

LISS: They don't own it. They have sites there. It's special. Like really beautiful. Impossible to get into.

SADIE: Camping FOMO is a very specific kind of FOMO.

JUNO: I actually like camping. Did it as a kid.

SADIE: We all did it as kids, Juno, not a reason to do it again. Used to eat boogers, too.

DANI: Not our thing.

LISS: Focus, please.

JUNO: You are about to have a baby and you want to go camping?

LISS: For NEXT year. I can book it. Would love to fight with my brothers about it tbh. I think it could be our thing. Every year.

SADIE: I'll bite. Where?

LISS: Up north. Green River. It's by the water. On the river. You can swim. Walk in the national park.

JUNO: Swimming and walking. Two things I can do in Sydney.

LISS: It's only an hour away. Honestly, it's the most beautiful place you've ever seen.

DANI: Send pictures.

Incoming pictures: Golden sunset over distant escarpment. Smiling people neck-deep in clear green water. Children play on palm-fringed beach.

JUNO: Okay. It's beautiful.

SADIE: Whoa.

DANI: Stunning. But still camping.

LISS: Think about it. Somewhere we can go, together, every year. Kids. Partners. Costs next to nothing.

SADIE: So nice of you to think of us plebs, my lady.

DANI: Hey!

SADIE: JOKING.
JUNO: It looks great. Does it have toilets? Showers?
DANI: That's a question?
JUNO: It's CAMPING. There are degrees of camping. Some places have pools and restaurants. Some places have drop toilets.
SADIE: I don't see any restaurants.
DANI: LISS! Come back!
LISS: No pool. No restaurant.
SADIE: I'm sorry.
LISS: NP.
SADIE: Was trying to be funny.
LISS: All good. Has toilets. Has showers.
SADIE: Who puts up the tents?
JUNO: Who even has tents?
LISS: We plan for next year. We get tents. Men will put them up.
JUNO: Oh, please.
SADIE: What men?
LISS: Lachy, Aiden, Seb???
DANI: Maybe Seb.
LISS: Of course.
JUNO: He's gone again?
SADIE: But the baby?????
DANI: He'll be here for the baby.
LISS: I'll call you.
DANI: Not now. He's here.
JUNO: Ask him if he can put up a tent.
DANI: There's no reality in which Seb could put up a tent.
JUNO: Then good riddance.
GINGER: Hey.
SADIE: Hey!
LISS: Hey! How's moving day?

HE WOULD NEVER

GINGER: I am hiding in the toilet.
SADIE: New house or old house?
GINGER: New house! We drove three hours with the goldfish on my knee.
LISS: What's it like?
GINGER: QUIET.
DANI: That's why you moved.
GINGER: TOO QUIET.
JUNO: Wait till the kids get settled. Not so quiet.
GINGER: I want to go camping.
LISS: Told you!
DANI: Whhhhhhhy would you say that?
GINGER: Because I'm going to miss you all and having something to look forward to will make it okay.
SADIE: You shouldn't have moved.
DANI: I think you've made that point, about fifty times.
GINGER: You should see the size of this house though.
SADIE: Yeah, but a home with no friends is just a house.
JUNO: I'm sure all her old schoolfriends are on their way over with fresh-baked scones.
GINGER: I fucking hope not.
LISS: FOCUS, PLEASE.
DANI: Liss, I can't think about camping. I'm thirty-two weeks. My brain can only think a day at a time.
LISS: Such lies, as if you haven't got a calendar for next year with all Lyra's kindy holidays and Seb's visits home, and all of our birthdays.
DANI: Okay, okay.
JUNO: I guess it's a project.
SADIE: I'm going to get a new boyfriend to come camping with us.

DANI: Please don't.

SADIE: Hey, thanks!

DANI: JOKING.

SADIE: Jacob might come. He says we're like Gwyneth and Chris.

DANI: Of course you are. Exactly like them.

JUNO: So when?

LISS: The summer long weekend. I'm going to ask my dad if it can be ours.

DANI: Why do I feel like you fighting with your family about camping might be your favourite thing about all this?

LISS: Can't imagine.

JUNO: You people are so strange.

GINGER: There's a mouse.

DANI: What????

SADIE: What??????

GINGER: Aiden just shouted through the door, there's a mouse in the kitchen.

SADIE: Stay in the toilet.

JUNO: Kill that thing. There's never just one.

LISS: I heard there's a mouse plague.

GINGER: Not helpful, Liss.

LISS: Sorry.

SADIE: Okay. We're in for camping. Why not? Can't be that hard to put up a tent.

JUNO: Said the woman who can't put up a beach shade.

SADIE: It was complicated!

DANI: Where do babies sleep camping?

LISS: Carrycot. They like the noise of the wind in the trees.

JUNO: That sounds like some top-level bullshit.

DANI: And the sound of the rain and storm and bushfire.

LISS: It's an HOUR AWAY. Not outback.

HE WOULD NEVER

DANI: Can an ambulance get in there?
JUNO: Why would you ask that?????
DANI: Practical.
LISS: Boat ambo from Pittwater. Five mins.
SADIE: How do you KNOW THAT?
LISS: My mum.
DANI: Shit.
JUNO: That's dark.
LISS: JOKING. My brother broke his leg falling out of a tree.
JUNO: You sick bitch.
SADIE: Sounds safe.
LISS: My brother is a dickhead.
GINGER: Mouse is dead.
DANI: Quick!
GINGER: Dog ate it.
SADIE: Eeeeeeuw!
LISS: Good boy, Goldie.
JUNO: If Pudding ate a mouse Emily would totally take him for a stomach pump.
GINGER: Goldie's a country dog now.
LISS: Okay, so we're on?
DANI: I guess so.
SADIE: Guess so.
JUNO: Yup!
GINGER: Yesssssssss!
LISS: Cool. Going to call Dad.
DANI: Enjoy that.
LISS: Oh, I will.
EMILY: FFS guys, 143 missed messages? Don't you people have lives????

17

Saturday, 12 pm

Green River Campground

Sadie

Sadie hadn't left the tent all morning, despite the climbing sun and stifling humidity. Despite both Juno and Ginger, at intervals, coming and calling through the flimsy walls. Despite the kids rolling out of there first chance they got when the sun rose.

Now, she found herself standing in the middle of the sweltering tent, having decided she was definitely packing up and leaving this place, but not having any idea where to start.

Everything was scrambled, starting with the vision of last night that was playing like a loop in her head, ending with how she'd ever get this flappy fabric house into two tightly rolled bags in the back of her car. Looking around, at clothes and sleeping bags and mess in every corner, it didn't seem possible.

'Trick!' she shouted, to the tent. To the trees. To the whole damn campground. 'Trick!'

She didn't know where he was, if he could hear her, or who else could.

HE WOULD NEVER

'Trick!'

Footsteps, fast. A rustle, a zip.

'Mum! What the fuck?'

She'd given up scolding Trick for swearing in front of her. It had seemed like the least of their worries over the past year or so, but still, it shocked her every time, these harsh words in her sweet boy's mouth.

'You have to help me pack.' Seeing his face, Sadie considered what Trick was looking at. His mother, wearing only a swimming costume, red-faced and sweaty, her hair a frizzy halo of chaos, standing in a mass of billowing sleeping bags, blow-up mattresses, soggy towels and scrunched-up clothes. 'I'm sorry,' she said. 'I know I'm peak crazy right now but I need your help to sort this out.'

'Mum.' Trick spoke slowly to her, like she was the child. 'We're not leaving.'

'Of course we are.'

'Mum, it's all fine. I promise. Everyone's chill. Why don't you just . . . go and have a shower or something? I can tidy up in here.'

'We can't stay here with these people.' Sadie didn't understand what Trick was saying to her. 'We have to go.'

'*These people*, Mum?' Trick looked tired, and irritated. She was a lot, she knew. A lot for him, a lot for Lucky. But if they could just get out of here, things would calm down. She would calm down. 'These people are our friends.'

'Not anymore, they're not.'

'Mum.' Trick stepped towards her and took her hands. It shocked Sadie, because, generally, he did almost anything to avoid touching her. Ducking his head when she went in for a kiss on his forehead. Spinning away from an arm across his shoulder. High-fiving her when she wanted a hug. But not now. 'Let's just calm down.'

'Calm down?' She watched the realisation that this was the wrong thing to say cross his face, but he kept holding on to her hands. 'You were there last night, Trick. You know what happened.'

'I know you think you know, Mum. But I just saw people dancing and, look, what you did is kind of fucked for Lyra.'

'Fucked for Lyra?' Again, Sadie's head felt spinny with confusion. 'How is this fucked for Lyra? I was trying to protect her.'

'Maybe,' Trick said, and he was still speaking slowly, 'maybe Lyra doesn't need you to protect her.'

'She's a child. And a girl child, so of course she does.'

Trick shook his head. 'Mum, let's just forget about it. I don't want to leave. Lucky doesn't want to leave. We want to stay with our friends. Please, Mum?'

It was confusing, not just the hand-holding, but her son being so interested in staying. Trick liked to be alone, these days. He liked to play video games and draw. He liked to lie on his bed looking at a screen. He liked to avoid the women in his house.

'Mum,' he said. 'Put some pants on. Let's go and have a swim. What about that?'

Trick suggesting they go swimming was so unlikely she actually laughed. 'A swim?' she asked him. 'What did you see last night? And where have you been this morning?'

'I've just been hanging out. Ginger made bacon. You should eat.' Her tall son let go of her hands and started looking around. 'Have you got some clothes here, Mum?'

'What did you see?' she pushed.

Trick looked like he was considering this question as he rummaged through the floor's clothes carpet, found a pair of shorts and handed them to her. 'I saw people dancing, having a good time.'

'And?'

'It was embarrassing, you adults, you know.'

HE WOULD NEVER

'I wasn't dancing,' Sadie said, indignantly.

'I know, small mercies. Well done, Mum.'

'And?'

'Lyra and Tia were kind of . . . joining in.'

His eyes softened for a moment, and Sadie remembered the way he was looking at Lyra Martin last night. How his eyes stayed on her, wherever she moved.

'And?'

'And then Lachy was being even more embarrassing than the other adults, I mean, seriously, that man cannot dance.'

Despite herself, Sadie swallowed a laugh. It was true. But also, coming from Trick, quite ironic. 'And?'

He looked at her. 'Then you went nuts.'

'Trick!' It felt like a gut punch, seeing herself through her son's eyes. Maybe through everyone else's eyes. 'That's not what happened.'

'Mum, it kind of is. And you know, I don't blame you.' Trick nodded at the shorts in her hand. 'Put them on. Lachy Short is a dick and everyone knows it. Even Tia.'

'What?'

'She's like . . . so embarrassed that he's her dad and everything but still, Mum, it was all okay and, truly, you just kind of lost it.'

Sadie balanced on one leg to put the other through the shorts. This was the longest sentence Trick had said to her in some time. The breathing exercises she'd been trying to do all morning, staring at the tent ceiling, finally felt like they might work now. She tried to breathe in and at the same time say, 'I didn't lose it.'

'Mum. You don't want to give him the satisfaction of ruining your weekend, do you?'

'I think,' she exhaled, pulled the shorts up, 'that ship has sailed. These people are delusional.'

He shook his head. 'Don't pack up. Lucky's having more fun than she's had in years, let's take the high road, Mum.'

Sadie knew she was being managed by her teenage son, but she didn't hate the sensation. Was this what she'd been teaching him, without even realising it? How to handle her?

These past few years had been tough for Trick. Stuck in lockdown while Sadie engaged in what her therapist called Red Flag Drinking. His dad starting a new family. Moving schools when they had to get out of their house. Being different.

But this was new. Mostly, Trick treated her like an annoying boss or nagging landlord. Other people assured her he'd emerge from this phase, that one day he might more closely resemble that toddler boy who'd climb into her lap to kiss her ears, but teenage Trick was someone who lived in her house half the time, created mess, consumed food, and told her she was doing things wrong. All kinds of things – saying words, wearing clothes, using technology, being a mother. Wrong, wrong, wrong.

When she looked at Trick she still saw that little person who'd turned her into a parent, a baby she'd wanted so badly she put up with all kinds of nonsense to get him, including something she'd always sworn she wouldn't – living with a man. She wanted to cover his head in kisses. He wanted her to feed him and fuck off. It was a lot. She was a lot.

Now, he was moving around the tent, putting things back into piles, shaking out a sleeping bag over a camp bed, pushing some of Lucky's errant T-shirts back into bags. 'Stop, Trick, you don't have to do this.'

'I'm just trying to get it a bit more sorted for you,' he muttered. 'It's too hot in here. Come outside. Come swimming.'

He picked up a purple hairbrush from Lucky's mess and passed it to her. 'Come on, Mum.'

And right then, Dani's voice. 'Knock, knock!'

Trick and Sadie looked at each other, Sadie's arm halfway to her head, almost comically poised to brush her hair. Sadie shook her head at him.

'We'll be right out,' Trick called, nodding at her, then lowered his voice to a whisper Sadie was sure Dani could still hear. 'Be cool, it's Lyra's mum.'

'Sadie,' Dani called. 'We're going to the rockpool. Come.'

Sadie didn't know what to say.

'Maybe we could drive off,' Sadie whispered to Trick, 'just leave the tent, I don't need a tent anymore.'

'Mum!' A hiss, and then Trick did that performance-loud voice again. 'We're coming, Dani!'

'I can wait. You okay, Sadie?'

She tugged the brush through her hair, feeling wildly nervous at the idea of facing Dani. Her breathing was back at a million miles an hour, her mouth as dry as if she'd been up drinking sav blanc all night. And why? All she'd done was tell the truth. 'All I did was tell the truth,' she mouthed to Trick, who rolled his eyes and shook his head at her.

'I can wait,' Dani said again.

Trick gave Sadie a very pointed look, handed her a towel and held open the tent flap.

Dani was standing on Site Eight with a navy and white towel draped over her arm, oversized sunglasses on, straw hat shielding her skin. 'Sadie.' She nodded, almost smiled. 'I'm glad you're still here. I thought you might leave.'

Sadie took a deep breath and started to walk towards the beach path, and Dani fell into step beside her. 'The kids,' she said, and only that, while she tried to keep her breathing steady and put one foot in front of the other, eyes down.

Trick charged past them, spinning to give his mum a low wave before heading towards the caves. And Dani, as if realising that Sadie was looking at the ground to avoid seeing someone she didn't want to, said, 'The men have gone fishing.'

Relief flooded Sadie's chest, but she kept her voice as steady as she could. 'Aiden will be loving that.' He would not. Pushed, again, to spend time with these men he didn't like.

'Yeah.' Dani smiled. 'Delighted about it.'

'And Liss?'

'She's at the pool. We wanted you to come, I was worried you were going to melt in there.'

We wanted you to come. Sadie realised Dani had been sent to collect her, to bring her before a floating tribunal. Again, Sadie had to remind herself that she had done nothing wrong, that this wasn't last year. She hadn't blacked out or forgotten or just not given a shit.

'Dani, I just said what I saw.'

'I know.' Dani kept walking.

The sun was directly above them, bearing down on Sadie's hatless head. She shook out the towel Trick had handed to her. It had cartoon characters on it, some kind of big-mouthed, big-footed monkeys, and it wasn't large enough to wrap around her body. She draped it over her shoulders, which were already turning pink.

'I was trying to protect Lyra.'

'I know you were.' Dani was unreadable under the hat and behind the sunnies with her straight answers. Then, suddenly, 'Thank you.'

It took Sadie by surprise. She knew Dani disapproved of her in general. Where Liss found Sadie entertaining, Dani found her irritating. Liss loved Sadie's stories – about her childhood, about dating, about Jacob and Charlie and her clients at her physio practice, but Dani always just raised an eyebrow, as if she didn't quite believe her stories. Sadie had always felt, in the friendship circles inside their friendship circle, that she and Dani had the least amount of overlap. And yet, here was a thank you.

'It's fine.' A few more steps. 'I think my boy's got a crush on your girl,' she said.

Dani just shook her head and smiled. 'Good luck with that,' she said quietly. 'I doubt that's going to end well for him.'

They broke through the shaded tunnel of trees into the glare of the beach. The rockpool was all sequins and rhinestones in the midday sun and the women looked like seals, lying in the shallows, sitting on the rock ledge, making short splashy swims to suspend themselves in the deep middle.

When the tide was just right, not too high, not too low, this natural hollowed circle filled like a bathtub and Sadie thought it was the only really good place to swim on the river.

Liss, sitting on the rock edge, raised a hand in a wave. Ginger and Juno were swimming. The smaller kids were studded about the place, poking in rockpools or neck-deep in the water. Sadie saw Lucky burying one of Ginger's kids' feet in the sand. 'Hey, baby!' she called as they got closer and Lucky looked up, raised a tentative hand, looked back down. Even Lucky knew Sadie had not yet been granted entry back in the fold.

'There you are!' Liss exclaimed as they got close. 'I was worried you'd melted.'

'Welcome, Sadie,' called Juno, a little too loudly, from the middle of the pool. 'Come jump into paradise.'

Sadie's heart was pounding and her breathing had completely escaped her control. The sight of the pool and the women ahead started to splinter in the unblinking sun and her vision began to blur at the edges.

'I don't think I can . . .' she whispered, unsure of her volume. 'I think I need to . . .'

'Sadie.' Dani stopped, and put a hand out to stop her. 'It's okay. We are your friends.'

It was unexpected.

'Hold my hand,' said Dani.

Sadie could make out Liss raising a hand over her eyes to see what was happening. 'Everything okay?' she called, that familiar voice both intimidating and warm at once.

Dani was holding her palm out, and Sadie surprised herself by taking it. 'I'm sorry,' she said. 'I have no idea what's going on with me . . . a panic attack, maybe?'

'Just walk with me, everything's fine.'

And Dani and Sadie walked the last few steps to the ocean pool together, Sadie getting a little surer with each footfall. 'Now,' Dani said, softly. 'Get in and put your head under.'

Liss just watched as Sadie dropped the ridiculous towel from her shoulders, stepped out of her shorts and slipped into the cool, blue-silver water. Her feet reassuringly found the weedy bottom and she bent her knees to slide her head under, exactly as Dani said to do. As she pushed herself back up, shaking her head, she saw Dani bend to collect her things and place them, neatly, next to Liss.

'Better?' she called from the side, standing beside Liss. The other women began to stroke towards her, the kids still leaping around in the rocky shallow end.

'Better.'

Sadie tipped onto her back, legs gently kicking, and looked up at the impossibly blue sky. Her thoughts were sorting themselves out, slowly. Yes, Lachy Short's hand on Lyra Martin's waist. Yes, the outline of Craig watching her as she retreated to her tent last night. Yes, the sound of Lachy's laugh echoing from Site Seven, bouncing off the shame she was sick of carrying around. All that. But also, Trick's face, in the tent, his big brown puddles of eyes pleading with her not to make his life

HE WOULD NEVER

harder, again. The sight of him bending to clean up her mess. And of Dani doing the same. She saw Lucky's face, just now, reluctantly greeting her mother in front of her friends. All these thoughts slid into order, like files, and she breathed out a big, steady breath, moving her arms and legs up and down, making river angels in the pool.

'You okay, Sadie?' asked Juno.

And Sadie found herself rolling over and swimming, her stroke as perfect as she knew it was, over to the side where Liss and Dani were watching. Liss picking at the spiky barnacles on the pool's edge, Dani following Sadie's progress, stroke by stroke.

Sadie stopped at the pool's edge, pulled her elbows up onto the side and rested her chin on her hands on the mossy ledge. 'So much better,' she said. *Breathe.* 'You know, Liss, I need to apologise. I think I was confused last night, overwhelmed by my sobriety, emotional about a whole lot of things.' *Breathe.* 'I'm sorry that I made that big scene about Lachy. I think I was mistaken and I'm sorry.' *Breathe out.*

There was a beat. Dani took off her sunglasses, looked directly at Sadie, something like a question behind her eyes. Cockatoos were having a shrieking match in the trees beyond the beach, and there was a hum of childish play and laughter from where Lucky was building towering dribble piles of sand for Gracie and Maya.

'Thanks, Sadie,' said Liss, eventually, reaching out a hand to touch Sadie's head. 'I thought that must be it.'

There was a sour taste in Sadie's mouth suddenly, like she was choking back an unwelcome flavour. She raised her eyes to Dani. 'Is Lyra okay?'

Dani nodded. 'Says nothing happened.' Folded her lips into a line, slid her sunglasses back on. 'So, there you go.'

Juno sighed and said, of course, what most needed to be said. 'Thank fuck for that.' She laughed. 'I thought we were in for a very awkward weekend.'

Liss laughed. 'Fucking Lachy. And his terrible dancing.'

'Yes.' Sadie went along with it. 'A lot to answer for.'

'I'm coming in for a swim,' Dani announced, taking off her giant hat. 'Let the weekend recommence.'

18

2015, Camp One

Green River Campground

Liss

'Does he think that's sexy?'

Liss could hear Juno whispering to Emily on the edge of the space they'd hastily cleared for dancing under a flimsy gazebo.

Liss did. The way Lachy, with hardly even a beer inside him, would stalk a dancefloor. She'd seen him do it at weddings and thirtieths, just as all the other men would stand off to the side, nursing their bottles and leaving the dancing to the 'girls' until they were definitely drunk enough to break out a move from their adolescence, perhaps tearing off their ties in the process.

Not Lachy. He loved to dance, and he didn't give a shit who was watching. In fact, the bigger the audience, the better. If others – Juno, clearly – might find it embarrassing, the way that Lachy was popping his shoulders and jutting his chin, shaking his hips, clicking his fingers, Liss did think it was sexy. And hilarious. A swaggering confidence coupled with a willingness to embarrass himself to entertain.

'He's always been a good dancer,' she said to Juno, leaning in to let her friends know she'd heard them. 'You should get up there.'

She watched Juno and Em exchange a look, swallow a little smile. 'Perhaps worth putting that in the consideration column about the genes,' Juno said, and Liss felt her own smile immediately falter.

They'd all arrived yesterday for the first Green River camping expedition. Liss had been so excited she could barely stop herself jumping up and down and clapping every time another car pulled over to the crop of campsites she hadn't visited for years.

She knew that her friends had been a little amused by the level of enthusiasm she'd invested in the site tours.

'It's tidal, you know,' she'd said, about a hundred times, when she took each arriving set of friends to see the beach, at its afternoon sludgy, muddy lowest. 'It's picture-perfect when it's high, I promise.'

By the time she showed Ginger and Aiden around, Juno was teasing her when she got back to camp.

'It's tidal, didn't you know?'

And Liss pushed down the irritated voice that wanted to shout, *But it is, and mud can be fun!* like the eight-year-old who used to have soggy-sand flinging fights with her brothers and dad out there, one of the only times she could remember her father being loose and silly. She was looking around as if she could see it all, she and her brothers as tiny little people, her tall, handsome dad carefree and dirt-splattered, scooping them up and splashing them down.

'I just want everyone to love it like I do,' she'd said to Dani, as she gave the last tour of the afternoon. Seb was back from New York, baby Brigitte strapped to his chest. The happy family charade that Liss had witnessed many times since Seb started 'working away' in full effect.

'I'm sure we will,' Dani had said, putting an arm around Liss's waist as they surveyed the mudflats under heavy grey clouds. 'We just have to adjust to the smell.'

HE WOULD NEVER

'The smell?' Liss had shrieked, and Dani had laughed and assured her she was teasing. Ever since, Liss had been walking around the campsite pulling in deep nasal breaths, worried she'd missed something.

Since then, everything had settled. High tide had coincided with a blaring sun in a cobalt sky, the water turning an inviting pale blue-green and everyone old enough to walk had tentatively waded into the river for the first of hundreds of group swims, as the smallest of the babies snoozed in muslin-draped prams up near the tree line. They had bush-bashed a little way into the forest to see Liss's favourite trees, let the saucy yolks of fresh bacon and egg rolls drip on their hands as they ate them straight from the barbecue, drunk red wine next to an illicit fire pit, and bonded over embarrassing song choices of their youth.

Oh, and Lachy had offered Juno and Emily his sperm.

Watching her husband now as he twisted himself around Ginger and Sadie, waving his imagined maracas to 'Sympathy for the Devil' – his father's favourite and his first request, always – Liss could see how hard he was trying with her friends.

Dani was a known quantity to Lachy. She'd been in and out of their home for almost five years now. There had been a little tension as Lachy worked through his jealousy over his wife's new confidant, but there was also affection and respect between them, which Liss loved.

But Liss knew the other women were little more than judgemental strangers to him, and there was nothing more motivating for Lachy Short than winning the approval of women.

He didn't seem to care a bit if he offended Seb, or dismissively spoke over Aiden, or had interrogated Sadie's Jacob when he'd been around. But Lachy Short wanted the women to think something about him, although Liss wasn't always sure what that was.

With Sadie, he was flirty, leaning into her energy. With Ginger, he acted curious, flattering her by asking questions about her rodeo relatives and life in the bush. And apparently, he'd decided Juno was one of the boys.

It had been cringy, last night, to watch his energy shift when he clinked his beer with hers, linen shirt open, baby Ollie rested on his hip.

It had been worse when Emily had come back from getting Bob to settle down in the tent and Lachy had said, 'Oh, so you're the mummy.'

And then things had got stranger again when Liss and Ollie settled next to Lachy as he told Juno, both of them now deep in a bottle of red, that he had heard they were trying to have another baby.

'You know, one of my mates is the best reproductive endocrinologist in Sydney,' he said, before stopping himself and rolling his eyes. 'Actually, his dad is. He's the second best. Went to school with him.'

Juno and Emily, Liss knew, were about to move out of Sydney's east and into the inner west, where there were fewer men like Lachy who would happily tell you who they went to school with, and more families that looked like theirs. She also knew, because Juno had told her, that the clinic they'd used when they'd conceived Bob had waiting list issues, high staff turnover and patchy patient care.

Juno had looked to Liss, her eyes wide. 'Good to know,' she said.

'He helped us, of course,' Lachy went on. 'You know, with all the miscarriages.'

There was an actual pain in Liss's chest at the casual way he said that, a little stab just underneath where baby Ollie was sleeping and snuffling. Here and safe, but not without scarring.

'Lachy,' she said, with what she hoped was a warning tone, the kind he hated.

'It's okay, Liss. You've got to share your privilege. Isn't that the kind of thing you say all the time?' He'd had more wine than she

HE WOULD NEVER

thought. 'Not everyone showered and wrestled and did fucking Latin with the best lawyer, financial adviser, skin-cancer dude or genetic endocrinologist. Not everyone has the right numbers in their contacts. Life's easier when you do. I do. Share the love, right?'

Liss's face had got hot. She knew what Juno would be thinking. She knew what she and Emily would be discussing, as soon as they were in their tent. People like Lachy Short were the reason they were moving out of the east. And Emily, lovely Emily, would say that they didn't want to live in a bubble, and that it was good to have friends with different world views and Juno would say something like Lachy Short's world view was from the time of the dinosaurs.

But actually what Juno said was, 'We couldn't afford it.'

'But we could.'

'Lachy!'

'Stop saying that.'

'It's okay, Liss, I respect his honesty.'

'Juno's American. Americans are more straightforward about this stuff.'

'But you don't go around offering to pay people's medical bills, Lachy. It's insulting.'

'Is it?' asked Juno.

Liss had shared careful conversations with Juno and Emily about their wonderful, well-meaning female doctor, at their wonderful, well-meaning bulk-billing fertility clinic. It specialised in same-sex couples, women who'd struggled with cancer, couples who couldn't continue to afford endless soul-crushing, bank account-draining IVF cycles. She had talked about it to Lachy, when they had been to see his schoolmate Bryson, because she didn't know what got you a baby – luck or money.

She had never imagined this was the campfire conversation it would lead to.

Lachy was beaming. 'See, Liss, not everyone's as uptight about money as you.' He laughed, relaxing into Juno's apparent approval. 'I've always wanted to be a sperm donor, you know. Help people have what they want.' He took another gulp of wine. 'I think everyone should get what they want.'

'I can't tell if you're serious,' Juno had said. 'You're a funny fucker.'

'He's not serious.' Liss had put a hand under Ollie's bum and pulled herself to standing. 'I'm taking the baby to bed.'

As she'd walked away from the gazebo, she could hear Lachy babbling on. 'I'm not God, Juno, I can't make it happen, but I can help make it more likely to happen than Doctor Turkey Baster and her hopes and prayers gang.'

Twenty-four hours later and the topic was coming back as they watched Lachy and Sadie and Ginger bump and grind. Everyone was a little more relaxed about kids' bedtimes on the second night, and the older children were jiggling around in their pyjamas, buzzing with the excitement of more sugar than was usual and their parents' good moods.

'Why did you ever stop coming here?' Emily asked Liss, clearly steering the conversation away from sperm. 'It's paradise.'

'Paradise is a bit strong,' Juno said into her glass. 'Paradise has a spa.'

'After my mum died it wasn't the same.' Liss could conjure exactly how empty that first visit after her mother's death had felt. 'Dad wouldn't give it up, I guess even he was sentimental about it. We came a few times with stepmother one and stepmother two, but neither of them were campers.'

'Their loss.'

'I tried to get Lachy to love it when we first got together and he made an effort when he was trying to impress me, but he's not the camping type either.'

HE WOULD NEVER

The three of them looked at him out there in the dusk, shuffling barefoot, arms in the air, a small child clinging to each leg. 'He's making an effort now, I guess.'

'I did have him down as more of a beach house guy,' Juno said. 'But this is an interesting side of him.'

'Oh, he's definitely a beach house guy.'

Before they married, the fraudulent ring she still wore blinking on her finger, there was a contract. Liss's father, entirely unhappy about the marriage but always willing to shift position to keep his avenue of influence open, told Liss to buy something big and expensive, like a home, and make sure it was only in her name, etched into the equivalent of a pre-nup, and locked down.

Liss hated to take her father's advice, but in a gesture of pragmatic loyalty to her dead mother she spent a hefty chunk of her inheritance on the Bronte house the year of the wedding. And she told Lachy that it was their home but it would always belong to her. He had signed the papers on the financial agreement without comment or argument and never spoke of it again. And then he immediately took a mortgage out in his name only on a holiday home on the northern beaches. They went there a couple of times a year, usually with his finance friends and their wives, and the rest of the time it sat empty, quietly gaining value along with damp, a musty monument to Lachy's ego.

'He certainly is full of surprises.' Juno looked at Liss, then Emily, then Liss. 'I suppose we should discuss his offer at some point?'

'I'm not the boss of him,' Liss said, pushing down her rising anger at her husband's attempts to make himself central to every situation, every relationship. 'Although I am surprised you two are entertaining it.'

'We're not,' said Emily, firmly. 'Absolutely not. It's ridiculous. Sorry, Liss.'

A rush of relief. 'Oh, don't apologise.'

'What's so ridiculous about it?' Juno demanded. This was clearly a continuation of an argument they'd already been having today. 'Our friends offering to help us? It's kind of beautiful, Em, when you think about it.'

'Juno.' As Emily spoke, her eyes were on Bob, who was trying to stand on his head in the middle of the dancers, kicking his little legs in the air. 'Can't you see that our friend is uncomfortable with this whole crazy thing?' She was nodding at Liss now. 'I swear, sometimes you are about as emotionally intelligent as a rock.'

Liss excused herself, headed over to her dancing husband, shaking her shoulders and hips as she went. She leaned in and whispered in his ear. 'My friends think your dancing's terrible.'

'Oh,' he said, picking up the edge of flirtation in her voice. 'And you?'

'I think it's hot as fuck,' she said. 'But you need to stop offering your sperm around. It's all mine.'

'So selfish.' He kissed Liss, and she felt a familiar rush of adrenaline as she spun out of his reach to usher Tia and Lyra off towards bed.

As she passed Juno and Emily, still hiss-arguing with each other, she saw Dani and Seb, standing under the camp kitchen's flickering fluoro light, baby Brigitte in a pram between them. Seb was leaning towards Dani, his illuminated face twisted in distress, and her friend looked so hollowed-out exhausted, so little and sad, pushing the pram handle back and forth, back and forth, shaking her head.

Lyra and Tia were dancing towards them, ahead of Liss, and she couldn't decide if it was better to stop them or let the little girls' energy puncture the moment.

'Good riddance to that guy.' Lachy's voice in Liss's ear, his arms around her waist.

'You think? For good?'

HE WOULD NEVER

'I told him he needs to make a call,' Lachy said. 'That Dani and Lyra seem happier when he's not around.'

A little rush of nausea flooded into Liss's mouth. 'Lachy, you need to stay out of other people's lives.'

'Why wouldn't you help the people you care about?' he asked, his mouth close to her ear. 'Or who your wife cares about? Sometimes people can't see what they actually need.'

The little girls had reached the puddle of light around Dani and Seb. Dani took her hand off the pram to extend it to Lyra. Seb looked over to where Liss and Lachy were standing, watching, and the look on his face was something like hatred as he turned and walked away, heading for their tent, perhaps, or the beach. But it was clear to Liss he wanted to get away from them. And from Dani, and his daughters.

'Do you mean Juno and Em, or Dani? How is telling Seb she's better off without him helping Dani?'

'That guy,' Lachy kissed Liss's neck as she watched Dani crouching down to Tia and Lyra, one hand on Brigitte's pram, 'just needed a little push. And she knows he's not the father those girls need.'

'Who is?'

Lachy gave Liss's hips a gentle shove. 'Go get the girls to bed. I've got more dancing to do.'

19

Saturday, 2 pm

Green River Campground

Lyra

'I would never.'

'Okay.'

'You have to tell them.'

'I did.'

Lyra Martin didn't want to be in a cave with Lachy Short. With his tallness and broadness, it felt like the rock walls were closing in. She inched a bit further towards the light of the entrance as her best friend's father looked at her with a very serious expression.

'You know nothing happened, right?'

Lyra didn't know what she knew, other than that she would like all the adults to stop talking to her about it. Aunt Sadie. Her mum. Aunt Liss. And now Lachy. It made her so uncomfortable she wanted to itch off her skin.

'I don't even want to remember last night, let alone talk to any of them about it.'

'But not because anything happened, right?'

HE WOULD NEVER

When Lachy Short was worried, apparently, he looked like a little boy.

His face was kind of screwed up, like his forehead was trying to meet his nose, and his eyes were rounder, and his mouth was pushed out into a mini duck face. His voice was a tight whine.

The caves gave her the creeps. It wasn't that they were very deep or even all that dark, they were just very obviously places where kids did things they weren't meant to do and although sometimes that was exciting, it was scary, too. There was graffiti, a melted-down candle stub, some empty Breezers on the ground and what looked like a water bottle with a bit of garden hose sticking out of it. Lyra felt a bit icky being in here at all, never mind it being the place where Lachy Short had insisted they meet.

Tia's dad was the first grown-up who made Lyra realise that adults didn't know everything. That they weren't in control, and that they sometimes did stupid, irresponsible things.

Her mum, she knew, was always trying hard to be adult. Or maybe it came more easily to some people than others. Maybe some people were just born grown-up.

'Nothing happened,' she said, hoping that this would be over soon. It would definitely be over sooner if she just said what he wanted her to say. She tried really hard not to think about his hand being on her skin. His fingers, pushing into her waist. *Stop it.*

'Are the kids talking about it?'

'They talked about Aunt Sadie.'

'Yeah, well, she's insane. Completely nuts. I'm sure even Trick knows that.'

'Trick's not said anything.'

'Not all adults have it together, Lyra.'

Lyra thought this was what her mum would call irony.

Even her dad, when he visited, gave the impression of being very together. The way he'd message her with dates and places and instructions. The way he never cried when he said goodbye, even though he always told Lyra and Brigitte he was sad to be going. He called her when he said he was going to call her, even before she had her own phone and had to rely on Mum, who would see his name flash up and immediately hand over to Lyra. 'Right on time,' she'd say. Dad was On It.

Lachy Short seemed more like a big mess. He lived in that huge flashy house with Auntie Liss but her mum said he didn't own it. He called Lyra's phone sometimes and said she deserved a better dad. Lyra thought he was probably drunk when he did that. He told her not to save his number and she didn't. Other times he bought her things her mum wouldn't. A pair of Dunks. A Stüssy T-shirt. A charm bracelet. A voucher to spend at a skincare shop her mum said she was too young for. Lyra had to be careful, because if her mum found out it was Lachy and not her dad buying those things she would lose her shit, so Lyra kept some of them at Tia's house. Lachy was also super-protective. He would tell her and Tia that they shouldn't go anywhere near boys. That they shouldn't go anywhere alone. Her mum always talked about resilience, but Lachy never did. He said girls had to be careful out in the world. That bad people wanted to hurt them and it was a parent's job to make sure that didn't happen. He said that if Lyra's dad hadn't fucked off he'd be doing that job. That someone had to.

Lyra hated it when Lachy said mean things about her dad. But there was a tiny part of her, if she let herself think about it, that liked that there was one person in the world who would say what Lyra secretly thought, sometimes. That it was a bit shitty to leave your daughters on the other side of the world for a job.

It was different for Bridge. She'd never known anything else. But Lyra had seen all the pictures from when Dad did live in Australia.

HE WOULD NEVER

She was in them, and she looked happy, on her dad's shoulders, or eating ice cream with him at the beach. She'd asked her mum what had changed, and her mum would just talk about Dad's work. She knew they had a deal, her mum and dad, not to say anything bad about each other. She'd overheard her mum say it to friends lots of times. Which was nice, but it was fake. Sometimes she liked that Lachy would just say it. It matched how she felt inside, on a bad day.

'I need you to stay cool, alright? Don't let anyone try to get in your head about it.'

Lyra wasn't really sure what Lachy was getting at. But the more he kept telling her that everyone was imagining a problem, the more she could feel the way he'd pushed into her on the dancefloor, like his front was still pressing against her back. The more he said it didn't happen, the more she could feel the way that it did. She really wanted to step out of here and into that big yellow sunshine square of the cave's entrance, just like she'd felt that need to spin away, last night, and be with Tia.

'Can I go?'

Lachy narrowed his eyes a little. 'Why are you asking me that? You think I made you come here? Of course you can go, you can go any time.'

Lyra stood to go and Lachy laughed. Like a short, barking laugh. His hand shot out and landed on her wrist, closing around it. 'Hold on, hold on! I didn't mean now.'

'Oh. I thought you said . . .'

'We just need to get this straight.'

'Get what straight?'

'Exactly.'

She had told the others, who were building a den in the woods, that she had to go back to camp to get a hat. That her mum would kill her if she got sunburnt, which was true. Tia looked at her a bit funny because you were less likely to get sunburnt in the woods than on the beach, but Lyra said she also needed a wee, which was also true, and she was much too old to wee in the woods around the boys now.

She knew all the adults were at the beach or the rockpool. It was that time of day, between lunch and dinner, when the camp became deserted. Just damp towels on the backs of chairs and empty mugs, glasses and the odd crumb-strewn plastic plate. Just scuttling flies and lizards and buzzing mosquitos and a chip packet flapping open. Just the sound of shouting and splashing beyond the trees.

All that was on the other side of this cave.

'What about Tia?' Lachy said.

'What about Tia?'

'Lyra, you just keep repeating what I say.'

'Sorry.' Lyra felt dumb. She could be so dumb.

'Some people,' he said, slowly, as if yes, she was slow to understand, 'would try to twist the fact that I look out for you. Help you with a few things. Give you a bit of advice, make your life a bit easier. Some people would make a big stupid fuss about it. That's why we don't go on about it, right?'

She guessed that Lachy had had to make an excuse about where he was too, because he'd just texted her, from the number he always told her not to save, saying, *Caves, now?* And he was twisting a cricket hat in his hands. Maybe he'd said he had to come back for a hat.

'Tia's okay,' Lyra said. 'She's just a bit upset.'

He looked irritated. 'What's she upset about?'

'I guess . . . people talking about her dad.'

'Jesus. I hope she's sticking up for me.'

'She's okay. She was there. She knows what happened.'

Was that the right thing to say or the wrong thing to say? Dumb, again? Lyra studied Lachy's face for a clue.

'She can be a bit weak,' was all he said. 'A bit *go with the flow*.'

Tia was her best friend but they were pretty different. They went to different schools, now. Tia went to a really posh school with no rules and Lyra went to St Diedre's, which was medium-posh but had lots of rules, mostly to do with God. Tia did drama and dance and Lyra did netball and soccer. So they didn't see each other as much as they used to, when they both went to Bronte Public and didn't have so much to do, but Tia was still the one who Lyra felt most comfortable with, of all her friend group. The others, you always had to watch what you said, or sometimes you might get to school and find out – through a feeling in your stomach or in the way one of the girls was talking to you, or in how they didn't answer or even open your messages – that there had been a shift. That's how you would find out you'd done something. You were out, and you'd have to work your way back in. It was tiring.

She was never out with Tia. They could be silly together, like babies, or they could be teenagers together, trying on who they might like to be next. It didn't matter. It was always easy.

Lyra used to envy Tia having a dad who lived in the house with them. But then she'd thought it would be kind of annoying, and a lot of pressure, to have two parents always up in your business, two parents nagging you about grades, two parents making sure you were where you said you were going to be, and when.

And then she'd got to know Lachy better, and she didn't envy Tia anymore. She'd seen him say really mean things to her, words like 'stupid' or 'lazy', that neither Lyra's mum or dad would ever say. He'd never do it in front of Auntie Liss but didn't seem to mind if Lyra heard. That's because they were family, she supposed.

'Trick's a bit of a spy,' she said, because she could sense he wanted her to say something else, and she didn't want to say anything about her best friend. Lyra was still standing near the cave's open face, looking down at her pink, painted toes.

'Really? What kind of spy?'

'Like every time I turn around he's there.'

'He probably likes you.'

'Why do adults always say that?'

'Because we know how boys' minds work.'

'It's insulting.'

'It's true.'

'You'd better stop texting me,' Lyra said, hoping this could be the end of it. 'My mum's going to be paying even more attention now.'

'Got it. Delete the messages, yes?'

She nodded.

'And tell me if anyone starts talking about anything crazy.'

'Okay.'

'Sadie's got an axe to grind.'

'A what?'

'She's got beef with me.'

She cringed at Lachy saying 'beef', but also, she knew this was true. Maybe Lyra had imagined how deliberate that hand on her waist had felt. But maybe the reason Aunt Sadie saw it was because she was tuned in to a version of Lachy who might do things like that. It was confusing.

'Have you ever heard her spreading lies about me?' Lachy asked, not making any move to stand up.

'Only the one everyone says.'

'What's that?'

'That you're Brigitte's dad.'

'What?'

'Lots of the other mums say it, and all the kids have heard it but obviously I know that's bullshit because Mum wouldn't do that. And, well, Brigitte looks just like my dad.'

HE WOULD NEVER

She watched Lachy's face as he processed this. There was a part of her that wanted him to be upset about it. He was never very nice to Brigitte. Not horrible to her or anything, but just . . . neutral. Like she didn't count. Which was why the rumour was even dumber, if you knew anything, like she did, and Tia did, although Tia really, really hated it when the boys brought it up. Stupid Bob and stupid James. They had no idea what they were talking about. The information seemed to pass over Lachy, into his ears and then out through his mouth in a little dismissive 'pfft' through his lips, and then he shook his head as if to get it off him.

'You kids talk a lot of shit in those woods,' he said, finally. 'And don't say bullshit.'

'But why would they say that?' Lyra asked. It just came out. Sometimes she felt like Lachy might be the only adult who told the truth.

'Small minds,' he said.

So, no, he wasn't that adult.

Lyra thought about the first time Lachy had spoken to her in a way that was different from how other grown-ups did. The first time she was confused.

She had been at Tia's, and they had all been in the pool, one of the first swims of last summer. Auntie Liss had a swimming pool with an infinity edge, like you saw in fancy hotels on TikTok. Auntie Liss said it made her feel like you were drifting out to sea, as if that was a good thing.

Everyone was getting out except Lyra, because there was nothing Lyra liked more than floating on her back, looking up at the sky. Tia and Liss and the little kids had all piled towards the kitchen to get some food, but Lachy had stayed behind, and he was looking at her.

'You look a lot like your mother,' he'd said, which wasn't what she wanted to hear but okay.

Then he said, 'You know she is extremely dear to us, don't you?'

And there had been something about the way he said it, words that people don't usually use, a question that didn't need an answer. Adults were always asking questions that weren't questions, but they usually used normal words.

'Liss would do anything for your mum. Me too.'

'Auntie Liss is very good to us.' Lyra knew to be grateful to the Shorts. The number of times, over the years, that she'd heard her mother say she didn't know where she'd be without Liss.

Lyra wanted to get out, to go and find Tia, but there was something about the way Lachy kept looking at her that made her want to stay covered by the water.

It was the year that eyes had started moving differently over her, at the beach, on the street. Lyra was wearing what she and her friends were always wearing, but suddenly it all meant something different. It was like a spotlight was suddenly pointed right at her and sometimes it felt good to be picked out, seen. But sometimes it felt scary. And she hadn't ever thought about it feeling scary with people you'd always known. That maybe all men had that light with them, and could shine it wherever they wanted.

'I should find Tia,' she'd said from the water, but she didn't move to pull herself up and out onto the deck. *Go away*, she remembered feeling. *Turn away.*

'Someone needs to look out for you girls,' he'd said. 'Now you're growing up. Your mum's so busy.'

'We're fine,' she'd said quickly, and then remembered. 'Thank you.'

Lachy had picked up a towel – Auntie Liss's house had the best thick, soft towels, big enough to wrap around your whole body – and took two steps towards the edge of the pool, where Lyra's arms were resting. She'd put her chin on them, and looked down at where the water was licking in and out over the shiny little square tiles. Anywhere but up at him.

'Come on, then,' he said, squatting down, holding the towel out. 'Let's go and get some food.'

How many times had Lyra jumped out of this pool and run into the kitchen, in a little sunsuit, in a swimming-lesson one-piece, in a bikini? Without thinking, without even being aware of herself, of her arms and legs and tummy and chest? Why did she feel, in that moment, when she glanced up and saw the crease around Lachy Short's eyes and the particular curve of his closed-mouth smile, like everything was different? She remembered the rough grout scratching her stomach as she'd pushed her whole self flat against the pool wall, hiding her bum, her thighs, her flicking feet.

Lachy hadn't moved. He'd stayed, so close, towel in hands.

'You girls should get bigger cozzies,' he'd said, and she could hear something like a tease in his voice. Friendly, maybe, a tone that suggested everything she was feeling was ridiculous. But then, 'If you don't want to be looked at.'

And she remembered feeling sick in her mouth.

Tia had stopped that moment, her voice yelling from the kitchen. 'Dad! Lyra! Come!'

And Lachy had laughed and dropped the towel, stood up and turned away. He moved quickly, and just as fast Lyra had pulled herself up, slippery feet hitting the wet deck. She remembered, now, how she had tucked that towel around her so tight it squeezed her chest.

'Let's go,' said Lachy in the cave, at last. 'You first.'

Thank God. She moved to the cave's entrance, but just before she left he said one more thing. 'We're cool, right, Lyra?'

She didn't feel cool, she felt completely crazy. Like maybe she had imagined the weirdness of that dance and maybe she should have told her mum that it had happened but that it wasn't a big deal. But maybe it was a big deal and maybe she was overthinking it because she could definitely be an overthinker, not as much as Tia, but still, her anxiety might be spiking. And maybe there was nothing weird about talking to your best friend's dad in a cave even if you knew it was a secret and your mum had always told you that you don't keep secrets for adults. But she knew there was something weird about it because it was weird how Lachy Short kind of pretended to be her dad but her dad, even from the other side of the world, never made her feel this confused.

She dashed through the open space into the light. 'Yeah, we're cool,' she called over her shoulder, and ran the few sandy steps back towards the campsite, and the toilet which she definitely did need now. Her breath was coming really fast but she didn't understand why, it wasn't like she'd been exercising. *Calm down, Lyra, you dumb-arse.*

Then, just for a second, just to the right of her, she felt someone, heard someone. In the slight snap of twig and the rustle of some grass. She whipped her head around, too quickly to consider who she might see. Someone who'd seen her coming out of the cave, someone who was about to see Lachy leaving just after her.

But there was no-one. Just a gap between two little saplings and some flattened grass.

Calm down, Lyra, you drama queen. There was no-one. That grass was probably always flat like that.

You haven't done anything wrong anyway.

Only what a grown-up told you to do.

20

2016, Camp Two

Green River Campground

Liss

Liss slid her arms around Lachy's waist and held her head against the exact spot where his cotton T-shirt was sticking to the sweat between his shoulder blades.

'Thank you,' she said, breathing him in. 'I know this isn't your place.'

'It's yours. And you're mine.'

Ollie was toddling around them, holding hands with Tia and Lyra, who had travelled up with them. The three kids singing and squabbling and squawking away in the back seat had left Liss syrupy warm, happy. She was pregnant again.

'How many positive tests is that?' Dani had asked her when Liss had told her, sitting at Bronte's Bogey Hole watching the kids splash around. 'No-one tells you that the number of times you've found out you're pregnant and the number of babies you'll have are rarely the same.'

'Oh, so many. I could play Jenga with them.' But what Liss didn't say was that she wasn't frightened this time. She had a sturdy instinct that this was their third baby, their last. The final character slotting into the family picture she'd always had in her head. Three little heads at the table, turning her way.

Dani had squeezed her hand. 'I'll never have to go through all that again,' she said. 'I guess that's a bonus, if there is such a thing, to being left.'

Liss didn't point out that Dani hadn't really been going through all that in the first place. Lyra was a happy accident, ahead of schedule. When Dani decided it was time to try to make Seb stick around with the second baby he'd always wanted, Brigitte apparently came easily. But Dani had other problems that Liss did not. Like being a single parent with a demanding job. That sounded like hell.

Lyra Martin almost lived at Liss's house these days; Dani was so busy and Seb was so gone. That's what friends were for, of course, and she'd rather have Lyra and Brigitte at her place than think they were with one of the babysitters Dani found from that online service, or with the chaotic au pair she'd had for five minutes. Liss would have hated missing all that time with her kids. She tried not to be judgemental, but sometimes she had to stop herself from asking why Dani hadn't just sucked it up, followed Seb to America and had a nice life. The one time she'd suggested this, Dani had told her she sounded like a person who'd never been to New York City with a toddler, and that was true. Liss had only been there on a shopping spree with Lachy when they were first married. But she'd seen a lot of movies. Nannies were cheap there, weren't they?

Lachy turned in her arms and bent to kiss her. 'I like to see you happy,' he said. 'It means I'm doing my job.'

They were in a good place. One of those moments to hold on to. Liss felt Lachy's lips, smelled her trees on the salty, brackish air, heard the rustle of wind through the acres of bush between her people and the real world, and vowed to remember exactly this.

HE WOULD NEVER

This was the year of three-wheelers. The year the kids would spend the entire weekend pushing themselves around and around the campsite's circular track on their little pink and green trikes and scooters, an adult or two trailing at the rear, beer or coffee in hand. The year the babies would be sitting up in the rockpool at the lowest of low tides, splashing their fat little hands up and down, up and down, until they got salty water in their eyes, and would scream until a mother, usually, would scoop them up.

It was the year pregnant Liss and Ginger were on the soft drinks and the year Sadie brought a boyfriend who lasted twenty-four hours before she sent him home. 'Soft,' she'd said, when he wouldn't get a huntsman out of the tent and she had to send six-year-old Trick in to do the job. Sadie didn't do spiders.

It was the year Dani came late because of a crucial work conference and Juno and Emily were barely speaking over their ongoing baby dispute. And it was the year that Liss's dad turned up unannounced.

Even Dani had never met Michael Gresky, but she had known exactly who he was when he climbed out of an old Land Rover that managed to look both incredibly elegant and incredibly trashed. Actually, she told Liss, he less climbed out than slid out. A long, lean streak slipping out of the big car – white cotton khakis and a white polo, the palest of skin, the whitest of hair.

'The whitest man you've ever seen,' was Juno's assessment to Emily that evening. But Emily wasn't speaking to her, so she wouldn't smile.

It was Saturday afternoon, and the children were running back up the beach path from a mid-tide swim. The only adults to witness the troop carrier grumble to a stop next to Site Seven were Dani and Ginger, who were chopping fruit and slicing bread in anticipation of the kids' ravenous arrival.

Liss was at the back of the children's parade up the petal-strewn path, her hair wet, her long skirt tucked into her pants, freckles bursting across her nose from the sun, holding on to her moment, just as she'd promised herself, when she heard Dani calling with a strange, almost polite, twisted strain in her voice.

'Liss! Are you far away?'

She wasn't. But when she saw who was standing there, looking at her big canvas tent, a cigarette in his hand, she wished she were.

'Grandpa!' Tia ran to him, wrapping her damp little arms around his pristine legs.

'Dad.' When she was Tia-sized, Liss had learned not to do what her daughter was doing. That disrupting her father and her father's space was never rewarded with anything other than irritation. She watched him glancing down at her daughter with a slightly confused look and patting her head cautiously.

'Tia, come away.'

The swarm of soggy, hungry children parted around Liss's father to reach the melon and oranges, sandwiches and biscuits. Their energy and chaos were in such stark contrast to his stillness it seemed impossible that her father had ever been a child himself.

Michael Gresky smiled. 'Alyssia. I thought I'd come and see what you've done with the place. What all the fuss is about.'

Liss gathered herself, shook her skirt out so that it fell around her bare legs, smoothed her hair with her hands and walked over to him, leaning to kiss her father on his offered cheek.

'What a surprise to see you here, Dad.'

She held her wet swimming towel in front of her stomach. She had no desire to taint the news about the baby by sharing it with him, yet.

'Daddy, these are my friends, Dani and Ginger.'

He raised his eyebrows. He didn't have to say anything to telegraph that it was unusual for him to be in the presence of people whose names were not Alice or Peter or David or Elizabeth.

Juno arrived from the beach behind her and Liss took pleasure in introducing her, too. She could see him, as clearly as if it were a speech bubble over his head, thinking *an American*.

'Well, what a party.'

This was not how the afternoon was meant to go. Irritation surged as Liss considered whether it was possible that there could be a positive reason for an unannounced visit from her father. None came to mind. Whatever he was doing here, it wasn't going to be good.

'Did I miss a message?' she asked, trying to sound calm. 'Or a call? Should I have been expecting you?'

'Oh no.' A wave of his hand. 'I just felt like a drive up the coast. It's been a long time.'

She'd been standing there, in the middle of the path, for a few moments too long. 'Lachy! Where's Lachy?' Liss hoped her voice didn't sound too panicked, which was the way she was beginning to feel with her father's focus only on her. Where the hell was Lachy? He was always an excellent deflection with her father, they hated each other so.

Cool and calm Dani stepped in, wiping her hands free of sticky-sweet honeydew juice and dropping the cloth in the middle of the horde of children.

'It's good to meet you, Mr Gresky,' she said, presumably in the voice she used with important people at work. 'I've heard so much about you I was hoping our paths would cross one day. I'm Daniella.'

'Oh, the Italian.'

'Greek,' Dani said, not missing a step, her smile only brighter. 'But, you know, been out here assimilating since 1984.'

Liss's dad smiled, dropped his cigarette on the ground, an offence almost worthy of flogging in the bushfire-prone Australian countryside, and stepped on it with a crisp white tennis shoe.

'Do you enjoy this place, Daniella?'

'Well, camping's not my first choice of holiday.' Dani was being charming. People always tried to be charming when they first met Liss's dad. 'But I've come back for more. This place is so beautiful it's hard to resist, even under canvas.'

A nod. A look across at Liss. 'Yes, well,' was all he said.

Liss's father had a trick of always staying separate from his surroundings. Children were milling and the sun was blasting and birds and insects were shouting a warning about something and yet he stood somehow unruffled, not a bead of sweat on his brow, moving and talking at his own pace.

Dani looked to Liss. 'Should I make your father a cup of tea?' It was a strange question, which Liss took to mean, *do something.*

'Yes, Dad, what can I get you?'

'A gin and tonic would be good.'

'Ah,' Juno called out. 'Your son-in-law makes a mean one of those.'

'Of course he does.'

Even if all the women here hadn't heard Liss talk about her father, anecdotes which never painted him in a warm light, the tone of his voice as he said this was as bitter as the twisted lemon Lachy swore by.

'But I can step in.' Juno shooed some shoeless children away and began to rummage for a clean glass. Michael Gresky observed her with open disdain.

'Only if it's no trouble.'

'Dad. Let's walk.' Liss decided getting him away from her friends was the best idea. 'I'll show you around. You can tell me why you're here. Dani, do you think you could find Lachy for me, please? I know he wouldn't want to miss Dad, and I'm sure he can't stay long.'

She had accessed it, the ability that flowed through her to speak like him, act like him. The whole family had this learned skill lying dormant.

HE WOULD NEVER

'Well, Daniella, before you scurry off like a good little maid to do what Alyssia tells you to, let me share a pertinent memory with you.'

Dani didn't flinch. She was probably more used to dealing with this kind of rude old white man than Liss had given thought to, working where she worked, knowing what she knew.

'Dad.'

'Alyssia's mother and I –'

'Dad!' Liss tried to take her father's arm. He shook her off in a quick motion.

'We found this place when we knew she was sick. Dying.'

'That's not true.'

'Not every story is yours to tell, Alyssia, please.'

Liss felt like the little girl with his hands on her shoulders. A familiar chastening. A familiar suffocation.

'And Alice loved it here. Specifically,' he looked around, 'she loved the peace. She was English, you know, came here so young, and she loved the Australian bush. She was romantic, spiritual about it. The trees, the water, the space. She saw a peace here she'd want to hold in her head through the times that were coming.'

The whole of HQ, including the chewing children, was silent, listening. Liss was willing him to choke on his words.

'It's not true. She wasn't sick when we used to come here. She was well, she was happy.'

'If that's your memory then we did it right.' He looked around at the plastic trestle table, the unkempt children, the toddlers sitting on the tarpaulin floor sucking melon from grubby fingers. 'She loved the simplicity. She was quite a simple woman.'

Why is he alive, and she isn't? 'Also not true. Come on, Dad, let's go.'

'It's painful to come back, I could never really bear it. Difficult memories.'

Liss thought of the two subsequent holidays to Green River with his two subsequent wives. They were very painful, for her at least.

'Well.' Dani cleared her throat, broke the spell. 'Liss is making new memories, with your grandchildren.'

'We bought these sites. You could do that, then. I suppose they're in her blood, and her brothers' blood, of course.'

The mention of her brothers landed like a thunk in Liss's muddled brain. The reason for her father's drive from the northern beaches to the tip of the peninsula, onto Liss's paradise.

'Dad, let's go,' she urged again. 'We need to talk.'

'At last!' Sarcasm dripped from the voice she knew he'd worked so hard to cultivate. The voice that marked him as old money, when really his wealth didn't stretch beyond his own parents. A voice that made him sound cultured and educated in the art world he'd hovered around his whole life, but that now marked him out as privileged and old and irrelevant in a world that wanted everything but that.

'Lachy!' she shouted now.

Her father laughed out loud and Dani reached out to squeeze Liss's hand. 'I'll find Lachy and send him down. You go to the beach with your father.'

His eyes were running over the various bare-chested children scrapping over buttered bread as if he were trying to pick out his relations.

'Mr Gresky, I know you'd like to see the beach.' Dani voice was firm, like she was talking to an unreasonable child who wasn't her own.

'I'd like that gin and tonic.'

Juno waved from where she was fishing through a half-melted esky for the gin. 'I'm working on it.'

'Thank you ever so much. It will be lovely to return to. Alyssia?' But Liss had already turned and started to walk back down the beach path. 'Oh, okay. Off we go then.'

HE WOULD NEVER

She felt her father's eyes on her back as she walked. He would be taking in her body, her figure, her size. He'd be cataloguing her many disappointments as a woman, her unfortunate unruliness, which started with her frizzy hair and made its way down to her muddy bare feet and their chipped glittery toenail polish, a remnant of one of Tia and Lyra's 'pedi parties'.

Fuck you, she thought with every step. She knew what was coming.

'Dad,' she called back to him. 'Are you planning on selling the campsites?'

'What was that? Slow down, Alyssia.'

He'd heard her.

'Did you come to tell me you're putting the plots up for sale?'

'Nothing so crass.'

'So?' She stopped at the beach and turned for him to catch up. He wasn't as fast as he'd once been, after all.

'I've had an offer. Several, in fact.'

Liss felt the words hang in the changing air. It had been still, but the breeze was picking up as the light shifted. The beach was momentarily in shade.

'The demand is enormous, darling, although God knows why.' He looked left and right, incapable of seeing what Liss was seeing. The dense, ever-shifting rainforest, the golden beach flats moving with scuttling crabs. The quietly lapping water, perfect for children's first swims. The rockpool and its natural flotation tank, the endless sky. Instead he slapped his exposed forearm, as if to flatten a mosquito, and squinted past the view to her. 'I've been contacted about selling the sites privately more times than I can count over the past few years. And you know, one day the Greens will get their way and this will all be part of the national park and the sites will be worthless. It's a good time to sell.'

A dealer. Not an artist. Someone who trades in beauty, incapable of creating it. Unable, even, to see its value beyond the literal sum of what it could bring to him. Paintings. People. Places. Views.

'Is it a good time to do it because my family has fallen in love with it, like Mum did?'

'So sentimental, Alyssia. There are a thousand river beaches in Australia. Pick another.' His eyes were paler than they'd once been, she noticed as he fixed her with them. 'You can't always get what you want.' A little smirk.

A tiny facial movement, a twitch of the mouth, might spark a fury so fierce it could make you push an old man over. It might make you want to slap him in his face. It also might make you say emotional things you know will give him a satisfaction you desperately want to withhold.

'You've always hated me living my own life.' You might try really hard to keep your voice from wavering.

'Please, Alyssia, your choice of holiday destination is not something that keeps me up at night. This is a practical decision.'

You might be made to feel tiny and insignificant in a way that seems outsized by the actual words spoken.

'I just don't believe that.'

To Liss it was clear that if her father could have prevented her from inheriting her mother's money he would have done it. That he undoubtedly had tried to unpick what Alice Gresky had painstakingly put in place. And not because of the money – although, yes, because of the money – but because of the control it afforded him. If he could have kept his daughter on a short leash, reliant on him, duty-bound to consider and defer to his opinion, he would have. But he couldn't. Liss's mother was too wily for that. It was a word he once used about her in Liss's presence, meaning it as an insult. As if a woman shouldn't

HE WOULD NEVER

be strategic and considered, and suspicious of her literal will being disregarded and discarded.

But those were exactly the things a woman should be in the eyes of a man like Michael Gresky. Liss's mother was soft on the outside, iron-rod strong on the inside. The words she'd left Liss with about men, about love and life and marriage and sex, seemed laughably archaic and soft. But her actions were those of a warrior.

The sun broke through and her father lifted a speckled hand to his eyes. 'Do we have to stay on this godforsaken beach? Can we not talk like civilised people, in shade, over something with ice cubes in it?'

'Do you need the money, Michael?'

It was Lachy. He came to stand beside Liss, putting his arm around her shoulder.

Her father looked from Lachy to Liss as if these were words he didn't understand.

'Hello to you, too, Lachlan. That's a rather common question, wouldn't you say?'

'Do you?'

'Is it relevant? Or any of your business?'

'Because if it's about the money, I'll buy them.'

Liss, startled, looked up at him. Of course.

'That's hilarious.' Her father snorted, and, still using his hand as a visor, turned to walk up the path. 'I'm going to get my drink.'

'I'm serious. Talk to my lawyer about how much you want for them.'

'Your lawyer. Honestly.' Her father stopped, looked back at Liss. 'This man.'

Liss smiled up at Lachy. 'This man.'

'I'm not selling them to you.'

'Then that seems to rather prove Liss right, doesn't it? If this is a purely practical decision, wouldn't selling them to me make everyone happy?'

Liss's father looked a little like he might explode in a shower of white diamond dust. A few beads of sweat stood out on his unflappable forehead. He sighed.

'Lachy, you can't outsmart me.'

'Certainly I wouldn't try.' Lachy smiled. 'I'm just a man who buys and sells things. Like you.'

Liss laughed, involuntarily.

'Or perhaps I could buy them, Dad, that would make Mum happy, wherever she is.'

'You're missing the point, Alyssia. Wilfully. I couldn't sell them to you without upsetting your brothers. Apparently you're all rather overly sentimental about this place.'

'So back to me, then.' Lachy, like Dani, had a voice he used for work. For talking to people like her father, presumably. 'My lawyer will call yours this week. Monday.'

'We'll see.' Liss's father set off up the path again and she noticed, for the first time, that there was a wobble to his foot. That he seemed lighter, more fragile. She let him walk ahead, let Lachy fold her under his arm as they followed behind.

Lachy smelled of the tennis game he'd been whacking out near the forest with Aiden. He had mud on his shins and sand in his hair. And he was excited, vibrating at a high frequency of steady loathing for the man who'd given her life.

Liss had never loved him more.

21

Saturday, 6 pm

Green River Campground

Dani

Case against Craig: He kept trying to steal romantic moments on a trip that was very definitely not about romantic moments. A campsite is a village without walls. A group holiday where there's so little privacy and every activity is communal, whether it's arguing or having sex or shitting or screaming at your children.

And yet, here he was, asking Dani to come down to the beach at sunset, at the precise moment she should be helping the others with Pasta Night.

'Let's go and watch the sun sink into the river,' he was saying, in that deep voice again, tugging at her hand in exactly the way that Brigitte did when she wanted her mum to leave whatever she was doing. *Come! Come!*

It was irritating, even though she knew it was a reasonable assumption that he should get to spend some time with her after he'd been banished on a boys' fishing expedition for the morning.

'I know you'll think I'm just saying this but the women are much more interesting company,' he'd whispered when they'd returned to camp, fishless. 'I feel like last year was more co-ed.'

Yes, but last year they hadn't been trying to solve the problem of whether Lachy Short had assaulted a teenage girl. Her teenage girl. *Assaulted*. She hadn't used that word, even in her head, about last night until now. Anyway. It hadn't happened.

It was reasonable for Craig to feel that he hadn't come away to spend hours and hours with men he neither knew nor liked very much. It was reasonable to assume that the woman you were in a relationship with might want to walk with you at sunset.

'In a minute, Craig,' Dani said, in exactly the same tone she would have used to Brigitte.

'But the sunset doesn't last forever, Dani.'

'Hold on!'

She had just a little block of cheese left to grate for the kids to spread all over their red sauce tonight. And she wasn't going to abandon her post. Especially with the way Sadie was looking at her.

Sadie was slicing tomatoes for a salad absolutely no-one would eat, with one eye on Dani and Craig. It was unnerving, and probably pointed. Yeah, she knew that some of the women thought that Craig was an odd choice for her. 'A poorer man's Lachy Short,' is how Juno had described him once, her guard lowered by gin. 'I know I'm a bit man-blind, but come on. Polo shirts and khakis and chit-chat about the markets? They're not twins, but they're brothers.'

That had infuriated Dani. Was that when she started finding fault with Craig's chosen words, with the way he spent money, with his *socks*, even?

'I always thought you would end up with another creative, like Seb,' Sadie had said, sometime during last year's trip. To which Dani had snapped, 'I haven't ended up anywhere, with anyone.'

HE WOULD NEVER

It all felt like judgement. But again, it wasn't unreasonable. If she still considered this a casual relationship, after almost two years it was fair that others thought it was more of a long-term choice.

Sadie was nodding at her, like *Go*, and Dani didn't understand why, when they were on dinner duty. If Sadie grilled a sausage, filled an ice bucket, or suggested a washing-up run, you knew about it. She was no domestic martyr, on or off the campground.

'I can get the water boiling, Juno and Em will be back with the little kids soon. Go see the sunset, Dani. I'm sure Liss is around, too.'

Liss had left the rockpool earlier to go for a walk to her tree, she'd said, as the air cooled but before the mosquitos woke. Dani had seen her briefly, coming back from the path to the forest, walking quickly, looking distracted. Still considering how to patch up the Sadie–Lachy problem, Dani imagined. And Lyra? Well, God knew where her elder daughter was, but since Tia and Trick and James and Bob were also all missing it was safe to say they were together somewhere. *Relax*, Dani told herself. Let's not have a repeat of last night's anxious search.

'Come on, Dani.' Craig pulled her hand one more time. 'I must insist my girlfriend walks with me.'

I have to break up with you, Dani thought. *I am not listening to who I am or what I want. I am not being fair. I have to break up with you.*

Still, she followed Craig down the beach path, out onto the expanse of hard sand being scrawled by the crabs, who scuttled away with every footfall. It was beautiful at this time, there was no argument. The pink-purple sky reflected on the wet sand, the water the silvery colour artists struggled to capture, the whirr of the insects just twitching to life in the lush tree line. Dani could breathe in and appreciate that, even if her mind wouldn't stop flicking through problems with the man walking next to her, holding her hand.

Case against Craig: Romantic.

Why was that in the minus column? Romance in the right hands was heart-filling, sexy. Like when Seb used to bring her a chocolate cupcake from that overpriced tourist bakery in Manhattan and offer it to her with a flourish and a sly smile. It had meant he was thinking of her when he walked past that place on the way to work. That he had made himself late by standing in line. That he'd borne the inconvenience of carrying a little cream-topped cake in a tiny box all the way home on the subway.

But romance in the wrong hands, the ones that didn't fit yours, that was cringe, as Lyra would certainly say. It actually made you recoil.

Why was she thinking about Seb's cupcakes now? The ones he was most likely still buying, but for a twenty-seven-year-old Pilates teacher from Brooklyn.

Dani hadn't noticed that Craig had stopped walking. That he had stopped talking about how beautiful the light was. She sensed that she was three steps ahead and looking much further out, and she stopped and turned and saw.

She had walked straight past it. A little card table, covered by a rough linen cloth, lilac, expensive-looking. A gold foil–topped bottle in an ice bucket. Two crystal glasses. Some flowers from the forest in a tiny white vase.

Dani's mind whirred. He must have packed that table, in one of the hidden cavities in the back of the red truck. And the ice bucket. And the tablecloth, which looked like it was from one of those expensive interior shops in Woollahra, the ones with the stacked wicker baskets and tiny, artisan-crafted white vases. Craig must have picked those flowers. He must have snuck away from the campsite to dress this set.

Oh no. Oh no.

HE WOULD NEVER

Time seemed to slow down as she took it all in. And then she turned to look at his face and there it was. An open, hopeful smile. Hand outstretched to her. A suddenly obvious box-shaped bulge in the pocket of his pin-striped sailing shorts. *Don't say it, don't say it, don't say it.*

'Don't say it!' she blurted, and Craig's face immediately collapsed in confusion.

He opened his mouth, but no noise came out.

'Please don't say it.' Dani hoped her voice was becoming less of a panicked shriek and more of a calm reassurance. She needed to think fast, dig deep.

When Seb had proposed to her, they too had been walking by water, in a metropolis on the other side of the world. He had never lived up to the stereotype of a demonstrably romantic Frenchman. They had been talking about her visa, about travel. They had been doing that thing couples do when they're first together, trying out versions of themselves and their futures on one another. Might they want to move to the west coast one day, live an LA life of sunshine and hyperbole? Might they want to try Paris, where his father's family still lived, and be a pair of bilingual sophisticates, living in a courtyard apartment? This was before Dani's pregnancy made her, like some hormonal homing pigeon, only want one particular, familiar nest for her family. This was back when everything was possible. And he just turned to her, on another cold evening, their faces framed by the hoods of their padded city overcoats, and asked her. *Would you like to? Why don't we?* It would make everything easier. And Dani just knew, like they said in the movies. She knew, *absolutely*.

Now, as time caught up with her, along with the reality of what the card table on the edge of the river beach meant, she realised how distant she was from that nodding young woman. Now she was someone who had created a relationship that was one thing to her, a completely different thing to the other person in it, and with nothing real at its centre.

'Craig. I can't.'

He laughed and looked at the ground, his hand now in the pocket with the box. He kicked at the hard sand with his tan leather boat shoe. He clenched and unclenched his other fist. She watched him, figuring out what to do with his body, his face, his hands and feet, and she wished she could disappear, or at least erase this scene.

'Craig, I'm sorry, I didn't know . . .'

'You didn't know?' His eyes stayed on the ground. 'That's the point, Dani. Proposals are meant to be a surprise.'

'I mean, I didn't know we were . . . here.' Dani was trying to pick words that didn't hurt, but she just kept bumping into the fact that this was ridiculous. The idea that they were going to pledge themselves to each other. Tie their futures together. Live with each other. She had never even thought about it, and he had gone out and bought a tablecloth and a little vase. And a ring. 'I didn't know we were that serious.'

'Serious!' Craig laughed again. Why did he keep doing that? 'Dani, it's been two years.'

'Yes, but we're just dating!' She knew she sounded silly.

'Isn't dating what you do before you get married? Isn't that what women want? A man who will commit?' Craig's voice was getting louder and higher and rougher. His soothing deep tenor was gone.

Dani reached out to grab his hand, but he pulled it back, his face red, his mouth twisting.

'You really don't want to marry me?' he asked. The words would be pathetic if they weren't so edged with disgust. 'You really didn't think this was going anywhere? Haven't I treated you well? Haven't I been nice to your friends?' He gestured around. 'Your kids? Haven't I done all the shit you're meant to do? That women are always saying they want? Jesus, I'm an idiot.'

Dani wanted this to be over and the easiest way she could see was to take this embarrassment from him.

'It's me,' she said. 'This is my fault. I'm all over the place. I should have been much clearer about my feelings. You haven't done anything wrong.'

'Wrong?' he shouted. He still couldn't look at her.

Dani stole a look around. There was no-one else on the entire beach. Not one other human from the campsite had decided this was the moment to come and see the sunset. Was that by accident, or design? Had Craig told people? She thought of Sadie urging her to leave the cheese ungrated. She knew. Who else knew?

'Craig, I'm so sorry.'

'Don't fucking pity me, Dani.' His eyes snapped up to hers. 'Don't pity me. Do you know how many women want a man like me? Plenty, I can tell you. All those women on the apps, all those women who want a man who can afford a ring.' He pulled the box out of his pocket and threw it on the sand.

'Craig, don't.'

'You know your problem?' Craig's anger was in full flight. Dani's plan had worked but now she needed a way out of this moment.

'I think I do.' She sighed. 'I haven't been honest.'

'You're arrogant. You think you're this superwoman single mum who doesn't need anyone except your precious Liss and Lachy and this whole incestuous mess.' He was still shouting. 'Crazy Sadie's the only real one here. And you think that these people love you, that you don't need anyone else –'

'Craig, I know you're upset.' Dani wanted to stop talking but also, his obsession with her friends was infuriating. 'This has nothing to do with Liss and Lachy. I know you don't like them, but they're family to me . . . Maybe that's another reason this could never –'

'You're so deluded,' he snapped, surprising her. 'You don't even know. You don't even know these precious people of yours. Did you know,' he stepped closer to her, within arm's reach, and grabbed the hand she'd offered him earlier. He pulled her in, dropped his voice. 'Did you know that Lachy Short has already sold these campsites?'

'What?' Dani felt a whiplash spike of panic. This was not what she was expecting him to say. 'That's not true, Liss would never –'

'I bet Liss knows nothing about it.' Craig laughed again. 'A developer mate of mine wanted my thoughts on the deal. I almost didn't look at the names because boring fucking property deals aren't my business, but then I did.'

'Why didn't you tell me this before?'

'Why would I?' Craig dropped her hand again, bent down to pick up the ring box. 'It's not that interesting to me. But being here again, with fucking Liss Short lording it over us all and going on and on about how much this place means to her soul chakra or some shit like that, it just makes me . . . They're fake, Dani. And apparently so are you.'

He opened the box. 'Good enough for you?'

A huge, violet-blue stone. It was beautiful. Expensive. Unusual. It would have looked dumb, Dani thought, on her neat little hand.

'It's stunning, Craig,' she said, so confused now that she thought she might lose her balance and topple over. 'Thank you. For making all this . . . effort.'

HE WOULD NEVER

'That's what you do, Dani, for people you love.' He snapped the box shut, put it back in his pocket. 'I thought you and me and Anders and the girls . . .' He trailed off.

There was a lull. Dani wondered if she could sit down. Not on one of the chairs at the proposal table, but right here on the ground. Would that be weird? She imagined so.

'What are you going to do?' she asked Craig. 'Are you going to tell Liss?'

'You're more bothered about that part of this, are you?'

'No, I just . . . I'm confused.'

'Your mate Lachy Short is a pig, Dani. I don't know what hold he has over you but he's just a standard, run-of-the-mill, entitled prick. And he's planning to screw over his wife, by the looks of it. Because having a beach house and a mansion in Bronte isn't enough. I thought maybe she was part of it, until we got here and I heard all her gushing.' He breathed out. 'Anyway, I don't give a shit about them. I'm going.'

'Where?'

'Home.'

Dani's brain jumped straight to the practicalities of getting her girls and her gear back to the city without that fucking red truck. She knew she should have driven her own car. And she realised that thought made it very clear that she didn't care about Craig anywhere near enough for any of this.

'Okay,' she said. And she did sit down, sinking into the sand, facing the sky that was blazing orange now that the sun had slipped itself down behind the black-green shoreline on the other side. 'I'm sorry, again.'

Craig stood there, jiggling the ring box.

'You shouldn't have asked me here,' he said.

'I didn't, you asked yourself.' She said it without thinking.

'Fuck you, Dani.' Craig turned and walked off up the beach to the path, away from the furious sky and the flimsy little table. And Dani stayed there, getting sand in her shorts and wondering how the hell she was going to talk to Liss about any of this.

22

2017, Camp Three

Green River Campground

Liss

At the far end of Green River Beach at low tide, oyster shells rose from an ancient, exposed reef like razor blades.

Liss knew, as a child, never to swim there. You wouldn't feel the shell slice into you until there was blood in the water and a million dirty microbes flooding your system. Unsuspecting visitors with bare feet and romantic aspirations could be seen hobbling back into the campground with a red-stained towel wrapped around a sopping foot.

The summer that Aiden cut himself was also the summer that Sadie brought a different man, a handsome trainer called Lewis. It was the year that Juno and Emily were vegan. The year the 'big' kids could be trusted to paddle in the shallows on their own. And the year Liss could barely walk because of the sciatica she'd been suffering since giving birth to baby Grace.

Dani was alternating cold and hot packs against her friend's lower back, providing a helping hand to lift and lower little Gracie into her cot and pram. Lachy, not a natural carer, would take Tia and Lyra, Ollie and Brigitte for river-camp adventures, so that Liss could rest and stretch and nurse.

For her, it was a quiet, uncomfortable year. Lachy had urged her to cancel, but she wouldn't. 'Once you get a tradition started,' she'd told him, 'you have to keep going, no matter what. That's how you build a shared history.' And he had shrugged at her, kissed her head, told her she was dramatic, and packed the car.

Saturday morning was the kind of beautiful they had learned to hope for. Hot but not so hot that the tents turned into little saunas. Glorious buttery sunshine with a breeze whipping up just enough air to freshen but not chill. Swimmable high tide coincided perfectly with the moment everyone tipped from their tents in their cozzies, and the rockpool remained blessedly seaweed-free.

Liss stayed back at camp, taking her doctor-prescribed short walks, jiggling the baby at her shoulder, and lying on her beach blanket while Grace kicked and cooed beside her. She felt like an invalid queen, as her damp friends came past to pay a visit in between swims and cricket games and child-chasing. They would wait on her a little and drop morsels of gossip on her blanket.

Juno stretched out beside Liss and played with Grace's toes. They'd stopped trying for another kid, she said. Nothing would take inside Emily. Juno refused to go again, insisting she was old, her shop was shut. Emily was angry about it. 'Maybe we should have taken up Lachy's offer,' Juno said, sticking out a playful tongue at Gracie. 'Before everything got so complicated.' Liss hadn't said anything to that, but reached out and stroked her friend's hair.

Sadie brought Liss a valerian tea and confided that Lewis wasn't as good in bed as he looked. Liss didn't say what she was thinking, which was that Lewis didn't look good in bed, he looked good at carrying you a long way on his back, but possibly lacking in the fine motor skills it took to bring an experienced woman to orgasm. Sadie patted Grace absentmindedly on the head while she fed and told Liss not to worry, they would all entertain Lachy. 'Not as thoroughly as you do, obviously!' Then she danced away to find Trick, who'd gone off sulking somewhere after James had kicked a ball at him.

Dani ushered Lyra and Tia over to show Liss the necklace they'd made from the pink pig-face flowers they'd found growing on the rainforest edge. 'So pretty, just for you, Mummy,' Tia said. 'Not for Gracie.' And Dani had whispered to Liss how she'd had to rescue the girls from Lachy's swim-stroke clinic in the rockpool. 'He told your girl she's got spaghetti arms and duck feet,' she said, which explained Tia's pink eyes.

And then Aiden came shuffling up the beach path, leaning on Ginger, his leg wrapped in a towel that was rapidly turning scarlet, his foot sliced on a blade of the oyster bed. Nurse Ginger was going to clean it out and wrap it, she said, and wait to see if it was worthy of a visit to Arcadia's emergency department.

Once his wife had administered enough Panadol, Aiden seemed relieved to have an excuse to sit out of man-play and hands-on dadding. He joined Liss on the camp chairs, his leg raised, and told her stories of their life in the country.

'Don't mind me, sickies,' Ginger said. 'I'll just make lunch around you.' And she did, pulling out the fixings for chicken wraps – slicing up tomatoes and carrots, chipping in to Aiden's stories as Liss patted Grace off to sleep in her pram.

Their new hometown was close but not too close to where Ginger had grown up. A pretty place with a top and bottom pub where the old high street was lined with wrought-iron verandas. One of those Australian country towns once full of farmers and their labour force, now full of single-origin roasters, wine-growers and artisan bakers. Bitingly cold in winter, blistering in summer.

But however chichi the town had become, the property they'd bought three years ago now was a hungry, dusty money pit. Ginger was working part-time at the town's general health clinic, and Aiden had got a good teaching job at the rural outpost of one of Sydney's most elite schools. It was the place young city boys were sent for a term at a time to be taught about the 'real Australia', and Aiden, who was not your guy for survival skill classes and multi-day hikes, was one of the 'ordinary' teachers keeping the usual curriculum going between sleep-outs, horse-breaking and orienteering.

'Some of them love it, you can see their eyes and minds just widen with the space and the freedom,' he said, wincing as he adjusted his leg on the chair. 'Others, well, you can tell they panic when the pavement runs out.'

Liss knew that Lachy's nephews went to that school. She knew a story that did not reflect well on her family was moments away. Her stomach fluttering at the thought, she kept trying to change the subject.

'I think you really do need to get that foot seen to, Aiden,' she said. 'Oyster shells almost always cause infection, even with your wife's professional cleaning skills.'

'He'll be fine,' Ginger called from where she was arranging cheese slices on a big plastic platter. 'It wasn't deep. I've got some pretty standard antibiotics in the first-aid box. Nurse stuff.'

Damn it.

Aiden suddenly looked at Liss as if something was just occurring to him. 'Actually, there's something I've been meaning to ask you about Lochs and Lachy's brother.'

Damn it. The dots had been joined.

'You know, I can't believe I never warned you about swimming at that end of the beach,' Liss said. 'It's so dangerous, isn't it?'

'Lachy's nephews go to Lochs, right? Primary?'

Liss nodded. She knew where this was going.

'But you're not sending Ollie there?'

'No,' she said quickly. 'Both his and Grace's names are down at Samara so he can join Tia. I really feel strongly about co-ed.'

'Yes, I thought that was it. Obviously I only teach Years Nine and Eleven.' Aiden kept looking at Liss like he was trying to work something out. 'Which is when the boys come to the bush, but I think Lachy's brother is involved in the school leadership? Richard Short? He's on the board.'

Liss swallowed. 'I think I know what you're going to say next, Aiden,' she said.

Ginger looked up from her salad plate, her nurse-issue rubber gloves paused midway through halving an avocado.

'The scandal?' Aiden looked left and right, as if expecting Lachy to come barrelling in, which he was likely to do any moment. His finite patience for swim school and the proximity to lunchtime meant his body clock was probably already propelling him back to base.

'What scandal?' Ginger separated the avo with a decisive twist.

'It's really nothing,' Liss said. 'One of those silly social media things. You know, a Facebook group getting a bit out of control.'

'Oh my God, I love those stories. Schools specialise in that shit, right? I can't believe you haven't told me this, babe.'

Liss sighed, closed her eyes, and Aiden, satisfied that Lachy wasn't lurking around a corner, gave Ginger what she wanted. 'Last year all the teaching staff got pulled into a meeting to warn us we might read stories about Richard Short on social media, and to ignore them and not comment to parents or kids. I think they were really worried the media might pick it up. I didn't put two and two together that it was Lachy's brother until recently . . . Should I not bring this up?'

Clearly, Liss's face was giving her away.

'Maybe you shouldn't,' Liss said. 'Not around Lachy.'

'What was the rumour?' Ginger asked.

'You know I don't gossip . . .' Aiden looked genuinely concerned. He really didn't.

'I know, it's infuriating. But you've started, so you have to finish this one.'

'I can tell you because it's over.' Aiden rearranged himself again, the pain shadowing across his face. 'The rumour had been that Short was having an affair with one of his sons' teachers. The school was convinced it wasn't true, but it wouldn't go away, and some of the staff in Sydney had a big issue with it because there were insinuations the affair hadn't really been an affair, but more of a harassment kind of thing, and the poor teacher – it was Linda, you don't know her, but she's so lovely – was deathly embarrassed about it all.'

'Poor Linda.'

'And then it kind of all went away because it became clear it was a grudge thing. Linda was so adamant, I think, and the school was so spooked they tried to track the anonymous online posts and how they'd got in the groups and could keep popping up about Richard Short . . . it was what they call a malicious actor.'

'Well, there you go.' Liss stood up, with some difficulty, desperately needing to bring this conversation to a close.

'But,' Aiden was still going, for fuck's sake. 'And this is what I wanted to ask you about, Liss, in the vault . . . All of a sudden it stopped. And the rumours all over the staffroom were that it was a family matter. Like, someone close to Richard had started the campaign. His wife, or someone . . .'

'Why would his wife do that?'

'She wouldn't.' Liss pushed through the burn spiking across her back and down her leg to grab the handle of Grace's pram and kick off the brake. 'I think we should stop talking about it, you know. It's over. We're just adding to the gossip.'

HE WOULD NEVER

And just as she had feared, or maybe even manifested, Lachy appeared at that very moment, shirtless, hair wet, lightly burning across the shoulders. 'What gossip?' he asked, smiling an extra-toothy smile at Aiden. 'You alright, mate?'

Liss knew how Aiden felt about Lachy. Ginger didn't have to say anything for her to understand there was a very long list of things Aiden would rather be doing, and people he would rather be doing them with, than camping with Lachy Short. They were such different people. It was like putting a dog and a cat in close proximity for the weekend and telling them to be mates.

Lachy considered teachers to be service workers. That they worked for the parents and performed as directed. The idea that a person – a man – would actively choose what Lachy considered a low-status job was something he couldn't comprehend. And his feelings about Aiden, about his profession, his influence, his status as a man, were not explicitly expressed but apparent in every interaction. Like now, with his over-wide smile and his pointed 'mate'.

Liss knew Ginger and Aiden were only here because Ginger was lonely in her new town. These trips were the connective tissue between Ginger and her 'old' life, to the solid friends she'd made at the most pivotal time. Liss had imagined the arguments that must proceed these weekends. Aiden asking if they had to go, really? And Ginger saying yes, do it for me, please.

Aiden was one of Liss's favourites in the group. He was good company, a great dad. But there was a part of her that got a kick out of seeing a man squirm in the presence of her husband. She wasn't proud of it, but it was true.

'I'm fine, Lachy, just a fight with a reef.' Aiden raised his water bottle as if in a toast.

'I'd get something else in that bottle if I were you,' Lachy replied. 'It's going to hurt like hell when the infection kicks in.'

'He won't be getting infected,' Ginger called.

'Anyway, what gossip? You can't stop now.'

Liss looked behind him. 'Where are the kids?'

'Coming up with Dani and Juno. What gossip?' Lachy was, she noticed, looking very directly at Aiden, his smile steely now.

'We were just talking about Lochs,' Aiden said. 'You know, and your brother.' It seemed like he'd decided to settle into the subject, take a jab. 'You heard about those rumours, right?'

'Yes, well.' Liss watched her husband turn and look at her, back at Aiden, back at her. 'My brother's a bit of a dickhead, let's be honest.'

Here we go.

'But it was all a beat-up, the school found,' Aiden went on. Ginger had stopped pretending to arrange lunch. 'Nothing to see and all that.'

'There's always something to see.' Lachy was standing in the centre of the space, still shirtless, still shiny. He'd pulled himself up to his full height. If he was a dog, his hackles would be up. 'So what were you saying about my idiot brother?'

Ginger began busying herself with urgent wrap-rolling, Aiden rubbed the bandage on his leg. Liss wanted to sprint away with the pram, but felt Lachy's eyes on her, willing her to stay put.

'Seems he was the victim of a smear campaign,' Aiden finally said. 'Close to home.'

'Very close to home,' Lachy murmured.

Shut up.

'It must have sucked, seeing people spread lies about him.' Aiden was trying.

'Who says they're lies?'

'Well, everyone, I think, in the end.'

'Listen, Aiden, my brother and I went to that school. It was my mother's singular fixation that we would. She thought it would change our lives and it did. Now my wife,' he looked over at Liss, who thought she might just vomit, 'is another mother with a very specific vision for her children's education, and that doesn't involve such a traditional institution. And look, we've had our differences about it. But just because my association with Lochs is over, it doesn't mean I don't care about the standards of the place. And if my brother, who's on the board, for crying out loud, is behaving like a horny little prick around the pretty young teachers, I think people need to know, don't you?'

'You're . . . jealous of your brother?' Ginger was the one who said it. 'Because his kids are at your old school, and he's on the board?'

Liss felt the need to step in. 'No, of course he's not. Let's get on with lunch, shall we? You could go and tell the others it's almost ready, Lachy.'

'I'm not jealous,' Lachy almost spat.

'And so you . . .' Ginger, fearless, straightforward Ginger, Liss could see, was going to call the tiger on its stripes. 'You sat around on Facebook, posting bitchy shit about him?'

'Of course not,' Liss said, instinctively defensive. 'Lachy, tell them. You wouldn't do that.'

Liss couldn't push away the feeling, almost as sharp as the pain shooting down her leg right now, that she'd had when Richard's wife, Beth, had called and told her that Lachy was ruining her husband's life. 'Call him off,' she'd said, as if Lachy were an attack dog with a safe word. 'Or we'll be involving the police.'

And Liss, who had been standing there with the phone to her ear, her big round belly full of baby Grace, felt her unconfirmed suspicion firming that her husband would do anything to settle a score.

'What did he ever do to you?' she'd asked Lachy that night, her head in his lap, his hand rubbing firm circles on her lower back. 'What did your brother ever do to you?'

'He got on the board of that school,' Lachy had said. And no more.

'Of course I didn't,' he said now, to Ginger, running his hands through his hair. 'But I've got a lot of sway up there, Aidie, you know. I could put in a good word for you about a promotion.'

'What promotion?' Ginger asked, looking up from the chicken as Aiden shook his head.

'Nothing, babe.'

Ginger went back to the chicken.

'Okay, so I'd better put a shirt on,' Lachy said. 'If the gossip session's over.'

Aiden looked down at his foot, where a bright red stripe was beginning to seep through Ginger's tight, white bandage. 'Babe . . .'

'Better get that seen to, mate,' Lachy said. And as he walked out of HQ towards Site Seven and a shirt, he ever so slightly bumped the chair Aiden's leg was resting on.

23

Saturday, 9 pm

Green River Campground

Liss

The palest of pinks and a glitter-sprinkled rainbow and a deep, dark red. The adults' toes had been painted by the little girls after dinner, ticking off the traditional pedi-party portion of the weekend.

The campground was newly dark, still and quiet, just the insects' whirr and snippets of conversations drifting over from other sites, a few notes travelling on the wind from someone else's novelty-shaped portable speaker, an occasional shriek from a tired child not ready to sleep.

Aiden had gone for green nail polish, Lachy for blue, and the two men were making awkward small talk side by side in their rickety bucket chairs, bellies full of pasta, one man down.

'Did you at least get a look at the ring?' Ginger was asking Dani. 'Was it huge?'

Liss could tell Dani wasn't ready to gossip about whatever had happened with Craig on the beach. They had all seen him coming up the path at pace, his face a mask of all the most avoided feelings: anger, distress, embarrassment.

It had been Sadie who intercepted Craig as he climbed out of Site Six's tent, blue-checked duffel bag in hand. Liss, trying to focus on counting bowls for the kids' dinner, watched them talking, heard Sadie swear and throw her hands up. Then Craig had climbed into the ridiculous red truck and driven away, not without spinning his wheels a little on the muddy path. And not without throwing Liss a look that she could still feel stinging her cheeks.

But Liss was feeling a lot of confusing things this evening.

'Dani turned him down,' Sadie had said to Liss back at the table, which was groaning under pots of red spaghetti and brown noodles and yellowy-white macaroni. 'Can you believe that?' But she'd looked at Liss with eyes that said, *Of course you can believe that*.

'Turned him down?'

'He proposed,' Sadie told her, bothering her pasta pot. 'Sundown. Champagne. Ring. He told me last night. Dani didn't suspect?'

'And you . . .?' Liss's eyebrows were up. If Craig had told her that he was planning to propose to Dani, Liss knew exactly what she would have said in return.

'I told him to go for it.' Sadie shrugged. 'Dani's a big girl.'

'Jesus.' *I should go to Dani*, was what Liss thought. Reassure her it was all okay, but she didn't think she could face it right now. 'I would definitely have told him not to bother.'

'Well, that's probably why he didn't ask you.' Sadie smiled.

Liss waited for Dani to emerge from the beach path, which she soon did, all pale face and pink eyes, holding an open bottle of champagne.

'Cheers,' she'd said to her gathered friends and some nonplussed pasta-eating kids. 'I'm going to need a lift home.'

HE WOULD NEVER

Lyra Martin almost looked happy, Liss thought, as she went to hug her mother. 'What happened, Mum?'

Liss didn't hear Dani's answer, murmured as it was into her daughter's neck.

Liss watched Lyra pull away, look into Dani's face and tuck her hair behind her ears and rub a thumb on her mum's cheek. Dani was looking at her with uncertain, wet eyes and Lyra was saying something to make her laugh.

Now Lyra had gone again, swallowed by the pull of the woods or a fire at the beach, Trick following at her heels, Tia by her side. The adults sat in the heavy evening air and chased their dinner with red wine, trying to prise details from Dani.

Liss knew that her friend would tell her the whole story when they were alone. But she couldn't possibly be alone with Dani right now. Because if she was, she'd have to tell her what else she'd seen Lyra do this afternoon.

This morning, Liss had wanted to follow her muscle memory up past the caves and into the wild edge of the national park. She'd wanted to sit on the cushion of a mossy log, or the smooth seat of a healed tree stump, and push her bare feet into dirt, and let it all go. Sadie. Lachy. Her dad. All of it. This beautiful weekend felt more complicated than ever and she couldn't shake the feeling that, somehow, this was the last one, the last time, that she and her friends would be here at Green River. That maybe, after all these years of braided stories, the rope that connected them all was too frayed, too threadbare. The feeling twisted in her stomach, and she needed to sit with it, and blow it off.

But Liss had barely made it to the caves before Lyra Martin almost knocked her over, all streaming hair and rushing legs. Liss had stepped back into the green cover of the tall fringing palms and hardly counted a beat until Lachy followed right behind Lyra, walking slowly, his breathing calm. He'd passed right by her, close enough that she could have reached out and grabbed him. By his hair, by the collar of his stupid polo shirt. She could have made him look her in the face and tell her why he was in a cave with a fourteen-year-old girl. The fourteen-year-old girl they had known all her life, who Liss considered a daughter, Tia considered a sister, and who Lachy had, only hours before, denied touching in a way no grown man should.

Liss had seen Lyra pause, turn, then run to the toilet block. She had watched her husband play with the hat in his hands as he headed back towards HQ, pull it onto his head against that high afternoon sun. Watched him check for her at their tent, even heard him call her name. And then Liss had gone into the cave herself. Sat there in the quiet, cool gloom and tried to make sense of what she had just seen, as if maybe the rock walls could tell her. As if there might be a trace of something, she had no idea what, that would signal the scene she had just missed.

'The ring was huge,' Sadie was saying now, cradling her soda water as if it were something precious. Her face, like all their faces, was in and out of shadow, illuminated by the solar lamps and string lights that flickered around and above them.

'How do you know?' asked Juno.

Juno was filming everything. The gumboot wine cooler, the pasta pots, the bugs that must be picked from Sadie's salad leaves, Emily's swaying hips as she danced to the table with a plate of cupcakes, somehow smuggled past the children and saved for dessert. Dani's shift from sadness to relief.

'He showed it to me.'

'Why would he do that?' Juno asked, as Dani looked over at Sadie with confusion.

'He wanted my reassurance, I guess . . .'

'And knew better than to ask Liss,' Ginger finished the sentence. Dani looked over to Liss. 'Did you know?'

Liss shook her head. She still didn't trust her voice. No-one seemed to notice that she'd said so little tonight. Or that she hadn't been urging them all into some card game or jukebox challenge now that the small kids were off watching screens in their tents. Or that she could barely speak to her husband.

Liss watched Lachy turning his newly blue toes this way and that in the golden light. 'Good riddance, I say,' he said, to a collective groan. 'We don't need any new husbands around here, do we? Pretty pleased with the ones we've got, hey?' He leaned over to punch Aiden lightly on the arm. Aiden cringed.

'You said that last time Dani lost a husband.' Sadie's voice was calm and clear.

'I didn't lose a husband today,' Dani said. 'It was just a misunderstanding.'

'A misunderstanding that you might want to marry a perfectly decent man who'd spent a small fortune on an engagement ring?'

'Sadie, drop it, please.' Dani sounded exhausted. 'I had no idea you were such a fan of Craig's.'

'Oh God no, not a fan,' she replied. 'He was much too boring for me, but I thought he might be just right for you.'

'Jesus!' Lachy laughed. 'And I thought you were a bitch when you were drinking, Sadie.'

'Sorry! I just meant . . . a normal, nice guy, maybe. Dani might want one of those.'

'Sadie, stop talking,' said Juno, raising her filming phone as she did. 'Sober you is too honest.'

Sadie pulled a face for Juno's camera then toasted with her soda water.

Lachy reached into the esky for another beer without leaving his seat in a long, well-practised movement. 'Let's change the subject,' he said. 'What do we think the teenagers are doing in the woods?'

Another collective groan. 'I don't want to think about it,' said Ginger. 'After all these years they deserve a bit of freedom out there, but I am so happy not to know. I did wonder, though if it was . . .'

'Was what?'

'Condom year.'

Huge groan.

In the glitchy gloom Liss was looking at Dani, then Lachy, then Dani, then Lachy. If she was going to bring up the cave, who would she speak to first? What would she say and how would she say it? After twenty-four hours of reassurance and denial and resetting, how could she be sitting here, thinking of upending everything, now?

'It's not condom year!' Juno screeched. 'That's horrifying. They're children. And they're like cousins.'

'Cousins can have sex.' Ginger laughed. 'I'm almost certain there are some kissing ones in my family.'

'I think they're just doing standard stuff,' Emily said, calmly. 'Vaping. Plotting our demise, you know, the usual.'

'Well, I know that Trick might wish he needed condoms around Lyra,' Sadie said. Her voice was still loud. 'But it's pretty clear you don't think he's good enough for her, Dani.'

Dani's head snapped around to Sadie. 'What are you talking about?'

Lachy leaned forward. 'Yeah, Sadie, what the fuck?'

'I told you earlier today, I think Trick has a crush on Lyra –'

'Ha!' shouted Lachy, and Liss's stomach clenched.

'And you made it pretty clear that was a non-starter.'

'Sadie, I just meant . . .'

'What did you mean?'

'All the things we've spoken about,' said Dani, her voice high, irritated. 'They're kids. They know each other too well. Lyra's oblivious to all that, anyway. Jesus, Sadie, it's been a rough night.'

Liss thought she heard Sadie snort.

'Yeah, come on,' Juno said. 'We've never fought over the kids, let's not start now.'

The tension wasn't fading and clearly Dani was done. 'I'm going to go to bed,' she said, standing and stretching. 'Not really in the mood after everything today.' She looked over to Liss. 'Walk with me, Liss? I need to talk to you.'

Liss couldn't move from her chair. A look of confusion crossed Dani's face for a split second and then Lachy was up, walking his blue toes over to Dani and wrapping her in a hug. 'You did the right thing,' he said. 'Didn't she, Liss?'

Liss managed a dumb nod and what she hoped was an encouraging smile.

'For fuck's sake.'

It was Sadie. Of course.

'This is ridiculous.'

'Sadie.' Juno's tone was warning.

'Well it is. It's obvious why Dani said no to Craig. He suspected it, it's what he came to ask me about last night, and of course I lied for you. But he's gone and it's clear what's been going on here for years, and yet we all just go along pretending that we haven't noticed.'

'Sadie!' Ginger was shaking her head.

For Liss, Sadie's words sounded a little like they were coming from behind glass. She just kept seeing Lyra Martin's face as she ran away from the cave. It wasn't happy. It wasn't calm, or amused, or reassured. She'd looked scared.

What if Sadie was right, and Liss was wrong? What if the edge of danger she was so attracted to in Lachy, right from the beginning, was not so impotent and harmless? What if she had made that terrible mistake, the one she thought she was steps ahead of, too smart for? Building a life that was entwined with his in great big ways and silly small ones. Sitting next to him at polite couples dinners, standing beside him at interminable company cocktail parties. Making him a home, feathering him a nest. Fucking him and hugging him and crying in his arms. Almost killing herself giving him children. Looking into his eyes and seeing something that wasn't there. Defending him. Laughing with him and laughing him off to so many of the people around them. Endlessly making small, uncomfortable excuses for him.

He would never.

'Oh for fuck's sake,' Sadie went on. 'Right in front of your face, Liss! They're right in front of your face.'

Oh. Sadie was yelling at her. Liss brought herself back to HQ, where Dani and Lachy were standing in the centre of the circle, and Sadie was leaning forward in her seat, her eyes glittering. To Liss, she looked as if she was shimmering with a furious energy.

'Here we go again.' Lachy had stopped hugging Dani, whose arms had remained by her side. 'Liss, I told you we should have asked her to leave.'

In contrast to Sadie, Liss knew she looked dumb, empty. It was how she felt.

'Dani is in love with your husband,' Sadie said, pointing a steady finger at Dani and Lachy. 'It's why she excuses his creepy behaviour. It's why Dani can do no wrong in the Short house. It's why the girls' dad left in the fucking first place.'

'Shut up, Sadie.' Dani sounded remarkably calm. 'You have no idea what you're talking about. No idea at all. Liss, come on.'

Why did Liss's tongue feel so thick and slow?

'Liss, I know you know,' Sadie pushed on, her voice trembling. 'I saw you all. I know the deal you've made.'

'Sadie. What about today, at the pool?' Dani asked in a voice much softer than Sadie's. 'What's wrong with you?'

'What's wrong with me is that I've been going along with this charade. And I'm living a different kind of life now, of truth. I know it's awkward for all of you, and even for my Trick, who just wants to fit in, but . . .' She choked a little, running out of fuelling fury at the thought of her son.

'Sadie.' Liss found her voice. 'Please.'

'I saw you that time, you know,' Sadie repeated.

'Sadie.' Liss realised now that she might finally be shouting, because the eyes that had been focused on Sadie had turned to her. 'Stop it.'

Sadie pulled herself up, put her glass down with the others on the crowded Formica table.

'I saw you all that day, on the beach,' she said. 'Everything I'm saying is true. And I'm going to bed now.'

Part Three

24

2018, Camp Four

Green River Campground

Dani

It was the year of the storm. The year the heat sat in the campsite basin like a sodden, heavy cloth, stinking and hissing out a low warning that something had to give.

By Saturday afternoon they were all exhausted, sapped by the relentless downward pressure of the humidity. There was no hint of a breeze, and the tide was so far out the relief of a swim had shrunk to a possible muddy roll in ankle-deep, coffee-brown water.

There had been an exodus to Arcadia, where the blissfully air-conditioned old art deco cinema was showing the second *Paddington*. The double-draw of Hugh Grant and choc-tops had left only a handful of stoics breathing through the afternoon at Green River with mozzie spray and iced water at hand.

By 4 pm, the storm was approaching. Even Dani could feel the edge of electricity cutting the solid weight of the air. Finally, the leaves on the palms were beginning to flutter with the slightest breath of wind.

She'd stayed behind because Lyra was feeling particularly bad in the suffocating heat, and was currently sitting with her feet in the paddling pool and a flannel on her head, being granted the very rare permission of connecting to Dani's wi-fi to watch toys being unwrapped on YouTube. Liss had stayed because she was a hostess who didn't leave her post. Emily because Bob had already seen the animated bear making marmalade in prison, and she wanted the peace to just read a book, even in a furnace. Lachy because he hated children's movies.

'Come and watch the storm roll in.'

It was the sort of thing Liss said on camping weekends. Determined that even the world's worst weather wouldn't dent the wonder of Green River, she jigged in front of Dani with a bottle of bubbly wine, eyes as shiny as the sweat slick on her bare shoulders.

'Day-drinking?' Dani asked, nodding towards Lyra. 'Is that responsible behaviour for the single parent of a sick child?'

'She's going to be fine.' Liss smiled. 'Emily's here and happy to keep an eye out. This weather's breaking any minute now. Come on!'

Liss was giddy and Dani was happy to let the silliness infect her. She had just put her signature to two significant life moments and she was allowing herself, just maybe, to breathe out this summer. She had the plans for a Bronte apartment, her very own home. And a new job. Leaving the bank behind and stepping into the role of chief marketing officer at a small but prestigious fund with big ambitions. It felt right, and it also felt like the result of many hours standing around Liss and Lachy's kitchen island, swapping industry gossip and gaming out strategy with Liss as cheerleader, lightening the mood, flitting about filling glasses with pinot gris and tipping pasta into bowls for the children. Sometimes Dani thought, *This must be what it's like to have a wife.*

Now she thanked Emily and trailed Liss down to the beach, picnic blanket under her arm, plastic wine flutes in hand. Lachy was already there, the legs of his camp chair pushed down into the sand like he was the only customer at an epic movie theatre. Beyond the far bank of Green River, the distant sky was billowing black. The light was an electric silvery-grey. Dani had never seen a sky like it.

'We should call the kids to see this!'

'Or we shouldn't.' Liss grabbed the rug and shook it out next to Lachy's seat. 'And just enjoy the show. It's going to be the sweetest relief when it hits.'

'If it doesn't blow us all away in the process.' Lachy took a slug of his beer and rolled his eyes for Dani. 'Only Liss could love the worst weather in the world.'

The champagne was opened, the plastic glasses clunked together and as the little cold pops of alcohol trickled down Dani's throat she tipped her head back and closed her eyes and let herself feel what Liss was feeling, what she imagined Liss often felt.

Three years since Seb had left and it finally felt like life was where she'd hoped it would be when she'd dragged him back from New York. And these people, Liss and Lachy, with their generosity and support, eccentricities and in-jokes, well, they felt like how family was meant to feel. As the bubbles went down and the dark clouds inched forward, Dani felt the need to say so.

'Liss, what if you'd walked into a different mothers' group, back when you were crazy?'

'Unimaginable,' Liss said, reaching for Dani's hand across the rug. 'I'd be locked away somewhere. Tia would be in care. Or, you know, living with Lachy and his second wife.'

'I've always wanted two wives,' Lachy said, throwing them a sly smile.

'Of course you have, Lachy Short, you're a greedy man.' Dani squeezed Liss's hand. 'I'm glad I didn't cut you loose when Anne lost her shit.'

The distant horizon lit up momentarily and rumbled at them. Liss let go of Dani's hand and jumped up, spinning around on the sand, glass in the air.

'Feel that, family? We're alive! The weather's changing!'

'My wife is insane,' Lachy said, but he was beaming.

Dani laughed, watching her friend twirl like one of the little girls, bare legs splattered with mud, her skin glistening, her hair two shades darker, stuck to her scalp.

'She's completely troppo.' Dani's eyes met Lachy's for a moment, their smiles matching.

'Why are you like this, Liss?' Lachy called over the gathering breeze. 'Why aren't we at a five-star resort in Byron? Or a beach house with air con? I know a lovely one, not that far away.'

'Because you didn't marry someone boring.' Liss ran over to him, put her hands on his knees and leaned in to kiss him. 'You married a wild woman.'

Dani rolled her eyes, pulled off the shirt she was wearing over her swimmers. 'You married a woman who likes to pretend she's wild. The Land Rover can take you to your beach house in twenty minutes, you know.'

'Pah! Your other wife is so sensible.' Liss spun away from Lachy and sank down next to Dani on the rug, grabbing her hand again.

Later, Dani would try to recreate a picture of what Lachy saw then that changed everything between them. She and Liss, lying side by side on the beach blanket that billowed with dark pink roses. She was wearing a bikini top and shorts, a combination she'd worn in his presence a hundred times before. Liss, beside her, in her strapless one-piece, the old 1970s number with the toucan she lived in when they were at Green River. Her curves and dimples and freckles as familiar to Dani as her own. Both women damp, laughing, breathing hard from the mood and the heat. Their fingers intertwined.

When Dani had opened her eyes, Lachy was kneeling between them. Like she'd woken up and was still in the slightly hazy reality of a dream. He was looking at her in a way she either hadn't seen or hadn't noticed before. She couldn't think of a better word for it than hungry. It made her uncomfortable, but it also made her stomach flutter, and that made her uncomfortable, too.

Liss, Dani saw, had propped herself up on her elbow and was staring at Lachy, saying nothing, her lips pushed together in a way that Dani couldn't read. Disapproval, or encouragement? Lachy had redirected his hungry look from Dani to his wife, but as his eyes locked with Liss's, his hand hovered over Dani's thigh.

'May I?' He was asking Dani, but he was looking right at Liss. He was asking them both.

He was beautiful. There was no question about it. Lachy Short ticked the boxes of tall, dark and handsome, the stereotypical romantic lead, but it was his confidence that either attracted or repelled you. In this moment, Dani felt his certainty as something she wanted for herself, something she could pull towards her and take a bite of. As she looked at Liss for the answer to his question, what flashed through Dani's mind was whether she had ever imagined Lachy's hand on her.

She had to admit that yes, sometimes she had.

There had been fuzzy evenings, when she and Liss and Lachy had been laughing together, playing music from their separate past lives, sharing stories, and he'd be spinning his wife around the kitchen, his hand on the small of her back, the place that only a lover puts a hand, and Dani had felt pangs. A longing, maybe, for a man like that? Or for this man? No. Not this man. Dani knew too much about him to ever be unguarded in his presence. To give too much of herself away. But right now, the way he was looking between Liss and Dani, and the way his fingers were just centimetres from the bare skin of her leg, she allowed herself, for a moment, to imagine being possessed by him, like Liss was.

Liss nodded her head. Just the smallest movement, and Lachy's hand was resting on Dani's thigh. She sucked in hot air as she considered its presence, what it meant to have her best friend's husband's hand on her skin.

She was still lying down, eyes on her friend. 'Liss,' she whispered. 'What are you . . .?'

'Can I kiss you?'

Lachy's hand moved from her thigh. His body shifted and he was above her, holding himself up, his body over hers, his face so close to her own.

'Dani,' Liss asked. 'Do you want to?'

She was, Dani realised, still holding hands with Liss.

The sky's rumbling was louder, nearer. Dani's eyes were now on Lachy's, as his face moved closer to hers. Their bodies almost touching, she felt the energy between her bare skin and his flickering and bouncing like the static in the air. He was so close. She had never noticed that dark freckle just on his top lip before, how full his mouth was, and how neat and sharp his teeth. Like an animal.

His lips brushed hers. His chest brushed hers. His thighs reached hers. Just a tiny bit more pressure and she would feel the weight of him on her. She wanted to, just for a second. To know how it felt. To remember.

Big, ugly drops of water began to pelt the ground beside Dani's head. She realised she had closed her eyes, anticipating Lachy's lips, and she snapped them open.

'Stop!' It was her voice, and it was Liss's voice, and they'd said exactly the same thing at exactly the same time. Liss's arms pushed at her husband in the moment Dani also shoved him with her hands and tried to pull herself to sitting as he rolled, with a loud, theatrical groan, onto his back, onto the wet sand.

The minute the rain hit Dani's skin, the spell was broken.

'Mum!' Lyra was standing just a few steps away, the flannel that had been pressed to her head dangling from her hand like a wet rag. 'Mum, I'm scared. Thunder's coming.'

Her daughter's hair was beginning to shine with raindrops. The trees were moving behind her as if there were others there, too. Lyra didn't look troubled, just irritated that her mother wasn't exactly where she wanted her.

What had Lyra seen?

'It's all fine, darling, storm's not here yet, run back to camp, we're just bringing everything in!' Dani was up, gathering the blanket, the plastic glasses; the cloud of Prosecco bubbles completely popped. It was just her, and her best friend, and their middle-aged bodies, and a dangerous man she had almost kissed, laughing hysterically on the sand.

'To be continued!' he called, from the ground, across the wind, as the girls turned and ran back to the tree line, the palms and ferns bending and waving with the weather.

'No!' was all Dani could manage, as she, arms full of blanket and clothes, followed Lyra back to camp.

The storm was short, intense, unforgiving, ripping tents from their pegs, flinging tree branches across paths and palm fronds across cars. Sadie and her kids had left the movie early, and the storm had chased them all the way back to camp, where mud and sand left a fine film of muck over absolutely everything. By the time the rest of the movie contingent made it back, Dani and Liss were two respectable friends dressed for the cool change, putting things back where they should have been, righting the mess.

'Where does it go?' asked Lyra, happily reunited with Tia, ineffectually sweeping to a Katy Perry soundtrack.

'Where does what go?' Dani asked, distracted, trying to keep herself moving, trying to stop herself from settling on a particular feeling that accompanied a particular image in her mind, the sensation of her lips being only centimetres from Lachy Short's, his body about to push into hers. Also, was it her imagination, or was Sadie looking at her strangely? *Stop.*

'The storm. Where did it go?'

'It just kept moving,' said Dani. 'And it will keep moving until it blows itself out.'

She was pulling the hot flesh from one of the supermarket chickens the others had brought back for dinner, piling it up on a plastic platter alongside bread rolls and packet gravy.

Liss passed behind her and squeezed her hand. 'You okay?'

No, Dani wanted to say. *I am not okay. I don't do that kind of thing.* And she wanted to ask her friend, *Do you?*

Did she? Did they? She rifled through all the conversations she and Liss had had about relationships, sex, fidelity, Lachy. Liss's mother's advice about always being in the mood to fuck. The casual way Liss would say her husband was always, always hard. Dani had assumed that their relationship was intense, sexual, monogamous. But why would she assume that when she knew the world of opportunity men like Lachy Short moved through every day? You never knew, not really, what deals couples struck between themselves. What they were prepared to do, to go along with, to tolerate. What they might learn they enjoy. Dani's fingers hit the chicken's breastbone. She wiped her hands.

'Dinner's up!'

'Yes! Peasant food!' Lachy was acting exactly the same as always, leaning in across the table from her to build his dinner. 'Delicious!' He looked directly at Dani, who immediately felt a nauseous lurch.

'I'm just going to clean up,' she excused herself and, checking the girls were where they should be, under Emily and Juno's eye,

HE WOULD NEVER

shovelling in plain bread with tomato sauce, she headed to the toilet block.

She shut herself in the cleanest cubicle she could find, rested her head in her hands and began to give herself a pep talk. *Idiot*, it went. *What now?*

'Day-drinking,' Liss's voice was at the toilet door, 'isn't always the safest pursuit.'

Dani smiled into her hands, a bubble of relief rising. Liss thought it was a mistake, too. 'Hi, friend.'

'I'm sorry,' Liss said, her voice thick, serious. 'I'm really sorry. About Lachy, about me, about all of it. You should never have been put in that position.'

Dani stood up, smoothed down her top, looked at her mud-flecked toes in her campsite sandals. Traces of the storm, traces of a very strange day. She couldn't feel the pressure of Lachy's body over hers anymore; it hadn't left a mark.

'It's like a very weird dream,' she told the door. 'I'm not quite sure what we do with it.'

'We keep moving,' Liss said. Dani could tell, from her stifled voice, that Liss was resting her head against the peeling chipboard door. 'You mean too much to me for this to come between us. Lachy and his dick.'

A breath.

'Is that all it was?'

'It was the storm,' said Liss. 'Weird magic. It won't happen again.'

Dani put her hand on the cubicle's sliding lock. 'Has it . . . happened before?'

Liss didn't say anything. Dani thought she could feel her friend's breathing as the cicadas started to sing outside, this day almost over.

'Liss!' Lachy's voice now, joining the insects in chorus. 'Liss! Are you in there?'

Dani unlocked the door and Liss almost fell on her. Dani folded her friend into a hug. 'It's all good,' she said. 'Let's just chalk it up to a strange day, like you said.'

The two women walked out of the bathroom block and into the darkening day. Lachy Short was standing a few steps away, looking at his feet, hands in the pockets of his board shorts. He looked around, clocking any approaching campers coming to wash off the storm.

'The kids want you, Liss,' he said. 'Something about puppy slippers and dry pyjamas.'

'You okay?' Liss asked Dani, squeezing her hand. Dani nodded. She was. But for this not to define or destroy them, she knew she had to say something to Lachy Short.

Liss nodded, started back towards HQ, not looking back.

Dani looked up at Lachy, and he at her. What she'd felt this afternoon, that magnetic drag to feel him against her, was gone. He was just back to being that guy, her best friend's charming, obnoxious husband, the one who thrived on chaos and told a good story, the one who had never liked Seb, the one who wanted her to owe him something, anything.

'We could still do that, you know,' were the first words out of his mouth. 'The door isn't closed. Liss would be –'

'The door is closed.'

'Didn't feel closed this afternoon.' The smirk around Lachy Short's mouth made her stomach do that nauseous flip again.

'Lachy, it's closed. I need you to respect that.'

'I don't think Liss would mind, or, you know, even really want to know. You're very special to us both. There's no need to deny yourself anything.' His voice was deep and steady but Dani could feel a simmer of frustration building underneath it.

'Liss is a sister to me,' she said, firmly. 'And the girls, all this,' she gestured around to the campsite, the others, the mob of children, the beach, 'is special to me. What happened today was a mistake.' She knew that for a man like Lachy Short, she was going to have to be plain, to not leave a glimmer of possibility, because he would see it there anyway. 'I don't want that. I didn't even want it in that moment. I was just confused.'

Lachy laughed. A short, sharp bark, throwing his head back and exposing those teeth. And then he stepped towards her, two steps, three. Closer than your friend's husband would stand to you, outside the toilet block of a bush campground, after chicken rolls and beer. Closer than men stand to women they are not intimate with.

Dani knew she should step back, recreate the distance between them, but she didn't want to give an inch to Lachy Short. If he thought his physical proximity would unsettle her, she would prove him wrong.

'Step back,' she said.

He didn't. The cicadas were deafening now. The clear, rain-washed air was beginning to gather and build again, the darkness closing in by the minute.

'Step back,' she said again. 'It's not happening, Lachy. It's not what I want.'

A noise, a footfall, a cough. And Lachy did step back, quickly, as Sadie came out of the gloom, holding a pink wash bag in one hand and a wineglass in the other, little Lucky by her side. 'Don't mind me!' she said, brightly. 'This one wants to go to bed. Imagine!' And she stepped through them, eyes down, and into the bathroom.

'That's it,' Dani whispered. 'Nothing happened. Nothing's happening.'

'Keep telling yourself that, Dani,' Lachy said from his respectable distance. 'I think you know that's not true.'

And he turned and walked back into the gathering darkness, with a cheerful little whistle.

25

Sunday, 9 am

Green River Campground

Liss

'I think we should call it early this year.' Dani was padding around HQ, filling small bowls with cereal while Liss and Juno were buttering toast that Ginger was ferrying from the camp kitchen's one functioning toaster. 'Everything's off.'

'No.'

'But, Liss, if you're not going to ask Sadie to leave . . .' Dani had her efficient voice on, the one Liss knew she used at the office, or when she had decided the girls were doing something they didn't want to do, no matter what. 'I don't think I can get through another whole day pretending everything's fine when it clearly isn't.'

'You are singing a very different song than yesterday,' Juno said, nudging Dani with an elbow. 'What happened to all that peace, love and understanding?'

'I think you know what happened to it.'

'Sadie's going through a lot,' Ginger said, putting another plate of dark brown toast on the table. 'I don't think we know how hard it's been for her.'

'Being on her own?' Dani asked, mockingly. '*I* know.'

'Come on,' Juno said. 'You don't have Sadie's . . .' she reached around for the word, 'issues.'

Liss had spent another night staring at the roof of the tent, listening to every rustle and scurry, every leaf-fall and dewdrop. Another night of waiting for Tia to slip through the tent flap and safe into her bed, of feeling her husband's weight on the mattress beside her. Another night of wondering if she was wrong about absolutely everything.

Sadie's declaration last night had sent Liss back to a moment she'd almost convinced herself hadn't happened. That version of her spinning around under lightning on the beach felt like a stranger. That version of Dani, lonely and longing, like an old acquaintance from school. And yet Sadie had been thinking about that image – the one three people had been dancing around and working through for years now – as if it was a real, meaningful thing. Maybe it was.

'She must have come down to the beach,' Dani had said, last night, after Sadie had stomped out of their circle and their friends stood around in stunned silence. 'She must have been there just before we came back up.'

'Nothing happened!' Lachy had said, to Ginger, to Aiden, to Juno and Emily's questioning faces, turning as if appealing to a jury.

'It was the storm weekend,' Dani had offered, as if that explained everything. 'And no, nothing happened. Sadie didn't see what she thought she did.'

'Again?' Juno had murmured, turning to Emily with raised eyebrows. 'She imagined things again?'

'No, not like that . . .' Dani had looked at Liss across the circle last night, as if to say *help me out here*. But Liss had lost her voice again.

No wonder Sadie thought Lachy was capable of the things she'd accused him of if, for five years now, she'd genuinely believed that Liss was the wronged party in . . . what? A soap-opera love triangle?

'These weekends are never boring,' Juno said, fishing milk from the esky. 'This latest chapter is in keeping with the canon.'

'I'm glad my reputation being trashed is so amusing to you,' Dani snapped, and Liss felt a surge of irritation at her friend's high horse. *Her* reputation? Still, Liss hadn't yet told Dani about Lachy and Lyra and the cave. She hadn't found those words lying next to her husband last night, nor making breakfasts for the kids alongside Dani this morning. Her irritation mixed with guilt mixed with frustration.

'This might be our last time,' Liss said, finding her voice.

Dani's head whipped in Liss's direction. 'What?'

'We don't know the future of the campground,' Liss said. 'My father's old obsession with it becoming part of the park might well be true. Or, worse, developers might get their hands on it.' Dani's eyes, she noticed, had returned quickly to the cereal. 'I just get a feeling, you know, that everything's going to change. I'd like us to have this weekend.'

She really would. She needed to think. She needed to make peace.

It was almost a year since Michael Gresky had died, maybe of cancer, or maybe of Covid, or maybe of Covid complicating his cancer, it wasn't clear. Maybe it was actually the cigarettes. Or the gin. Like many things involving Liss's father, there was a cloud around his death – a haze of keeping up appearances and payrolled gatekeepers and her last stepmother, the predictable woman of a certain age and fading glamour, claiming to protect his privacy.

HE WOULD NEVER

Liss had mistimed her goodbye. Meaning, she'd missed it altogether. The call summoning her to his bedside arrived just that little too late. She could still feel the sharp stab of anger that had surprised her, arriving at that grand old house to a door closing, to not being able to say what she'd wanted to say to him, not that she'd known what that was.

Lachy and Dani had both been there for Liss when she had fallen apart in spectacular fashion. Lachy was like a solid tree she could lean her back against when she felt too weak to stand through the funeral arrangements she was cut out of, the squabbles and accolades and sudden stabs of loss. He also reminded her, often, that although Michael Gresky was, in Lachy's words, a cunt, he was the cunt who had brought her up, and that was not nothing. Dani had whirled into practical action, organising a fancy meal delivery service for the kids, pink wine delivery for Liss, insisting that she leave the house and walk off the stinky film of grief that had settled on her most days there, for a while.

It was one of those times in her marriage that Liss was most grateful for Lachy's sly smarts, because he had stepped in, spoken to her brothers, dealt with the details, mobilised their lawyer to talk to his. All of that money side. She didn't care about it, not really. It was a basket of things she couldn't face because she was confused and consumed by her own strange reaction – a mixture of relief and sorrow she didn't know how to name.

She didn't believe her father's ghost lived here at Green River, in the way that her mother's still did. The last time he'd set foot here, back when Grace was just growing inside her, that was the last time they'd spoken, really. There had been family things – her brothers' birthdays, a Christmas or two, when she had moved around rooms in a carefully choreographed avoidant dance, limiting interactions to hellos and distant nods, to the polite ushering of wiped-down children in his direction. But that was all. Every other overture was carefully rebutted. He wasn't good for her to be around, everyone from Lachy to Dani to her therapist said so. And so it had been, right up until the call from her brother. *Come, now.*

It had shocked Liss that she found losing her father profoundly altering in ways she hadn't quite expected. She was an orphan. It was a word that stopped her. A word for little lost children, not adult mothers-of-three, but that was how she felt. Abandoned, rootless. Also, she felt like someone she had railed against her whole life had stepped out of the fight and now she had a lot of resentment with nowhere to go.

And it was only now, perhaps, looking around her beloved Green River with her friendships crumbling and a grinding question in her gut, that Liss knew she wasn't ready to leave yet, and that her father did still walk here, that version of him playing mud fights at a low sunset tide.

Lachy walked into HQ, grabbed a piece of toast and took a hungry bite. He was dressed for a run, all short shorts and tech-loaded trainers.

'We're going for a man jog,' he said, through his mouthful. 'One down, obviously, since Dani wielded the axe.' He bared his bread-filled teeth in an ironic grin at her. 'I see the accuser isn't up yet.'

'Shut up, Lachy,' Dani snapped. 'Go run off a cliff.'

Liss stood up, put her hand on Dani's arm. 'It's okay, Dan, everyone knows it was nothing.' And she looked around the table at her friends, authoritative and pleading. 'Don't you?'

Juno and Emily and Ginger nodded, slowly. Aiden, who was also dressed for running, in long boardies and tired Nikes, but with an expression that suggested he would rather be doing literally anything else, nodded at the edge of the tent.

HE WOULD NEVER

'I want,' Liss said, 'one last weekend, one final last-night party. If this is the last time we're all together here, because the park expands, because we can't get past . . .' she waved a hand in a gesture that encompassed *all this shit*, 'I want to remember this season for all of us. It's been too important. To us, and to the kids.'

'Nothing lasts forever,' Emily said, quietly. 'We would have had a good run.'

'Bullshit,' Juno replied, nudging her wife with a hip. 'There is no reason why this can't last forever, why we won't all be coming back here with the kids and their kids one day. No reason at all.'

'There seems to be one big reason,' Lachy said, and he nodded over to Site Eight. Sadie and Lucky were leaving their tent, heading for the toilet block, towels over shoulders, wash bags in hand.

The others watched, saying nothing, for a moment. Liss felt the weight of all their eyes on Sadie and her daughter. 'You know, things got so bad this year Sadie sent the kids to live with their dads for a while,' she said. 'It wasn't ideal. Jacob has a new partner, Trick's dad has a new baby. Nobody, including the men, wanted it to happen, but Sadie felt they'd be better off with anyone but her while she sorted things out.'

Liss knew this because Sadie had told her. She was the only one who stayed in touch with Sadie between camps anymore. In calls and texts and the occasional coffee, the odd doorstep care package when she knew things were bad-bad. It hadn't been easy after last year, but she could see that Sadie was drowning. Others might struggle with the fine line between meddling and helping, between judgement and counsel, but Liss couldn't let Sadie sink. Because of what she'd meant since that day she'd rallied the women, babyless, in a sterile shopping centre cafe, and also because Liss's husband had been part of what had sent her under. Perhaps.

'She didn't say.' Ginger's forehead was creased in concern.

'When would she have?' asked Liss. 'When we didn't invite her to your place for the weekend? Or when we didn't ask her to come to dinner when you were in town visiting Aiden's mum? We stopped including Sadie in anything other than this weekend years ago.'

'Because she always creates drama,' said Dani, gesturing around the table. 'Case in point.'

'Sometimes drama is needed,' said Juno. 'Because it's what the truth brings.'

'That wasn't truth she was telling last night, Juno,' Dani said, 'and she's had five years to ask me what really happened that day, if she had given a shit about finding out.'

'That's not what I mean.'

'Let's go, Aiden,' Lachy said, with a performative sigh. 'The women are making irrational decisions on our behalf, best leave them to it. How's your pace these days, anyway?' Aiden threw Ginger a yearning look as he followed Lachy out of HQ, and down the path to River Road.

Liss watched the men retreat, watching Lachy's straight shoulders and sure feet pad away as if there were no problems in his world at all.

'Dani, you're right, Sadie should have asked us about the storm weekend years ago, but we haven't exactly been there for her, have we?' She felt her heart picking up pace as she went on. 'While she's been trying to make big changes in her life, we've been backing off. Her problems were inconvenient for us, weren't they? And now we're acting surprised that some of that resentment is coming back our way.'

Dani, Liss could see, was softening under her words, blinking a little as she fiddled with the cereal boxes, making sure, as she always did, that all the labels were aligned and facing the right way. Liss stopped one of Dani's hands on the boxes with hers.

'One more night. It might be the last one.'

HE WOULD NEVER

Dani smiled. 'You've always been good at a guilt trip.'

'I don't want to go anywhere,' Juno said. 'Another shot at disco night will be great for content.'

'I don't know if it's up to us.' Emily sighed. 'Sadie's probably thinking of packing up right now.'

'I'll deal with that,' Liss said, and she meant it. She couldn't have Sadie thinking the things she was thinking about Lachy. Or about her. Her marriage. Her family. 'We'll wipe the slate clean.'

'That slate's been rubbed almost to nothing.' Juno snorted. 'You might need to lower your expectations.'

Breakfast was ready, the stage set for another invasion of hungry children. As Ginger whistled loudly to bring the kids running, Liss wiped her hands on a tea towel and started for Site Eight. She nudged Dani with a gentle shoulder. 'It's okay, Dan.' She hoped it was true.

As Liss leaned on the bonnet of Sadie's car and waited, she took in the familiar chaos of Site Eight. There were towels on the muddy ground and dangling from the car's wing mirrors. There were plastic laundry tubs crammed with a hotchpotch of pans and plates direct from a home kitchen. The tent was leaning heavily to the left, straining at its far pegs. And a plastic bag hastily tied to a pole to serve as a bin was ripped, flapping open, showing its contents of biscuit wrappers and aspirin packs.

'Hey.' It was Trick. Appearing from the tent, a hoodie over his ears despite the building heat. 'You looking for Mum?'

Liss nodded. 'You okay? There's breakfast over there, you know.'

He looked away quickly. 'I'm coming. Just been talking Mum into staying. Again.' Liss hadn't expected a full sentence out of Trick, never mind one as honest as that.

'Then you and I have something in common today.'

'Lyra's mum yesterday, you today.' Trick lifted his head and looked Liss in the eyes in a way she hadn't seen before. He'd probably seen a lot, and Liss got a heart pang at the thought. Tia seemed like a clear-eyed baby next to this mature young man.

She shrugged. 'We want everyone to enjoy the weekend.' It was a bullshit thing to say to a teenage boy and Liss was irritated with herself as soon as it came out of her mouth.

'Yeah.' Trick passed her, heading towards HQ and food. 'It would be nice not to have to do so much rebuilding every morning.'

Liss was still staring after Trick's back when Sadie and Lucky returned. Sadie didn't seem surprised to see Liss leaning on her car. Even with her newly scrubbed face she looked tired, beaten down, and Liss knew she hadn't been the only one who'd spent the night staring at the tent's canvas instead of sleeping.

'Have you come to ask me to leave?' asked Sadie. 'I wouldn't blame you.'

'No. I want you to stay,' Liss said, not moving to touch or hug her friend, but trying to strike a balance with her voice between kind and a little formidable. 'I don't want to lose you.'

Sadie nodded, swallowed, moved from foot to foot. Behind her, Lucky hung back, as if waiting to see if it was safe to head off to get breakfast.

'You really didn't see what you thought you did on the beach that year,' Liss said. 'I know exactly what you did see, and I know exactly what happened next, and what's been happening ever since. It's not that.'

Sadie shrugged. 'Okay.'

'Let's just revert to the original plan,' Liss said. 'We give Lachy a wide berth, we enjoy ourselves because this is our break, our holiday, our place.'

'It's your place,' Sadie said, quietly. 'But the kids do love it here. I'd have to tear Trick's fingernails out to get him to let go.'

HE WOULD NEVER

'Well, then.' Liss pushed down the last remaining twinge of uncertainty. She would tell Dani about Lyra and Lachy as soon as she found the words. She just needed some more time. 'Let's make sure this last night's a doozy, yes?'

Sadie laughed. 'You're very forgiving, Liss. Lachy and Dani are beyond lucky, I hope they know.'

'Oh, they know.'

26

2019, Camp Five

Green River Campground

Liss

Liss was weeing on her tree.

She was nervous, spending longer than she needed, kicking leaves over the little puddle like a puppy, looking up at the spreading branches of the fig, running her hands over the knotty curves of its trunk, tracing its roots with her toes, killing time before she returned to Site Seven.

Dani hadn't arrived yet and Liss was jumpy. In the year since the storm weekend, plenty had changed in their cosy little blended family. Dani wasn't such a regular fixture at the house anymore. If she was there when Lachy arrived home, there was no lingering over wine and pasta, only Dani making polite excuses, gathering bags and keys and children and leaving. Lachy would say nothing, watch Dani disappearing down the front path, and always be just a little sulkier on those evenings.

Liss and Dani had stuck to the agreement made outside the toilet block that night. They would not let that glitch of an afternoon come

HE WOULD NEVER

between them. They would push through Liss's discomfort and Dani's embarrassment to talk about it. They would laugh about it. They would rid that afternoon of its power to dismantle their friendship by drenching it in sunlight. Their friendship, and their daughters' friendship, was too precious to let crumble away.

Generally, their commitment had worked. They still spoke almost daily, still shared their own rituals and rhythms. They were solid. But there was something about being back here, in the steaming, salty cocoon of Green River, that made Liss nervous. Dani, too, clearly, because she had called, last week, and said how busy she was, how there was a campaign launching in March that she was behind with and she couldn't guarantee that she wouldn't be tied to her phone, that her sick mum might take a turn and that Seb might be flying in on that Sunday this year for the girls and that it might just be easier if –

'Dani, stop.' Liss had been in her study, standing in front of an easel she'd just pinned a lesson plan to. When the school term began she was going to start working three days a week at St Mary's up the road, as an assistant to the art teacher. She was nervous. She was inspired. She was sure it was Dani's fault she was doing it.

'You're coming. Please. It's not going to be weird, I promise.'

Liss knew Dani was also genuinely worried about her mum, who was ill and being cared for at home by Dani's sister and aunt. Dani drove over there twice a week after work to sit in the downstairs bedroom, brush her mum's hair and be told she should come more often. And then, Dani said, her mum would generally lose patience with any coddling and tell her to leave, to get back to those beautiful girls of hers. Dani and Liss, whose father was drip-feeding dark hints about his health to her through her brothers, shared what could never be shared elsewhere: they were bad daughters from different worlds, clinging together, still.

'Okay, okay. We'll come. But if Seb does turn up, I might have to leave early.'

'He can wait a day. The girls wait for him for months. Your mum would want them to see their friends. Come, relax, stay. You know I won't enjoy it without you.'

'Okay, okay.'

Liss didn't know, as she picked her way out of the forest, if it was true that it wouldn't be weird. She wasn't sure she was in complete control of that.

And now she was waiting to hear the tyres of Dani's sleek white Mazda pull up on the stony path alongside Site Seven. To hear her god-daughter's voice. To hear Dani complaining about the traffic, saying she had to take a call.

'Liss!' A voice through the trees. Lachy would be looking for something. Something that would be right in front of him, but that his eyes couldn't find. Her whole family was like that, convinced only she had the special sight to locate lost things.

'Coming!' She picked her way through the tree roots and dangling vines back to Site Seven. Indeed Lachy was standing in front of the open boot, his eyebrows low, his mouth pursed.

'I can't find the fucking poles.'

She rubbed his back, pointed at the poles. 'You okay? You remember what we talked about?'

'Of course I do. Give me some credit.' He was tetchy. On the drive up he'd been listing all the reasons they needed to ditch this camping tradition. It had been cute for a while, he said. A novelty. Now it was too much work at a busy time of year. He didn't want to have to spend three days talking to Aiden. Ron and Shell were neglecting the place and it was becoming a mosquito-riddled death trap. His leg hurt from that squash thing. Fucking crazy Sadie. It was all too much.

HE WOULD NEVER

But Liss knew he was still smarting from last year. Unsettled at the idea of having to spend a few days in close proximity to Dani, a woman who'd rejected him.

'We just have to move past it,' she had said to him, speaking in code to confuse little ears in the back of the car. 'It's behind us.'

They had put it behind them, as a couple. Liss was savvy enough to know that Lachy needed some distraction, and she organised that for him sometimes, on her phone, just like she organised his skin-cancer checks and her yoga classes. He liked her to be involved, even if it was only in the planning and the telling. She liked the control, the knowing. It was a season, she was certain of it, something he would move on from.

That year everyone arrived before Dani. Liss, Ginger and Juno were already cutting up onions to fry for sausage sandwiches when the white car rolled in. Liss knew she was being too eager when she dropped her knife and almost ran to meet it.

'I thought something had happened to you,' she said as Dani stepped out and they hugged. The wind was picking up and the gums were waving their highest limbs in celebration.

'Calm down,' Dani whispered. 'People will think I'm sick.' But she pulled away laughing, and Liss felt a warm thrill spread through her chest as the other women came to embrace Dani, marvel at the kids' height, and offer to help her set up before dark.

'I'll get the tent up for you,' Lachy said, appearing seemingly from nowhere.

'No thanks.' Dani shook her head. 'I'll manage.'

Aiden was permitted, eventually, to help Dani set up so the disco could begin. Lachy looked like a kicked puppy over at the barbecue, turning sausages as Ginger talked about the promotion Aiden had got at Lochs. Sadie kept turning the music louder and Juno kept easing it down. Children fought with their siblings over watermelon and grapes and salty chips.

Dani looked tired as she sank into a chair next to Liss and put out a hand. 'Bubbles me, friend.' And Liss was delighted to pass her a glass as the kids, still small enough to dance with abandon, or toddle about in circles until they fell on their bums, began to spin around the makeshift dancefloor.

Liss watched her husband cross the space to crouch down in front of them. 'Dani,' he said, 'will you tell my wife it's time to stop pretending that camping is fun? Will you tell her she's got it out of her system and it's time to drop the charade?' His face was serious, his mouth twitching with a smile, his voice faux stern.

'I will not,' Dani said, her voice relaxed, playing along. 'You both need to mix it with the commoners every now and then, it keeps your guy ropes tethered.'

Maybe it was all going to be fine.

'I reject the entire premise of that statement.'

'I'm sure you do, Lachy Short, man of the people.'

'And I want my beach house.'

'Of course you do, darling.' Liss patted her husband on the head. It was like the old times – teasing, flirtatious, calm. 'Go and dance with your daughters.' She gestured to Tia and Grace, jumping around to Taylor Swift.

'Those are not my daughters,' he said, with mock indignation. 'What are you suggesting?' And he was gesturing to Dani's girls, who were dancing alongside. Liss's stomach plunged. Dani looked down into her drink.

'Lachy, don't be a dick.'

Confusion crossed his face. Maybe he really didn't know that attempting a joke about questionable parentage at this particular moment, on this particular evening, was a terrible idea. Maybe he thought he was breaking some ice. Either way, Liss wished he'd disappear, and leave her with her friend.

'Jesus.' Lachy huffed at the look on Liss's face and stood. He crossed the floor again, jigged with the girls for a moment, and then, throwing a look over his shoulder at Liss and Dani, approached Sadie, who was still wrestling with the phone's playlist. He tapped her on the shoulder and she turned, responding to his grin and his exaggerated shoulder shake, and followed him with a wiggle as he backed onto the dancefloor, beckoning her to follow.

'How do you do it?' Dani said, quietly, after a moment.

Liss could have asked, *Do what?* But it was Dani. 'I know what I'm doing.'

'And what is it?'

'He would never do anything that would truly risk us.' Liss took a sip of her drink. It was true. Too much of Lachy was tied up in what they had. In the status of her and the house and the money and the beautiful kids. The whole perfect package of enviable success that he'd wanted since he was just a skinny boy trying to get his dad's attention.

'Do you know that, for sure?'

'Dani, I know him better than he knows himself.' Liss wanted to move on. This was dangerous friendship territory, even for her and Dani. Maybe especially for her and Dani. They watched Lachy and Sadie dancing, mouthing the lyrics with exaggeration, all big arms and twisting hips. All performance. All fakery. 'He's just flirting. There's a difference between a man who wants everyone to want him and a man who will act on it –'

'He nearly acted on it last year.'

A spike of anger. Liss looked around. Everyone was busy, everyone was distracted. Everyone was listening to Taylor. 'Come on, that was different. That was *us.*'

Even as she said it, she wondered how it made any sense, but to her, it did. She knew he'd always been jealous of the easy intimacy she had with Dani, one that he would really rather she had with no-one other than him. Muscling in on it made perfect sense to Lachy Short.

'Anyway,' she said. 'There's something to be said for not having any illusions about who you married. That's all I meant.'

'Sure.' Dani shrugged.

Liss rocked her chair so it knocked into Dani's, puncturing the tension. 'We should get the little ones to bed, yeah?'

'Oh, just a moment, I need to sink into being here.'

The insects, the night, the sound of the river at high tide, lapping beyond the trees. Liss knew Dani was coming to love it here too. That she had wanted to come, really. It made her feel warm, safer than she'd felt before Dani arrived.

'It's going to be a big year,' Liss said, raising her glass. 'I've got a fucking job!'

'Mum!' Tia exclaimed, hearing her mother at the exact moment the music stopped and before Taylor was followed by 'Old Town Road'.

Dani tapped her plastic glass on Liss's. 'Proud of you, friend. To a life outside your mansion.'

Liss felt her smile tightening.

Then someone barrelled past her chair, bumping her glass, spilling some bubbles. It was Emily, who Liss hadn't realised was missing. She'd seemed distracted today, fussing over Bob's sunscreen more than usual, spending a long time setting up the inside of their tent, declaring she was going for a walk alone at sundown. Still, Emily and Juno had a lot going on. They were planning a wedding. It made Liss emotional to think about how seeing her friends marry wasn't even legal when they all first met. Lachy teased her about her liberal warm and fuzzies when she expressed excitement about going to her first gay wedding. Dani told her not to say 'gay wedding', but she wasn't sure why.

Emily's face was a little drawn, her forehead creased in a frown. Maybe gay weddings were every bit as stressful to plan as straight ones, Liss thought. 'Hey, Em,' she called, as Emily passed, 'did I tell you about my job? Dani's just congratulating me for not being a super-lame boring housewife anymore.'

Dani's head turned sharply to Liss, but Emily kept moving. There was something purposeful about where she was going. She walked right up to Lachy, and tapped him on the shoulder, in much the same way he had just done to Sadie. Except she didn't want to dance.

Emily pushed Lachy – shoved him, more like it – and Liss was out of her chair and stepping over the oblivious children before she'd realised it.

'You,' was all she could make out Emily saying, by the time she was close enough to hear. 'It's your fucking fault.'

Sadie was standing between Lachy, who looked slack-jawed with shock, and Emily, her face curled in disgust. 'Hey, guys,' Sadie was saying. 'What the fuck?'

'It's his fault!'

Juno stepped up and took Emily, mild-mannered, always reasonable Emily, by the arm, pulling her away, out from under the tarp into the lamp-studded gloom.

'What?' Liss shouted, over the music. All the kids' heads were popping up now, eyes on their parents, sensing tension, danger. 'What?'

'She said something about him costing them a baby,' Sadie said, half-giggling, still fizzing with the surprise of it all.

'Oh Jesus.'

'Liss, I have no idea what she's talking about,' said Lachy. 'I'm getting blamed for fucking everything today.'

But Liss was already walking, past a stunned Dani, along the path with the little solar lamps she'd carefully pushed into the ground to guide the kids to the bathroom. Over to Site Five, where a silhouette of Juno and Emily was projected on their yellow tent. They were inside, and even from their black shadows, it was clear that Emily was crying, and Juno was soothing.

'We can't blame him,' Juno was saying, through the thin, shiny fabric. 'Em, seriously, we can't blame him.'

'I can fucking blame him,' gasped Emily through tears and snot. 'He cost us time.'

The head of Juno's shadowy outline lifted, as if she could sense Liss on the other side of the wall. 'Hold on, Em.'

'What happened?' Liss asked, straight away, before Juno reached her.

'She had another miscarriage.' Juno's voice was low, with a crack in it.

'Oh no.' Liss had a muscle memory of what Emily was feeling. Her stomach ached, her hands tingled, her throat closed just a little tighter thinking about Em speaking through those sobs. 'I thought you two had stopped trying.'

'We had,' Juno said. 'I had. She wanted one more round.'

'I'm so sorry.'

'It's not Lachy's fault.' Juno shrugged, to a new cry from inside the tent. 'But Em's got herself stuck on it.'

Baby grief was wild, Liss thought. Unable to be tamed or channelled. If Emily, the most rational and reasonable and reserved among them, could be here, years later, then every day had mattered to her. Every hour.

'I understand,' Liss said. And she did. Lachy, she knew, had distracted these women for a time with his hero complex, sending them off to the waiting list of a fancy doctor friend who had ended up being no more successful than Juno and Emily's clinic. She also understood the part she had played herself, putting her foot down about Lachy being a donor when he kept on pushing it. It was infuriating, his need to insert himself into their lives, to control and help and perform as the golden saviour. It could be seductive, endearing, and completely devastating.

'She doesn't want him at the wedding,' Juno said, dropping her voice another decibel. 'I'm just telling you that. Maybe she will calm down before then. It was hard to get her here.'

Liss pulled Juno into a hug. 'Of course,' she said, a ball of frustration pushing against her ribs. Smoothing over his messes, always.

'Of course,' she whispered, her mouth at Juno's ear. 'Lachy will have the flu on your wedding day.'

27

Sunday, 11 am

Green River Campground

Dani

Aiden's face was still tomato red from his run with Lachy, sandy-blond hair still plastered to his freckly forehead. The threadbare John Butler Trio T-shirt he'd pulled on over his board shorts this morning had dark patches under the arms and around the collar, his stomach pushed a little at the fabric around his waist.

'Dani!' Ginger was calling, dragging her sweaty husband across the beach. 'We have to talk to you!'

'Ginger,' Dani could hear Aiden protesting. 'Ginger, can we just –'

'No, we can't.'

Dani stood up in the water. This morning, after Liss's plea for unity, for one more night in her beloved Green River, Dani's instinct had been to get the hell away from everyone and try to wash off her irritation and confusion. Her anger at Sadie, even after all Dani's effort with her yesterday, yet again showing herself incapable of shutting up. Her anger at Craig, for not understanding her at all. And her anger about Liss. How was she going to tell Liss, delusional, determined Liss, that the reason she might be right about this being the last trip to her magical soul haven was not because of 'greenies', or evil developers, but because of her husband.

Lachy Short. Who just couldn't help himself to meddle and mess and push, but also, perhaps, to destroy?

Peace. Wasn't that what Dani had said she was wishing for, on that first afternoon, standing right here, in this water, with Liss and the other women, blindly optimistic about the weekend ahead?

The tide was up now, high and clear, cool and light green on a day that was already hotter than the day before. And Dani had snuck away, asking Brigitte if she wanted to come and being roundly rebuffed by her tween, leaving the others packing beach bags, reading under trees, rearranging tents and taking stock of what supplies needed to be eaten up in the trip's last supper. As if everything was completely normal. They were good at that, after all these weekends. Pushing aside big and small tensions, pretending things weren't happening that clearly were. Liss and Lachy set that tone, Dani knew. Rich people were very good at pretending. Maybe it was in the DNA of how they got rich in the first place.

'Dani!'

She'd known it would only be a matter of time before the others came down to the water, but she'd hoped by then she would have reset, calmed to a place where she was happy to resume usual service – smiling, nodding, small talk.

Ginger and Aiden did not look like small talk. She raised her hand and waved.

Ginger didn't stop walking, she just let go of Aiden's arm, pulled off her T-shirt and walked straight into the water in her lopsided bra. Dani blinked.

'You okay?'

'We need to talk to you.'

'Clearly.' Dani dropped back down into the water and swam a few strokes towards Ginger, who was impatiently motioning to Aiden to come in, too.

'I've got to take my shoes off, for fuck's sake!' he shouted, wobbling on one leg before sitting down and huffing away at the laces of his trainers.

Dani and Ginger swam to each other, meeting in the shallows, down on their bellies, hands pushing along the sticky, muddy bottom.

'What is it?'

Ginger shook her head, took a gulp of air and sank under the water for a disconcerting second. Then she shot back up and bobbed, their faces inches from each other's now, glittering with river drops.

'Ginger, what is it?'

'Lachy and Aiden just came back from a run.'

'I can see that.'

'He needs to tell you something.' Ginger looked over her shoulder impatiently at where Aiden was pushing his rolled-up socks into his tired running shoes. 'Come on!'

You usually knew, Dani thought, in that moment between being told someone needs to tell you something and someone actually doing the telling, which scenarios were most likely. You calculated as many of them as your brain could manage in the allotted time.

Was Aiden sick? Were they divorcing? Was it James? Had their overconfident teenage son done something the other parents would need to know about? Sexting? Revenge porn? Drugs?

Aiden and Lachy just came back from a run. Oh. Of course. They knew about the sale.

Aiden reached them and said, with a slight breathlessness, 'It's about Lachy.'

'Of course it is.'

HE WOULD NEVER

Dani loved Aiden, all the women did. It couldn't be easy being one of the two regular males in this intense group of longtime female friends. Especially when the other one was Lachy Short.

Aiden was steady and kind. He didn't patronise. He was attentive and adoring to Ginger, without being obsequious or coddling. He had stood with all the women in the shade of a spreading oak at Juno and Emily's wedding and, like them, had cried when Juno spoke her vows. When Dani and the girls had visited them out on the farm, she had felt a considerable pang of envy. She admired how they had built this life around their steady union, and how much genuine joy it seemed to bring them, despite its difficulties, inconveniences and dramas. Dani envied it even as she would rather eat a box of hair than live where they had chosen.

So they all loved Aiden, who was not given to drama, and here he was, being rushed into telling her something urgent about Lachy. Dani instantly felt sick.

'We were running,' started Aiden. 'And you know he likes to talk when he runs.'

'I did not, but go on.'

'I think he likes to prove that he *can* talk when he runs. And that I can't. But that might be in my head.'

'Aiden, come on.' Ginger hustled her husband along, tapping his bare arm with her hand.

'Okay, okay. My point is, I don't say much.' He pushed his wet hair back on his head. 'Which actually is my general strategy around Lachy Short, but running is particularly annoying.'

'I think I know what you're going to tell me,' Dani interrupted. 'It's about the campsites.'

'What?'

Oh. Okay.

'What about the campsites?' Ginger asked.

'Never mind.' Dani folded her mouth tight and looked at the water. 'God, the river's so clear at this time of day.'

'This isn't easy to tell you,' Aiden said, shifting on his muddy feet again. 'I'm struggling.'

'Just do it!'

'Okay. So he's talking, and he talks a bit about Sadie. Standard issue. She's crazy, driven by revenge . . .'

'You guys talk about that stuff?' Dani was surprised.

'Of course they do!' Ginger was not.

'Okay . . .'

'And then Lachy brings up Friday night, and the disco, and what Sadie said had happened.'

Dani felt sick again. In fact, her stomach flipped, an expression she suddenly understood with great clarity.

'Lachy said – and I just really need you to know that I do not agree in any way with this, it's why I'm telling you –'

'For fuck's sake, Aiden.' Ginger grabbed his arm and shook it, sending him a little off balance.

Aiden's face, textured with ridges and freckles, creased at the forehead and around his mouth with concern, or revulsion. He started to speak in a tumble.

'He said that I was lucky I worked in a boys' school. He said that teenage girls are the most infuriating creatures on earth. He said that they want attention from adult men, but when they get it they complain. He said, is it any wonder that sometimes grown men get confused around them, because they act like whiny little children but look exactly like the women men have been chasing their whole lives . . . Well, he said, since our balls dropped.'

Dani was losing her breath. She put a hand to her chest, hoping to hold in what she could feel building there.

'He said that, in the old world, we knew when a girl turned into a woman, but now we're trying to rewrite biology, deny nature.' Aiden looked confused. 'I have no idea what the fuck he was talking about.'

'I know what he's talking about,' Ginger said, her hands raking through her hair at a furious rate. 'He's trying to justify himself.'

'He said,' another big gulp of air for both Aiden and Dani, 'that sometimes a man forgets all the modern rules that have been forced upon him. That sometimes men just act how they were designed to, rather than how they've been conditioned to, and that always, when that happens, women freak out. Because they think they've domesticated us. And they're reminded that really, we're wild.'

Dani was picking through Aiden's words even as they fell out of his mouth. 'Did he say what he did to Lyra?'

'Dani, he never mentioned Lyra's name.'

'And what, what did you say?'

'I said . . .' It was like Aiden exhaled; he knew the answer to this question, a man certain of that, at least. 'That there was nothing confusing about knowing you have to act like an adult around a child. I said that I didn't relate because I found that line pretty clear. And I said that he should stop talking.'

Dani felt dizzy, like she might just fall into the water and never come up again. She also felt an almost unbearably urgent need to get to her girls on the other side of the trees, and to wrap them in her arms, and to never let them go.

'And what did he say to that?'

'Oh you know what he's like, he sort of punched me on the arm as if we were both in on a joke, or as if maybe he was only joking, and then he said I didn't understand yet because my daughters were still young and hadn't started bringing all their friends home in their bikinis.'

'Oh my God.' All Dani could see, suddenly, was Lyra at Liss's pool. The bright white-gold light of a hot afternoon blasting the deck.

Little bare feet hopping across it. Dropped towels. Shrieks and jumps and wrestles. One-pieces, two-pieces, Marco Polo and handstands. One hundred afternoons like that. Ones Dani was there for. Ones she was not.

'I told Aiden he had to tell you,' Ginger said, her voice steady, her face concerned. 'It's insane.'

'I would have told you,' Aiden added, solemnly.

'I can't believe Lachy said all that to you,' Ginger replied. 'Like you wouldn't tell us.'

'I don't think he considers me much of a person at all.' Aiden didn't look sad when he said it. 'I also think he believes any real man would agree with him.'

Dani turned to look out at the far bank of Green River. She thought of Lyra's insistence on 'nothing' happening. She thought of the way her beautiful girl had learned to hunch her shoulders and fold her arms across her stomach when she was out in the world in clothes she'd felt powerful in, before men's eyes singed and curdled it for her. She thought of Lachy Short's body above her own on this beach years ago. And she thought of Liss telling her she knew exactly who she'd married. Her friend, Dani now blisteringly saw, in a wave of rage as strong as the sun she was shielding her eyes from, was an idiot. Or worse.

She spun back around to Aiden. 'Why didn't you ask him what he did to Lyra?' Dani hadn't meant the words to come out so angrily, and she immediately saw the forceful effect they had as her friends rocked back on their heels. 'Why didn't you ask that?'

'Dani.' Ginger put her hand on Dani's arm. 'Come on.'

'Seriously,' Dani spat. She couldn't help herself. 'What good is your bromance chat if we have no evidence?!'

'Dani, I don't know if he did do –'

'Please. After all that?'

HE WOULD NEVER

'Men . . . talk.' Aiden shrugged, and he looked pathetic doing it. 'He wasn't actually saying –'

'You know what he was saying,' said Dani. 'That's why you came straight down here to tell me.'

'I know you're upset,' Ginger said, cautiously. 'I think we should talk to Liss.'

'So the fuck do I,' said Dani. And she stood up from the water with a force that sent streams of river drops in every direction, and headed for the beach.

28

2020, Camp Six

Green River Campground

Lyra

'What does a virus even look like?' Tia was asking through a mouthful of jelly snakes, contraband lifted from the esky by Trick.

'Like a big spiky ball of snot. I saw it on the news,' Lyra told her. It was true. Her mum was trying to keep her away from it, she said that between the American orange man and spreading sickness, the news was just anxiety.

'They seem worried, the grown-ups,' Tia said. 'My mum says that there's a place in China where people aren't allowed to leave their houses.'

'Well, that would be okay in your house,' Lyra said, thinking about all the rooms at Auntie Liss's house they didn't even really use, and the swimming pool, and the big lawn. 'If we ever have to stay in our houses, I'll just come to yours. We could get a dog.'

Lyra and Bridge and their mum were in Bronte now. It was cool, because everything in it was new and her mum got this dreamy, smiley look every time they walked in and she looked around.

HE WOULD NEVER

It wasn't far from Auntie Liss's either. It was annoying that Lyra wasn't allowed to walk to Tia's on her own yet. Lyra walking places on her own seemed to be high on her mum's worry list. Also, they weren't allowed a dog, because they were upstairs. They had a balcony, but a dog couldn't poo on a balcony, her mum said.

The other thing her mum seemed worried about was her dad. He was supposed to be coming for a month, but everyone was talking about travel maybe becoming a problem, because of the spiky ball of snot. She'd heard her mum telling Liss that Seb was worried about getting 'stuck' here. Maybe that meant her dad would come and never go home. Which would be weird, but fine with Lyra. When Dad was home he treated her and Brigitte like it was the weekend every day – imagine months and months of ice creams and iPad time and presents just because.

'My mum thinks everyone is overreacting,' said Trick, who was poking about under a log with a stick. 'Worrying about nothing.'

'What are you doing?'

'James said there was a snake here.' Trick was on his belly, skinny little legs sticking out of the bottom of his black shorts, his chin on the scrubby ground. 'I want to see a snake.'

'No you don't,' said Tia, jumping up from where she'd been sitting cross-legged on a mossy rock and looking around with suspicion. 'Snakes bite, you idiot.'

'And James is a liar.' That was true. James was a liar. Especially this year. It seemed like James and Bob were more into teasing and playing tricks and running away than they were interested in hanging out and building secret dens. And Trick didn't seem to be invited when they ran off.

The five of them were the OG Kids. That's what their mums called them. The babies who had brought the mothers' group together. There were more kids now, but they were still all little and annoying, and the OGs were all ten now, so Liss said they could play in the forest as long as they didn't go far, and stamped their feet, and didn't make fires. The little ones still had to stay with the parents all the time.

Lyra knew that if her mum didn't like Lyra walking round the block to Tia's house in the city, she probably didn't like her disappearing into a forest either, but Auntie Liss could sometimes get her mum to agree to things she wouldn't usually. Sometimes it was like she was the boss of Lyra's mum.

'Do you want to go see if there's any chocolate in the esky?' asked Tia, her jelly snakes now just sticky memories on her gappy teeth. She was going through a mad lolly phase. Now they were ten they'd worked out where treat things were kept, how to get to them, that you could help yourself or maybe even buy stuff from the convenience store with your pocket money if the parents weren't paying attention. It was mind-blowing, really, because you realised why your mums were keeping this stuff from you. It was the only thing worth eating.

'Not until I've found the snake.' Trick gave his stick a big shove and it snapped on the craggy edge of the rock. 'James lied to me.'

'Of course he did,' said Lyra. 'Come on, let's go back.'

The weather wasn't great. They'd had a day of showers and a day of clouds, and the parents were all complaining about their beach time and their tans. Lyra didn't mind though, because when it was too hot it was hard to sleep in bed with her mum, and Brigitte always got sunburnt and whinged.

But the overcast day meant that the forest was darker than usual. The trees always blocked out the sunshine anyway, but now it felt positively gloomy as they made their way out of the clearing and back towards the caves.

Trick whistled a tuneless whine as he walked behind Lyra and Tia, waving a new stick. He loved to thrash at stuff, which made Lyra paranoid that bugs were going to fly out and into her eyes.

HE WOULD NEVER

She hated bugs, and a kid at school had told her they could lay eggs in your eyes if they got to them. This was going to be the second-last year that she and Tia were going to school together, and she didn't know who she was going to talk to about where bugs really laid their eggs once she didn't see her every day.

There was a rustle and shuffle in the scrub beside them and suddenly Lyra realised that she was seeing what she thought she was seeing. James' snake. A thick, shiny black snake sliding onto the path in front of her.

She stopped, gasped, and Tia bumped into her back. 'What?'

Trick bumped into Tia. 'What?'

Lyra couldn't talk, but she could point. It was magnificent, actually. So big and round, muscles rippling under the scales, black as black, with red curling up from its belly, the snake was crossing in front of them, and then suddenly it stopped, the whole path blocked by its length, head in the scrub to the right, tail in the scrub to the left.

'Oh my God,' Trick breathed, his stick in midair. 'It's a red-bellied black snake. They're deadly.'

Lyra's heart was pounding. 'What do we do?'

She thought about what she'd been taught about snakes. At school, on *BTN*. Stamp your feet. Never step over it. It's more afraid of you than you are of it.

It didn't look very afraid; it had just stopped there, making them wait.

'How do we make it go?'

'Maybe we could catch it?'

'We're not going to catch it, you just said it was deadly.'

'Stamp your feet.'

'We can't tell my mum about this, she'll never let us go into the forest again.'

Trick stamped his feet, as hard as he could, and the girls joined in.

The snake, as if just woken from a nap, raised its head from the bush and Tia screamed. Lyra elbowed her in the ribs but the snake heard. A rustle and a flick and it was gone as quickly as it had appeared.

'I can't believe it. James wasn't lying.'

'Let's go.'

Lyra started running, and the three of them didn't stop until they were down past the caves, into the campground and all the way to the edge of HQ. She didn't know, because she didn't look behind her, if she was the only one lifting her feet really high in case of more snakes.

It was weird, because they were expecting all the parents and all the little kids to be at camp. But things were quiet. There was no sign, as they came up the campsite's edge, of trikes and scooters and mums shouting about hats. It was quiet, the only noise coming from Ron's buzzy buggy somewhere and kookaburras shouting.

Then, as the three of them walked towards the tables and chairs and treat-filled eskies, some laughter.

'Hey there!' It was Tia's dad and Trick's mum and they were sitting in two camp chairs very close to one another, which Lyra thought was strange because there were so many empty ones all around the circle. They had drinks, the kind of drinks Lyra knew the kids weren't allowed to taste, with ice cubes and a slice of lemon. Looked like lemonade but was not.

'We saw a snake!' Trick shouted, and both the adults laughed, although it wasn't funny.

'Trick, we weren't going to tell.' Lyra shoved him.

But he wanted his mum's attention, she could tell. Wanted her eyes away from Tia's dad, to him.

'It was a red-bellied black, Mum! They're deadly.'

HE WOULD NEVER

'And it was this big.' If they were telling, Lyra wasn't going to be left out of this story. She had been the one at the front, after all. She spread her arms out as wide as they would go. Tia's dad and Trick's mum just laughed more.

'A red-belly?' Tia's dad said, a chuckle still in his voice. 'That's very impressive, kids. Did you know what to do?'

'We stamped our feet and shouted and it went away,' Tia said, quietly, looking at her father. 'I think that's what you're meant to do.'

'Good girl,' he said, and Tia's whole face seemed to split open with a smile. 'That's exactly what you're meant to do.'

'Where is everyone?' As Lyra asked this, she noticed that Trick was looking at his mum with a strange expression on his face. He was staring at the adults' knees, which were almost touching, Tia's dad in his tennis shorts, Trick's mum in her short sundress. Bare knees, like theirs.

'The little kids are riding their scooters down on the hard sand, it's low tide. You should go too.' Tia's dad's voice sounded a bit different from usual. Thicker, somehow. 'We thought we'd have a little sundowner.'

'It's not sundown,' said Trick, his face serious.

Tia's dad laughed again. Seriously, what was so funny? 'Your son's a smart boy, Sadie,' he said. 'Busted.'

Tia was edging her way around the table to where the esky with the chocolate might be.

'Go on, Tia,' her dad said. 'Grab something and run off down the beach. Tell your mothers about the snake and we'll hear the shrieks from here.'

Tia couldn't believe her luck at being given permission to get something from the lolly box. Neither could Lyra. Tia's hands went into the esky at record speed, grabbed a plastic packet and a bar wrapped in gold foil and showed them to Lyra, who nodded.

'Let's go.'

Trick was just standing there, looking at his mum. Lyra pulled at his sleeve. 'Come on, before they change their minds.'

The grown-ups were laughing again. Heads together, knees touching. The kids dashed back out onto the path, sank down behind the nearest tent and ripped open the lolly bag. Strawberries and cream.

'I don't like the way your dad's looking at my mum,' Trick said, shaking his head at the sweets. 'It's weird.'

'They're drunk,' whispered Tia, and Lyra was surprised. Did adults get drunk in the daytime? 'That's all.'

'I don't want Mum to be drunk,' Trick said. 'Who'll look after us?'

Lyra thought that was a weird thing to say. Trick could be so weird. Weren't they looking after themselves right now? They'd just fought off a snake.

And then a burst of hooting laughter from HQ, a few metres away.

'If this virus happens,' Lyra could hear Trick's mum saying, loudly, 'I wonder how you catch it. Touching? Breathing? Kissing?'

Lyra's stomach flipped and Trick's face knotted into a deeper frown. It was uncomfortable listening to the adults talking, and hearing what they were actually saying, rather than just the blah-blah sound they were usually making around the kids.

'Come on!' said Tia. 'Let's get out of here. Yuck!'

'Don't say yuck about my mum,' said Trick, his face dark.

'I'm not,' said Tia, sharply. 'It's my dad's voice, when it's like that . . .'

They stopped talking for a moment, to listen. Now it was hard to make out all the words that Lachy Short was saying, but the deep tone was like the one he used on Auntie Liss, when he was saying something nice to her and Tia would blush.

HE WOULD NEVER

'Touching, I think,' they heard him say, and then something mumbled, and then a giggle, and the noises were just so awful that they started running down towards the beach, lollies left on the ground behind HQ, running as fast as they could to tell their mothers about the snake in the grass.

29

Sunday, 2 pm

Green River Campground

Liss

There was graffiti on the inside of the cave walls. Scrawled and chiselled onto the overhanging lip of its entrance.

Sals a slut

Arc Boyz 2017

Locals only fkn tourists

There had probably once been rock art on the insides of these shelters instead of scrawled inanities, Liss thought. Symbols that meant something, signposted a food source, transferred tradition. The sitting ledge smoothed from millennia of exchanging stories; the smoke-blackened ceiling. This cave had seen a lot.

Now though, the cave was seeing two adult mothers sitting side by side, trying not to hit each other.

Liss wasn't sure why she was focusing on graffiti when her beloved best friend was sitting beside her, sobbing as if she was broken.

The anger was simmering when Dani had told Liss about her

conversation with Aiden and Ginger. Those words made it impossible for Liss not to tell Dani about what she'd seen yesterday. Lyra running from this cave. Lachy leaving behind her.

In the sheer, wild rage that followed, Liss had to grab Dani's hands and hold them down at her waist to stop her from – what? Clawing at Liss's face? Pulling her hair? Punching her? It was only the sheer difference in their size that had allowed Liss to hold her friend off, continually saying her name, until the fury broke into something else. Sadness, fear, betrayal, devastation. And then Dani had told Liss the secret she'd been keeping, that Lachy had bought and sold Green River.

And now they sat, Dani sobbing, Liss oddly numb.

'You didn't tell me,' Dani spluttered.

'And you didn't tell me,' Liss replied.

'It's really not the same.'

It had taken Dani almost two hours to find her, apparently, after she ran from her river conversation with Aiden and Ginger straight to the campsite in search of Liss, to tell her about the things her husband had said to Aiden on that long, hot slog of a morning run.

Allegedly, she wanted to add, in her head. *What her husband had allegedly said to Aiden.* But Liss knew it was true. She knew it not only because she knew Aiden, and she knew, despite his patent dislike for Lachy, that he owed her husband something. She also knew because it was exactly the kind of thing that Lachy would say, and she might have chosen not to believe, or to have laughed it off, until yesterday when she'd seen Lyra and Lachy leaving the cave. And until what Dani had just told her about the campsites.

It had taken Dani two hours to find her because Liss had driven off with the teenage girls for a few late supplies for the last-night party. Boring things, like milk. Less boring things, like chocolates and champagne. She never went on the supply runs to Arcadia. For

Liss, once she was at Green River, she stayed at Green River. Finding herself in a strip-lit shopping centre within a thirty-minute drive rather punctured the fantasy of her personal wilderness, so she left it to the others to decide if they couldn't live without another type of breakfast bread or an extra bottle. But today, she had needed to get in that car. Wanted to put some distance between herself and everyone else, and the heat, and the eyes on her.

Dani had been wild, apparently, but somehow resisted going straight to Lachy with her fury. Liss had no idea how.

Liss had felt Dani's rage the minute she and the girls climbed out of the car, Lyra and Tia clutching the skincare-spoils of an impromptu chemist visit with Liss's credit card. She had put down the milk and alcohol and felt the simmer between Dani, Ginger and Aiden, sitting around in camp chairs waiting, like animals crouched to ambush. Lachy was at the beach with the younger kids, mustering a game of cricket. Juno was making some spon-con over in the kitchen, filming herself turning two-minute noodles into ramen over a camp-stove flame. 'Boil an egg for as long as you want, and you're done!'

Liss had seen Dani's face and known. 'The caves?' she asked her friend, who gave a tiny, furious nod and followed her, offering only a restraining palm to Ginger. *Stay there.*

Now, here it was.

'You are married to a monster.' Dani's voice was thick and choked. 'You are married to a fucking monster and you've been making excuses for him all this time.'

Liss just sat, staring at *Sal's a slut*. She bet that Sal had seen that. She bet those words were for Sal's benefit. A punishment, not a warning.

'You know, you could have left him. You could afford to leave him. Does being alone look so awful? Do I make being alone look so fucking sad?'

Liss kept sitting.

HE WOULD NEVER

'I need to talk to Lyra. I need to talk to her now.' Dani didn't move. 'Why would she lie to me? Why wouldn't she tell me if there's something happening? Why wouldn't she let me protect her?' Dani's voice was devolving back into a sob.

Liss lowered her eyes from the words to the view. This cave, the one that she had seen Lyra and Lachy leave yesterday, the one she had sat in afterwards, trying to feel something, anything, about what had happened here, had a large opening out onto a scrubby patch of forest between the park and the campground. It was right on the edge of the path down to the kitchen and the toilet block, and yet it was almost completely concealed. A space where you could see people coming, but they couldn't see you. A place you could observe but not be observed. The perfect hide. When she was little, her brothers would dare her to go in here alone and try to jump out and scare them as they walked up the path. She would agree, delighted to be included in her brothers' plans, and then the boys would go off to the beach or go climb a tree and leave her sitting here, lying in wait, for hours. She felt like that now – a tiny, insignificant person, being tricked. Someone who didn't matter in the big boys' games.

'Dani, I'm just so sorry.'

Dani waved a hand, swallowed a sob.

'I'm so sorry, but we can sort this out.'

'I will not . . .' Dani was gasping through her tears, 'be doing that *with you*.'

Liss flinched. She deserved it. After today, she was going to lose everything. Her husband. The picture of a perfect family she'd been carrying around and polishing for so long. This beloved place. Her best friend. There wasn't really any alternative. Or there was, but she no longer had the stomach for it.

Still, her tears wouldn't come. She felt clear-eyed, right-headed.

'I have to find out if anything has actually happened.' Dani choked on the words. 'I have to talk to Lyra. Where are the girls?'

'Skincare haul,' Liss replied, and smiled, despite herself. She had spent the afternoon watching them skipping about through supermarket shelves and coffee shops and the aisles of a chemist lined with jars and tubes and potions. They had seemed so innocent. Young. Silly.

'For fuck's sake.' Dani was gulping, wiping her face on the back of her hand, trying to pull herself together. 'This is bullshit.'

'Dani,' Liss said, still looking out at the view, 'I'm so sorry.'

'So you've said.'

Liss knew her friend's head was whirring, that she was calculating her next move. She knew Dani wouldn't go and talk to Lyra until she was composed and calm. Dani felt the responsibility of being her girls' constantly present parent like an extra ten kilos on her back. She couldn't put it down, because what would happen then? But Liss knew she was wrong. Lyra and Brigitte had been in her kitchen, her house, her bath, her pool, her holiday home, her sacred campground for their entire lives. They had slept and played and cried and fought in her home. Liss had picked them up and dropped them off from daycare, from school, from sport and parties and trips to the mall. She had wiped tears and bums and patched knees for them. Lyra Martin, Liss felt deep inside herself, was her child too. She had done half the mothering for Dani.

And now she had to face that she may have put Lyra in danger. She wanted to kill Lachy for that.

Tia, too, of course, in a different way. She saw how her girl cowered around her father. At least, she saw it now that the scales were falling from her eyes.

HE WOULD NEVER

'I know those words aren't big enough,' Liss said, finally. 'But I need you to know something. My loyalties are not divided. My loyalties are with you and Lyra. And my kids.'

Dani sniffed, covered her face with her hands. 'I have to get myself together.'

'We do,' Liss said. 'We do.'

Lachy had managed to convince her, for decades, that she was the one thing he would always need. That he would never be successful enough, rich enough, important enough to betray her. That any other interests were safe, frivolous dalliances. She had genuinely believed, all this time, that she had the upper hand. She had believed that until . . . when? Friday night? Yesterday? Today?

Her father, making a deathbed deal with a man he hated. Her brothers, keeping it from her. Her husband, trusted, for once, with a piece of her mother's legacy. All these men, playing her.

How much were these campsites going for? That was her price, she supposed. A stupid, petty loss compared to the dread she felt for Lyra, but a stinging devastation of any remaining trust. A compounding realisation that this man was capable of anything.

'How can I not have seen this?' Liss asked, out loud. 'How can I not have understood all this?'

Dani was not going to do what Dani always did, Liss knew. She wasn't going to say, *It isn't your fault. Don't worry, it will be fine. Don't be so hard on yourself.* Dani was trying to piece her own reality back together, right alongside her.

Nothing was going to be the same after today.

'Dani,' said Liss, 'I think I know what to do next.'

'Liss, this is not one of our just-move-on moments. We can't rally around this. We can't gloss over it or leave it until tomorrow so we can have one more disco. We are so far beyond that.'

'I know, Dan, I know.'

'So what are you thinking?'

'Well.' Liss stood up, eye-to-eye with *Sals a slut* above the cave's exit. 'First, we need Juno. And we need Sadie. God knows I owe her an apology.'

30

2023, Camp Seven

Green River Campground

Sadie

Somewhere between Lockdown One and Lockdown Two, Sadie's glass had turned into a bottle.

Now, on the first weekend back at Green River since the pandemic hiatus, she could see that she was refilling her plastic tumbler twice, maybe three times as fast as the other women. She also knew it wasn't a problem; her tolerance was higher these days, that was all. So sue her. Everyone had indulged a little too much over the last two years. Now that life was almost back to normal, she'd sort it out, cut back. After the long weekend, though. This was her last hurrah.

She'd said as much to Trick, as he'd watched her load a case of her favourite red into the back of the car from under his heavy fringe.

'How many last hurrahs is that, Mum?'

'Don't be a narc, Trick. Life's hard, don't know if you've noticed. I need some little treats.'

She didn't tell him that under Lucky's unicorn squishy and his skateboard were also several bottles of Prosecco and some gin.

Although, let's face it, he probably knew. He seemed to know most things these days.

Now they were sitting on the beach after a low tide sunset, breaking first-night disco tradition with a full-moon campfire Liss had somehow wrangled permission for from Ron and Shell. Sadie was feeling safely warm and blurred around the edges as the kids collected driftwood to add to the small triangle of flames, and she watched them flitting about in the glow of it, like little jumping fleas.

She knew they'd all felt relief that everything was still here after their pandemic skip. The circle path was still rough and wide, the gums were still leaning in, breathing heavily over the campground's shorn sites. The tide was still seeping out and creeping back, just the other side of that tangled line of figs and palms. The kitchen still stood, with a toaster and kettle whose numbers and settings had worn off years before. The caves were yawning their warning mouths on the edge of the national park. Webs were spinning, mozzies were whining, Sadie's site across from the toilet block was still just a little too smelly.

For the past two years, every time it looked like the families might be able to escape to Green River, the virus would shift. A new strain. New regulations. Newly drawn borders that could not be crossed. The national park would close. The campground would close, open, shut for good. Someone got sick.

For Sadie, it was the least of her worries, whether and when they'd get back here, but Liss, she knew, had been obsessed by it.

Now Juno was going around their circle, asking everyone how 'their Covid' had been and filming the answers, and as far as Sadie could see, everyone's was better than hers.

Even Ginger, who had cancer, for fuck's sake, had all that space out there in Woop Woop, so many fewer stupid rules and restrictions on them. Liss had her mansion and her swimming pool and her beach house. Juno had become an influencer, apparently, if Trick was to be believed. And Dani had somehow found a fucking boyfriend.

Sadie wasn't really impressed, as she looked over at where Dani and Craig were sitting, his arm around her as the flames jumped and danced, her head on his shoulder and her eyes on her girls. He looked boring; he looked arrogant. He looked like Lachy Short.

'My Covid,' she'd happily told Juno, 'was absolutely fucked.'

Her physio practice could barely operate. Tightly controlled masked appointments that were almost always cancelled at the last minute were both impractical and undesirable. She'd had to give up the treatment room she was renting in a shared practice and try to make the box room in her apartment work. That meant ejecting Lucky from her bedroom, so Sadie shared her bed with her ten-year-old daughter for months, which didn't work out well for either of them. Now Lucky didn't like to be out of Sadie's sight, but also couldn't seem to stand her. It was like the kind of toxic, co-dependent relationships she'd had too many of.

Supervising remote learning was a nightmare. She didn't know if it was stress or stupidity on her part, but Sadie couldn't make it through Lucky's Year Four maths worksheets. Trick spent his entire day in headphones at the laptop his father had bought him and she couldn't say with any confidence that she knew if he was in class or watching porn. It was too much: too much expectation, too much failure, too much being inside all day with bored, angry children and glitching technology. Wine time crept a little earlier every week.

'If we ever have another pandemic,' she told Juno's phone screen, 'I'm moving in with the Shorts.'

'Not likely, Sadie,' Lachy said, coming to sit beside her. 'I couldn't handle the temptation.' The way he said it, half-joking, half-leering, was typical of the way he always spoke to her, which was different from the way he spoke to any of the other women in the Green River group.

'How was your Covid, Lachy?' Juno asked, turning her camera to him.

He smiled, looked down, looked up. 'My Covid taught me you can still make plenty of money without putting on a suit and going to an office.'

'Amen,' called Craig.

'Ugh,' said Liss, who'd come to sit beside her husband. *That's* your takeaway?'

'Yes, and that I'm happy we own two homes, both of which have pools. Our successes paid off.'

'I think you mean,' Liss said, and Sadie could hear the panic in her voice as she sensed the looks her friends were exchanging in the moon's glow, 'that you're grateful for our privilege.'

'That's not what I mean.' Lachy laughed, sipping his beer. 'But you can say that if you want to, darling.'

'I admire your honesty, brother,' said Craig, the newcomer. 'There's too much feeling guilty about success in this world. You shouldn't have to apologise for your hard work.'

Lachy raised his glass towards Dani's boyfriend, and Sadie made a little vomiting sound. 'Oh spare me,' she said, raising her cup to her lips and realising it was empty. 'You men make me want another drink. Anyone got the red?'

'Sadie is grateful,' Lachy said, steadily, 'that Covid didn't close bottle shops.'

Sadie felt a flush of shame hit her cheeks, and burn a little harder as no-one jumped in to defend her. The bottle of red, all the same, made its way back around the circle.

Sadie filled her cup and scanned for Trick, who would doubtless tell her to drink some water if he were close. He'd become such a prude lately.

'Dani?' Juno shuffled around the circle, handed Dani the camera.

Dani untangled herself from Craig. 'Do I have to do this?'

'We all do. It's a historical document,' Juno said, with dramatic flourish.

'Okay.' Sadie watched Dani, neat little Dani, purse her lips and decide what to say. She noticed, as she always did, that Lachy Short was watching her intently. He never spoke to Dani in the way he spoke to Sadie. Sometimes, she was flattered by that. Sometimes, she realised flattery wasn't his intention.

'Okay. My Covid was hard on my girls,' Dani said. 'Their dad lives overseas, they saw him once in two years. That was tough.'

'But so are you,' Craig interjected.

'I learned I am flexible.'

A coughing laugh from Craig, which made Dani, Sadie noticed, visibly cringe.

'Because at work we changed everything. It made me proud of how resilient my girls are. But most of all . . .' She raised her glass to Liss. 'It made me grateful I live in the same postcode as my best friend, so we could bubble.'

Sadie's head swam with red mist. She lived one postcode over, and yet, she'd barely heard from Liss or Dani or any of the Green River group during lockdown. No single-mum care packages appeared on her doorstep. No invites to socially distanced al-fresco drinks at the beach, the park, someone's garden. She'd been surprised, if she was honest with herself, when the old mothers' group chat fired up again, with talk of when they might finally get back here, to Green River. She didn't know if she was part of this circle anymore. Or if she wanted to be, when it felt she was so secondary, and she felt so second-rate in their presence. Fuck them.

She pushed herself up off the sand. 'Going to look at the moon,' she said to the group. She didn't think she slurred when she said it, but she noticed a couple of heads turn her way.

The kids were scattered across the beach. Little ones near the fire, poking its base with sticks, scrapping over the few remaining marshmallows, rolling around in the warm evening air. Some of the teens were gathered near the shoreline, phones up towards the full moon. Where was Trick?

Gosh, it was hard to walk on the soft sand. Harder than she remembered when they'd walked down here. Maybe it was deeper near the waterline. She kept going, needing to put distance between herself and the others. Fucking Dani, bringing her boyfriend, boasting about her Covid bubble buddies. What an incestuous mess that was. One day, she was going to tell someone what she'd seen that day on the beach, however many years ago. Three? Four? She was sick of pretending these people were so perfect . . .

'Sadie, where are you going?'

It sounded like Lachy's voice. She turned around, and it took a moment to focus, further away from the fire and the torches, the only light the moon's steady spotlight. It was Lachy, looming in the dark. She often forgot how tall he was. It was rare she needed to look up into someone's face.

'To look at the moon,' she said, careful to round out and finish every word. 'Bit of peace.'

'The moon's everywhere, Sadie,' Lachy said, and he stepped towards her, reached for her arm and closed his hand around it, as if he was steadying her, but she didn't need steadying. 'Don't go wandering off into the dark.'

He was looking right at her. Into her, somehow.

'The others sent me to bring you back.'

HE WOULD NEVER

'Ha!' Sadie felt her red mist rolling back in. 'Worried about me, are they? All the perfect people?'

'Sadie, come on.' Lachy took another step. He was much closer than other men with wives would stand to a single woman. She was an expert in this, after all, being viewed as a threat or a warning, in a sea of couples. She had never liked coupledom. She knew men couldn't be trusted, just look at her father. She knew that the wife-guys at the school gates weren't what they seemed when they were alone with you. She knew that Lachy Short was just another one of those.

'Why do you always look at me like that?' she asked.

'Like what?' asked Lachy, while looking at her exactly like that.

'You don't look at Dani like that, and you love Dani.'

'Sadie, you're drunk, I think you mean Liss.'

'I know what I mean.' Sadie dropped her wineglass on the sand. It was too dark to see it, but she knew the dark red stain would be spreading out onto the lighter sand, making a mark like a bloodstain.

'You've always been different,' Lachy said. He was still too close. She could smell him, even out here with the salt of the river and the dirty edge of the seaweed underneath. She could smell his skin, a sort of clean, gritty smell. And she could look right at his mouth as it moved, those full lips. 'Not like any of the other women.'

Sadie stepped forward. They were now so close that their arms, their chests, were almost touching. She looked over to where the others were still sitting around the fire, doubtless still swapping stories of their not-so-bad Covids. None of them seemed to be looking this way.

'Are you okay?' Lachy Short asked her, but his voice was warm and teasing. He let go of her arm.

'I know you,' Sadie said, leaning in a little more. 'And men like you.'

'You do, do you?'

'You want to fuck me. You always have.'

'I do, do I?' Again, with the teasing tone.

'Stop pretending you don't.' As she said it, Sadie put a hand on Lachy's chest, as if to push him backwards but somehow instead of pushing, she grabbed a handful of his polo shirt in her fist, and pulled this big man, with his big, shit-eating grin, even closer to her. He let himself be pulled.

'You should kiss me,' she said. Moment to moment, she wasn't sure what she wanted. She wasn't sure who she was talking to, even. Or how long they'd been here. But in this moment, she wanted this big, tall man to kiss her. To want to kiss her. Like he wanted to kiss Dani. And Liss. But also Dani. 'See if it's like you think it is.'

'Sadie,' Lachy said. 'My wife is over there.'

'I don't think that's stopped you before.' Sadie was surprised at what she said, and she was surprised to find herself pulling him to her, her hands pulling on his clothes now. She was surprised how easily she could stand just a tiny bit taller and kiss him, getting her lips on his, feeling his beery breath, the slight stubble of his chin. She pulled him in and didn't want to let go. She wanted to put his hands on her body. She grabbed a hand, pushed it into her breast. 'It didn't stop you with Dani,' she found she was muttering, as she pressed her mouth onto his.

And then she felt his hands on her and she was confused for a moment, in the muddle of the wine sloshing around her mind, on why he wasn't pulling her in, but pushing her back.

'Sadie, stop,' he said, loudly, a moment after he'd shoved her away. 'Stop!' It was a shout.

She felt for a moment like she was falling far. The sensation of hitting the sand, so much harder than it looked. Slamming into the ground with her bottom, her lower back. It took a moment for everything to clear, and then she realised the moon's spotlight would pick her out sprawled on the sand. Her hair everywhere, her shirt yanked up, her mouth red, her eyes wet.

'Sadie, are you okay?' a man's voice asked. It was Aiden, maybe. She didn't want to open her eyes, the realisation of what she'd just done piercing the fog in her brain.

'Sadie! Are you alright?' It was Liss. They were all coming. 'Lachy, what happened?'

Lachy's voice, the mocking edge still there. 'She fell. Just a little overzealous on the wines tonight, right, Sadie?'

Who saw?

'Mum?' Trick's voice. And the tone of it. Shock and shame and worry. She didn't ever want her son's voice to sound like that. 'Mum. Get up.'

31

Sunday, 4 pm

Green River Campground

Lyra

Trick thinks hes so dark
  I know rite

Lyra put her phone down on the log next to her as Trick re-emerged from the dark green of the forest, back to where the girls were lying on the mossy ground of the clearing, feeling the sun find its way to them through the shade of the canopy.

'Golden tops,' he was saying, 'are the ones you want, but it's totally the wrong time of year.'

'As if you know what you're talking about,' Lyra said, extending a pointed foot towards Tia and poking lightly at her thigh. 'There's no way your Bay High friends are doing mushrooms.'

'You underestimate me, Lyra Martin.' Trick came to sit as close to her as he dared.

She'd figured out now that Lachy Short had probably been right, and Trick did *like* her like her. And she couldn't decide if she liked that or not.

HE WOULD NEVER

She spent so long looking at her own face these days. They all did, it was just there staring out of her phone all the time, and Lyra couldn't really see what she looked like anymore. Well, she could see what was wrong with her face. How you could see her pores. And she had these weird dark patches on her cheeks. And her nose was too big. But the only way to tell if you did look at all decent was in knowing what other people thought of what you looked like. Working that out through people like Trick, she guessed, was better than through people like Lachy Short.

So it was interesting, seeing how Trick acted and what he would do. It was like learning the cheat notes for how to tell if a boy liked you, and what they would do if they did. If they were Trick, they would try extra hard to be funny, or deep, and they would hang around you but not so close that they wouldn't care if they bumped into you. Trick, she could tell, would care a lot if he bumped into her.

And after the conversation she had just had to sit through with her mum and Auntie Liss, the idea of any person wanting to touch her felt very dangerous.

'I'm worried your mum's going to come and find us again,' Tia said, grabbing Lyra's probing toe. 'She's so mad.'

'Can you even imagine what's happening back there right now?'

She and Tia had been taking snaps of their newly unboxed chemist haul when both their mums came right into Lyra's tent and started asking more questions. They were all about Tia's dad and they were ten times worse than the ones her mum had been asking yesterday.

The words they wanted to hear were sort of stuck in Lyra's throat. Like she couldn't drag them out, and then Auntie Liss had lowered her voice, tilted her head while Lyra's mum covered her face in her hands and Liss said, 'I want you to know that whatever has happened, no-one blames you and you are not going to get into trouble.'

Pause. No-one said that kind of thing unless they definitely blamed you and you were definitely going to get into trouble.

'Did Lachy do anything to you in that cave yesterday afternoon?'

And that question kind of blew everything open. Lyra knew, then, that Auntie Liss had been the person outside the cave. The one she'd tried to pretend she imagined.

'Or any other time?' Lyra's mum added, pulling her hands away from her face which Lyra kind of wished she hadn't. She just looked so worried, and so sad, and Lyra knew she had failed, again, to make her mum's life easier, not harder.

Lyra knew what they were asking her. She knew the answer was no. She also knew that it didn't mean there was nothing weird or scary about the things Tia's dad did, and she didn't really know how to say that. Especially with Tia sitting right there. She thought the adults should have figured out a way to let Tia leave. It really wasn't any fun hearing people talk shit about your dad, Lyra knew.

'Lyra?' her mum had pushed.

'No, he's never done anything bad,' she said, and watched the women exchange a look. Maybe they understood. Or maybe they didn't believe her. 'He's never touched me, or anything.' And then she remembered Friday, and it was confusing again. 'Except when we were dancing, and Auntie Sadie saw.'

It made Lyra want to disappear even thinking about saying that now. It had made her mum put her face in her hands again.

'I didn't lie to you,' she said. 'When you asked me. I just didn't know, wasn't sure . . . I'm sorry.'

Auntie Liss had done her head tilt thing again. 'You don't need to be sorry, Lyra. Like I said, you've done nothing wrong.'

But the truth was, when Liss had told her that she had seen Lyra and Lachy leaving the cave, Lyra had felt a flood of relief. First of all that she wasn't going crazy for feeling like someone had been there.

HE WOULD NEVER

And then she'd felt relief at telling them the truth. And then she'd felt relief at their faces, even though they were sad. Because they were expecting something worse. Which was so gross.

Honestly, adults could be so disgusting. Lachy Short was an old man.

So she told them the truth-truth. That she didn't know what happened, that she was confused about it. But also that, yes, Lachy Short's hand had done those things that Auntie Sadie said. Lyra just didn't know what it meant, or whether to make a fuss. Everyone was so . . . *much* about it all. She didn't want all that.

Her mum continued being a mess. Which Lyra hated but was also a little bit relieved about. Even her mum didn't have it all together. That was the truth, too. And she'd cried, which Lyra hated but, again, it was kind of nice that she was so upset.

Tia, though. Tia was being really weird. Now she suddenly sat up on the forest floor. 'Will you take my hair out?' And she shook her head so her braids swung. 'I don't want it anymore.'

'It took me ages!' Lyra was annoyed, but also, she couldn't blame her, they did look kind of basic, and she wasn't sure why Tia had wanted her to do them in the first place.

'Yeah, I'm sorry.'

The girls shuffled themselves together, Lyra sitting up on the log throne, as they called it, and Tia slipping in between her knees. She could feel Trick watching them.

'You girls are so dumb,' he said. *Another way to identify if a boy likes you*, Lyra thought. *Insults*. Which was so stupid because no-one liked insults. 'Worrying about braids when dead-set your parents are about to divorce.'

'What?'

'Well, don't you think your mum is going to drop your dad after all that?'

Tia went quiet. Pulled out her phone.

I hate him.

Lyra's hands were full of Tia's hair, but she saw the message flash up beside her where her phone rested on the tree.

'Who?' Lyra wasn't sure, did she mean Trick?

Dad.

'Shut up, Trick,' Lyra said. 'You weren't even there.'

'It's a *campsite*, Lyra, everyone can hear.'

He's ruined everything

'Your mum can't stay with your dad if he's a pedo.' Trick was talking to them but looking down at something he was turning over in his hands.

'He's not a pedo!' Tia snapped.

'Are you sure? Because it sounds like what he's been doing with Lyra is *grooming*.'

'Shut up, Trick,' said Lyra. She'd heard about grooming at school. Was that what Lachy Short was doing? Showing an interest? Buying her presents? Winning her trust, her mum had said. Yes. All of that.

'You know,' Trick said, moving a little bit closer, squatting near where Tia's legs were straight out in front of her. 'My mum does some fucked-up stuff.' He stopped himself. '*Did* some fucked-up stuff.'

The girls both looked at him. They knew, of course, that this was true. Lyra, unpicking a tiny, thin braid, looked back down at it. 'That must suck.'

'It did.' Trick held up the thing in his hand. A long, thin silver vape pen. 'It's weed,' he said. 'I swiped it from James.'

Lyra laughed. 'James is an idiot.'

'I think they're in the rainforest, looking for it. He dropped it near that fig tree.'

'He's going to kill you if he finds out you've got it,' Tia told him.

'I'm not scared of James and Bob,' said Trick. 'Meatheads.'

HE WOULD NEVER

Lyra looked up at Trick, who was looking at her when he said that, just as she knew he would be.

'Should we have some?'

'No,' said Tia.

'Maybe,' said Lyra, and Tia immediately looked up at her. 'Hey, keep still!' Tia looked back down.

NO WAY, Tia texted. *Mums all over us*

That was true.

'Stop texting each other. It's rude.' Trick sounded like a whiny little boy.

'It's easier, isn't it,' Lyra said. 'Talking is awkward.'

'Tragic but true.' Trick put the vape pen back in his pocket. Pulled out his phone.

Both the girls' phones buzzed at once.

Should we get hi tho?

Lyra laughed. She couldn't help herself.

'I think,' she said, a worried feeling fluttering in her stomach, 'maybe we're a bit stressed out for that. A bit . . . paranoid.'

Trick pondered, made a little *hmm* sound.

Relax us?

'No,' Tia said, frustrated. 'I hate my dad. I don't think getting high's going to fix that.'

I hate your dad too. It was Trick.

'Yeah, I guess I'm on board with that.' Lyra tried to remember what it was that had made Lachy mad with Sadie, or the other way around. He always talked about her like she was disgusting or something. It was horrible, really. 'Your dad's caused a lot of drama.'

'At least he pays you attention,' said Tia. 'That must be nice.'

Lyra didn't know what to say to that. She squeezed Tia's shoulders and kept going on the braids.

'He thinks I'm boring,' Tia went on. 'And ugly.'

'Whoa,' said Trick. 'That's a lot, Tia.'

'It's true.' Lyra had never heard Tia talk like this before. Tia didn't talk a lot about her dad, and Lyra sometimes wondered if it was because she felt bad, because Lyra's dad wasn't around. 'He makes me feel stupid. And he's embarrassing, but he thinks it's everyone else who's embarrassing. And . . .' Tia's voice faltered, and Lyra stopped playing with the plaits and just rested her hands on her friend's shoulders, hoping she could feel them like a hug. 'My mum doesn't deserve this. She's a good mum.'

'She is,' Lyra agreed.

'She's not *that* nice,' Trick said, but both the girls whipped around and glared at him so fast he put his hand up in surrender. 'Okay, okay, she's pretty nice.'

'What's it like,' Tia asked, tipping her head up to look at Lyra, 'to get my dad's attention?'

Lyra really wished Tia hadn't asked her that. She thought about it for a minute. 'Uncomfortable.'

'Yeah.'

There was a silence again. Only the birds and the leaves in the wind.

'So that's a no on the weed vape then,' said Trick, putting it back in his pocket.

'For the best,' said Lyra, going back to Tia's hair.

'What do you think they're going to do?' Tia asked, looking down at her fingers and thumbs, which she was turning around each other in her lap.

'The mums?'

'All the adults. Do you think we're all going home?'

Lyra looked up at the sky, above the trees. It was beginning to turn a little goldy. 'I think they would have done that by now,' she said.

I dont think I can go back there, Tia texted. *So cringe*

HE WOULD NEVER

'Worse than cringe.'

I wish he wasn't around

'Maybe they'll ask him to go,' Lyra said. 'Maybe they'll throw him out.'

Is life easier without a dad?

At that message Lyra and Trick looked at each other. It was weird, Lyra knew, that they had that in common. Bob, too, but that was different.

'We have dads,' said Trick. 'They're just not the main event. But I think maybe a lot of families are like that.'

Tia nodded.

'I wouldn't have said this,' Trick went on, 'if you hadn't said you hated him, but once I thought maybe I might kill your dad.'

Lyra laughed. It was such a stupid, dramatic thing to say, she didn't even look up from Tia's almost-done head.

'Why?' asked Tia, and she wasn't laughing, which freaked Lyra out a bit.

'My mum,' said Trick, shrugging and picking at some dirt on his black jeans. 'After last year, she had a breakdown. I had to go live with my dad. And then there was all this therapy shit and she's had to try so hard and work so hard and I see it on her face all the time, like she doesn't think she should be here, or that it's too hard to be here and . . . it's your dad's fault, I think.'

How?

'How what?'

How would you kill him?

'Tia, don't be so dramatic, he's joking.' Lyra laughed again, although actually what Trick had said made her really uncomfortable, and a bit scared. And sad for Auntie Sadie, who was always so lovely to her.

'Don't know,' said Trick, straight-faced. 'All my ideas were terrible. I don't think I'm cut out to be a master criminal.'

Surprise.

Lyra's mum had told them they had to be back at camp at five. Lyra felt sick about what might happen when they got back there. Everyone would look at her. Would she have to speak in front of people? Would she have to speak to Lachy? She really hoped they had asked him to go.

'It would be easier if he wasn't there,' she said, and tapped Tia's shoulders. 'It's finished, shake it out.'

And she did, her mousy curls falling back around her shoulders, all angles and waves. 'Better.'

Then Tia bent back down to her phone and began to type another message.

Lyra and Trick's phones both pinged. This time, Lyra picked it up first.

Trick. What happened to your grandad?

32

Sunday, 8 pm

Green River Campground

Lachy

Thank fuck this is the last time, Lachy Short thought, fastening a flimsy, bright pink button, that he would ever have to put on a loud Hawaiian shirt and pretend to enjoy the company of his wife's terrible friends.

Thank fuck this place would not exist this time next year.

Thank fuck all that drama with crazy Sadie was forgotten, that tool Craig had been dispatched and Lyra Martin had kept her silly little mouth shut.

Just one more night, a few more hours, and everything was going to be, as his father would have said, roses.

Or was it gravy? Lachy squinted into the misted mirror over this disgusting public-bathroom sink and tried to conjure his father's voice.

His dad didn't live long enough to see this iteration of his eldest son. Which was a real pain, because Lachy had listened to plenty of shitty feedback about the other versions. The schoolboy who was never quite good enough to be an automatic pick for the first fifteen, the late-developing skinny teen who sometimes still wanted his mum, the student who wasn't smooth enough with the chat to convince those 'lady teachers' to give him top marks, the young man who hoped that finance would be an approved choice, only to be told it was a business for cowards in suits. All that bullshit.

He heard his father's voice that time he'd managed to get him to come and see his city apartment. The one he was living in when he met Liss, all sharp edges and conspicuous consumption. He had been so proud of that place when he'd moved in. A visual representation of being better than the average, with their sad little suburban three-beds. But he'd got that wrong, too. 'You're an idiot,' Dad had boomed, his voice bouncing off the shiny finishes. 'Invest in bricks and mortar, space, a garden, something you can build on. This is just a poofter's palace.'

Yeah, thanks, Dad.

This version of Lachy, though. The house, the wife, the family, the money. Answering to no-one, soon enough. Surely his dad would have admitted that this version was doing okay. You know, if you didn't mention the camping.

Sometimes you've got to give to get, Dad. Sometimes. Even you.

Gravy.

Lachy ran a hand over his hair and smiled into the mirror. He looked good. Some of his mates the same age – and bloody Aiden, of course – were really losing it around the edges. Thinning hair, soft bodies. That wasn't going to be him, because discipline shows up in everything you do, and your will was all you had. Lachy told Ollie that all the time, but so far his son just looked at him blankly and went back to sketching, or reading, or playing one of those imaginary building game things. So much of Liss in that one. Too much, really, for a boy.

HE WOULD NEVER

It was time for the last hurrah.

Lachy left the toilet block and headed back to HQ to grab another beer and swing his wife around what they all pretended was a dance-floor. She deserved to enjoy this, the final trip to Green River, even if she didn't know that's what it was.

There she was. Liss could have made more of an effort since he was wearing this ridiculous shirt. She had that long floaty skirt that didn't show off enough of her legs over the one-piece swimsuit she should have thrown out years ago. It didn't do much for her boobs, which were still pretty great, truth be told. It wasn't like she couldn't afford a new bikini, but this entire weekend was an indulgence of Liss's sentimental side, and the outfit was part of it.

She was smiling at him, though. She had this big, generous pink mouth, his wife, and those lips being happy to see him was one of the absolute pleasures of his life.

'Come, dance!' she said, waving her hand over her head. 'I want to dance with my husband!'

There was a moment earlier today when Lachy thought maybe he'd fucked it. He sensed something had shifted in the atmosphere when he'd brought the kids up from their afternoon cricket game. An edge with Aiden and Ginger maybe. A side-eye from some of those cocky teenagers. But then Liss and Dani had come back from whatever pow-wow they'd been having off in the rainforest, the latest in a long line of far too many peace talks, in his opinion, and everything had been smiles and rainbows again. He didn't know what had to happen between these women for them to finally see that these long weekends had become an empty charade.

Anyway, what he'd been worried about, that maybe he'd been a bit too frank with Aiden on that excuse for a run this morning, turned out not to be true. Which he should have known, because Aiden didn't have the balls to talk out of turn. Because Lachy had got him that promotion at Lochs, of course, and also because men like Aiden knew their place in the pack.

Dinner was done and cleared away. 'Everything Platters', what they always ate on the final night. 'Leftovers' is what Lachy Short would have called them, the rubbish no-one had wanted all weekend, laid out as if it were a sumptuous banquet. Interesting how there was never any of the aged wagyu he paid for every year left over for Sunday night. Hilarious. He played along for Liss. Like when she'd asked him to stop bringing the really good wine because it was making the others uncomfortable. Really? They hadn't looked that uncomfortable drinking it.

That's what marriage was though, wasn't it? Working out a way to get what you wanted while convincing your partner they were getting what they wanted. He had known, since the minute he found Liss at the party he only went to to meet her, that it was time for a wife and she was the perfect choice. He also knew he was going to have to spend a lot of energy making her feel like she was in control, which suited the part of him that liked a challenge. It was a testament to her that it had taken him this long to finally learn how to outplay her.

He grabbed a cold beer from the nearest open esky and took a swig as he looped an arm around his wife's waist and kissed her neck.

'Happy?' he asked her.

'Very.' She swayed into him, pushing her bum against his thigh in a way she knew made him a bit wild. 'All my people are here.'

She threw an expansive arm out to the crowd. The teenagers hovering around the perimeter, ordered to be here by their mothers, heads down to the glowing lights of their phones. Smaller kids jiggling to the music, which appeared to be some sort of hellish girl-pop angst set to a techno beat.

Sadie was leaning against the cold barbecue, talking into Juno's ever-present phone for whatever pointless video she was making now.

The woman was bold enough to be dressed in head-to-toe flamingo pink for the last night party, jabbering away as if she wasn't the same person who had tried, more than once, to destroy Lachy's family. It was a shame that Sadie was such a mess, because back at that first birthday party in Centennial Park, when he'd met all these people for the first time, blissfully ignorant that they were going to become permanent fixtures in his life, he had thought she was the Hot One. Tall and loud and confident. She was like a less cultured version of Liss. Happier to wear something a bit slutty, drink too much and flash you a little peek. He'd known then that all that 'I don't need a man' stuff was bullshit. And he was right. Because look at her now.

It was one of the things that made these weekends bearable, really, flirting with Sadie, reeling her in, pushing her out, trying to spike a little jealousy in Dani. It was sport, until she got too messy and then it was just sad.

He wasn't proud of how he'd handled that, last year. But he couldn't believe Covid hadn't killed this weekend off, and he'd really, really hoped that Sadie trying to fuck him in front of the entire camping party might just do it. The fact she was back this year, and had made it through to Sunday night, was testament to his wife's unfathomable capacity for forgiveness. Also known as doormat disease.

The night was hotter than yesterday. Every day the heat and stink and godforsaken insect population multiplied. He knew his wife saw tropical romance where he saw soul-sapping humidity and the potential for Ross River Fever. Imagine, he thought, when this was a complex of twenty air-conditioned condos, with a hatted restaurant and a riverside cocktail bar. He might actually want to come back then. Although, probably not.

He couldn't quite believe his luck that Liss had dropped the ball so badly after her father's death. His old foe. The man he'd most enjoyed proving wrong. It was Michael Gresky's fault that Lachy had no claim on the Bronte house. It was Michael Gresky's fault that Liss had a pre-nup when no-one else in Australia did. And it was Michael Gresky's fault, Lachy knew deep down, that Green River was even a thing for Liss. Some kind of siren call to a time before she had lost her mother, when she had the kind of father who got muddy and delighted in your giggles as he threw you up in the air to catch you with safe hands. Before he was bitter and uptight and status-obsessed. At least, that was Liss's version of the story. Lachy suspected that Michael Gresky had always been a cunt.

The kind of cunt who would sell his daughter's dream from under her to a man he couldn't stand. He had asked Lachy what he was going to do with the sites and Lachy had told him – whatever the hell he wanted, once all the legals were out of the way.

Maybe Liss's defences were down. After all these years of making sure what was hers was hers and what was Lachy's was also hers, she had completely trusted him when it came to dealing with her father's estate. An uncharacteristic lapse that was going to cost her. But if Lachy played it right, and he was playing it so right so far, she would likely never know he had anything to do with Green River Dreaming. And oh, how she was going to hate that name.

That was too bad, but she loved this place too much. Chose it over him, it felt like. He wasn't going to stand for that.

'Enjoy tonight, Lachy!' Juno called over to him, holding her phone up.

Lachy performed for the camera, giving a little bicep flex and shoulder shake in his silly flowery shirt. *Give the ladies what they want.*

'Might be the last one, hey?' she yelled, raising a glass. Lachy thought he caught Liss giving her a sharp look as she said it, but Juno just laughed. 'I mean, YOLO, who knows what tomorrow brings.'

Juno said all kinds of shit. Americans.

HE WOULD NEVER

Ginger was dancing with some of the kids, spinning around in her full cowgirl gear, standard dress-up for country bumpkins. She had no idea, of course, that the farm-saving pay rise Aiden had got from that promotion was all down to him. *Don't say I never do anything for anyone*, Lachy thought, as he watched Aiden swinging their youngest in circles, her hair and skirt flying, a grin as big as her head. *I like people to get what they want.*

He was feeling nostalgic knowing this was the end of an era. Or several eras. There was the era when Emily wasn't talking to him because of that whole misunderstanding with the baby doctor. He thought he'd been clear that he wanted to be the donor, not just the fixer. And although he knew Liss hated the idea, he'd done his best to go around her and make it happen with the girls. His wife, though, wasn't always a doormat, and that was one of those times she'd put her foot down. He was the good husband for taking the fall, although it did get him out of that wedding.

Liss kissed him on the mouth and spun away, leaving him lightly jigging, surveying the scene, finishing his beer. He'd like to dance with his daughters, he thought. Like a good dad, rounding out another family weekend. Where were they?

Well, there was Dani. She was talking to the teenage girls, to Lyra and Tia, and the three of them, heads leaned in together on the edge of the party, looked almost the same age. When Lachy had met the women, and decided Sadie was the Hot One, he had not yet understood the extent of Dani.

She, actually, was what kept him up at night. The grit in his oyster. Another of his dad's sayings, he was sure. Or was it the spit in his beer?

I'm going over there, he thought. *I'm going to dance with my daughter.* He saw Tia raise her eyes to him and quickly look away. She was a disappointment, really. He didn't like to say so, he certainly wouldn't say so, but he didn't understand his oldest. She didn't have any oomph about her. Wasn't as beautiful as her mother, didn't have Liss's easy way with people, either. Liss was the kind of wife you wanted if you were a bit of a prick. The kind who made people like you, made your home more welcoming, knew how to bring people together, how to talk to a billionaire or a bum. She liked to think she was wild around the edges, but deep down, Liss was just a northern beaches princess, a trophy as well as a challenge. Tia wasn't like that, and she didn't have his edge, either. It was like she was scared of him, and Jesus, he knew what it was to be scared of your father and he'd never given her reason to shrink in his presence. Good dad, he was.

Lachy bent down to scoop up another beer, chipped it on the table's edge to flip off the top and broke into the gang of three. 'Hello, ladies,' he said, with an exaggerated dip of the head. 'I would love the honour of a dance.'

Tia looked down. Lyra looked away. Dani looked right at him. Chin up, a challenge in her eyes. 'Looking beautiful tonight, Dani,' he said. She was, of course. Always. Tiny, tidy little dark thing. She was in a bright green floaty top and pants, a stripe of taut skin showing at her middle. Discipline and will. She was like him. It was part of what drove him completely mad about her. That, of course, and the fact she could see right through him. That his wife loved her too much. And she didn't want a bar of him.

'Well, thank you, Lachy,' she said, her eyes glittering in a way he hadn't seen for a while. 'I'm not quite at dancing stage, but I'll get there.' She raised her glass to him. Her smile was as sparkly as her eyes. It must be because she'd got rid of that drip Craig. Thank God. Not quite as painful as the Frenchman, but maybe that was because it was always clear to Lachy that Dani didn't really give a shit about Craig, in the way she had about Seb.

Maybe all hope was not lost that one day he would get what he wanted, what he deserved, from Dani. And if not, well, he had

Lyra Martin in his pocket. She would come in useful one day, he just knew it, fatherless little thing that she was. A perfect pawn for payback. He just had to be more careful than he was on Friday night, losing himself for a second in the memory of that day in the storm on the beach. Discipline.

These women. They had no idea, with their sisterhood, and their boundaries, and their belief that together they were stronger and all that bullshit. They had no idea that he had them all played.

'Tia, come dance.' He put his beer down on the table, grabbed his daughter's arm, thought he saw Dani flinch a little. 'We'll get Gracie and your mum, make it a family thing.'

Lyra Martin turned away and Dani with her, after giving Tia a patronising smile that seemed to him entirely unnecessary. Were they pitying her for having to dance with her father?

Lachy spotted little Gracie across the floor, raiding a rogue chip packet, hand in almost up to her elbow. 'Grace, put down the salty fat and come dance with us,' he bellowed, enjoying this display of expansive fatherhood. He turned back to his beer, took a big swig. The three of them stepped into the middle of the dancefloor as Madonna's 'Holiday' pumped out of the little shit speaker.

Where was Liss? To complete the picture, put the finishing touch on the portrait of this nonsense camping era. Of pretending they were ordinary people, like Ginger, like Aiden, who he could see now, holding his younger daughter in his arms, swaying and watching Lachy with an expression he couldn't quite read.

'You alright, mate?' he called, and Aiden smiled and nodded slowly. Juno had the camera up, of course, filming each dancer in turn.

'Show us your best moves!' she called, and Sadie stepped up, water bottle in hand, and dropped it like it was hot. Embarrassing.

He saw, in the darkness, beyond the edge of HQ, Sadie's weird son Trick standing back, watching, not even looking at his phone.

He was probably hoping Lyra would dance so he could perve, that little creep.

His girls moved alongside him, Tia looking like she was sucking a lemon, Gracie jumping up and down on her tiptoes. 'I don't want to go home tomorrow, Daddy,' she said.

'Liss!' he called out, scanning again for his wife. She could bring Ollie in, Juno could capture the perfect family moment.

Lachy Short spun around, feeling like the man his father had always dreamed of being. Rich. Loved. Respected. Feared.

He grabbed his beer from the table, took another thirsty chug.

And everything went black.

33

Sunday, 8.30 pm

Green River Campground

Dani

It was the noise.

Even under the music, under the shouting insects and the chattering children, Dani could hear the strangled scream as it went up. And Dani could see it coming out of Lachy Short's mouth, because she'd been watching him just before he fell.

An intense flash of surprise, a mouth forming an O, a hand to a throat – a split second before Lachy collapsed.

And then, when he fell to the floor, legs pumping, Lachy's hands kept flying to his neck, as if trying to pull at a tightening scarf. Then he stopped. And the next noise was everyone else's screams.

Tia and Gracie stepped back, Grace's little hands to her mouth as adults rushed in. It had taken Dani a moment to move from her spot. She was with Lyra, after all, which was where she wanted to be, now, before, always. Where had she been, all the other times? But Lyra seemed calm and Dani touched her daughter's hands. 'Get Tia and Gracie out of here,' she said.

Somehow, in that strange swirl of time moving at all different speeds – the slow motion of a big, heavy body falling to the ground, the rush of panic at hearing breath so hard fought for, the shock of trying to understand just what it was they were seeing – Dani had a moment where she looked up and caught Liss's eyes. Her friend was standing, just back from a kitchen run, a clutch of soft drinks in her hands, her face a frozen mask, her mouth open.

Of course, their eyes seemed to say, in that second. *Of course this happens now.*

Tomorrow Lachy Short was going to be exposed. Dani and Liss had come out of the cave and found Sadie and Juno. A walk to Liss's fig tree. Truth-telling in low voices among the ancient roots and branches. A hunt through Juno's phone. A call to Dani's boss, a man six degrees of separation from every major property deal in the state. Another call, to a locksmith. Another to Liss's lawyer, from the same trusted firm who'd drawn up her mother's will all those years ago.

It was astounding what these women could set in motion in one hour on a Sunday afternoon, now that they could see clearly.

Tomorrow Liss would leave Lachy Short. He would be locked out of his home. He would find that the developer deal for Green River was under review. A sale perhaps secured by illegal means. He would see the footage buried in the background of Juno's film of Emily dancing on Friday night. Dani had barely been able to look at it, his hands on Lyra's skin, his face at her daughter's neck. He would be told this would be taken to the police. To his professional partners. That Lyra was no longer keeping his secrets. The gifts. The texts. The hands.

Tomorrow Liss and Dani and their children would start a new chapter. And all they'd had to do was to keep Lachy Short calm and happy for one more night, for him not to suspect a thing as they pulled it all together.

HE WOULD NEVER

And now, this.

Time collapsed back on itself, back to Liss's bottles hitting the floor and she and Dani running towards him.

By the time Dani had reached Lachy, still squirming on the dusty plastic sheet of the floor, his eyes were bulging and his lips were swollen. He seemed to be gasping for breath and finding only whispers.

Who had been standing over him? Sadie, Ginger.

'It looks allergic,' Ginger was saying. 'Lachy, can you hear me? We're going to need an ambulance, who's got a phone?'

Of course, they all did.

But before those calls could be made, Lachy took in a huge jagged breath and pushed out a growl. He was rising, pushing the hands away. Shoving. Throwing. Dani felt herself fly backwards, her back hitting the metal side of the table in a spike of pain, her head smashing into the ground.

She watched Lachy Short pull himself up to one knee, to standing, and then stop, panting like a racehorse. His face was illuminated by a lantern swinging from the centre of the makeshift roof, his eyes spinning, unable to focus on anything. His forehead was wet with sweat, the muscles in his neck were twitching. He looked dangerous.

It went quiet. The children's crying faded to soft whimpers. The mothers backed away to stand in front of them. Aiden's feet stepped in front of Dani's eyes. Liss ran to crouch beside her.

'Lachy, mate.' It was Aiden, his voice breathless but calm. 'Are you okay?'

He sounded concerned, but his stance, Dani could see, was one of defence. He was standing between this wild-eyed man and the women and children who had, moments ago, been trying to save Lachy Short.

'What?' it sounded like Lachy shouted. 'Whaaat?'

Liss, one hand on Dani, tried to speak from her position on the floor. 'Lachy, you need to calm down,' she said, with as much authority as she could muster, her voice trembling. 'Let Ginger check you out.'

Her husband did not appear to hear.

The pain in Dani's head was making her close an eye, although perhaps not by choice. But even with only one open, she could see that Lachy was vibrating.

She heard Emily saying to the children, 'Let's go to the kitchen, kids. Let's just walk calmly to the kitchen together. It's going to be fine.'

And then Lachy roared again. Did he charge, like a bull? It felt like he did, as everyone screamed again, and there was a thunk of bodies hitting each other as he flew past Juno, who was filming, phone raised, into Aiden, through Aiden maybe, towards where, Dani would learn later, Tia and Lyra and Trick were standing tightly together, watching everything.

She saw Aiden on the ground, and Lachy Short running, stumbling, charging towards the beach path and then veering into the rainforest, the sound of him crashing through the trees audible over the music that was still playing, as if everything that had just happened had not happened, and there was still a collection of happy families dancing to Madonna under moonlight.

And then the track finished, and there was silence for a moment, before all the crying started again.

He didn't come back. Not in the first few minutes as Ginger crouched over Aiden and Liss over Dani. Dani's good eye could only see her friend's face. Could only say, 'What just happened?' And Liss, tears pouring, wiping at Dani's forehead with napkins, shaking her head with no answer.

Lyra and Tia came to their mothers, kneeling down next to them, wet faces, frightened eyes.

HE WOULD NEVER

The little ones, corralled by Emily into the camp kitchen, made hot chocolates and were assured of things that no-one could actually assure them of.

'Aiden?' Dani asked, and Ginger looked up, grimaced. 'He'll live. Punch in the face, fell on his arm. You're okay, aren't you, mate?'

Dani heard Aiden grunt, and make something like a 'Sorry' sound.

'Is Lachy . . . dead?' It was a voice none of them were expecting.

Trick. Standing in the centre of the space between Dani and Aiden and the people gathered around them. His pale, determined face set in confusion. 'Did he go off to die?'

'Trick,' said Lyra. 'Shut up.' Her voice was sharp, scolding. It took Dani by surprise.

'What do you mean?' Dani asked.

'Poisoned rats,' Trick said, slowly, as Lyra shook her head at him. 'They go away to die.'

Liss and Dani looked at each other, some slow gears clicking into place.

'Trick,' said Liss, and Sadie, suddenly, was with them. 'What are you talking about?'

'Nothing,' he said, turning his phone over in his hands. He was looking, though, from Lyra to Tia.

'What do we do now?' Sadie was asking. 'Are we just waiting for that lunatic to come back and beat us all up? Liss?'

Even now, after everything that had happened, they were looking to Liss to make the rules.

Ginger and Juno had propped Aiden up against the barbecue, a handful of ice cubes at his temple, cradling his arm.

'Was he drunk? Was that drugs?'

'Did he know?' Sadie asked. 'Was that rage?'

'Did he know what?' asked Tia, and her mother shushed her with a hand.

Dani was trying to think, but everything was too blurry. She, too, looked to Liss.

'I think we need to call the police,' said Liss. 'And an ambulance, I suppose. I think that's what we need to do.' She looked into Dani's eyes, across to Sadie and Juno. 'Bring the plan forward.'

The women nodded, and Dani felt a wave of relief along with the breeze that was kicking up from the river now, as it often did in the evenings, quieting the cicadas, whistling up a rustling lullaby.

'No.' A yelp of a word, wrapped in a teenage girl's sob. 'You can't call the police. You can't.'

'Tia!' It was Lyra.

All the adults' faces turned to Tia Short. Lachy's quiet daughter, with something to say.

'It was us,' Tia said, softly.

'It was me, Tia,' Trick spoke up. 'Really. It was me.'

'It was us.'

Dani was looking at Lyra, at the face she could look at forever, the one she knew better than her own, and tried to understand what her daughter was saying.

'Mushrooms,' Trick said. 'We made mushroom poison.' At the word poison, Dani saw Lyra flinch. Not Tia, though. Tia was crying, her mother's hand on hers.

'What?'

'Like grandad,' said Trick, and Sadie made a noise. A low moan.

It took a moment for Dani to unravel those words and understand them.

'Tia?' Liss moved in front of her daughter, hands on both her shoulders. 'Why would you do that?'

'Trick, you have to tell me.' Ginger's voice was clear, she was next to Sadie, an arm around her shaking shoulders. 'You have to tell me what the mushrooms were, where you got them, and what you did with them. Exactly.'

'Lyra,' Dani asked, lifting her daughter's face to hers. 'Is this because of what he did?'

'I wanted him gone.' Tia's voice. 'He doesn't deserve you. Us.'

'The forest,' Trick said. 'We made tea. The mushrooms are called yellow stains. There were about six of them. We . . .' He looked down at his phone. 'We googled.'

'I don't know,' said Lyra. 'I don't know. There was just so much. So much drama. So much noise. We,' she looked at Tia, 'we wanted it to stop.'

'We were handling this, kids,' Dani said. 'We had a plan. It didn't involve *poison*,' she almost choked on the word, 'but we had a plan.'

She looked to Liss, who still said nothing.

Juno waved her phone. 'I've got it – Lachy hurting Dani, punching Aiden. We were attacked by a drunken, violent man, and we have evidence.'

'Yellow stains aren't deadly,' Ginger said. 'Just very unpleasant. Judging by Lachy's reaction, he's allergic. He'll probably lose consciousness.' She looked cautiously at Tia and Liss as she said the next part. 'He's probably not going to die.'

'Did you tell anyone about this?' Dani asked. 'James? Bob? Did you send any messages?'

'James and Bob haven't hung out with us all weekend,' Lyra said. 'They're always off,' she raised her eyes to Juno, Ginger, 'getting stoned. Like now.'

'Hardly the time for the moral high ground, Lyra,' said Juno, with something that was almost a laugh. 'Trick, send me your video.'

It was just Liss, now. Liss who was going to get to make the call, as always.

What to be done about her husband. About these children. About all of them, and this beautiful, terrible place.

She was just sitting there, still holding Tia's hands. Her face blank, her mouth slightly open.

'Liss, darling?' Dani asked, her hand heavy on her friend's leg. 'What do you want us to do?'

Epilogue

Sunday, 11 pm

Green River Campground

Liss

Liss was sitting in the dark, her toes just touching the edge of the cool water.

She was listening to the gentle slap and suck of the river as it pulled in, pushed out. It did it when she wasn't here. It would do it when they were all gone, tonight. It didn't need her to be here to keep going.

She was counting out the minutes until she would go and find her husband.

Liss had performed her parts of the plan. She had pulled the kids' old kayak from its hiding place, just inside the tree line. She'd had to brush the leaves and webs and scuttling insects from the plastic bench seat, marvelling at how quickly the forest had begun to reclaim it.

She had considered its weight – surprisingly light, like the toy that it was – and for a moment wondered if maybe it wouldn't hold a woman with adult thighs and an unusual amount of baggage. And three phones. Wrestled from guilty teenagers distraught about their loss even after everything, now wrapped tightly together in a sandwich bag with a rock in it.

She'd had to walk across the water's silty bottom until she was up to her knees, and then sit in the flimsy canoe and paddle just beyond the fishing boats out to where the water was black, the high tide keeping her hollow oars clear of rocks and reef. Twenty strokes to reach the deep water of the channel, where the river moved everything along.

And then, *plop*, she had dropped the package.

She'd had to turn the kayak. Liss knew how to turn a kayak. Even in the dark, illuminated only by the tiny guide lights on the few boats bobbing at high tide. She was her mother's daughter. She wasn't a splash-about. She knew to push the oar down vertically to make the boat spin back towards the beach.

And she had sat there for a moment, rocking with the water in the quiet, in the calm, to say goodbye to her beach, her river, a place she had attached to that had never been hers. All the versions of herself, and of her mother and her father, of her husband, of her ever-changing children. All of those ghosts, running and dancing and swimming and fucking up and down this beach.

She'd had to paddle back, another twenty strokes, until the boat bumped onto the sand and she could step out and pull it in. Give it back to the forest with an extra shove. *Here, make your nests and twist your vines and weave your webs.* Cover it, hide it, until another group of barefoot children banged a knee on it, and decided to make it theirs.

And she'd had to sit back down, with her toes just touching the water, feeling her bottom wet on the sand, and wait a little while for the others to hastily pack up. The whole group had to flee in the middle of the night. It was for their own safety. There was a crazed man out there. A man caught on camera in a drunken rage.

HE WOULD NEVER

It was true, this would be a fitting place for Lachy Short to die. But he wouldn't. All that would die here tonight would be his reputation, his ability to convince anyone ever again that he was anything other than an abusive, uncontrollable monster, drugged and drunk on a family camping trip, groping teenagers and attacking men and women. Ask anyone how he'd been this weekend. Ask Sadie. Ask Aiden. Look at the footage Juno had filled her phone with.

It wasn't the true story of the kind of monster Liss had shared her life with, but it was a simpler story to tell. And the world liked simple stories.

So Liss would wait. And then she would walk back through the thick rainforest she knew so well, and she would find Lachy at the base of her fig tree. And once she was certain, she would run to Ron and Shell's and tell them that the dangerous man was collapsed in the forest. That it was time for Ron to haul in the ambulance boat.

And then she would drive away. She and Dani and their babies who were no longer babies, crammed in the old Land Rover with whatever they could fit, leaving the rest behind, strewn around Sites Four to Eight.

The best sites in the park.

Acknowledgements

My daughter Matilda was a tiny baby of all peach and gold with lungs the size of rottweilers' when I first took her to Mothers' Group at our Early Childhood Centre.

Fifteen years later, it's difficult to conjure just how impossible that task felt. Transporting her in and out of a car from our home to a second location on time, fed and dressed and clean and awake but not crying. Making myself presentable enough to be viewed by strangers, awake but not crying. In the cyclone of the early days of parenthood these felt like undoable things.

I remember the circle of plastic chairs, I remember the brusque but kind nurse who answered our questions calmly, despite having heard these same queries about eating, sleeping and shitting at least a thousand times. I remember that some of the women in that circle seemed to know exactly what they were doing, an air of capable calm rising from them like fine steam. And then some women seemed more like me – flustered and unsure and messy, certain only of how overwhelmed we were. By love. By fear. I was confused and sleepless and a touch hysterical, and I remember making it home and telling my partner, with wonder, 'These women have the same problems I do!' No-nappers, no-feeders, no-pooers. Babies struggling to put on weight. We all had questions about milestones and rashes and stimulation and sleep, sleep, sleep. Turns out, there was nothing that special about us, and the women in that circle were exactly where I was.

Weeks went by and every Wednesday morning it got a tiny bit easier to make it to the clinic for this little pocket of support, of gallows humour, of help. And then we were cast out, and some of us pledged to keep meeting on Wednesday mornings. In the park, in a cafe. Friendships were formed – some duos and trios and foursomes. Some who lived close to each other, some who shared the same, particular challenge. Some who just got each other, who would have been friends no matter where or how they'd met.

Some of us went back to work. Some of us moved. Months and years went by, with group dinners and joint birthday parties for this gang of children brought together only by proximity of postcode and birthdate.

And then, a handful of us started camping. Every Easter, for nine years now, a non-negotiable three-night date in the diary. Requirements: adjacent sites. A beach nearby. Hot water in the shower block (we only made that mistake once).

These days, it might be the only time of the year that we're all together. We've scattered across suburbs and cities and states, and everyone is predictably busy. The kids were little and now they are not, but they remain connected like distant cousins, bonds rebuilt within hours of all the cars pulling up, all the tents taking shape, all the ground rules being renegotiated.

I promised my camping Mothers' Group that this book was not about them, and it isn't – none of us brings a Lachy to the party – but those friendships formed in the early days of the biggest shift of all of our lives is, of course, inspiration for Liss and Dani and these women who see each other through so much.

So thank you to my group, to Mel Ware and Rebecca Rodwell and Sam Marshall and Ciara O'Neill and Sarah Sutton and of course Leanne McLaughlin who won't sleep in a tent but did send her kids along that one year . . . I will always be grateful that I didn't allow the tales of toxic, competitive mothers' groups to deter me from making it out of the house that first day.

Female friendship is the bedrock of almost everything great in my life, so I have to acknowledge the women without whom life is so much less. Lindsay Frankel, Penny Kaleta, Karen Flanagan, Angie McMenamin, Sally Godfrey, Helen Campbell, Katie Hodkin and Tara Nicholson, Claire Isaac, Jo Willesee, Lenka Kripac and Heidi Fletcher.

My work wives and constant sparks of motivation and inspiration Mia Freedman and Jessie Stephens. To the Outlouders we talk to all week, every week. Your stories inform everything I do and we are so grateful for them. Now I can add MIDs to that list. Talking and listening to women for a living is a privilege I don't take lightly.

My fellow glimmer-chaser and wisest counsel Lucy Ormonde. In awe of you always, and not because of *that*. Monique Bowley, whose advice is always confronting in its correctness.

My wise writer sages Sally Hepworth and Tori Haschka, generous, funny and smart beyond measure.

Books need more than writers, and this one needed more help than some. So I offer enormous thanks to my publisher Ingrid Ohlssen and agent Catherine Drayton. To the editors who polished the raw material, Brianne Collins and Deonie Fiford, and to Christa Moffit, who makes books beautiful. And to Cate Paterson, whose encouragement means the world.

And of course, thank you to my family, to my parents Jeff and Judith Wainwright whose calm support is my constant, and to my brother Tom and to Lila and Louie.

And most of all, to the family in our little yellow house with the garden that brings me so much joy: my Brent McKean, without whom nothing happens. And Matilda and Billy, who sizzle and sparkle more every day and are the very best reason to do anything at all.